DRAGONSTAR

By Barbara Hambly
Published by Ballantine Books

The Darwath Trilogy
THE TIME OF THE DARK
THE WALLS OF AIR
THE ARMIES OF DAYLIGHT

MOTHER OF WINTER
ICEFALCON'S QUEST

Sun Wolf and Starhawk
THE LADIES OF MANDRIGYN
THE WITCHES OF WENSHAR
THE DARK HAND OF MAGIC

The Windrose Chronicles
THE SILENT TOWER
THE SILICON MAGE
DOG WIZARD

STRANGER AT THE WEDDING

Sun-Cross
RAINBOW ABYSS
THE MAGICIANS OF NIGHT

THOSE WHO HUNT THE NIGHT
TRAVELING WITH THE DEAD

SEARCH THE SEVEN HILLS

BRIDE OF THE RAT GOD

DRAGONSBANE
DRAGONSHADOW
KNIGHT OF THE DEMON QUEEN
DRAGONSTAR

DRAGONSTAR

BARBARA HAMBLY

BALLANTINE BOOKS • NEW YORK

A Del Rey® Book
Published by The Ballantine Publishing Group
Copyright © 2002 by Barbara Hambly

All rights reserved under International and Pan-American Copyright
Conventions. Published in the United States by The Ballantine Publishing
Group, a division of Random House, Inc., New York, and simultaneously in
Canada by Random House of Canada Limited, Toronto.

Del Rey is a registered trademark and the Del Rey colophon is a trademark of
Random House, Inc.

The Cataloging-in-Publication Data for this title is available
from the Library of Congress.
ISBN 0-345-44121-4

Manufactured in the United States of America

For
Lester and Judy-Lynn
with love

DRAGONSTAR

What Passed Before

The tale of John Aversin and Jenny Waynest, and their involvement with dragons and with the Realm of Belmarie, begins in the book *Dragonsbane*, when Gareth of Magloshaldon, heir of King Uriens Uwanë II, rides north to the desolate province of the Winterlands to seek John Aversin's help. Aversin is a Dragonsbane, the only warrior outside ancient legends ever to have slain a dragon, and the black dragon Morkeleb has descended upon the underground kingdom of the gnomes, the Deep of Ylferdun, close by the King's city of Bel, and is spreading havoc and death.

Aversin at first refuses to go. He is the Thane of the Winterlands, the last repository of law and government in the ruined and nearly empty province upon which the Kings in the South turned their backs nearly two centuries ago. However, Gareth promises him that if he slays the dragon, the King will send garrisons to protect the people of the Winterlands against both the barbarian Iceriders, and the incursions of bandits, which have plagued the land in the absence of royal law. Aversin assents, and he, his wife, Jenny Waynest—a witch of little training and severely limited powers—and Gareth ride south together.

In the city of Bel they discover that the true enemy is not the dragon, but a beautiful witch named Zyerne, who has enchanted the King with powers she is drawing from a Drinking Stone, a secret powersink of magical force that the gnomes had kept hidden in the Deep. She summoned the dragon to drive out the gnomes so that she could have the Stone all to herself. Since she derives her power not from slow learning but from the borrowed force of the Stone that she is not wise enough to use, she can now not get rid of the dragon, who is much stronger than she thought.

John Aversin fights the dragon, and is mortally wounded. Jenny, in her desperation to save John's life, makes a bargain with Morkeleb, who was likewise mortally wounded in the fight: that she will use her magic to save the dragon's life if Morkeleb will guide her into the Deep to find the medicines of the gnome Healers, so that she can then save John. In doing so she discovers the secret of the Drinking Stone, and in saving a dragon's life, she learns the secret of the dragon's name, and acquires mastery over him. *Save a dragon, slave a dragon,* runs the ancient spell, and Morkeleb is bound to do her bidding.

Jenny, John, Gareth, and the dragon Morkeleb forge an alliance with Gareth's cousin, the rebel Master of Halnath, and with the gnome-witch Miss Mab, to defeat the evil Zyerne and destroy the Drinking Stone that gave her power. Morkeleb, who has fallen in love with Jenny, offers to transform her into a dragon herself, so that she may share the life of a dragon with him. Only after she agrees does she realize that she loves John more than the dragon, or the magic that has become hers when she took on dragon form. She asks Morkeleb to release her from dragon shape, and so great is the dragon's love for her that he does.

Because Zyerne's spells broke King Uriens's mind, Gareth becomes Regent of the South and sends the garrisons, and the strong rule of royal law, that he promised. For four years, another of Gareth's royal cousins, Rocklys of Galyon, commands the garrisons of the North. Then Rocklys is convinced by an old suitor of hers, the wizard Caradoc of Somanthus Isle, that Gareth is incompetant and that she, Rocklys, would make a better ruler, and it is at this point that the book *Dragonshadow* begins.

Unbeknownst to anyone at that time, Caradoc has been possessed by a demon named Folcalor, who seeks to gain mastery over the human realms of the earth by setting up Rocklys as a pawn. Folcalor, in Caradoc's body, summons other demons to possess the bodies of wizards and dragons, forming an all-powerful corps to lead against Gareth. One of the first wizards seized by Folcalor is John and Jenny's twelve-year-old son, Ian, taken when Jenny herself is away from home helping one of the garrisons deal with bandits. After desperately trying to get in touch with Jenny, and failing, John goes to the Skerries of Light, the islands in the far western ocean, to seek out Morkeleb's help.

From Morkeleb he learns that exactly the same situation occurred a thousand years ago. Though ordinarily demons can be controlled by wizards with ward-spells, then—as, suddenly, now—demons acquired unheard-of powers, and, led by a demon-ridden wizard named Isychros, possessed both wizards and dragons to take over the ancient realm of Ernine. Folcalor, and his master, Adromelech the Arch-wight, were called in by the ancient wizards of Prokep to defeat the demons ruled by Isychros, demons who were banished behind a mirror wrought of indestructible meteor-iron. When the demons within them were destroyed, Morkeleb says, the wizards and the dragons all died.

Desperate, John and Jenny go south, to both warn Gareth and rescue Ian. Jenny discovers too late that the demons trap wizards through their magic; that in using her magic, she makes herself vulnerable to possession herself. She is possessed by a demon named Amayon, while her true soul is imprisoned in a green crystal that Folcalor is keeping—unknown to his King Adromelech—for secret purposes of his own. In trying to free her and Ian, and the other possessed wizards, John and the gnome-witch Miss Mab go to Ernine, and John passes beyond the Burning Mirror into the Hell that lies behind it. There he makes a bargain with the Demon Queen for the spells and the implements that will free the possessed mages from the demons' influence. In return she demands a teind, a tribute: a piece of a star, the tears of a dragon, and a gift freely given to him by one who hates him. If he cannot bring her all three, he will become her slave in Hell.

Though John eventually tricks the Demon Queen and wins back his soul from danger, he is branded a trafficker with demons by Gareth's councilor, Ector of Sindestray. The spells he obtained from her free the wizards Folcalor has trapped. In pursuing Folcalor—still in the body of the mage Caradoc—Jenny and Morkeleb slay Caradoc beneath the sea in a battle whose virulence strips Jenny of her powers. Morkeleb cannot help her, for between his love for her and his own battles with the demons, he has renounced most of his own magic, as he once renounced the gold to which all dragons are addicted. He has passed beyond material existence and become a Dragonshadow, a creature of the legends of the dragons of whom few mortals have ever even heard.

The demons appear to have been defeated, but the psychological toll on everyone concerned is devastating. Jenny and Ian—and the other surviving wizard of Folcalor's corps, Bliaud—discover that once one has been possessed by a demon, one is plagued by desperate feelings of longing and grief. At the outset of *Knight of the Demon Queen*, Ian begins to hear the demon Folcalor whispering to him in dreams, trying to take him over. He tries to kill himself to prevent this from happening, and John and Jenny, their love strained to the utmost by the emotional aftermath of what they have been through, quarrel. Jenny returns to her own small house on Frost Fell, where she lived alone for many years before living with John; John nurses Ian at his castle at Alyn Hold. Through the bitter weeks of winter, Jenny wrestles with the worst of her depression and dependence on the memories of the demons.

Before Jenny can return to speak to John, John is visited by the Demon Queen, Aohila. The Queen extorts his services in looking for a man who, she says, betrayed her. She sends him on a quest through various Hells, with Jenny's former possessing demon, Amayon, as a guide. In freeing Jenny, John captured Amayon and turned him over to Aohila for torture and vengeance; Amayon is an equivocal companion at best.

On her way to Alyn Hold, Jenny discovers that the demons, far from being gone, are growing in numbers, possessing the bodies of the dead. They are also buying slaves from the gnomes, slaves who have no apparent use in the gnomes' mines—John was warned of this earlier by a former mine-slave named Brâk, whom he helped to free on his way to the Skerries of Light. Realizing that Folcalor is still at large and still plotting, Jenny and Ian seek to retrieve the talisman jewel that still holds the soul of the mage Caradoc, which was lost in the sea during the final battle. Though the whalemages bring it to her, Jenny is forced to drop the jewel, which falls back into the sea and takes over the corpse of a drowned sailor. In this corpse, Caradoc attempts to drown Ian so that he can take over the boy's body and thus have the use of his magic. Jenny drives him away, and he flees.

After passing through several Hells, John comes to another world, where magic does not work and where Aohila's betrayer is hiding. He is a scientist of ether physics named Corvin NinetyfiveFifty, and demons working for both Folcalor and Folcalor's ruler, the Archwight Adromelech, are hunting him there. John falls in with a group of men and women, the League of the White Black Bird, who claim that they would be wizards if magic existed. One of them, Shamble, gives him a sword, which he says is spelled against demons. John knows that this world is a true world and not simply another Hell, because the stars are the same, including a comet that has appeared, which is called the Dragonstar, and that appeared also in the sky a thousand years ago at the time of the demon-wars in Ernine.

Returning to Alyn Hold with Ian, Jenny finds the place besieged by bandits who have allied themselves with demons. Because the demons can use a wizard's magic against him, Ian cannot use his own magic to keep the Hold from being destroyed. Jenny and Ian, at a safe distance, use Ian's magic to transform her into the shape of a dragon, which Morkeleb once showed her how to do. In this shape she drives the bandits away, but in becoming a dragon she is in danger of forgetting her humanity. Returning to human shape nearly kills her, and she is healed by Morkeleb. The Dragonshadow takes Jenny south to Bel, to warn the regent Gareth that the demons are taking the bodies of the dead.

They arrive to find the city in the grip of a terrible plague. Gareth's wife, Trey, dies, and to Jenny's horror is resurrected by the wizard Bliaud, who, weaker than Jenny or Ian, has given in and accepted another demon into his body and mind. Trey's body is the possession of a demon; when Jenny goes to the Deep of the Gnomes to consult with Miss Mab, she is cornered by demon-possessed gnomes and shot with a poisoned arrow.

At the same time John traps Corvin NinetyfiveFifty in the magic box that the Demon Queen gave him for the purpose. But because he doesn't trust Aohila, John had the League of the White Black Bird manufacture a duplicate box, with a magical gateway between the two boxes. Upon his return to Bel, John is betrayed by Amayon and captured by Ector of Sindestray's men, and condemned to be burned at the stake. Gareth, exhausted and shattered by Trey's illness, death, and resurrection, promises John that he'll be broken out of prison and smuggled out of the city, but the demon Trey drugs Gareth, and the plan is not carried out.

Chapter 1

The Demon Queen came in the dark hours before dawn; she shined in the blackness with the moony radience of rotting wood.

Chained, John Aversin raised his head and squinted at her; his breath came fast. The King's guards had taken his spectacles from him when he'd been brought to the cell beneath the prison tower, and even at three feet—the cell measured barely six—she was blurred to him, which made him sure that this was no dream. That fact was perhaps the most frightening of all the things that frightened him that night.

Prince Gareth, Regent for the mindbroken King of Bel, had promised he'd return Aversin's spectacles to him with the guardsman he'd send to smuggle him out. That had been that afternoon, while the King's men and those of the King's councilor, Ector of Sindestray, were building a pyre in the square before the city's market hall to burn him alive for trafficking with demons. "He'll come with the midnight watch, when the courtyard is quiet," the young man had promised, pushing his own thick-lensed spectacles up onto the bridge of his nose. "He'll bring you a horse and food," for it was customary to starve prisoners condemned to the stake. After three days in the dungeon, John was too light-headed and short of breath to put up much of a fight or run very far even if he could escape from his chains. "The man I'll send—Captain Tourneval—is loyal to me, and will ask no questions."

By the dirty yellow torchlight that fell through the grilled trapdoor overhead—the cell's only entrance, nearly twelve feet from the clayey rock of the floor—Gareth's face, even to John's myopic perception, had appeared haggard. Days without sleep deepened the lines that rulership and responsibility had put in the features of a boy who'd once ridden to the Winterlands to fetch John to the aid of the Realm, a boy who'd gone looking for the Dragonsbane of his precious ballads. That boy was twenty-four now, and carrying the burdens of a man.

A man's grief had turned those facial lines to gouges, showing what Gareth's face would look like in old age. Plague had swept the Realm and especially the capital of Bel. The fever seemed to come from no source, and it killed rich and poor alike. The Lady Trey, barely twenty-one years old and the mother of Gareth's daughter, had died the day before.

Had died—and had returned.

"It's all right," Gareth had said, his light voice shaky with relief and exhaustion. He'd passed a nervous hand over his face. He was built like a fence-rail, and up until the start of his Regency five years ago had done little but study ancient ballads and modern fashions, a gawky and well-meaning dandy whose elder cousin, only the previous summer, had nearly taken the Regency from him by force. "There's a healer, a very great doctor, in the town. He—he brought her back. She's all right. . . ."

And at the words, John's heart sank, and the memory of them made him shudder now. In other worlds, in the alien Hells and alien realities to which the Demon Queen had sent him on errantry, he had seen how demons entered the bodies of the dead. He had seen what those people became, and what they did.

Gar, no. No . . .

And in the young man's eyes, sick with relief that the woman he so adored had not after all gone out of his life, John saw that he could not speak. For if he said, *She's a demon, Gar, and you must burn her alive as Ector seeks to burn me,* the young Regent would have turned away. Would have made his choice of what to believe, and left John to face the fire.

But as John heard the midnight shift arrive and begin their rounds, and later start up games of dominoes and dice to pass the time, he thought, *I might just as well have had me say.*

Laughter overhead, and patrolling footfalls that didn't pause. Anxiety turned to suspicion, then to despair.

Had the demon who now dwelled in Trey's body dosed Gareth's wine? Drugged him before he'd met with this Captain Tourneval? Or had it only been sufficient to whisper love-words to him, draw him to her bed? Exhausted, the young Regent would sleep like a dead man afterward. His dreams would be sweet with relief and satiation, with demon-painted visions that now everything would be well forever.

Demons were good at that.

Small odds, anyway, John thought as the night dragged into its final hours. The muttering of the other prisoners along the corridor faded, the sounds he'd heard for three nights now. Curses or weeping, or the gluey persistent coughs of pneumonia. A few yards away from the grilled trapdoor a single torch leaked little of its light down into the cell, four elongated brazen trapezoids on the stones some two yards above John's head. Here, under the central tower of the old section of the palace, the damp cold seeped to the marrow. The river wasn't far away. Though it was impossible for Aversin to hear anything but the murmur of the guards, the occasional cries of the other prisoners, his too-vivid imagination—the bane of his thirty-nine years—manufactured for him the footsteps of the men who dragged wood to the pyre in the market square, the harsh rattle of tinder being stacked, and the clack of the ladders raised against the stake.

Trafficked with demons, he did, he could hear them saying, like voices in a nightmare. *Got to watch them. Demons started this plague, the way demons possessed them wizards, that evil Caradoc, that tried to raise a rebellion in summer and slay the old King. Never trust those that have words with demons....*

And they were right, of course. That was the worst of it, that John agreed with everything that was being done. As a ruler himself it was what he'd have done.

He gazed in the darkness at the sickly phosphorescent specter that stood before him, smiling—even without his spectacles, he knew she smiled.

Her hair clothed her, wreaths and coils like sable sea wrack and like sea wrack gemmed with pearls and creeping with nacreous life. Thighs, shoulders, coral-tipped breasts lifted through it like alabaster, and the spells of lust and yearning ran off him like rain. She said nothing, only looked at him with those golden goat-like eyes. He knew she was waiting for him to speak.

Get me out of this!

Since the age of ten he'd read every book and fragment he could get his hands on of law and judicial proceedings. As Thane of the Winterlands it was part of his duties to bring as much justice as he could manage to those in his care. He knew exactly what would be done to a man who trafficked with demons, and why it had to be that way.

Don't let them burn me!

He'd been Thane of the Winterlands for twenty-three years. He'd seen men die by fire.

It is the whole aim and purpose of the Hellspawn to find in the world of the living a servant who will be theirs, the encyclopedist Gantering Pellus had said centuries ago. *Who will open for them a gateway through which they can pass out of Hell. They amuse themselves with human terror and human pain, drinking them as beasts and men drink water. They seek power and destruction to protect themselves and to wage war against others of their kind, but this is always true: that they will do anything they can to enslave human souls to their will. Never forget this.*

Gar, come and get me out of this!

John knew by then that he would not.

Jenny ...!

But Jenny Waynest, even had she known he was imprisoned, had lost her power in the summer. Her magic had been stripped away in the battle with the demon Folcalor, who had possessed Caradoc the mage. Wise and clever, Jenny had been in Bel only days ago. Gareth had said as much, but none knew where she was now.

This slim, tall semblance of a woman, beautiful as moonfire and corpselight, was his only hope. As he, John Aversin, was Gareth's only hope. *I'm the only one who truly knows, who has seen demons take the bodies of the newly dead. The only one that can warn him.*

This thing that looked like a woman ...

And he had only to speak.

Don't let me die. Don't let me burn.

He had tricked her once, putting his soul in pawn to her in order to defeat the demon Folcalor and then redeeming it with Jenny's help and that of the dragon Morkeleb.

He had served the Demon Queen once, fetching for her from the Hell of the Shining Things the water that would show her where the

Otherworld scientist Corvin NinetyfiveFifty was hiding. He had gone to fetch this Corvin—who had once betrayed her, she said—in an enchanted box of silver and dragonbone. Maybe this would have been enough to bargain with her for his freedom, but the box had been stolen from him by Amayon, his demon guide.

So he had nothing to bargain with now, nothing to trade. Except himself.

She stayed in the corner of the cell, like the reflection of light on the stones, until the stamp and scuffle of guards' boots in the corridor above marked the end of the midnight watch, the coming of dawn. Then, still smiling, slowly, like a dream, she faded away.

A guard lowered water to him, down through the grille on the end of a rope. It was the first water John had had in three days, but he poured it onto the floor, guessing it would be drugged. He was the slayer of at least one dragon, trained all his life as a warrior, however unwillingly. Even at the end of three days' starvation and thirst, the guards were ready for trouble. Because demons could sometimes enter into the bodies of those who were drunken or drugged, he guessed that whatever was in the water wouldn't cloud his mind, but there were herbs aplenty that could be counted on to double a man up with cramp or wring him out with purging or dry heaves so that he'd offer no resistance as he was stripped and shaved and dragged to the stake.

He was aware of the man watching him down through the grille, and knew he'd carry word of it back to the guards.

Bugger, thought John, lying back on the verminous straw tick and closing his eyes. *If they want to do this the hard way, let's do this the hard way.* Under other circumstances Ector of Sindestray, Councilor and Treasurer of Prince Gareth's Council, might simply have bricked over the grille and let it go at that. But so long as Gareth was alive, this wasn't possible. And the command to burn those who trafficked with demons had been instituted precisely to be sure that the physical body was destroyed beyond the demons' use just as—and no later than—the departure of life and consciousness.

Would the Demon Queen still come, he wondered, if he now called on her name?

He was afraid she would.

That was the problem with demons. The wizard Caradoc had fallen into the trap of it, and started this whole deadly game. Once you called on them, you never knew what they would demand. Caradoc had probably only wanted a little more power. There were any number of ward-spells to hold demons at bay. True, all the grimoires ever written warned against calling on demons, ward-spells or no ward-spells, but Caradoc was vain of his abilities.

Caradoc's ward-spells hadn't worked. John still didn't know why—at a guess, Caradoc didn't, either. The demons had somehow reacquired power they hadn't had for a thousand years, and nothing had stopped them so far, except the spells John had bought from other demons. . . .

Always a bad idea.

John didn't put up a fight when the Councilor's guards came for him. From his days of friendship with Gareth he knew the layout of the prison tower: It was the ancient core of Bel's original palace. He knew there was no way to flee. He would only be hurt, probably badly enough to prevent a break later, between the old gate on the Queen's Lane and the square before the city's market hall where public burnings were customarily conducted. It wasn't hard to act as if he were too exhausted and debilitated to be any threat when the guards cut off his hair and dressed him in the thin white shift of the condemned. A squad of six soldiers in the red cloaks and trousers of the House Uwanë came to do this: "You're joking," said John as they all came down the ladder into the cramped cell. "Somebody thinks I *could* take on *five*?"

His hands were manacled behind him. Just as well he hadn't put up a fight in the cell, he thought—always supposing there was room for one—as he was manhandled up to the corridor above, and led along to the watchroom. Whoever built the place probably had him in mind. There wasn't an inch of cover. The walk, over flagstones worn uneven by two centuries of military boots, seemed two or three times longer than it had when they'd brought him in; he was dizzy when they reached the round stone room at its end. Hunger and dehydration made all things unreal, and he felt unable to picture anything clearly beyond each separate moment. The details of his capture and imprisonment blurred and segued into the battle that had preceded it: a battle against garishly painted men possessed by demons and wielding the horrible weapons of the bizarre, waterlogged city in another world where he'd gone to find Corvin NinetyfiveFifty.

In the aftermath of the carnage from which he'd rescued the little scientist, he'd opened the dragonbone box and dropped into it the demon's golden beads. Corvin had screamed once, and whirled into the tiny container like smoke. Later, John had stepped through a door in the flooded subway tunnels—a door marked with a demon rune— and had been in the King's city of Bel again.

And in the hands of those who knew only that he'd worked at the behest of the Demon Queen.

Only the hunter's instinct that had kept him alive for thirty-nine years in the Winterlands let him focus his mind on details now: how close together the guards walked, how many doors were on each side of the stone-flagged passageway, and whether the men holding the wrist-chains did so attentively or not. His dizziness lent a dreamlike quality to the walk, and for an awful moment, as the leader of the squad opened the door into the watchroom, John expected the Demon Queen to be waiting for him there, smiling. . . .

She wasn't. Instead, the demon Amayon sat there in the watch captain's big chair, and beside him stood Lord Ector of Sindestray.

How John knew this was Amayon he wasn't entirely sure, especially without his spectacles. But he knew. The demon had been his guide through the doors of three Hells, and he'd seen him in several different guises. Most of the time there he'd worn the shape of a beautiful girl—he'd never given up his efforts to seduce John. But on occasion he'd occupied the body of the beast John had ridden through the red and black horror of the Hell of the Shining Things.

At the moment, Amayon was wearing the body of the dead Lady Trey.

It was the closest John came to being sick with sheer shock.

The blue eyes met his, unmistakably the demon's eyes. The red lips of the thoughtful, rather shy girl John had known curled in a lazy smile, daring him to speak.

"I'm told you refused to drink the water that was given to you this morning," said the King's Treasurer, folding his chubby arms. Ector of Sindestray was built along the lines of a tree stump, clothed in the blue and white velvet of his House and made more square yet by an enormous set of Court mantlings that draped around him like an embroidered curtain. His gray curls were worn long, after the fashion of the oldest Houses in the Realm, and dressed as if for a State occasion. He smelled of scorched hair and pomade.

"I wasn't sleepy," said John. There was no point now in husbanding his strength or reckoning chances for an escape in the light of the terrifying enlightenment about just which demon had taken over the body of the dead Lady Trey. He guessed what was coming, and despaired

Ector glanced across at Amayon, who was stroking the round belly of her pregnancy. When she had died, Trey had been carrying Gareth's second child. When the demon guide had betrayed John to Ector, he had worn the form of a slim, curly-haired boy of fifteen or sixteen—Ector had seemed at the time to believe the boy was his nephew, an illusion John guessed the demon had planted in the older man's dreams. Amayon caught John's eye and winked at him, then turned back to Ector and nodded. Ector gestured to the squad captain, and though John knew perfectly well that the outer door of the watchroom was barred, he hooked his bare foot around the booted one of the man behind him, tripped him, elbowed the next man holding the chains that bound him, and made a run for the door, all while the other members of the squad were picking up the clubs that lay on the watchroom table. There was nowhere to run and pretty much no hope of getting out of it at this point, but he couldn't go without a fight.

As the blows hammered him and his consciousness fractured away, he heard Amayon laugh.

The Demon Queen waited for him in that clouded gray borderland on the other side of the pain: *Don't be a fool,* she said.

I'm doin' me damndest not to be, he replied, and her pale mouth tightened. He had a dim awareness of being roped to something—a ladder?—and carried shoulder high, but it was all hazy now, and all he saw was her face.

You'll let others die, because of your stubbornness?

Lapsing entirely into dream he found himself momentarily in Gareth's room, windows opening onto the terrace of the Long Garden to admit the smoke of plague-pyres still burning beyond the palace walls. Gareth slept, a heavy and unnatural sleep, his graying, thinning

hair scattered on the linen of the pillows and his face furrowed with
concern even in sleep. Trey sat beside him, the demon-Trey, Amayon-
Trey, robed in royal red and white with her small jeweled hands rest-
ing on her swollen belly. Another man was in the room, and John felt
again that cold, sick jolt of shock, for he recognized Gareth's father,
the old King Uriens. The King's mind and consciousness had been
eroded, stripped away, reduced to childhood five years ago by the
spells of the witch Zyerne, but now he moved briskly. The blue eyes
that had seemed so puzzled during last summer's rebellion were
bright, sparkling with demon fire. His lips curved under the fleecy
amber curls of his beard. "Do you think he'll be surprised?" The King
nodded down at his sleeping son. Trey's evil grin echoed his own.

"Why should he be? If old Bliaud the Wizard can wake a girl
from the dead—not to speak of her sweet little son"—she patted her
belly complacently—"why shouldn't he be able to wake old Grandpa
from mere imbecility?" And she reached up to tweak the King's gold
beard. "The people will be delighted. I'm sure after the rebellion of his
cousin, and plague, and his precious Dragonsbane turning out to be
in league with demons, Gareth will leap at the chance to step down
from the throne and out of the council-chamber, and go back to collecting ballads."

They both laughed, the ribald gloating mirth of demons, and
John tried to cry out, as if under the muffling weight of sleep.

"They are my enemies, too, my love," whispered the Demon
Queen. She stretched out beside him on the ladder that the guards
bore through the barred and guarded gate of the Old Palace, down
the cobbled slope of the Queen's Lane, where the crowds trampled
last week's snow to thin mush. The air was bitter on his flesh under
the thin linen of the shift, and through it he could feel the heat of her
flesh. "Folcalor and the one he feigns to serve, the Hell-Lord Adromelech, imprisoned me and mine in the Hell behind the Mirror a thousand years ago. What makes you think I would not do all in my power
to avenge myself on them for that defeat? What makes you think I
would not help you against them, if you will help me?"

Her fingers stroked his cheek, touched the silvery runes she'd
written on his flesh when first he'd sought her help behind the Burning Mirror. The vision changed, and he saw his sons.

They stood on the wall of Alyn Hold in the Winterlands of the

North, the place that was his fortress and his home. His heart leaped at the sight of Ian, whom he had last seen fragile and wasted, battered by the aftermath of demonic possession as Jenny had been battered. Ian was on his feet, and though thin and too serious for a thirteen-year-old, he looked well. Adric stood beside him, sword in hand—a boy's sword, but though only nine he handled it like a man—and they were looking down over the battlement. Behind them the roof of the kitchens had been burned, and marks of fire scored the stone walls. Men moved about outside the walls, bandits, besieging the Hold as it had been besieged many times since the power of the Kings had waned in the North. But there was something else in the smoke that wreathed the burning village of Alyn, something fearful that scuttled like a huge rat among the smoldering houses. Something that defied all John's efforts to watch.

"Can you see it?" Ian whispered, and his young brother shook his head.

"It spoke to me last night, though," breathed Adric. "Spoke in a dream. Said I should kill you, and run down and open the gates. I told it to go bugger itself. It did." The boy looked queasy. He was John's son, in his red-brown coloring, and even more the grandson of old Lord Aver, stocky and barrel-chested already, though like the black-haired and blue-eyed Ian, he had John's thin-bridged curve of nose. "But it still kept looking at me, and laughing; waiting for me to get my sword and kill you. Only I knew even then that you wouldn't really die."

"No," said Ian quietly. "No. And that's what it's waiting for."

One of the guards bearing the ladder stumbled; John felt the cold again, and heard the crowd shouting, their voices bouncing off the walls of the tall houses around the market square. Looking up, he saw the cold gray of the birdless winter sky.

Then the sky turned to darkness, the darkness beneath the earth. Something in the smell of the wet stone, coal smoke, and cooking thick with grease spoke to him of the Deeps of the Gnomes. *Ylferdun,* he thought. The Deep beneath Nast Wall. Its gates lay a half-day's walk from the King's palace in Bel, one of the great strongholds of the Gnomes in the West of the World.

The place he had gone to five years ago, to fight the dragon Morkeleb, with such curious results.

He smelled blood, too, and the sulfur-stink of blasting powder. Through the Hell-Queen's spells he saw Jenny in the darkness, broken and bleeding in a hollow of the stones. Morkeleb the Dragon was somewhere near—he knew this as one knows things in dreams—but the black dragon had been trapped like her when the gnomes had blasted the mine tunnel.

She is dying, said the Demon Queen. *The gnomes shot her with arrow poison. This, too, was the work of Adromelech and his minions. None knows she is there but the demons . . . and now you.*

John's mind cleared, and he heard again the shouting of the crowd. He was bound to the stake—he'd been dimly aware of the six guards doing it, though it had felt like someone else's body through the cloudy horrors of his visions. The cords cut into his arms and ankles and throat, and the air was ice-water cold on his flesh and the raw skin of his scalp. Ector of Sindestray was reading the charges, savoring each with the morbid relish of a doomsayer who has been proven right. "He has trafficked with demons. . . ."

Even had he been inclined to, John couldn't very well argue with him.

It was to defeat this other lot of demons, see. . . .

Who would believe that, except Gareth stupefied in his crimson chamber? And maybe the Master of Halnath, wherever he was. But the Master of Halnath, the scholar-lord Polycarp who was Gareth's cousin, had voted also for John's death, knowing the things that had been done in the past by those who dealt with demons.

It was to save Jen, and me son; to keep them from being possessed by demons who would use their wizardly powers. . . .

But those who called upon demons to aid them frequently did so out of the best of motives.

Such as now.

It was Amayon, bright-clothed in garnet velvet and sparkling with jewels and malice, who handed Ector the torch which he drove into the kindling.

At this distance John couldn't see clearly, and the crowd beyond that flame-like crimson form was only a blur. But he heard their voices, wild over the cracking of the fire. Furious voices, relishing as Ector did the vindication of themselves. They'd been told that the plague was his doing, or the doing of the demons he'd worked for, and they were doubly angry, for there had been a time when he'd been popular in Bel. *Dragonsbane*—the only man living who had slain a dragon. He had fought the demon-possessed dragons that flew down at the command of the demon mage Caradoc; he had defeated them.

"... pawn of the Hellspawn," Ector was shouting above the rushing crackle of oil-soaked tinder. "Author of the plague that has swept this land ..."

The smoke billowed thick and greasy. The heat was suffocating, and in the smoke she took shape. Beautiful and hideous, wrought of fume and fire, she held out her hands to him, waiting for him to call her name.

I won't. He closed his eyes—not that that did a lot of good; he knew she was still there—and turned his face aside. Airless, all-encompassing heat and pain. *I won't. I will die, and Jen and the boys and all the Realm die with me....*

Someone screamed.

He thought, *Do they see her?* and someone else took up the shriek. More howls—terror, panic. Wind bent the flame around him, whirled the smoke, and he opened his eyes and saw a dragon, huge, fifty feet or more and with a wingspan twice that, silver-streaked and tabbied with black and opal-green blazing eyes. It was almost on top of him already, and he could do no more than stare up at it in shock as the silver claws lashed down, caught him up, stake, ropes, and all, scattering burning hunks of wood and hay over the heads of the trampling crowd. The beating shadow of wings, the flash of the winter sunlight as they rose above the city's walls and the bitter, freezing cold after the fire's heat. With his hands still tied, John felt a stab of pure dread that the dragon would drop him—*Fat lot of difference that would make, given the day I've had so far*—and turning his head he saw the city fall away, mossy ice-slicked roofs and bare trees; city fields and the silver loop of the River Clae, shining in the Magloshaldon woods. Brown fields, then brown steppe, then gray sheets of cloud that enveloped them like damp muslin and cold that shredded his bones.

The dragon carried him tucked up under its breast, and without the heat of its flesh John thought he probably would have slipped away into death from the cold, *Which I wouldn't have bet two coppers on last night . . .*

Weightless exhaustion. Consciousness that came and went, slipping away to drop him suddenly back to an awareness of hanging suspended in damp gray clouds, over a barely glimpsed landscape of formlessness below. He was only marginally conscious when the dragon descended to a gray-yellow desolation of sand and scattered boulders, of flint hills without vegetation and of twisting scoops of pebble-filled stone that had been watercourses long ago. These he saw only dimly, for the gray light was fading, and his eyesight wasn't good enough to discern details. On a wide plateau in the desolation stumps of pillars marked where a city had stood. Crumbled foundations and lines of broken walls surrounded a stone platform two hundred feet by nearly five, a square rock island in the sand—even he couldn't miss it.

The dragon balanced in the air like a kite and, reaching down, laid John on the ground before the remains of the platform's wide stair. Evening turned the vast sky yellow, lilac-stained and fading. John felt the stone under him chill as snow through the torn rags of his shift, and knew the night would be brutal. He couldn't imagine where he was, or how far they had come:

Please don't make me walk home.

Still hovering weightless above him, the dragon extended its swan-like neck and with a bill like Death's scythe bit through the ropes that bound him, the chains that fastened his wrists. Then it ascended with no more flurry than a cloud of smoke, wheeled on its silken wings, and flew away toward the west.

Aching with cold, with bruises, with hunger and exhaustion, John raised himself to one elbow and shouted, "CORVIN!" His voice echoed hoarse in the emptiness, not loud enough to startle rabbits, had there been any. The ancient authorities—Dotys, and Gantering Pellus, and others who'd written of dragons—said that to name a dragon's true name would call it, though these true names were in fact airs of music. . . .

Save a dragon, slave a dragon, went the ancient granny-rhyme: To rescue it from death put it in bondage to its rescuer.

John had never quite known whether this applied to ordinary

people—he'd only ever seen wizards do it—and he prayed his guess about the dragon's name was correct. "Corvin NinetyfiveFifty, by your name I charge you, come back!"

He saw the flash of distant silver in the last western sunlight, and the glittering shape of the dragon returning. But before it reached him he fainted from exhaustion and cold.

Chapter 2

In the dark beneath the earth, Jenny Waynest dreamed of the Dragonstar.

John had told her about it, on and off, for three years, and in her dream they lay together on the platform he'd built above the moss-fouled leads of the Alyn Hold tower, on one of those hot summer Winterlands nights when the whole world breathed magic and the stars leaned down close over the desolation of moor and stones. "A thousand years ago was the last time it showed up, when Ennyta the Great was the King of Ernine," John was saying to her. The starlight flashed in the round lenses of his spectacles, and his voice was deep and velvety with odd undertones of huskiness to it, like rocks in a plowed field. Jenny would know it in her dreams, she thought, until she died. In this dream he had half a dozen of his crumbling old volumes scattered about him: He'd spent a lifetime ferreting them from the ruins of old fortresses and towns. The lantern he'd brought up to read them by had gone out.

"Accordin' to Dotys, anyway—if that thing I have really is a fragment of his *Second History*—it reads like Dotys, no error, the fussy old prig. He claims he was writin' from the *Golden Chronicle* of the Kings of Ernine, but—"

And Jenny asked, "What does he say about it?" because even in her dream John was apparently ready to explain at vast and meticulous length why he thought the author of the forty or so sheets of mildew-stained vellum he'd bought from a peddler were in fact Dotys's *Second History* and not one of the other ancient authors' and she wanted to hear about the star.

"Well, anyway, it's a double-headed comet," John said, called back from historical exegesis that could easily have taken the remainder of the night. "The first comet showed up in spring, and the second, in the same place in the sky, in fall. The dragon's head an' his tail, they said."

On the southern horizon a pale streak showed where the sun was dozing, and all around them the cornfields of Alyn Village resounded with the twitter and warble of sleepless summer birds. In her dream, Jenny still had magic. She could feel the radience of it, glowing golden in her bones.

"Accordin' to my calculations ..." He rolled over and grubbed among his books for a much-scratched wax tablet. Only Jenny's mageborn eyes could have made out the scribbles on it, in the starlight. "... the first head should show itself, the year after next, right there in the Sign of the Dragon...." He put his head close to hers so that she could site along his pointing finger at the cluster of stars hanging low above the toothed black notches of the Wolf Hills. They had been together a dozen years on this particular night, but she still loved the smell of his flesh, and was deliciously conscious of the warmth of his shoulder against hers.

Oh, my love, how could I have turned away from you?

Shadow folded around her, like cradling hands. Morkeleb the Dragon had said to her once, *Endure,* and she now tried to say to him, *I will, my friend.* The dream faded away. She became aware that she was underground, in darkness, in the gnomes' Deep at Ylferdun. That she was dying. Around her the darkness of the Deep was very cold. She was conscious—from what felt like a great distance away—of lying on stone. Gritty dust clogged her throat and her nose, and a small star of cold pain radiated from her left shoulder, pain that no longer seemed to be part of her body. She had been shot with a poisoned arrow, she remembered. Morkeleb had come to save her, whipping down through the passageways of the mines that lay below and to the north of Ylferdun Deep. But it had been a trap, and the gnomes had set off an explosion, caving in the tunnel around him with the blasting powder.

She felt his mind reach out to hers.

Endure till I come. He had said that to her before, when they had parted after the loss of her magic, in those terrible days when she could meet John's silences and anger with nothing more than silence of her own.

No, she thought now. Morkeleb would try to use magic, the strange powers of a Dragonshadow, to save her and himself. Magic is the heart and the flesh of dragons, and she knew there were demons in the Deep, waiting for him to do just that. In the summer just past she had seen how the demons could use the magic of a wizard as a bridge into that wizard's mind and flesh, thrusting aside all protective spells as they had never done before. Thus the demon Amayon had entered her. *Back when I HAD power,* she reflected, without even bitterness, now. The demon lord Folcalor had come close to conquering the Realm of Bel through the wizards he had seized. Had he not, for reasons of his own, chosen to imprison the souls of the mages thus possessed rather than simply drive them out to dissolve, Jenny knew she would never have regained her body and her life.

Better that she herself should die, she thought, than that demons seize Morkeleb's mind and power to use as their own.

Nightmares pulled her back into darkness. The memory of what Amayon had done with her magic tormented her, acts of cruelty and wantonness. The memory of being trapped in her green crystal prison, feeling the hot brilliant rush of demon magic, pain, and shame. The memory of what the world had looked like when Amayon had been within her mind.

In nightmare she heard, too, Amayon's screams when John had turned him over to the Demon Queen behind the mirror, to be tormented forever. Felt anew the blasting shock of utter grief, when in killing the wizard Caradoc—in driving Folcalor from his body—her own magic had been seared away to ashes.

Desolation and cold washed over her, the recollection of having nothing left of the power that had been hers.

She wondered, as she sank into deeper darkness, whether death would liberate her from those nightmares. Or was that what death consisted of: helplessly reliving horror, over and over again?

"Jenny my child," a soft old creaky voice whispered in her ear, "Thou art what thou art." Someone was with her in the darkness, someone whose strength touched that cold, disembodied pain and slowly melted it into nothingness. Someone whose strength kept her from sinking beneath those black waters.

"Past and present and yet to come, this thou art. All of it, fire and water, earth and air. All of magic ariseth from understanding this."

The voice was familiar, and Jenny thought, *Ah.*

Her past was clear to her, as clear as the old scars on her back. Caerdinn, the bitter old wander-mage who had taught her spells, had often struck her in his anger, but it was he who had made her a wizard. He who had taught her the uses of power.

She had been a witch-child, knowing from earliest awareness that magic was in her. She could look at a lamp and call flame to its wick, or find her mother's thimble when the cat had knocked it under the wood-box. She could see in the dark, while others groped and blundered in that gloomy little house in the lower village, beneath the walls of red-bearded Lord Aver's Hold. Lord Aver had had a prisoner at the Hold when Jenny was small, a black-haired Ice-witch he'd captured in a raid on an Icerider camp one year when those nomads had come raiding down from the North. This Ice-witch was a shaman among those northern nomads, she had told the child Jenny, and had been cast out from her people. She could not go back.

Kahiera Nightraven had been Jenny's first teacher.

Past and present and yet to come, this thou art . . .

Sweet incense and warmth slowly returning to the innermost hollows of her flesh. The cold star of poison pain slowly fading. The sweetness of herbs.

The Nightraven had not been a good woman, or an easy teacher. Coldhearted and beautiful, she had laid spells over her captor, so that Lord Aver had loved her even when they fought. His sisters, Jane and Rowan, had hated her like death. When she had disappeared, leaving behind her a son, a puzzled, wary toddler who never quite trusted the world, the spells on Lord Aver had remained: He had never loved another woman, not even his former longtime mistress Hollyberry, the town blacksmith's wife.

Jenny, too, had been left with a hole in her heart.

It was old Caerdinn, the half-mad and rage-filled old hedge-wizard Lord Aver got for his son John's tutor, who took Jenny as a pupil when she was thirteen. Caerdinn took her into his crumbling stone house on Frost Fell, and taught her how magic was organized. Showed her how to draw power from the sun and the earth and from her own flesh and bones and blood. How to observe, and to name each tiniest flower and grass blade by its true name so that they would be within her power: how to call power from these true names. How to weave Limitations on each spell, so that cows would not run mad, nor birds forget how to fly, nor thatch roofs take fire two villages away when she summoned Power; and how to harmlessly disperse the power she'd called, after her spells were accomplished, lest it linger in the place where she'd raised it and mix with later spells. This was how Spaeth, his master, had taught him, and all the wizards of their Line back to the shadowy ancient warlock Herne.

All magic comes from understanding, Caerdinn had told her, staring at her with his huge pale blue eyes, like a demented goat's beneath white brows. He seized her by the shoulder, small hands but terribly strong. The long nails stained yellow with the herbs he smoked dug into her flesh. *Know the names of each pebble underfoot, and you can call even their tiny magics from them at need. The more of them you know, the more accurately you know their nature, the greater will be your power.*

In the darkness, in her pain, in her forty-sixth year, she thought now, *There is power in me still.*

She breathed in deep, feeling the demons nearby. Their minds circled hers like ravens. She felt the presence of Morkeleb the Dragonshadow, who in his days as a dragon had nearly destroyed this Deep. He had dwelled here for a time after driving the gnomes forth, and knew its every passageway and chamber. His calm strength upheld her, flowing into her lungs and blood.

As her mind and body relaxed she felt the warmth return. *Past and present . . .* the glimmer of cold disdain that had been the Nightraven, who had given her the first knowledge of what power was.

Caerdinn's resentment and bitterness, that had not stopped him from teaching her all the little he knew. Even though they were dead—Caerdinn for certain, and Nightraven for all she knew—Jenny felt them still, a part of her body, her self as surely as Morkeleb's magic had once been a part of her bones and blood.

And a farther mind, that sweet creaky little voice again, said, *Linger till we come, child. Hold my hand.*

Mab, thought Jenny, clasping that strong, gentle shadow. Miss Mab, the men of Bel called her: Taseldwyn of the House of Howeth-Arawan, the tough little gnome-wife whose spells had enabled John to pass through the Burning Mirror at Ernine—to survive his first encounter with the Demon Queen.

Mab was still far away. The Wise Ones of the Deep had put her under house arrest in the warrens of her own clan, but in her dream Jenny felt her hand. It was no bigger than a child's and hard-muscled like a blacksmith's, thick with the gaudy rings in which the gnomes delighted. There was comfort in her grip, reminding Jenny of all those nights when she'd gone to sleep holding John's hand.

John, she thought, giddy and frightened. *Where is John?*

She saw him riding away from her through the blowing snow of a coming storm. Riding down Frost Fell after they'd found their son, Ian: The boy had taken poison, to keep the demons from returning to his flesh. She saw John ride away and felt the darkness that she'd felt then, too despairing even to speak to him or to anyone of her pain.

Morkeleb lifted her. She heard the slither of boulders pushed aside, smelled the brimstone residue of blasting powder and the choke of rock dust. From a great distance she heard the dragon speak her name in that voice like the dark behind the stars, and though she'd already wandered a long way into a quiet gray country beyond the borders of sleep, she could still speak to him, for she was still holding Mab's hand. *I'm here,* she said.

His body was warm. Like sleeping near a stove on a freezing night. It flashed through her how cold she was, and she tightened her grip on Mab's hand: *I'm cold,* she said.

Endure. The word flowed over her like the tides of the sea.

She didn't know how she would, but she thought again, *There is power in me still.* Not really magic, she thought, but power of a kind. She tried weaving a little skein of magic from the name of that black-haired girl-child, running after Kahiera Nightraven along the battlements of Alyn Hold. To that she added a thread of power from the awkward, un-pretty thirteen-year-old who had fetched Caerdinn's breakfast porridge for him all those mornings when he'd been too crippled with arthritis to rise from his bed. Who had endured his slaps and curses because he was the only one who could teach her spells.

She colored the magic with her endurance then: *If I could stand living with him, I can surely stand this.*

Magic from understanding. Know the names of each pebble....

The name of this pebble was Jenny Waynest, she thought. *What I am is that person who was.*

She breathed a little easier, and some more of the coldness in her limbs seemed to abate.

After a long time—more dreams—she smelled herbed smoke and

sheepskins. Much closer now she heard Miss Mab say, "Lay her down. A well lies farther along that passageway. Fetch water. I brought a hothwais of heat...." She named the spell-stones of the gnomes, which could be charged sometimes with heat, as if they'd been baked in fire, and sometimes with glowing light: sometimes with other things. "She must be kept warm."

Jenny had a clear picture in her mind of the place where she lay, though she had not the strength to open her eyes. It was a cavelet barely larger than the smokehouse at Alyn Hold, a nodule deep in the rock of the mines. Air flowed through it, tracking across the stubble that was all that was left of Jenny's hair after the fight with Folcalor. So the cave must be near the ventilating shafts that riddled all the gnomes' workings like worm-tunnels. Reaching out with her other senses, she smelled water not far off. Miss Mab had brought blankets and sheepskins as well as her medicines. Even large burdens were of little account to a gnome. She laid some of these down as a bed for Jenny, and moved her onto them. From a box she took a stone as big as a man's fist, and set it beside her. Passing her fingers across it she whispered the True Name of heat. The stone gave forth no light, but the chill of the cave, and the bitter cold in Jenny's flesh, grew less.

Will she live? asked Morkeleb. Jenny heard the slosh of water in a gourd, smelled it as it dripped on stone. In her half-dreaming state she could not tell whether the dragon wore his human guise or the serpentine semblance of a dragon in miniature as he sometimes did. He might even have been completely invisible, a state he had returned to more and more since giving up his magic lest the demons take hold of him. In the darkness Jenny was aware of his diamond eyes, no more.

She could see Miss Mab, in any case, a bent little gnome woman with a round face seamed with wrinkles, and eyes the color of sunset beneath a jutting brow. Her pale gold hair she wore dressed in elaborate rolls and bands over a padded frame, and she was dressed in silky trousers, tunic, and a quilted jacket, as both males and females among the gnomes clothed themselves. Only her family's influence with Balgub King of the Deep had kept her from being killed for abetting John's quest for the Demon Queen. As it was, she had been imprisoned for a year and a day.

Demons could, of course, being deathless, wait far longer than that to make their presence known in one they possessed. But they never did. Like children they were impatient, and greedy about their pleasures, even to their own detriment. If one immediate plan failed, there was always another.

The Lady Trey is dead, Jenny tried to say. *Prince Gareth is sending for one in the city who is said to raise the dead.*

But all she could do was whisper, "Dead," in a voice no louder than the scrape of dried leaves blown across a marble floor. Human ears would not have heard her, but she felt Morkeleb draw near.

Is this what you learned when you went into the city, my friend? Claws touched her, light as spider feet. Tender.

She gathered images together like a sheaf of dried flowers. Herself at Trey's bedside, and Gareth stretched weeping over his wife's body. The stink of pyre smoke on the rainy air and Polycarp, Master of Halnath, saying, *I don't like it,* as they sat in the Long Garden. Like flowers she handed them to the dragon, thankful that she need do no more than that.

She had been a dragon, once upon a time, transformed into that shape by Morkeleb's power. For a time the magic of a dragon had filled her veins and her flesh. She remembered how dragons spoke.

With those images, others: the horror of the drowned sailor rising from the water of Eldsbouch Harbor, with the soul of the wizard Caradoc glaring hungrily from its ruined eyes. The tall, gray-haired form of the Baron Pellanor, leading bandit slave hunters through the Winterlands months after his death in battle. Trying to trap her sons.

They are raising the dead. Tell Miss Mab. The demons are raising the dead.

She slipped away into sleep.

She lay for a long time in the cave, like a child in the womb. Morkeleb never left her side. Miss Mab came and went, bringing water sometimes, or gruel, or once another hothwais, this one imbued with white light so strong, she kept it wrapped in several layers of leather sacking. With a silver knife barely as long as a finger, she cut Jenny's wrist and drew sigils around the cut in ocher and ink. The spells of healing were a whisper rather than a shout, for demons still lurked in the mine. In her dreams, Jenny felt them, slipping green and shining far away among the rocks. Mab was forced to work slowly, dispensing tiny sips of magic, drawing forth the poison a little at a time. In the long periods between, Morkeleb's smoky presence wrapped Jenny around, and held her in life.

Sometimes Mab spoke to her as she worked, gentle words like a mother, telling her about the road back to healing and life. "Power lies in thee still, child; in thy heart, in thy bones. Call it from what thou art, what thou truly art NOW, not from anything thou wert before."

When I had the magic of the dragon in me, I had power, thought Jenny. *That dragon power was all that I saw. What am I, truly, now? A woman who formerly had the power of a dragon: This I am. A woman who has borne three children, and who loves them now more than she did at their births: This I am.*

She took even the headaches and the little spurts of nausea that had tormented her for years, the flushes of heat and the migraines of her changing body, and sought in them for power instead of calling on the power of her youth to suppress them: *This I am.*

She laughed in her dreams, to feel that power respond.

Once she even called on the power of the poison itself, slowly working out of her body: from death and pain whose name and nature she now understood, weaving strength. *This I am.*

Opening her eyes she looked up at Mab and though she could not speak, she smiled. The pale golden eyes smiled back.

"Walks the plague still in the City of Men?" Jenny heard Mab ask later, through the dim shadow of sleep.

So deep lies this place within the stone of the mountain, even I cannot hear. Morkeleb's voice sounded in Jenny's mind, as she knew it would sound in Mab's. *When I reach forth to listen to those who walk the thoroughfares of the Deep, the rumor is confused. Some say the plague there is ended, and the man who brought it upon the city was killed. Others say no, the demons saved him from the fire, sending a dragon to snatch him away. Others yet say stranger things. The old King who was ill and broken in his mind is now restored, they say, and takes up the reins of power again in his hands. The Warren of your Clan lies closer to the ways of your brethren than this hiding-place, Gnome-Witch, and the tongues of servants are ever ready to gossip. Surely you have heard?*

"I listen in the stillness of the nights." Mab's warm, stubby fingers paused in drawing the sigils of healing along Jenny's veins. Her voice was barely a murmur, as though she feared who might overhear. "These rumors have I heard, and others as well. In the City of Men, they say, evildoers rove the streets killing men in their own gateways without reason, without concealing themselves from the justice of the King's guards. No man now trusts another, nor children their parents, nor wives their husbands. Those whose loved ones were resurrected from the dead try to pretend that the ones who were re-stored to them were indeed those who were taken away, but they weep in their fear, and dare not speak. All this I have heard."

Ah, said the dragon softly. *This is as it was a thousand years ago, in the Realm of Ernine.*

And having been a dragon once herself, Jenny saw into the dragon's mind, as he had been able to see into hers. She saw the columns of smoke that rose above the walls of that lost golden city, seeing in its prime what she had only glimpsed as ivy-smothered ruins. She saw flame and smoke rising from the roofs in Morkeleb's memory, and no one came to put out the blazes for fear of the demons they might meet. She saw the bodies of young girls and chil-dren left mutilated by the waysides, and how, in time, gangs in the streets would kill without a hand raised against them, until at last barbarians swept in from the East and looted the undefended town.

"Were you there?" asked Mab, and she used the form of words that gnomes use to address Kings, or gods. Somehow to Jenny this did not sound strange.

The dragon replied, *I was there.*

Then he was silent. Jenny saw the mad wizard Isychros riding at the head of his corps of dragons and wizards, demon light burning from his eyes, as Caradoc later had ridden. The possessed dragons sparkled in the sunshine, crimson and golden and blue and bronze, their magic transfigured by the magic of demons. The wizards scried in water and glass and crystal with fivefold power for any who would plot against them, and those plotters came to terrible grief.

Polycarp, Jenny thought. Fear sliced her at the thought of the Master of Halnath, who had sent her here to the Deep to tell Miss Mab of Trey's death. Polycarp knew too much of demons for his own safety. Had he been able to escape from Bel, Jenny wondered, before things came to the pass there that they had all those centuries ago in Ernine?

The High King of Ernine had become the pawn and slave of the demons, she remembered, seeing through Morkeleb's eyes. His two daughters had killed him, but too late to save the Inland Realm from the terrible cancers of mistrust and blood-feud. Even the destruction of the dragon corps, and the death of the wizards whom the demons had taken, came too late. Working against them with demon magic, further damage was done, though no human magic was found that would prevail.

"How was it ended, in the end?" asked Miss Mab at length. She sat on a corner of Jenny's sheepskins, and Jenny could smell in her clothing the scents of lamp oil from the Warren of Arawan, and the dried herbs of healing. "How were the demons—and the other demons who helped to defeat those called up by Isychros—finally bound?"

That I know not, returned Morkeleb. *It was nothing to me, these squabbles of men. In those days I had the sense not to remain in a place of danger, no matter how much gold there was for the taking. I followed the dragon corps south and east, to gather up the gold of men....* And in his thoughts Jenny felt the warm, deep strength of that love for gold that is the heart of every dragon, the intoxication of the magic that dragons can breathe through the refined metal, and drink back again in almost unbearable ecstacies of dreams.

When I saw what the demons did, that dwelled within the dragons, I was disgusted, and came away. I returned to the Skerries of Light, to the islands in the western sea where the dragons dwell. I had no more to do with them, nor with the wars of men.

"Were you not concerned," asked Mab, "to help your fellows among the dragons, who were enslaved?"

Morkeleb did not reply for a long while. Jenny saw them sitting together, though her eyes were closed in sleep: Miss Mab in her green velvet jacket and bright pink trousers, her curly-toed blue slippers glinting with jewels. The dragon curled near the hothwais of heat, like a great half-visible dog before invisible flames. He had been black as a thing of carven coal when first Jenny had seen him, and huge, forty feet from the tip of his nose to the cruel spiked club of his tail. She had not known then that the great dragons, the mages and lore-masters among that kind, were capable of changing their size. Among the dragons Morkeleb was foremost in lore, in the spells and wisdom passed along from mind to mind for centuries and millennia, wisdom and power growing in him until at last he had given up his magic, and passed entirely beyond dragon shape.

Now he had the semblence of a dragon, insofar as he had any semblence at all—or perhaps, thought Jenny, it was only her perception in dreaming that saw him thus. The shape of him that she saw was the thin, snake-like body of a dragon, with its long tail like a muscled whip and great thin-boned silken wings folded along his sides. All his joints and spine bristled with spikes, and great scales like razor-edged fans. In the narrow, beaked head burned crystal eyes, mazes of diamonds that you could fall into forever. Among long horns and tufts of mane, antennae flicked lazily, the points of light at their tips the only thing about him that could be clearly seen.

Not human, she thought. But not a beast, as so many humans considered dragons. The young among dragons were beasts. But they grew, and passed on, with the years, to become other things.

As Morkeleb had.

A man would have gone back for fellow men, replied the dragon slowly. *Indeed I have met a man who would go back for them, though they were no kin nor friends of his. It is not a thing of dragons, to concern oneself overmuch with the safety of others. I knew their minds were enslaved, and there was little that I could do. We are creatures who look after ourselves.*

Jenny opened her eyes at that. Turning her head, she saw the dragon regarding her with his diamond gaze. "Save a dragon, slave a dragon," she murmured, and held out her hand. "You saved me in the North, when I was in dragon form, as once I saved you."

He did not ask her how she was. He knew that—better than she knew herself: She felt the chill scrutiny of his consciousness touch her bones. But she thought the shadowy outlines of his form became more distinct with the passage of thoughts in his mind. To Mab, he said, *She must be moved as soon as may be. And yourself also, Gnome-Witch. Sense you not the passage of demons within these mines? Hear you not, in the still of the night, the scratch of their glass shells upon the rocks as they emerge from whatever pool hides their gate? Smell you not the stink of them, like blood poured onto hot iron? They wait and they listen, and they are strong. Soon or late they will find this place, and take you in the darkness.*

"They are strong," agreed Miss Mab, rising. "This was the question a thousand years ago, Dragonshadow, and is the question again. That they are strong. Ward-spells that once defeated them, and held them in check, now leave them untouched. Are these new demons, then, bred somehow from the old who destroyed Ernine?"

Jenny said, "No," with such conviction that both gnome and dragon turned to look at her in surprise. "No. Amayon remembers the Fall of Ernine. He was there." It surprised her that she could name the demon who had possessed her without a break in her voice. Without wondering where he was, and what had become of him after John had given him over to the Queen behind the mirror. Without a pang of concern as to whether he was in pain. Perhaps the poison had burned the longing out of her, or the healing had strengthened her heart. She did not know.

"In possessing me," she said, her voice barely a whisper, "he not only occupied my body, while my mind was imprisoned elsewhere in a green jewel. He occupied my mind itself, the portions of my mind that remained in my body, side by side with his. That—that portion of me shared his thoughts. Some nights I have dreamed *his* dreams. . . ."

She grimaced at the dirty memories, the hellblaze of passions and power that still could heat her flesh if she let them. Yet she realized that in her poisoned dreams she had not once dreamed of him. Only weeks ago she had been literally incapable of dreaming about anything else.

"He was there." She struggled for breath to speak. "He was one of Adromelech's demons, that devoured and defeated those of Aohila of the mirror." She drew the fleece up close, though the cave was warm now, the warmth kept in it by a straw mat hung over the door. A feather of light was allowed to leak from the wrapped hothwais, just enough that she could see. Farther off, on the flowing draft that everywhere ventilated the Deep and the mines below it, she smelled water and stone, and farther off other fires, where the gnomes dwelled, or their slaves who worked the mines.

Morkeleb tilted his narrow head—he had shrunk himself to little larger than a stag, and sat coiled in the shadows like a gleaming skeleton of diamonds and pitch. *Then were I—or another—to search deeply enough in your dreams, it might be that we could understand how the demons were in the end defeated?*

Miss Mab raised her brows, turned her golden eyes to Jenny. "Is this so, child?"

"Maybe." Jenny shivered, not liking the hidden suspicion about what she would see.

"I will search, then," the old gnome said, and stood, "for spells of dream reading. For spells, too, to guard *your* mind, child, from too close a sight of the demon's heart." When she put her hand on Jenny's shoulder, Jenny felt how sharp her own bones were under the gnome's thick palms. Even in the warmth of the cave she felt chilled, as though she had barely any flesh left to her. Her combat with Folcalor beneath the sea, near the gate of the Sea-wights' hidden realm, had left her scarred, her long black hair burned away and her hands crippled and twisted. As she fumbled weakly to return Mab's clasp she saw that though her short fingers, her brown square wrinkled palms, were still marked by the blasts of steam and fire, they were no longer drawn together like claws, but able again to spread and flex.

There was a touch of arthritis in the joint of her right thumb, where for years she had ground pestle to mortar in preparing herbs for medicine. That was all.

"Thank you," she said softly. "When Morkeleb takes me from here, you will come? He's right, my lady. It isn't safe for you anywhere in the Deep."

"And how safe will any be," asked the gnome. "Did I leave the heart of the Deep, and flee away to a place where I could not hear what passes beneath the earth? I can come and go from my prison if I am careful, enough to send thee word. I am not in a cell. It is true that there are demons here in the Deep, Dragonshadow"—she turned to Morkeleb—"it is true, that I hear them chitter and scrape in the night. And my question is, What do they *here*? What seek they in the Deep, that they cannot have in the City of Men?

"This would I learn. King Sevacandrozardus has sent for Goffyer, the greatest of the mages of the gnomes and my own old teacher, from Tralchet Deep, in the North. If any will know how to look into your dreams for the memories of the demons, my child, it will be he."

Jenny nodded, but shivered again as Miss Mab gathered up her medicines and took her departure. The thought of delving into that part of her consciousness, her memories of Amayon, filled her with a sickened dread. She lay among the skeepskins and tried to sleep, with Morkeleb stretched across the foot of the pallet, chin upon his paws. The last she saw was the lights of his antennae, flicking back and forth in the dark.

Chapter 3

J ohn woke in panic, thinking, *Jenny!*

And lay in the warm glow of a small fire, trying to breathe.

The dream had been blazingly clear. Jenny in darkness, bleeding, an arrow through her shoulder and the sweat of death on her face. The Demon Queen's voice, *She has been poisoned....*

He hadn't been there to protect her, to help her. It was his fault.

And he would never see her again.

He tried to sit up, and his head spun. He lay back down, blinked at the stone walls around him in the apricot whisper of the fire. A frieze of what appeared to be human figures marched around the four sides of a room not much bigger than his cell under the King's prison tower—at least in the gloom they seemed human, though without his spectacles it was difficult to be sure. The background stone was pinkish, and whatever the painted shapes carried in their hands— treasure, presumably—threw back the firelight with gold leaf's unmistakable dusky brilliance.

He lay on a springy mound of fresh bracken, covered by a red velvet cloak so thickly gemmed and embroidered as to look like a blanket of embers in this ruddy light. A ewer stood by him, silver mountings embracing a red-and-white shell bigger than a man's head. A beautiful thing, of a species he'd never seen before. There was also a clay cup, and the meat of two or three rabbits, cooked and lying in the cracked curved section of a painted jar.

There was no one else in the room.

Jenny ...

In the dream he'd seen her also with the dragon Morkeleb. She wore the dragon form he'd once seen her take, not white but crystalline, as if wrought of crystal lace and bones. They flew low over the ocean, the black dragon and the white, shadows running blue before them on the waves, as alone among humankind he'd seen the dragons fly in the Skerries of Light that lay westward across the sea. The memory of that dream calmed his pounding heart, filled him with a sense of peace.

An old memory? An illusion, sent up by his mind to reassure him?

The vision, perhaps, that both Jenny and Morkeleb had perished in the cave-in, and that in death her soul had become a dragon's soul at last?

The thought left him desolate.

He had traveled, he realized, for so long since leaving the Winterlands that he had become confused about time. Time in Hell wasn't the same as time that is ruled by the sun and the stars. On his errantry for the Demon Queen he had crossed from Hell to Hell, the magic of one unworkable in another, and at last from the myriad Hells into that other world where the dragon Corvin had taken refuge in human shape. John felt like he'd been lost for years. Capture, imprisonment, and the specter of an agonizing death had come between him and the longing ache he'd felt, just to see Jenny, to speak to her. . . .

If she'd listen. If she wouldn't turn away.

When last he'd seen her, at her old house on Frost Fell, it had been the morning after Ian's try at suicide. He heard his own voice lashing at her, saw her crumpled beside the hearth, beside the nest of blankets they'd made up for their son.

God, I might just as well have gone over and kicked her, he thought, trying to wriggle away from that memory, that shame and pain.

Back then, even with his experience of dealing with the Demon Queen, he hadn't understood what possession by a demon did to those who survived it.

He wanted to walk back into that room, that time, and knock that man who was himself upside the head and scream at him, *She's hurting, too, you nit! Let her alone!*

Don't let her be dead, he prayed, to the Old God whose name and nature were mostly no longer remembered, save in backwaters like the Winterlands. *Don't let her be dead and not knowing how sorry I am.*

He closed his eyes and watched the play of the reddish light on the lids, breathed the fusty sweetness of the bracken and the moldery earth-stink of the covering cloak. His body was covered with bruises like a windfall peach. After a time he rolled gingerly up onto one black-and-blue elbow and devoured rabbit and water, and as he did so saw that broken pieces of wood had been heaped near the chamber's stone doorway, ready to be fed to the blaze. Boughs thicker than his calf had been snapped into short billets, as if they had been twigs.

Corvin NinetyfiveFifty, he thought, and rubbed a half-healed bullet graze left over from that final firefight in the lab. His shoulder was bruised black from the kick of one of those noisy chattering horrendous guns that could kill a roomful of people in moments.

A dragon hiding in human form. Working as a scientist, of all things, in that alien half-drowned world. Changing identities whenever it became obvious that he wasn't growing old like everyone else.

He must have been hiding there—or somewhere like it—for a thousand years.

The old granny-rhyme was right. Save a dragon, slave a dragon, at least for a time. Cold flowed through the doorway from the dark of the passage beyond, and with that cold the harsh scents of dust and sand. John gathered the robe about himself—a King's robe, certainly finer than anything he'd ever had as Thane of the Winterlands, the gods could only guess at where it came from—and limped barefoot and aching down the passageway, the cold growing sharper and more penetrating until he came out under desert stars.

The room was built into that huge granite foundation that rose like a mammoth bench in the midst of the ruined city. Sand had flowed in the inconspicuous doorway, duned against the walls and piled over the threshhold so that John had to climb, feet slithering in freezing powder, and bend down under the lintel to emerge.

The city lay before him, reminding him of an old drawing sun-faded nearly to extinction. Between starlight and myopia he could see only suggestions of the nearer walls, and portions of three pillars that stood duty for some vanished palace. A dimple in the ground marked where a lake had been. Some distance away an immense plaza was demarcated from the desert by a ring of stones, water-shaped but uncut by human hand; a minor cavalry skirmish could have been fought inside it. He thought something glinted in the middle of that ring, like a palms-breadth of ice, but it was impossible to see what.

A dance floor? The temple to some god whose very name was forgotten? Wind skated across the barrens of hard-packed earth and around the snaggletoothed rock, everything either silver or blue-black in the moon's blanched light. How long had it been since the smell of growing things had weighted the night here?

By the taste of the air, dawn wasn't far off. The cold stung John's bruises, and his scalp, raw where the guards had shaved off his hair. He wrapped the earth-smelling robe tighter around him and wished his vision were good enough to see stars, so he'd have some idea of where he might be. They'd be winter stars still, only a month or so advanced from where they had stood when he'd ridden out from Alyn Hold in the freezing sleet, to do Aohila's bidding lest she harm his people and his son. The weeks he had spent following Amayon through the terrible Hell of the Shining Things, through the Hell of Winds and the ghastly dangers of Paradise, all these had dissolved like dreams. Only time had passed when he'd been in the other real world, with its bitter rain and its crowded streets and a woman he might have loved.

High above the first yellowish blush in the eastern sky a comet danced, bright enough to be visible even to him. He had to take it on faith that it was the split-tailed Dragonstar he'd been reading descriptions of, and observing since the summer. Jenny had put a spell on his spectacles that they wouldn't get broken or lost: The guards had taken them off him when he'd been arrested, and he wondered where they were now and if the spell still worked.

Would a jackal appear in a day or two, carrying them in its mouth?

He'd be in serious trouble if it didn't.

Not, he reflected, that he wasn't in serious trouble now.

He retreated down the passageway to the painted chamber, sand whispering under his frozen feet. *Save a dragon, slave a dragon,* he thought again, *and if this is his idea of savin' me life I only hope he left a couple more rabbits and a map to the nearest subway.* Subways were a thing he'd learned about in the Otherworld, strings of metal chambers that whipped along through tunnels in the earth propelled by the emanations of etheric plasma.

He'd have to ask Jenny about etheric plasma.

If she would speak to him again.

If he managed to get out of this place alive.

He added a couple more logs to the fire—marveling that he

could come within three feet of the flame without flinching—and stretched out carefully on the bracken again. He thought he'd lie awake for hours worrying about Jenny, or trying to come up with a scheme to get himself back to the Realm of Belmarie from wherever the hell he was now, but the only thought that went through his mind was, *Where'd he get the bracken?* And that only lasted for the four seconds between lying down and sleep.

When he woke, Corvin was there. The dragon wore his human guise, the shape in which John had rescued him from demons in the flooded city that had seemed to extend forever: a spidery little man with a paunch, his hair dark-streaked silver. In that hammering chaos of burning laboratory and demon gunmen, John had gotten a brief glimpse of Corvin's eyes, which were like green opals, but he knew better than to meet them now or allow them to meet his. One could get lost in a dragon's eyes, and stand confused until it struck. Even at twenty-five and in full possession of his wits, John had barely escaped a much smaller dragon's claws and tail. Fourteen years later he still carried the scars on his back and thighs.

"You got out of the Queen's prison box, then," said John, easing himself gingerly up onto his elbow again. "I didn't know if that Gate-rune I had them put inside it would work. Thank you for coming for me."

Corvin said nothing for a time. Nor did he turn his head from his study of the procession of painted tribute-bearers on the pink-tinted wall. His arms he had wrapped around his knees, lost in the folds of the plain, voluminous robes that seemed to be part of a dragon's illusions of humanity: Morkeleb's, when he appeared as human, were black, and so Corvin's were black and gray mixed, merely something to satisfy the eyes and minds of human beholders.

Demons did the same thing, of course, and John was familiar with it. Still, at least he did not have the horrible feeling—as he did in his dealings with the Demon Queen—that the moment he took his eyes off her she reverted to her true appearance, like something in a ghastly dream.

In human form the dragon spoke in human voice, light and dry as bleached bone. "I did not think," said Corvin slowly, "that I had been gone so long."

Morning light filtered through the doorway. The fire had burned to ash. John felt a momentary flash of anger—*Couldn't you have banked it, you silly oic, so we won't have to light it ...?* Then remembered that lighting fires was the least of his problems, as long as the dragon stayed around.

What had Corvin expected to find, returning to this abandoned city? What had he expected to see?

"I knew the lives of men were short." In the hazy reflected brightness the scientist's thin-boned human face did not appear very human at all. "Their memories shorter yet. *Forever* means, *during my lifetime....* And time is not the same, when one is in Hell. Yet I thought I would find this, of all places, still safe."

He regarded John, who sat up very carefully, the bracken crunching under him, and pulled the cloak up over his shoulders against the morning cold.

"You were one of the dragons then," said John conversationally, "weren't you? One of those Isychros enslaved with the help of Aohila's demons, when he took over the Realm of Ernine."

"I was the only one to survive," Corvin replied. "And that, only because the demon who dwelled within my brain understood that the Sea-wights could attack through the magic that was used against them. The others—dragons and wizards alike—died screaming, as the Sea-wights devoured the demons already in possession of those bodies. Devoured them as demons do, taking their substance into their own. Burning up themselves in the process, many of them. The war between demon and demon is too much for the flesh and the mind to survive. It was not pretty to see, even to a dragon who has seen the evils that lurk in the darkness behind the stars. The demon who rode within my brain turned me loose and fled. But afterward she called to me in dreams."

"And that's why we're here?" John leaned his back against the wall and drank from the clay cup. The water was cold from the night air, even so near the fire, and tasted faintly of iron. "Because you thought in Prokep you'd be safe from Aohila? Or I'd be safe?"

"Even so." The dragon rose in a fluid movement, like a dancer, and walked down the passageway toward the light. John wrapped the jeweled cloak around himself and limped at his heels. He ached in every muscle and limb but felt much better for last night's food. *And just as well,* he thought. That Corvin owed him a life didn't mean the dragon wouldn't abandon him here, and half-blind and weaponless he didn't suppose he'd last long.

Corvin had resumed his dragon form by the time John reached the outer air. In the brittle desert light he flashed like a mountain of ash and diamonds, every joint armored with silver spikes, the bird-like head tassled and tufted and horned in subtle colors, irridescent purples and stripes of ivory and red. In the *Encyclopedia of Everything in the Material World (Volume III),* Gantering Pellus had related that as they age, dragons' colors and the patterns of their scales become more complex and beautiful, then grow simpler again, as their magic strengthens and shapes. John had seen Morkeleb the Black, eldest of the dragon kind on earth, colorless and powerful as night; had seen what neither Gantering Pellus nor any other human save Jenny had seen, how Morkeleb was passing now beyond even that darkness, into the realm of shadow and invisibility as his magic transformed past or-dinary maturity to somthing else.

Corvin was probably as old as Morkeleb, and as strong. But the difference was there, in the flashing shape of silver muscle and sable wing.

"What does she want of you?" John asked.

The serpent head slewed around, but John was gazing out across the dun formless land to the circle of stones.

"Aohila," said John. Most men would have been intimidated by the mere presence of fifty-five feet of lethal strength and magic any-where in their view, let alone within a yard of them, and he suspected Corvin thought that he would be, too. And he was, for he knew better than most men what a dragon could do. But he'd participated in the killing of one dragon, and had more or less befriended another, and he was damned if he'd let Corvin know his fear. After one has had dealing with the Demon Queen, even dragons lose some of their ter-rors. Besides, he reflected, at this point he didn't have a hell of a lot to lose.

"She possessed you, yes. But why take the trouble to send me to Hell and back to destroy you? To keep you out of Adromelech's hands, or Folcalor's, obviously . . . but how could they use you against her? You weren't her servant in Hell, were you?"

No. The dragon's voice was a drift of wind in his mind, but even so was remote with distaste. *When one gives one's service in Hell, one does not emerge.*

John had guessed that. He wondered how many other men had, given that choice of being burned alive, or calling on a Demon-Lord's name. He turned his eyes from the dragon back toward the stone circle, but could not find it. He thought—he wasn't sure without spectacles—that the lay of the ground had not changed, and somewhere had the impression of that blink of reflected light, but when he looked in the direction he thought it was, there was nothing there.

It appeared to him, though, that the dust-devils veered aside as they neared the place. But that could only be the result of wind currents chaneled through the dark-stained broken hills.

"Why take that trouble to trap one dragon," he went on, "when the Skerries of Light are creepin' with 'em, and all young and bright and too stupid to fly the other way when a demon starts sendin' 'em dreams? They're all creatures of magic. If the demons could trap you, they can trap them twice as easy."

He felt the flex of contempt in Corvin's mind, like dark music flowing through his. Most of the dragons with whom he had spoken had talked thus, with few words, like images in a dream. He wondered what their voices sounded like to one another.

But Corvin had masqueraded as human for many years, and the words that came into his mind still rang in that sand-whisper voice.

They? I would crush them. This Aohila knows.

And with the images of his mind John saw clearly what he had guessed before, that it had been the Demon Queen who had possessed this dragon. That her mind had taken root within his. She had used Corvin's magic, and his lore, and his memories as Amayon had used Jenny's.

Looking up at the small bird-like head in its cloud of green-and-silver mane, he wondered if Corvin had longed for the Demon Queen after she had fled, the way Jenny—in spite of herself and in spite of her hatred for the demon and what he had done to her—had longed for Amayon.

Long before Isychros wrought his unholy mirror to open the gate of Hell, I was the most powerful of the star-drakes of the earth. Corvin's antennae flicked, bright-hued whips in the wind. *My lore is the deepest. Now added to that lore is the knowledge I have gained in the years of guising myself as human. Alone among the dragons or demons or mages of this world I understand ether-magic. This magic demons cannot touch, for it is sourced from other realities, in the other world. That will be what the demons want of me.*

"You think so?"

The green-opal eye slid sidelong to regard John, and the Dragonsbane felt the heat of Corvin's annoyance at the query, but the dragon deigned no reply.

"If demons can't touch ether-magic—don't ken it at all—why would they want it? They're dead lazy, y'know. I can't see 'em takin' the trouble to learn about it from you."

You speak like a human, Dragonsbane. All the demons have to do is enter into my brain again, to learn all that I know. And this I will never permit, if I have to remain here in Prokep forever. The dragon bristled his scales haughtily, for all the world like one of Jenny's cats, and turned away.

Then, after a time of silence, he asked, *In the other world, you told the wizardlings—the League of the White Black Bird—to make the Sigil of the Gate upon a piece of dragonbone, and put a like mark within the Queen's prison box, that I could pass from one to the other, and so be free. What did you think to gain by cheating her?*

"Dunno." John shrugged. "But demons lie, an' somehow that story about you lovin' an' leavin' her didn't listen right to me. I figured somethin' she was that fired up to have me do for her was gie likely to turn out badly for the folk of my world, one way or another. But I didn't know enough about it to be sure, an' in the end it was just a guess." The carnage in the GeoCorp headquarters, where demon henchmen had tried to seize Corvin, came back to him like a nightmare: bullets shattering those expensive mirrors, tearing through innocent flesh. The smell of blood, like any village raided by bandits or Iceriders. Worse: Three quarters of the people in that room had been too relaxed with liquor and drugs to even dive for cover.

That was what demons did. "Was that what let her trap you in the prison box in the first place?" he asked. "That she'd been in your mind, an' knew all you knew, at least at that time ... includin' your true name?"

It is how such things work. Grudging anger, like a bass note under the music of the dragon's thought. Fury at Aohila, as if his subjection had been a few days ago and not ten centuries in the past. *My true name was written within the catch box. In its presence I would be called to it, irresistably.*

North and west, rising sun razored shadows among the stones. Details of the landscape unfurled exaggerated ribbons of blue-black, throwing into prominence each minute pebble and hillock. Another dust-devil appeared out of nowhere, skated frenziedly through the piled sand, then petered itself out in the desert beyond.

I confess I was surprised that the magics of those little wizardlings who haunted the computer nets actually worked. I took refuge in that world precisely because magic no longer operated there. The energies of etheric plasma by which those people power their machines has a tendency to damp certain other forms of magic—because of course it is itself a form of magic. But that world's own magic was so attenuated that it was easily snuffed out.

"Doesn't mean people aren't still being born there who could have worked it, had it still existed. You got out of the second box with no trouble, then?"

As if recalling a dream, John glimpsed the image of the dragon emerging like smoke from the duplicate box, which was tucked behind a complete set of Clivy's *Speculations*. On the same high shelf were concealed the silver bottle in which Aversin had dipped an extra cup or so of the water from the spring in the Hell of the Shining Things, the rune-written sword given him by the League of the White Black Bird, and all the notes he'd made on his travels, grimy rolls and wads of parchment and papers all creased from being stuffed in his doublet pockets. Gareth must have gotten hold of them from Ector's guards.

And like a second dream he saw the young Regent sleeping, as the Demon Queen had shown him, with Amayon in the guise of the Lady Trey sitting smiling beside his bed.

John's belly clenched.

"Take me back."

Don't be a fool.

"You think every day you delay the demons won't get stronger?" John shaded his eyes to look up at the dragon's haughty profile, high above his head. "Whether Folcalor wins out over Adromelech or t'other way around, whichever one ends up Lord of the Hell beneath the Sea, he'll come after you, son. And either way they'll do whatever they have to do, to get out of you whatever they went into the next world to get. And if you think they won't, you're joking yourself."

They cannot come at me here.

The dragon spread his wings, and evening sun speared John's eyes, when it had moments ago been only an hour after dawn. The dry air turned moist and thick in his nostrils, laden suddenly with copal, plumeria, and frankincense. He heard men murmuring, and saw the city before him restored in its myriad beautiful hues. Painted walls, pillars of porphyry and malachite, rivaled the flowers on a thousand terraces and vines. Everything was startlingly clear, too, and he understood that he was seeing the dragon's memories. Watching with the dragon's hyperacute sight.

The circle of stones stood where it had been last night. With a dragon's far-reaching perceptions, John could even make out the faces of the ten people in that vast ground, seven men and three women, the youngest of them probably over sixty. They held hands, forming a ring that looked tiny in that open expanse of dun-gray dust. The chip of brightness in the ring's center was indeed water, a puddle that seemed barely larger than John's palm. But it caught the light of the torches, as it had caught that of last night's waning moon. The air above that fleck of water wavered with the greeny-silver luminosity of the Sea-wights; John felt their power, smelled the metallic vileness of them even at this great distance—the dragon's sense, not his own. Wind scoured from the hills, made dust-devils among the encircling menhirs.

Where the comet had wavered in the sky last night, only clean, pale twilight glimmered now.

They were astronomer-priests, as well as mages, said the dragon's voice in his mind. *They understood enough of the nature of the Dragonstar so as to be able to hold against the magic the demons derived from it, until the Dragonstar ceased to rise, and its alien power faded away.*

Outside the Henge walked others, yellow-robed like those within. Some of them were very young. Some bore the marks of combat, burns and scars and half-healed claw-rakes. One had been marked, as John had been marked, with the silvery half-seen tracery of demon runes, that gleamed strangely in the sun's dying light. Two or three wept as they paced.

They bent to draw signs in the sand between the stones with sticks of what looked like wax or chalk. *Jen'll skin me if I don't give her a sketch of that,* John thought, and concentrated his borrowed eyesight on the marks, memorizing as he had taught himself to memorize the small differences of animal tracks in the snow of the Winterlands, and the coded signs of hundreds of bandit and Icerider gangs. All these mages chanted and whispered as they traced the symbols, words that John could not make out, and within the stone circle the ten priests swayed, lined, calm faces blanched by the sicklied demon light.

When that light faded, leaving only the shining handbreadth of water, the ten priests retreated from one another, each drawing a circle of protection separate from the others. The silence in the city square beyond the Henge was like doom, though far off John heard a man in the hushed crowd weep.

Each priest within the Henge—within each separate protective ring—took a bottle from the robes they wore. Men and women, they knelt in their individual ward-rings, and drank. Then they lay down, and covered their faces with their cloaks. The torches carried by the warriors who lined the city square burned smoky in the waning daylight. The priests outside the barrier stones were still as the uncarved rocks.

John watched as, one by one, each of the ten mages whose strength had forced the Sea-wights into the shining water at the Henge's center went into a brief convulsion, and died. As each died, faint light licked and glimmered along the edges of the encircling stones, seeming to leap from stone to stone like brightening fire. John said nothing, but he trembled as if he had witnessed a great battle. As indeed he had, he thought. A great battle's end, and victory at a price he wasn't sure he'd have had the courage to pay.

Then he was looking at the empty sands of morning, and the dust-devils that whirled and twisted where even the ruins had mostly perished.

The spells they put on the Henge permitted nothing to leave, said Corvin after a time. *Not demons, and not the mages themselves. They wove their webs of spells upon the whole of the city, surrounding the Henge in an unbreakable Maze, and the magic that locked Henge and*

Maze they sourced in their own deaths. There is magic—tremendous power—in any human soul, that can be used when the soul dissolves in death. Greater magic still, if the soul be that of a mage.

Bugger, thought John. Grief for the lost mages pierced his heart as if he had truly seen their deaths and not merely a remembered echo ten centuries gone. As if they had been his friends, when he did not even know their names. Grief for knowledge that had been lost with those ten mages, knowledge that they had almost certainly lacked the time to pass along. The horrors he had seen in the other world, where demons had stalked their prey in the flooded streets, these seven men and three women had seen in their own world a thousand years ago. They'd given their lives to stop it, as he'd have given his life rather than call on the Demon Queen.

When the trouble started, he thought, they'd have had no time to teach their yellow-robed adepts anything but what they must know to do their own part in the spells of ward and mazery. No time to write anything down of all that other knowledge that had made up the length of their years.

Time is long, and words unsaid remain unsaid forever.

"How'd they get out, then?" John asked, determined not to let the dragon hear the sorrow in his voice. "Adromelech, an' Folcalor, an' the rest? I understand about the Dragonstar comin' back, an' the demons usin' it to source spells, but if the spells the mages put on the Henge an' the Maze are still that strong . . ."

The dragon turned his tassled head and regarded him in surprise tinged with impatience.

They did not escape, he said. *Adromelech is still there, with the greater part of his demon horde. Did you think you were dealing with the full might of the Sea-wights, Dragonsbane? What you thought of as the Hell of the Sea-wights is only an enclave, to which Folcalor and his cohort escaped when the Star set for the last time. The gate of the true Hell still lies within the Henge. What else has Folcalor been waiting for these ten centuries but the chance to free his Arch-wight lord; the chance to take command of that Hell for himself?*

John thought, *Bugger.*

All this time we've only been dealin' with the advance-guard.

God's grandmother . . .

"So to come to power over Adromelech"—he was astonished at how casual he sounded, through the dizziness of horrified shock—"to take true command—Folcalor has to break the Henge."

Break the HENGE? The words were barely articulated, only the curling wave of the dragon's incredulous scorn. *BREAK the HENGE? You speak like a human—think you that anything can break through the magics of ten mages' deaths, like a bumpkin kicking his way through a stable door? Folcalor is a fool.*

"Folcalor had a good try at puttin' together the deaths an' souls of at least seven mages," replied John. "Not to speak of what he'd get if he devoured Aohila—no wonder she sent me along to get you before they did."

His demons would never have taken me, snapped Corvin, as if he hadn't been trapped by the demons in his burning laboratory in a world where his own magic would barely function. *Nor shall he, Dragonsbane. Not me, and not you.*

Wind breathed across the remaining fragments of wall, the broken pillars and dry pits, and it smelled of emptiness beyond the endurance of man. John had heard of the deserts that lay east of the plain and steppe that were the farthest marches of the Realm of Belmarie, but had heard of no man crossing them. No tribes or hunters roved them as the Iceriders roved the cold tundra to the north. "Take me back," he said again, and tried to keep the fear out of his voice.

To the demons that run squeaking through the halls of the palace where I came forth from the prison box? Scorn rippled in the dragon's hot music. *You think much of yourself if you fancy you can keep silent when they ask you where I went.*

"My friends are there." John saw Gareth again, asleep in his demon wife's arms. Saw Gareth's daughter Millença, only an infant in white satin when last he'd seen her, she must be three now—and Trey with a dead child in her womb that would be a demon as it was born.

The dragon regarded him blankly, truly not understanding what he meant by *friends.* In a thousand years, thought John, Corvin had not had friends. Perhaps never. Maybe it was *not a thing of dragons*—as the dragons said—to have friends, as it was not a thing of dragons to love.

You saved my life, said Corvin. *Therefore will I preserve yours. You need not fear that I will not bring you food, and water, from the moun-*

tains, though they lie far. For myself there is gold here, abundant gold, hidden in the palace's ancient crypt and the secret treasuries of a thousand nobles. Sweet gold, each coin and necklet and ring singing its own song of the earth it came from, the hands that wrought it, the fire that refined. You will be safe.

"I don't want to be safe!" snapped John. But the dragon spread his wings and lifted weightless from the earth, like a thistledown of silver and black. Like a thistledown, Corvin rode on the desert wind, higher and higher, until he was indeed no larger than dandelion-fluff in the harsh blue desert sky.

Chapter 4

Jenny listened to the demons as they whispered in the dark.

So tangled were the passageways of the mines, the narrow tunnels that supplied ventilation and water, that near sounds and far were confused. Even a trained mage like Miss Mab had trouble casting her senses very far into the darkness of the mines. Sometimes a chance whisper near a ventilation shaft a half-dozen levels down would repeat a word nearly in Jenny's ear, startling her to sweat-drenched alertness. Other times the sheer cold massiveness of the mountain's rock deadened even the footfalls of the slave-gangs barely a hundred yards away.

Lying in the darkness, Jenny had a long time to accustom herself to the tricks and echoes of the mines.

Long ago, as a girl-child in the bandit-haunted Winterlands, she had learned to still herself to nothing. To listen, and sort sound from sound, until on summer nights in the attic of her house on Frost Fell she could tell the difference between the rustle wind made in the big hand-shaped leaves of the solitary oak on the south slope of the hill, and the lighter hissing of the birch leaves to the north. Just that sound would tell of the weather for days to come. In those days her powers were slight—this had been before the time of the dragon, before Morkeleb had transformed her into dragon form to fly with him, and in doing so had given her a strain of dragon magic. She had made up for her lack of ability by the most painstaking attention, by long meditation, the study of each star and pebble and raindrop. As Caerdinn had said, the more she knew, the greater would be her power.

This attention, this meditation, returned to her now in the dark. She sorted sound from echo, built words from inflection and rhythm of speech. The stillness in which she listened was like a dream, as if, in sleeping, she passed into the nothingness of the darkness itself. From this nothingness she reached toward the demon voices, bodiless as smoke.

She understood them. That was another thing that the demon Amayon's possession had left in her mind.

"... seven hundred slaves here." A gnome's voice, deep and vaguely familiar. She thought it might be one of the guards who had shot her when she'd fallen into the pit-trap in the mine. He spoke in the tongue of the demons. "Folcalor will bring another two hundred at least."

Two hundred? Jenny gasped, appalled. All through the North she had heard rumors for weeks of gnomes buying slaves. Not, as they ususally did, to work in the deeper levels of the mines, but paying good silver for children too young to work, cripples whose families wanted to be rid of their upkeep, grandparents who could no longer contribute to the harsh endless work of the Winterlands farms. The gnomes, as usual, denied these rumors as they denied all rumors of ever having human slaves. John had freed a band of them when he'd passed Tralchet Deep in the North—they'd warned him then of more sinister goings-on. The days were long gone when the King could send men into the mines to investigate—or do anything about whatever he might find.

But two hundred slaves? And seven hundred ... *where? In the Deep?* The tunnels, Jenny knew, extended much farther north than most people knew, and there were entrances scattered through the great jagged mountain range of Nast Wall. With the Realm's northern province of Imperteng in rebellion against the King all last summer, it would have been easy, of course, to bring in any number of such slaves. But *seven hundred ...?*

How would they even *move* them unseen?

Morkeleb, she thought. He would know how far the tunnels of the Deep extended to the north; Morkeleb or Miss Mab. The dragon had gone to the surface, to lie on the black rocks far above the tree line, scrying the wind. Would he take note of a coffle that large coming out of the Wyrwoods? Or a succession of such trains? Or would he consider it *not a thing of dragons,* to care whether gnomes enslaved humans or not?

"And no luck with the dragon?" A man's voice this time. Again, the timbre was familiar, as if Jenny had heard it before, speaking human words. The gnome must have shaken his head, because the man added a curse. "Unless we find the dragon, we're wasting our time. All this ..." By the flex in his voice Jenny knew he gestured to something—*what?* "... won't give us a toad's spit without her secret name. And you know Folcalor won't listen if we say we can't find him."

"We'll find him. Stinkin' snake. Even if we don't, those'll give us power to find the catch-bottle that old Arch-Seer made."

Those what? Surely if they'd blasted a tunnel to trap Morkeleb, they'd have known he escaped. . . .

"What, in Ernine? With *her* power over all that land?"

Catch-bottle? The phrase was an old one, a spell Jenny had only heard of in the lore handed down by the Line of Herne. Since Caerdinn hadn't been clear himself what it meant or how it worked—his master Spaeth having left the North with the last troops of the King's last garrison—Jenny didn't know, either.

"Her power can only reach so far. We know the bottle was lost when the mages went into the mirror-chamber. For certain she was never trapped in it, the bitch. So all we have to do is find it. How far can it have rolled?"

The man's voice cursed again. "I'm not going after it, I can tell you. . . ."

"Folcalor will go, and you'll go with him or I'll know why. With these here and the ones he'll bring, that should give him the power to see through whatever blinds *she* can weave."

These what? Jenny's mind groped, and she wondered if she'd missed something in the shifting echoes, and the voices faded as the speakers moved away.

"... two days ..." and "... Kings ... damned glad to get the gnome-witch at last ..."

Folcalor.

Jenny sat up, straining to follow the voices, but only the whisper of air moving in the vent shafts met her ears, and the cluck of subterranean streams.

Two days.

She felt absolutely cold.

Another two hundred slaves ... seven hundred HERE. Here in

the mines? Obviously in concealment with the collusion of one or several of the Lords of the Deep, but ... *seven hundred?*

Those will give us power ...

Those what?

Shakily, Jenny pulled on her skirt and her boots. To get to her feet she had to lean on the curve of the wall. The hip she'd twisted when she fell in the pit-trap twinged hard, making her stagger, but that, too, was already responding to the spells of healing Mab and Morkeleb had laid. Mab had brought a staff so that Jenny could limp as far as the latrine-bucket. Its tip was muffled in leather. Jenny groped it from beside her nest of blankets and hothwais, and stood.

Those will give us power.

Seven hundred slaves.

She listened in the darkness again but heard nothing. Not breath, not the murmur of voices, not weeping, not curses, not cries. Wherever the seven hundred slaves were, it was nowhere near where the two demons had been. So what were "those"?

From beneath the blankets she dug the little chip of hothwais Mab had left for light, and wrapped the cold-glowing stone in the folds of her overskirt, two and three thicknesses deep. So piercing was its light that by unwrapping a fold or two she could keep a muffled glow, like the faintest starlight, just enough and only enough to see.

I was once able to see in darkness, she thought. *I should be keener-eyed now in dim light, even if not nightsighted as once I was.* She focused her mind on calling that power to herself, calling it out of herself, and wrapped another fold of skirt around the stone. Then she slipped out of the chamber past the layers of straw mat, listening along the corridors for the direction in which she'd heard the voices.

It wasn't far. In the long hours of silence and listening, she'd heard voices coming from that direction before. This was a section of the mines that had been worked out, short tunnels cut like the legs of a centipede off the long main lode. Jenny worked her way carefully from tunnel to tunnel in the darkness, listening and scenting. Even the most silent of slaves must sweat and breathe and piss. The smells of the mine were thin and cold around her, wet rock and clay and the old wood of the props. The sulfurous drift of blasting powder. Now and then the breath of the vent-shafts brushed her face, or riffled the silky black-silver stubble of her hair. She neither heard nor smelled demons, but wrapped another fold of her skirt over the hothwais nonetheless, fearing even the farthest glimmer of light that might alert them—or the mine-guards—to her presence.

How could they POSSIBLY have seven hundred slaves here? Bring them here, feed them, keep them silent . . . ?

She smelled straw. Wet straw and clay.

And the next instant sensed the presence of others around her, other souls, other thoughts. It was as if she'd walked suddenly into an immense crowd, silently watching. But the thin stream of air along the walls had not altered. The echo of walls close on either side of her was unchanged.

No sound of breathing. No scent of sweat. Only the echo of weeping in her mind, the broken clamor of terror and grief and pain.

Utterly silent in the dark.

No smell of demons, either, nor the whisper of claws on rocks. Nothing of the faint shivering chime that their glass shells made when they scraped against stone. Cold air eddied out of the denser darkness of a tunnel mouth, and Jenny made note of her directions, counting right and left by notching the side of the staff with her knife. She slipped around the corner and advanced into the almost absolute dark.

People. The tunnel was filled with people. She knew it. Impossible, she could touch the walls with her hands! Yet she sensed people all around her, felt their presence. But not a whisper did she hear, not a sound. And no smell save that of damp baskets, of clay pots.

Fearing yet to risk more light, she strained her eyes, shifting the focus of them as once she'd learned to as a mage. The tunnel took another turning, and opened into a little chamber of the kind to which Mab and Morkeleb had carried her, a sort of catacomb whose ceiling made her stoop. The movement of the air there spoke of a small space, not a large one.

A few pots and baskets stood against the wall.

And that was all.

Kneeling, Jenny went to the nearest basket and removed its lid.

It was full of jewels.

Jenny blinked. A dream-vision came back to her . . . when? At the Hold? In the night-camp in the Snakewater Marshes, when she and Morkeleb were on their way here? It had been a dream of Folcalor, whom she'd recognized through Amayon's memories of the demon rebel: Folcalor dipping his hand into a dish of jewels. A gnome's hand, she recalled, powerful, the short fingers adorned with huge rings, slabs of opal and turquoise. She saw again how those stubby knotted fingers had stirred and rubbed the jewels, savoring them. This vision had made no sense to her when she'd had it: Folcalor had imprisoned the minds and souls of the mages he'd enslaved in jewels, Jenny's mind and soul among them, but in her vision there were far, far too many jewels for that.

There hadn't been that many mages born in all of time.

Hundreds . . .

She crawled a little farther and opened the next basket. It, too, was full of gems. Rough-cut crystals, glittering coldly in the darkness.

They mine gold in Ylferdun, she thought. *Not gems.* She scooped up two or three for a closer look.

And nearly dropped them in shock.

Dear gods!

The souls were in the jewels.

Not mages' souls. She would have felt the magic there, the minds still clear and thinking and aware. But souls nonetheless. Weeping, some of them, as she had wept in her prison. Calling out to their husbands, or wives, or children, or parents, or friends, as she had called John's name in despair.

She felt their deaths, too—deaths in agony and horror. She recalled enough of her demon sensibilities to recognize that.

Seven hundred, she thought, first blank, then burning with an all-consuming rage. *SEVEN HUNDRED . . .*

She sat down between the two baskets in the dark, feeling as if she could not breathe.

"Any who wish to rid themselves of old folks, or cripples, or the simpleminded," the innkeeper at Eldsbouch had said to her not so long ago, "can earn good silver by giving them over to the brother Kings. . . ." And as the northern winds had whipped and screamed at the walls of that old stone inn, Jenny and her son Ian had looked at each other in bafflement, wondering why the twin Kings of the Deep of Tralchet would purchase slaves so patently useless. "I think you should let Lord John know of this," the innkeeper had added.

Dear gods, if only I could!

Jenny's small hands shook as she pressed the jewels between them, held them close to her lips. *Your cries are heard. Your cries are heard. Be at peace.* She tried to will comfort to them, but she understood that they were dead, and they could not hear. Tortured by demons, murdered by demons, the moment of death prolonged and suspended in the jewels . . .

What would become of their souls?

Damn them. DAMN THEM . . .

It was forbidden to all the ancient Lines of wizardry, to generate magic by the sacrificial death of a human being. But it was known to all of them—certainly to the demons—that it was possible to do so.

Folcalor trapped those deaths, as he trapped the souls of the wizards, and for the same purpose.

To transform into weapons. To use against the Demon Queen, or against Folcalor's Lord Adromelech . . .

Those will give us power.

Jenny scrambled to her feet again, trembling, glad that she had the staff to support her shaking knees. She felt as if she had been struck over the head, understanding everything now, sickened and shocked and unable to do a thing. She looked at the jewels in her hand—rough crystals, mostly, hunks of quartz and amethyst and a few garnets, rudely hewed and most with bits of their native rock or dirt adhering to them. Wanting to do something, but not knowing what she could do.

Carry them all away with her? It wouldn't take the demons, in their gnome or their human bodies, long to track her down if she did that. Destroy them all? It would take hours. . . .

Hide them? There were two baskets and two pots, none very large or heavy. John had spoken of escaped slaves hiding in the worked-out galleries of the Tralchet mines, and had helped some escape. Presumably the same situation existed in Ylferdun, and the theft could be blamed on them. Jenny stooped to lift the first of the baskets, then froze, scenting, far off, the metallic whiff of demons in the moving drift of the ventilated air.

The tunnel was a cul-de-sac. She slipped the loose jewels still in her hand into her skirt pocket, caught up her staff, and fled. In the main tunnel the smell was stronger, and she flitted back along the way she had come, counting the side-shafts that were like separate abysses, darkness within dark.

Mab would know what to do, or Morkeleb ... or John. Surely there had to be something that could be done.

Dear gods, she thought as she made her way back to the comfort of her own small niche, her rock womb in the great rock and darkness that seemed to constitute all the world now. *Dear gods, where is John?*

And she saw him again as last she'd seen him, disappearing into the blowing snow. Saw the battered grimness of his face and the bitter lines around his mouth as he helped Ian onto a horse, the long wet strands of his hair caught with flecks of sleet. His dark plaids billowed around his body as he mounted his horse, and when he moved suddenly, the thin silvery ghost-trace of the Demon Queen's marks on his cheekbones caught the faded afternoon light.

On that bitter afternoon he'd been preoccupied with Ian, with getting him back to Alyn Hold before the storm got worse. She hoped that was the reason he hadn't appeared to notice when she'd slipped her own horse back into the stable, and returned to the house. During the storm that followed she had sunk back into her dreams of the demons that in those days had possessed her with a ferocity that she now could barely conceive.

When the storm was over she'd gone to the Hold, hoping and fearing to see him as well as seeking to see her son. They'd said John had ridden out. Had ridden out after burning his workshop, something he never would have done, she knew, had he not conjured something there that he feared would harm whoever later entered that ramshackle, junk-crammed shed.

She had a terrible feeling that she knew what he had summoned there.

In all the weeks since—through bandit-siege and darkness, during her journey to Eldsbouch and her own disastrous conjuration of what was left of the wizard Caradoc and on until her departure with Morkeleb for the plague-haunted South—John had not been seen.

The Yellow-Haired Goddess, the Horned Goddess, Balyna of the Sea, who was called Hartemgardes in the North, was the goddess lovers prayed to, to reunite them with their loves. But Jenny prayed, as she had come more and more to pray, to the discredited God of

Time, the thirteenth God whom old legends said had dreamed the other twelve; and she did not know exactly what it was that she prayed. *Time come around,* she thought, *and make the circle whole; time come around and make the circle whole.*

But only the God of Time knew what that circle was.

We have to get you out of here, Morkeleb said when he returned. *The tunnels between this place and the warrens of the Arawan clan on the Ninth Level creep with demons.* Jenny saw into his mind, and saw the silvery salamander shapes darting along the bases of the rock walls like unwholesome quicksilver in the blackness. She smelled the foul sharp pungence of them, felt the tingle of their dreadful magic, probing for her.

We cannot leave Miss Mab. Nor can we forsake those whose deaths are suspended within the crystals, without trying at least to get them away. The Master of Halnath may know what to do to release them.

The gates of Halnath are shut. Through Morkeleb's mind she saw from far off the black rings of the university fortress's walls, adamantine on their black knee of mountain rock. The smoke of cook fires fingered into the gray overcast. *The Master is not there. Rumor has it that he is in hiding in Bel, either to traffick with demons and further spread the plague, or to attempt to murder the King or the King's Heir . . .*

That's absurd, said Jenny. *It was Polycarp who sent me here to the Deep, to learn of the demons from Miss Mab.*

The patent absurdity of any rumor, replied the dragon drily, *has never yet halted its spread, and I have observed such matters for many lives of men. I look to the palace of the King of Men and I see only the glamours of the demons about it, like shining clouds. Moreover, as I lay on the glaciers above the mines and cast my mind down into the city, rumor came to me that the Dreamweaver of whom you are so fond was taken by the King, and would have been put to death—*

John? Jenny's breath stopped, and she stared disbelieving into the diamond infinities of the dragon's eyes, which were all of him that were visible in the cave's dark. *How came he . . . ?*

That I know not. Had they not been friends, and after long acquaintance used to passing thought back and forth like sisters trading hair ribbons, he would have closed his mind against her, to shut out her awareness of his regret. But she knew the regret was there, and the sadness, that she had chosen mortality and the loves of mortality: even the love of one who had cursed her in silence over the body of their dying son.

The names of dragons are music, threnodies embodying all that they truly are. She heard the regret woven in his name and his soul, at the way her heart skipped just then, hearing John's name.

Regret and amusement, at himself and at her.

It was he: I heard his name. They say in the town that the demons sent a dragon to carry him off to safety; many in the marketplaces accuse ME of the deed.

He is safe?

This I know not. The dragon may have been a minion of the Queen behind the mirror. Or it may have had a score of his own to settle with your husband, or wanted to discuss with him the Analects of Polyborus or the breeding of pigs. I listened long for him, scrying the winds of heaven. I saw him not.

Jenny sat silent in her blankets, the hothwais of warmth cupped between her frozen hands. Even had she unwrapped the hothwais of light it would have done her little good, for Morkeleb was probably invisible. Still, she saw him clearly in her mind, spined and dark and serpentine, with his antenna-bobs glowing in the blackness, coiled in the small space of her little cave. The dragons she had saved from Folcalor and his demons all owed her fealty, though she had released them of any debt to her. One of them might have saved John—he had drawn out the spikes of quicksilver and adamant from their skulls, where the demons had dwelled. Nymr and Centhwevir, Hagginarshildim and Enismirdal . . .

But in that case why could Morkeleb not find him? He had said that from the glacier where he lay, on the Wall's high crest, he could scry vast distances. He knew John well, having come down with him from the Skerries of Light in the summer, dragging John's sagging and battered flying machine by its ropes. The dragon's mind saw clear, like a hawk that can identify a rabbit from hundreds of feet in the air. John must be far off indeed if the dragon could not detect the beating of his heart.

And Miss Mab? she said again, and Morkeleb sighed. She put her palm on his narrow, bony forehead, and his thought enfolded her; she felt him cast his mind along the dark of the corridors, seeking for Miss Mab.

But the gnome-wife, when she came at length to what appeared to be a saucer of water on a table in her lamplit room—Jenny saw this only distantly, like a half-recalled dream—refused again to flee from the Deep. "None do I trust here, and none do I let come near," she said, and she glanced around her, as if at shadows Jenny could not see. "My uncle the Howeth-Arawan, Patriarch of the Ninth Deep, and my cousins and brothers hold too much power for King Sevacandrozardus to send any here, against my will. In fleeing I will lose what I have here—a position in which I might yet do good."

"Folcalor will be here in two days," said Jenny. "I think he must be traveling in the train of your Master Goffyer of Tralchet. Miss Mab, it is not inconceivable that Folcalor has taken over the body and the soul of Goffyer himself, for Goffyer is a mage and this would be the demon's goal. Could you stand against Goffyer, if you had to?"

Mab was silent. Jenny saw, through Morkeleb's eyes and Morkeleb's mind, the flicker of refusal in the gnome-wife's wrinkled-apple face as she pushed the thought from her that her old master would be enslaved as others had been enslaved. Then she said, "If this be so, all the more reason for me to remain. To help him if I can. To help others here, if I cannot. My clan will protect me, as well as any can. I would not have thee, child, nor you, Dragonshadow, put yourselves in danger trying to reach me here, or to rescue me if I encountered demons in the mines in my attempt at flight. So long as I remain here in the warrens among my family, I will be safe. Goffyer . . ."

Her golden eyes grew sad. "Goffyer was a gnome of great age, a master of lore and a mage of tremendous power. If they could take him . . ."

Their strength is the strength of the one who fights them, said Morkeleb. *It is like shining a light into a mirror. Do not think, gnome-wife, that you can stand against him by strength alone.*

And she said, "I will do what I can."

From that they could not move her. Nor, to tell the truth, could Jenny imagine how they would get to her to take her out of the warrens on the Ninth Deep, for when she listened into the darkness, she could hear the scritching of demon claws on the rock in the silence, in every passageway and tunnel in that direction.

As Mab must hear it, she thought. She wondered how much of the gnome-wife's refusal to be rescued was due to awareness of that danger to the rescuers, and to herself if she tried now to leave.

After that, Jenny listened long into the darkness of the mines, casting her thoughts to the mains of played-out rock that surrounded them, focusing her attention on the sigh of the vent shafts, on the drip of water from underground springs. Lying on the floor beside her bed like a dog, Morkeleb listened, too, his dragon senses reaching farther and his mind following those senses, like tendrils of smoke through the air. *Hear you aught of the Hellspawn, Jenny?* murmured his voice in her mind, and she murmured back,

Not north of us in the mine. In the Deep, yes, everywhere.

Nor I. Nor yet footfall of guard or scout. Let us see what we can carry away, of these seven hundred dead slaves you feel such pity for.

By the notches she had carved on her stick Jenny was able to find the place again, familiarity aiding her in seeing the shape of the rock walls. She found herself able to identify the little landmarks of ceiling dips and bends in the passageway, barely to be seen by the glow of her thick-wrapped hothwais as once she'd identified sprigs of blossom or saplings beside some Winterlands trail. But the little chamber was empty when they reached it. Not one gem remained on the slimy uneven floor.

Can you scry them? she asked, in distress. *Scent them, find them?* And she took the two or three crystals she carried in her skirt pocket and held them out to him, for him to feel and sense what they were. He breathed on the stones, his breath velvet on her hand. Then he fell silent for a time, reaching with his mind. She called upon the disciplines he had taught her, and those Mab had spoken of, the powers within her changed flesh and mind, and reached out likewise. She heard, far behind them, the scrape of boots on rock, and a gnome's voice say something about straw matting. Her heart beat hard, knowing her hiding-place had been discovered.

Morkeleb said nothing. But when he moved off it was northward, not back to her shelter, and she followed. The ways they took, up steep stairways and narrow twisting shafts, told her that he, too, had failed to find any trace of the prison-crystals, for they were going upward through the mountain to the old watchtowers on its flanks. Breathless with her long recuperation, Jenny stumbled, and the dragon's clawed grip bore her up—she still could not tell whether he wore a dragon's shape or a man's. At last they came to a chimney through the heart of the stone, whose hot rising air lifted Jenny's ragged clothing around her and breathed on her face like some great beast. Morkeleb stepped out into the darkness before her and she saw him hanging there in the utter blackness, dark within dark, with his diamond eyes glittering and his wings spread out like sable silk and all the glowing bobs of his antennae swinging and flickering like fireflies.

In his clawed hands he grasped her, holding her against him as they rose through the abyss, up and up with the rock tube narrowing around them. At last they came out into true night, and freezing air, stars burning hard above Nast Wall's jagged rim of basalt and ice. This was the world as dragons saw it, clean and untouched, uncomplicated and magical; the world Morkeleb had once asked her to enter, through a door that she was not sure, now, that she would be able to re-pass.

To the east above the horns of the mountain she saw the glowing streak of the comet, the Dragonstar John had watched for these three years now. An unknowable thing, she thought, different in nature from the stars, from the moon, from any thing on the earth. But John, being John, had spent a good deal of time trying to understand it, when it had nothing to do with the duties he had been bequeathed by his father, nor with the affairs of Kings, nor the struggle to survive in the Winterlands.

Morkeleb said nothing, letting her speak first, waiting for her thought.

Jenny said, "Let us go to Ernine."

Chapter 5

John Aversin was in Prokep for seven days before the demons came.

Having been told by Corvin NinetyfiveFifty that it was impossible for him to get anywhere close to the Henge, the first thing he did when the dragon flew away to hunt was to wrap himself in his velvet cloak and walk down to where he calculated the Henge had been last night by moonlight and in that morning's vision. There were places in the Winterlands that were said only to exist under the light of certain phases of the moon, or things that were visible only when the sun and the moon were together in the sky or on certain days of the year—a standing stone on Moonfairy Hill was one of them, two days' ride north of the Hold. He'd spent the best part of two years visiting the place, again and again, whenever his other duties gave him time, until he'd seen it, in a dell he'd visited a dozen times before.

His recent journeys through Hell had certainly taught him how to look for gates into places that sometimes existed and sometimes did not.

Being so shortsighted that he could barely see his hand in front of his face didn't help the situation, of course. He considered marking where he thought the Henge should lie with something large enough for even himself to see at a distance, but aside from the fact that the only thing he had was his cloak, which he needed to keep from freezing to death, he couldn't be sure when Corvin would be back.

It was just as well the dragon not know what he was up to.

So he took careful sightings on all the stationary landmarks he could, on the shape of distant hills and the exact lines of sight of the corners of that huge stone foundation—it would take an earthquake to shift it—and then began to work his way around the perimeter of where he thought the Circle should be.

Looking for the places where the dust-devils appeared to come from.

According to Gantering Pellus's *Encyclopedia*–and his own observations–the gates of Hell are seldom completely tight, and the temperature of the air there is generally either warmer or cooler than that of the real world.

John crept, either on his hands and knees or squatting and stooping in a way that made his knees and back feel as if someone were driving red-hot nails into the bones, back and forth across the huge grayish-dun expanses of what had been the center of the city of Prokep. It was the slow way to do it, but with a clear field of vision that ended less than a foot from the tip of his nose he couldn't devise a better one. And, for that matter, he reflected, what else did he have to do with his day?

He found the first gate by the flowers.

There were dozens of them, wilted to shreds of brown string on the ash-colored sand. Just a tangly little patch of vegetation that had no business being where it was. *Like the Henge,* he thought, *this gate into the Maze is only in existence–or only visible–at certain times or under certain conditions: I'll have to watch, and see when the wind sets from this direction.* The dessicated wisps of grass, the parched finger-lets of fern, grew in a rough semicircle, as if someone had laid a military cloak on the sand. *The gate opens, seeds drift through. They root, they claim a little moisture from the air the next time the gate's open, but a few suns kill 'em.*

He crept back and forth along the flatter edge of the semicircle until he found the place where the small ghostly tracks of what looked like worms or slugs came from and went to, mysterious weav-ings around the sand that ended as sharply as if smoothed away with a trowel.

The threshhold of the gate, he thought, uneasily passing his hand through the air over the spot–of course nothing happened to his hand whatsoever. He drew in the sand the sigil of the gate, which he'd seen Amayon draw, often enough, in their journeys together through Hell. Still no result.

Wrong time of day.

Or of year.

No, he reflected, crawling back to find the most recent of the dead flower stalks. *This hasn't been dead but a few days.* A little green lingered at its base. He sat back on his heels, back aching, and squinted at those few stones, pillars, and hills large enough to register in his vision. *It opens often, at the time of day when the wind sets from between those two notches in the hills.*

Whenever that is.

In addition to three more rabbits and a mountain sheep—which John hung in what had been a ruined guard-chamber beside the foundation's great stair—Corvin brought him clothing that evening, striped breeches woven in a pattern with which John was unfamiliar, a shirt and sheepskin boots that were all too big for him, and a coat of black and white goatskins. The coat had blood on it. John didn't ask from whence it had come. Corvin also brought more wood, and when John cooked the meat he rendered what little fat he could out of it, to pour on the ends of sticks to make torches.

The second day he found the treasury, deep in the crypts where Corvin would lie up most of the night on a bed of gold. Sacks of coin long rotted away, so that the bright metal lay in drifts, palanquins and statues and chairs and mirrors of gold or electrum or bronze scattered about and rising through it like the ruin of the city in miniature, gems flashing somberly in the orange glare of the torch. John knew better than to cross the threshhold or touch so much as a toothpick. Corvin's soul would know, and pursue gold anywhere—it had been no coincidence that Aohila, who knew the dragon best, had triggered the spells of his True Name with beads of gold.

In another room he found swords, knives, and arrowheads, though the shafts and bows had all perished. He felt better, once he had weapons, though he knew they'd be little use to him if demons showed up.

And they would show up, he knew. Corvin said they feared Prokep, which had a way, he said, of trapping demons. But John knew better than to believe that Folcalor would give up his dream of ruling both Hell and earth. It would only be a matter of when he would strike.

Better than the weapons, John found spectacle lenses, some of ground yellow crystal and others of brownish glass. Some were set in frames of horn or bronze, mounted on sticks like carnival masks, others lay loose in boxes. He braided a strap from the rags of his discarded execution shift, and mounted the best of them in a bronze frame, but he took care to wear this contraption only after Corvin was gone for the day.

After that, it was easier to seek for the gates to the Maze.

In the end he found several, mostly by sitting on the edge of the palace foundation and observing the dust-devils. The second day he made sure to be poking around in the ruins south of the foundation—on the side away from the Maze—when Corvin flew away in the morning, so that the dragon would think nothing of it if he did not see him before he departed: And where, John thought, would the dragon expect him to flee, anyway? Even the ridge of hills that surrounded the city in a vast basin lay unendurably far off. Flight would be madness, like a child running away from home with two bannocks and an apple wrapped in a handkerchief.

Cautiously, John began to probe at the Maze.

He located three other gates before he entered the one through the Garden of Dawn by observing the dust-devils, but it was the Garden of Dawn he entered through, near the withered flowers, on the fourth morning of watching. The garden was of the same nature as the Hells, a place outside the world of sun and stars. When he wrote the sigil of the door at the moment of sunrise, and smelled the dew and the flowers, he experienced a qualm of apprehension—*What if it's like a lobster pot, that I can walk into but can't escape?*

But given the length of time it had taken a dragon to fly from Bel to Prokep—from mid-morning till sunset without stopping—the city in the desert was something of a lobster pot itself. John stepped across the sigil, and found himself in the Garden of Dawn.

Amayon—and every book he'd read on the subject as well—had repeatedly warned against eating or drinking anything in Hell. Whether this applied to an unworld enclave like the garden John wasn't sure, but he guessed he'd better not chance it. Fountains bubbled among hillocks of mossy stone, and in places trees bent under the weight of peaches so ripe, he could smell them from the winding pebbled path. It seemed to be midsummer, strange vines and familiar ones bearing gaudy flowers, and the moist air stroked his dusty skin. When a yellow butterfly danced across his path in the soft dawn light he nearly bolted, for he remembered all too clearly the deadly butterflies of Paradise. He listened, but could hear no sound; only the faint stirring of willow leaves in the wind.

The gate was clearly visible behind him. He could see the desert—and a corner of the palace foundation—through it, washed with the first pink flush of the new sun's light, and the gibbous moon just setting above the hills. The wall around the garden was black basalt, laid without mortar, and disappeared among thickets of ivy and poplars. John followed it around as well as he could, and ascertained that the garden itself was some half-mile in diameter, roughly circular, and contained five gates.

Three were in the wall. One was in a stone pavilion on an island in the garden's miniature lake. The fifth was in a clearing: He located it, as he had the entrance to the garden itself, by the withering of the moss beside it. When he drew the sigil, and passed through, the enclave on the other side was dark and bitterly cold.

The gate behind him disappeared the moment he stepped through it, and he thought, *Torches, next time. If there is a next time.* Winds savaged him, cold slicing through his jacket and clothing as if he were again clothed only in the thin shift of the condemned. He dropped at once to his hands and knees, felt the contours of the ground behind him—unpaved, rough, rock or dirt—and drew the sigil of the door immediately in the place over which he guessed he had just passed.

Nothing happened.

Damn it, he thought, shivering desperately, *don't do this to me....*

The wind must have knocked him a step or two as he'd come through. He patiently crawled upwind and tried again, and then again. The Old God—who knows everything—only knew what was in the darkness with him, or how far this Hell or enclave extended. If there was a stricture against eating anything you found in Hell there was probably not one against something you found in Hell eating you. After what felt like an hour, John located the gate again and crawled through.

It was still dawn in the garden, delicious with the twittering of birds. And, to judge by the leaf-mold beneath the trees, the relative clarity of the paths among the shrubberies, it was still the year of the last appearance of the Dragonstar, ten centuries ago.

Any gate that'd have a pavilion built over it, he thought, contemplating the spot in the strange little multiroofed structure where the slightly sulfurous stench lingered, *can't be the one the chaps in the yellow robes didn't want me to walk through. Let's take a miss on this one.* The three in the walls were all neatly kept: None looked more neglected than the others, or more used. In the tangles of white-flowering shrubs that grew to either side of the central of the three gates—they were about a dozen yards apart, all on what appeared to be the north wall of the garden—he found two insects, or what looked like insects. Dead, fortunately, since they were the length of the knuckle of his thumb and equipped with the most comprehensive sets of chewing, stabbing, and gripping mandibles he'd ever seen in his life. He'd encountered such creatures nowhere else in the garden, but a search of the area around the central gate yielded five more dead ones and a live one that struck him, wings roaring, from a tree, dug its claws into the side of his face—it had gone for his eyes, but fortunately he was wearing his spectacles—and began to chew.

When he cut its head off, the head continued to chew. He had to strike fire with the flints and steel that had been in the coat's pockets, and burn the thing off his cheekbone.

Let's not go through that gate unless we really, REALLY have to.

John didn't check the other two gates until the next day. He didn't really feel up to it.

When he came out of the garden gate it was still dawn. Still—by the finger-mark he'd drawn in the sand, unblurred by wind—the day he'd gone in, which was a relief. *Be a bit embarassin' if I was gone for a month or a year ... I know dragons don't think much of time, but even Corvin'd notice that.* He trudged back to the painted chamber in the palace foundation and made a dressing of rags and sheep-fat for the torn, blistered flesh of his cheek. Then he rested for a time, inventing an explanation for the injury, should Corvin ask, and life-stories for three more of the tribute-bearers who decorated the wall: the chap in the blue with the feathers was named Browdiestomp and had a wife at home whom everyone called the Beautiful Coco, who was fonder of her birds than she was of him—little yellow and green ones who whistled, and a red and black one who told her stories of things far away, which it made up of course because it had never been out of its golden cage in its life. But the Beautiful Coco believed them because she wasn't much smarter than the birds.

Later he took a box from the armory and in a nest of earth and rags stowed a couple of smoldering coals from last night's fire, took a couple of unlit torches and went exploring for other gates in the city. He found none that day. In his seeking he had a long while to think of the things the Demon Queen had showed him on his way to the pyre, of Amayon lying in Gareth's arms, smiling and whispering love and poison into his ear. Of King Uriens greeting the Lords of the Great Houses with hearty cheer: He'd always been a more impressive King than his shy, pedantic son. The Lords of Greenhythe and Yamstrand and the islands would fall over themselves with delight, wanting to believe that he was back and therefore things would be back the way they'd always been.

Of Ian and Adric—and their tiny sister, Maggie, too—trapped in Alyn Hold by the deadly shadows of magic and banditry outside. *Did you see it?* Ian had whispered. John didn't like to contemplate what "it" might have been.

Of Jenny, dying in darkness.

He had asked Corvin the second night—when the dragon had returned with the sheep and the clothing—of Jenny. Corvin had said, *It is a night and a day since Aohila showed you these things, Dragonsbane. Do you think your woman has lived so long?*

"Please," John had said. "Aohila might've been lyin'—she does that. If you can't see Jen, can you see Morkeleb the Black? He'd be with her, he's her friend. . . ."

And had felt Corvin's incredulity, and, a moment later, like a gust of sea-scent on the wind, the enmity the silver dragon bore for the black. A tangle of opinions—*sly, unscrupulous, haughty*—sparkled in the music of the silver dragon's thoughts, and with them, envy and anger, and the ringing sweet music of gold and gems that the black dragon had taken, which the silver wanted, some time deep in the abysses of the past.

To live forever is to remember slights eternally.

Corvin had sniffed, and turned away.

In the painted chamber that night, watching the firelight on the walls, John thought of Jenny, as he had thought of her every night in

Prokep. She had told him once—the first time she'd returned from taking the form of a dragon—that she had returned because she knew that if she remained a dragon in body, she would become one in her heart, and would forget what it was to be a woman, and to love.

He saw her then—as she had been then, with the midnight oceans of her hair lying over his shoulder where her head rested, and her small square face like a sunburned acorn looking up into his—as she said, *I did not want to forget you, my love. I did not want you to grow old, with me not there.*

Her voice was deep, grained through with sweetness, like silver in rock. He couldn't imagine never hearing it again.

Ah, love, if we either of us live to grow old, it'll be more than I'd bet on tonight.

When he was young, and she would not come to the Hold to live with him, he used to scream at her, curse her, as he had wanted to curse the Icerider witch who had been his mother and who had left him, too: *It's all you care about, isn't it? Your magic and your power.*

He couldn't imagine why she hadn't turned him into a toad, let alone why she'd borne him not one child in those days, but two.

Let her be alive, he prayed to the Old God, watching the dim firelight shift over the shapes of the tribute-bearers on the walls. *You can have all that tribute those fellers are carryin', I promise I won't keep a penny of it, if only she'll be alive when I get back. . . . If I get back.*

But he'd lived in the Winterlands too long to believe that things ended happily. He had seen too many people he knew die.

The chap in the red boots there on the end, he thought, turning his eyes back to the wall. *He has a wife who's a witch, and she loves her power—well, not more than she loves him, but as much. Yet she came to his life, and bore him two sons and a daughter, which has to have hurt . . . she loved him that much. Then one day she turned into a beautiful white dragon and flew away. And she was happy forever.*

John reached the Henge of Prokep the following day.

It helped enormously, that time stood still in the enclaves. He could search patiently, drawing the sigil of the door over and over, until he got through; he'd learned to keep a torch burning in one hand the moment he stepped through a gate, and a drawn sword in the other, and—if nothing attacked him, and usually it did not—to immediately turn and mark where the gate lay. He brought water with him, too, in a clay jar slung over his shoulder on a strap of braided rags. At least, from enclave to enclave, there was no worry about whether it was half an hour after noon or not.

The gate on the left, the one immediately to the right of the Gate of Dawn, passed him through into the Salt Garden: stone pavement, beds of glittering salt stretching hundreds of feet in all directions under a pitiless golden sky. There was no gate to be seen there, but at noon, when he had returned to Prokep and was investigating the other gate locations he'd found, he passed through one of them and found himself in the Salt Garden again, and spent a grueling eternity in the heat there until he found by sheer patience where the invisible gate was, that let him into the Maze beyond.

Sometimes the walls of the Maze were hedges—knee-high in places, head-high in others. Sometimes they were stone: gray smooth river stones, or harsh hunks of black basalt like the garden wall. Sometimes the Maze itself was just a gravel path raised between mossy ditches where a little water glittered, curtained by a very fine scrim of mist. John knew better than to step off the path or touch the mist in any fashion. He didn't know what would happen if he did, but had an idea he wouldn't like it. From a number of points in the Maze it was possible to see the Henge, huge dark uneven stones showing through whitish fog. As he'd seen by moonlight, and again in Corvin's vision, they seemed to be about twice his nearly six foot height, rough-hewn and, as he drew nearer, he could see that some of them were embellished with the same crude carvings that he'd sometimes seen on standing-stones on the far northern moors in the Winterlands, spirals and rings and crosses. There were ninety of them, when he counted them from a break in the tall hedges of the Maze. When he came out to where the hedges were shorter and counted again, there were eighty-seven.

Intrigued, he began to count from wherever he could see them, and quickly discovered that if he was on the correct path there were ninety; if the path was leading him to a dead end, or to one of those places where the level of the ground dipped down under sheets of still silvery water, there were either more or less. Why the makers of the Henge would have created a Maze in the first place, John wasn't sure—it was a far less effective form of defense than the nodes of choice in the gardens—but in two places mists covered the path, and he felt himself watched from the hedges by unseen eyes.

Watching for demons, he wondered? Corvin had set electronic alarms on his Otherworld property that would be triggered by a demon's presence, and had spoken of such things still active in Prokep. Or was this only his own imagination, fueled by nerves and exhaustion?

The Henge itself stood where it had stood for a thousand years, in the midst of the ruined city. Standing next to its stones, John could see across the barren ground, to the three pillars where a temple had stood, to the pit of the dry lake. To the palace foundation, where Corvin brought new gold every evening from other caches in the city to lie upon; where tribute-bearers walked eternally around the walls of John's painted room. Standing beside the circle of stones, John wondered if he would be invisible to someone standing in that sand-clogged doorway in the foundation, where he and Corvin had stood four days ago. Wondered if he would have to go back through the Maze to return to the place, and what would happen if he simply tried to walk cross-country to it.

Would the Henge disappear behind him?

Would he disappear?

It was noon, the hour at which he had stepped across the threshhold into the Salt Garden.

At a guess, the third gate he'd detected could be opened at sunset. Would the Maze be the same?

He peered cautiously between the stones, into the center of the Henge.

He couldn't see the little flash of water at the center—probably in a depression in the ground. There was a slight distortion of the air over where it would lie, like a heat-dance. Corvin had told him he couldn't get into the Henge, and in any case John had been married to a witch far too long to casually step over the boundary of any magical enclosure, let alone one containing even worse demons than those he'd already met. Instead, he walked around it, keeping close to the stones where the air was still, counting the stones: There were ninety-three when he walked sun-wise; eighty-eight when he walked widdershins the first time. A second count yielded still different numbers, to his intense delight. As he'd seen at a distance the stones had been rough-hewn and some of them were carved—he made notes on the clay side of his water jar—and they were all of the same close-grained, faintly bluish stone. They bore no marks of weathering, and varied in height from about eight feet to over twelve.

The sun was visible from beside the Henge, and the shadows of the stones crept out over the sand, but still John backtrailed his way through the Maze, through the Salt Garden and the Garden of Dawn, to reach the city of Prokep again. That night beneath the late-rising half-moon he stood on the great stone foundation and looked out toward the Henge, and saw it clearly, black shadows on the formless ivory of the land.

And now what?

He turned his palms up. In the moonlight the silver traces the Demon Queen had left gleamed thinly on his skin.

You know the way through the Maze. You know what Folcalor has to be planning, you know what Adromelech has all these centuries been waiting to command his servants to do.

You are here in Prokep, a prisoner, and you will die in the desert before you will escape.

Grimly, John returned to his painted room, and by firelight cut the gems from the red velvet cloak, to sell for money should he ever reach human lands again. The tribute-bearers on the walls stalked impassively with the movement of the fire, and didn't offer him so much as a penny.

In the days that followed, John explored the city, and the Maze, stubbornly turning his mind from the futility of what he did. In time, the demons would come, no matter what their fears of the city's ancient, hidden traps. Adromelech would bring them.

Folcalor, greedy for vengeance and power, would not stay away.

In the night he dreamed, over and over, of walking that narrow, windless zone around the outside of the ring, and in his dreams he could see the demons inside.

Adromelech, gross and savage, a silvery green shape whose belly moved with the dying remains of those lesser wights he'd devoured, who lived inside him, crying, still. The Arch-wight's silver eyes watched John as he walked from stone to stone, clever greedy unhuman eyes, with rectangular pupils like the Demon Queen's: watching and waiting. Sometimes in his dreams John could see

Amayon in the ring, as he'd seen him in the Hell of the Shining Things, when terror of true death, real death, had broken his concentration from the illusion in which demons lived, and left him in his actual shape, wizened and shrunken and silver. Sometimes he saw the Demon Queen herself, smiling at him through the pyre-smoke.

In the evenings, when Corvin returned from his flights, John would tell him, "The demons will come. The Dragonstar hasn't got that long to stay in the sky—accordin' to my calculations it'll be gone by the Moon of Winds. If Adromelech's had his goons out workin' to stir up whatever power-sourcin' they can for this long, you can bet he's not gonna sit back an' say, *Oh, too tough, well, let's just stay here for another thousand years. . . ."*

But Corvin, lying among his gold, only blinked sleepily at him and spoke in that whispery voice in his mind: *They will not come. They cannot. The Henge was formed and sourced in the deaths of the ten greatest mages of that time, and there are traps in the city that make it perilous for them to linger here. They cannot find their way through the Maze before it destroys them. They will not come.*

And John learned that it was foolish, to try to speak to the silver dragon when he lay dreaming among the music that he called from the gold, even as he'd learned early never to argue with his father when Lord Aver sat late over his wine. He could only return to his chamber and lie awake, watching his painted friends march in their eternal procession, listening for the first sound of trouble and wondering what the hell he could do about it when it came.

On a night of wind he dreamed of the Demon Queen. He saw the Burning Mirror in its chamber beneath the ruins of Ernine, the black enamel that covered it cracked, light and smoke streaming forth. The Demon Queen stepped out through those cracks as if through a door, and as she stepped, fire blasted all the chamber's rock to splinters. When she walked each step took her miles. She flew with her dark hair a tangled wrack in the night; she lifted from the ground, spread out her arms into the wind, and laughed. Wind and fire surged around her, the air a maelstrom of heat and carnage, and in it John heard a queer, musical zinging, a sigh and whisper, far-off silver chimes. Flying things moved in it, some formed of dust and others of fire; formed, and blended away to dust again.

But fire flickered in the dust.

And the Demon Queen quickened her stride to outrun the fire.

John woke to the metallic whining, and the smell of dust in the wind.

He slipped his makeshift spectacles on, and wrapped around him the cloak that he used as a blanket as well; he slept in his boots. From beneath the bracken he pulled the ancient sword he'd hidden there, and the dagger, hung on a sash of braided rags, though he knew the arms would do him no good against the things he'd sensed in his dreams. He strode down the passageway with the choke of dust in his nose and lungs, and the firelight glowing behind him in the painted chamber showed him the air filled with glittering black specks like blowing sand.

When they struck his face they cut heavier than sand.

Beyond the doorway the night was like falling into a bag of soot. Far off in the darkness he could see flecks of what looked like silver fire, and in the direction that he knew the Henge would lie, a single, tiny greenish flame. Wind lashed and tumbled the air, the grains that blew in it cutting his skin like tiny knives. When John retreated back into the passageway and touched his cheek with his fingers, he brought them away smudged with blood.

Metal? he thought.

And then, *Dear gods.*

He bolted back to his own chamber, unearthed a torch, and lit it, strode for the Treasury as fast as he could go without killing the wavering flame. As a Dragonsbane, he knew that when you attacked a dragon in its lair, you had to reach him fast, reach him before he got clear of the covered place so that he could not rise in the air above you, either to attack or to get away. He shouted as he ran, "Corvin!" but knew he wouldn't be heard.

Corvin would be dreaming, breathing his dreams of past joys into the ocean of gold and drinking back the beauty of them a thousandfold, magnified by the gold's music.

The flying specks of sand in the air were gold.

John knew it instinctively, guessed it. It was what he would do if he could, to trap a dragon and render it too drunk and confused to escape. No dragon could think clearly around large amounts of refined gold—Morkeleb was the only one he knew who had renounced gold completely.

He knew, as Aohila knew, that a dragon's heart would follow gold, even unto doom.

Dust and particles of sand—gold—hazed the air, even in the treasury. Not being mageborn himself—or any more sensitive than an old boot, John would have added—he could not feel, as Jenny could, the sweet-singing emanations of the magic blended through and magnified by the gold. All he saw was the great black and silver shape curled on its bed of coin and gems and statuary, glittering in the lamplight like an extension of the treasure itself. Even the bobs of light that would flick and move on the ends of the dragon's antennae in normal sleep were dimmed, hanging like the grimed raindrops of the other world in which Corvin had hidden so long. The room was thick with the hot, faintly metallic smell of the dragon, and in sleep the hooked silver claws tightened spasmodically, reflexively, around the coins.

"Wake up!" yelled John, walking over and kicking the dragon's nose. (*Bet THAT's one the heroes of legend never got round to.*) "Wake up, damn it, they're coming!"

And how long's it going to take them to get round to me, after they've got Corvin all secure?

He thought of the Demon Queen and went cold with panic. Even if the demons moving in the dust were not her minions but those of Folcalor, he'd seen demons turn aside from their intended task in order to disembowel bystanders simply for the immediate gratification of hearing them scream.

Demons were dangerous, but they were sloppy hunters. Being deathless, they knew there was always time to go after escaped prey another day. They would not forgo the pleasure of another's pain, even for their own ultimate benefit.

He'd met people like that as well, of course.

He picked up a silver statue, whacked Corvin on the side of the face, on the blank dark purple-tinted eyelids, with all the strength in his arm. "Wake up, you brainless worm! Demons!"

Still nothing. To the dragon the whole atmosphere must be a drowsy glory of happiness, drowning in gold, forgetting all other things.

"Damn it," John muttered, picked up the biggest and gaudiest piece of gold he could see—a lamp stand nearly his own height, wrought like a tree with crystal fruit—and, staggering under its weight, started to carry it to the door.

And dropped it, ducking a cat-paw swat from the dragon's clawed forefoot that would have broken his bones against the wall if it had landed. "Demons!" he yelled, rolling out of the way of Corvin's slashing teeth. "Demons, coming here!" And fetched up, gasping for breath, against the jeweled back of a golden chair, sword in hand for all the good that was likely to do him.

Corvin stared at him, blank with shock.

"They're forming up from the dust, they've got gold dust in the air for miles! *Damn* it!" he added, looking down, for a trickle of dust was flowing into the room now, thin and swift as water pouring down the stair.

Corvin seemed to shrink and elongate in size, slithering like a snake up the stairway that was the Treasury's only entry, moving with a dragon's terrible speed. John pulled the strip of rag he'd been using for a scarf up over his nose and mouth and followed, throwing aside the torch when the wind snuffed its flame, and ran up blind in the dragon's wake, one hand on either wall and praying nothing more solid than dust was waiting for him between the Treasury and the top.

There wasn't, but the wind struck him as he emerged from the stairway onto the top of the foundation, taking him by surprise and spinning him around before throwing him to his knees. The night was utterly black, but above the howl of the wind he could hear a voice calling his name: Gareth's, he thought.

What the hell was Gareth doing here?

Orange light, like a wind-torn torch. Gareth's voice shouting again, with a desperate note of panic. "John? *John!*" And something about Jenny.

The white dragon that was Jenny's onetime dragon-shape could have brought him here.

Or the demons could be toying with him, eating up the surging throb of his heart at the thought of rescue and waiting for him to run toward the phantom torch and pitch off the edge of the foundation. The cream of the jest would be that the fall wouldn't kill him. It would amost certainly break his legs, though, and he'd be weeks dying of thirst at the bottom.

John crawled forward on his hands and knees, feeling the stone before him. Sure enough, the edge dropped off about two feet away, invisible in the gritty darkness. But having reached the edge he was able to grope his way along it, knowing there'd be a stairway eventually—there was one on each of the foundation's four sides. From there he'd be able to feel his way along the wall....

Aye, he thought, at the glimpse of a flash and flicker of silver-green. Could the demons counterfeit the silvery glow that rushed up from the pool in the heart of the Henge?

He didn't know, but the wind and dust were hammering him harder, and if he stayed in the open he'd be blinded in no very long time and suffocated soon after that. If nothing else the air within the Maze would be still.

The fourth gate that he'd found—the one that could be opened at midnight—had been in the palace itself, and stood just on the edge of the foundation platform not far from the northeast corner.

Dust-devils tore him, wind raking his face and his stubbled scalp. Sometimes he thought gritty hands pawed him, seized him, hands wrought of silver fire and dust. He slashed once with his sword, barely able to see, and of course the great looming things in the darkness simply dissolved, to re-form instants later, green phosphor glimmering in their eyes. Once he thought he saw Corvin, or what would have been Corvin, illuminated by the ocherous flare of the burning slime that the dragon spit. Saw a writhing shape high in the air, muffled in a cloud of blackness—dust in his eyes, in his nostrils, the singing hum of the gold confusing his senses, demon-voices ripping through his brain to his heart.

Waiting for him to use magic, so they could seize him through it.

Then darkness again, and John saw no more. But the wind grew stronger, driving him to his knees on the broken stone of the platform. If Corvin had any sense—if he could break free of the demons at all—he'd rise straight up over the dust storm like a balloon and head away fast toward the North. He'd done his duty, fulfilled the geas that binds dragons to their saviors....

Blinded, John lost sight of the Henge, then saw it again, mercifully in the same place and at the same distance, which unless the demons were being clever with him probably meant it was actually the Henge he saw. . . .

He fell again, groping at the stone underfoot—the gate was almost exactly at the edge of the platform and you stepped through it as if you were stepping off into thin air. The first time he'd tried it, the night before last, he'd had a braided rope around his waist, which had impeded him severely when he'd stepped through onto the solid ground of an orchard of savagely animate thorned trees. It had been midnight there, too, and if he hadn't had a torch with him he'd have been cut to pieces before he saw the path away from the gate.

But better that than this, he thought now. In any case, he knew the path ran away to the right and the thorned trees could be dodged, to get to the next gate into the Maze. Monstrous shapes loomed and dissolved in the whirling dark around him, reached ephemeral hands for him, and smiled with malicious, glittering eyes. *And why not smile?* he thought. From being a prisoner in all the city of Prokep he was now a prisoner on the foundation, and if Adromelech in fact guessed that he knew the way through the Maze, it wouldn't be long at all before they'd be on him.

Quicker, if they could run him off the edge of the foundation and break his legs for him. After about a week of lying at the bottom he'd probably be pretty happy to talk about which door to choose and where it lay.

Jenny's voice cried to him, trapped in the hammering storm. Crying his name, crying "I forgive you . . . ," in a voice that tore his heart. "Please—John, please . . . !"

He groped along the edge of the platform, sighting on the blurred silver fire of the Henge, wondering how long it would be till midnight or if it was already past. He didn't think so, but there was no way to tell, and he didn't think he'd make it until dawn even if he could get down to where the other gate was. Dust smothered him, trapping him in a vortex of winds that circled him like a dust-devil, sucking the air from his lungs. Flecks of flying metal tore his face, and he staggered, feeling hands catching at him, claws cutting his flesh.

The wind changed notes. Lightning split the darkness, the crack of thunder like an ax cleaving the bellow of the wind, and a cold, hard blast of rain struck John in the face. Wind drove the rain, wind straight out of the north, shattering the circling column around him, and lightning struck again, spearing from clouds to earth. Its purple glare showed him the rain, hammering the dust back into the ground; the darkness afterward was like being struck blind.

The next flash showed John the wet shining black and silver shape of the dragon plunging down from the pouring heavens through the rain. He stepped to the edge of the platform and held up his arms; all the demon-light within the Henge had died. The dragon's claws snatched him hard around the ribs in the darkness, and the ground jerked away beneath his feet. Lightning rimmed Prokep one last time, a skeleton city in blackness.

Then they were flying west under the streaming rain.

Chapter 6

For close to a thousand years—according to John's copy of the third volume of Juronal, admittedly incomplete—the Realm of Ernine had dominated the meadowlands along the River Gelspring and the prairies that stretched east to the sunrise. In those days the city of Bel had been a fishing village, subservient to the vassal kings of the Seven Islands, whose true wealth lay in trade from the south. Through Ernine, amid its luxuriant hinterland of crops and cattle, had flowed the gnomes' silver from the Deep at Droon, and the furs of the northern forests; the Kings had raised palaces there pillared in the golden sandstone of the eastern deserts, and the priests worshiped unremembered gods in marble temples open to the sky. Long after Ernine had fallen to raiders from the steppe, a second city was built on the low knees and foothills above the Gelspring: Its foundations stood on the more ancient stone, but few recalled what it had been named or how it had met its end.

Descending with the dragon through the pink-gold radience of morning, Jenny Waynest could make out the outlines of this second city's temples, tangled in brush and thickets of pine all powdered with snow. She'd seen them before only at night, when in the autumn Moon of Sacrifice John had come here to pay his teind to the Demon Queen, the tithing that would purchase back his soul.

On that occasion Jenny had been too shaken, too sick from the wresting-away of her own demon, to remember much of the city's appearance. But she recognized now the long stairway that curled up the low hill's flank, and that inconspicuous cave under the vines. She'd sat on the marble step at the top, shivering uncontrollably in the autumn night, hating John and hearing Amayon scream in her mind. Above the stair a hollow square of pillars crowned the hill, their decorated capitals broken and white as the lingering snow patches among the brown of last year's sodden bracken.

This, the Master of Halnath had told her, had been the temple of the Moon-God Syn, who was worshiped in the North in the form of a black sow.

After long days underground Jenny's eyes ached in the glory of morning light. Everything seemed to sparkle and shout with color, even in these leaden weeks of granny-winter. Rowanberries on branches a hundred feet away blazed like fire. Wood that to ordinary view would have been silver-gray appeared to her as a mottling of a thousand subtle hues, lavender and snuff and cobalt. Among the bare trees she glimpsed broken pillars, pink porphyry and marble, and the flash of ice in what had once been ornamental fountains and ponds.

Morkeleb spread his dark wings to circle above the Temple hill, Jenny leaning from his back. She traced the descending stairs and the courtyard near at hand with its frozen pool. "Would the mages—this Arch-Seer the demons spoke of—have come up by the main stair to attack Isychros?"

The palace stood on the hill in those days. In her mind she saw the stair as it had been in her earliest dream of the place—her earliest dream of Amayon. Saw the rich pillars of sandstone and marble that ringed what had then been the Queen's Court, where ladies wove bright-colored cloth and sang among the colonnades. *Isychros was the King's Mage, helping the Most High Lord Ennyta to keep his vassals on a leash by means of scrying and cantrips and blackmail. The chambers cut from the hillside were traditionally given to the Court Mage.*

Had the dragon walked those courts? she wondered. Climbed that long footworn stair in human guise? How long had he been in the custom of walking in the shape of humankind?

"Would there be a back way in?" she asked. "When Isychros took over power in Ernine, with both mages and dragons at his beck, I can't imagine even an Arch-Seer coming at his stronghold from the front."

Images shifted in her mind. She saw the palace again as it existed in Morkeleb's memory, like an image painted on silk and hung before present reality. Strange-shaped roofs with painted rafter-ends rose above red-flowering trees whose names she did not know. The shape of the land had not changed much, though the profusion of flowers spoke of warmer summers. Ernine spread farther down the Gelspring Valley than the city that had subsequently covered the spot. The pillared hall that reared on the hillcrest above the Court Mage's chambers—where the Moon-god's temple later would stand—had wide windows on all walls glazed in small panes of clearest glass, so that the building glittered like a heap of diamonds. Jenny smelled the cook fires of the town, and heard an ass bray far off.

"Any wager you like," said Jenny, shifting her balance between the spiked scales of the dragon's shoulders. "There was a stair coming down to his quarters from the hall above. That was the library, wasn't it, with all those windows? Were I Court Mage it's what I'd have. By the foliage it rains a good deal here."

And she felt the ripple of Morkeleb's amusement as he banked low over the tops of the bare trees. *It is a thing of men, to put themselves in danger by leaving a back way into their dwellings, only to avoid a little water. See where there was a fountain even in those days, hard by the stair? It was out of that water the Sea-wights came, when the mages of the city of Prokep reached a bargain with Adromelech, to drive back Aohila's demons behind the mirror.*

Wind snapped in the baggy folds of the trousers Miss Mab had brought Jenny in the mines, and in the thick fluttering ends of the plaid she'd worn down from the North. After the warmth below the ground the air stung her face. Morkeleb turned above the higher flank of the mountain, and Jenny saw behind the jumbled roofs of glowing red and gilt the exquisite manicured wilderness of the garden, and all around its edges the workaday buildings of stables, servants' quarters, kitchens.

They would have come in through the kitchen gate—the path up from the town was even in those days much overgrown with trees. She could see where the back ways among the storage quarters provided a safe, quick route from the kitchen to the library.

Then she was seeing the ruin again, the palimpsest of old walls and foundations cloaked in leafless vines.

"There," she said, pointing. "If a way down to the Court Mage's quarters existed from the library, it would have been somewhere there."

When the forehead of the palace hill had been cut back, to build

the later crypt of the Temple of Syn, the sealed door of the Court
Mage's quarters had been covered over by a wall. Only the subsequent razing of Syn's city had opened the way again. Jenny and
Morkeleb picked their way down the curving slope that turned into
the old sandstone stair, and from there descended to the door behind
its curtain of blackened vines flanked by the faded ghosts of frescoed
gazelles still dimly visible on the face of the rock. Jenny's own footsteps, and John's, scuffed the corridor's dust.

The doorway from the corridor into the round mirror chamber
had been bricked shut in ancient times, the brickwork later stove in
by who knew what impulse of foolishness and greed. The hothwais
Jenny carried shed a wan light, in which the stars painted on the ceil-
ings of corridor and chamber seemed to dance.

A second set of tracks obscurred those she and John had left
last autumn. John's again, and recent. There was no mistaking the
patched boots.

He'd been here—why? Morkeleb had said he'd been in Bel. When
she'd gone to the Hold only a few weeks ago, Sergeant Muffle—John's
blacksmith and muster-chief and illegitimate brother—had told her
John had gone scouting in the Wraithmire marshes, after first burning
his workroom and taking with him only a few days' food. He'd left his
horse with old Dan Darrow at the marshes' edge, had gone into the
snowy mire on foot. Only ten days ago Jenny had talked to Darrow
himself, and the old farmer had been sure of what he saw. Given
the nature of the Wraithmire, and Dan's watchfulness of those evil
lands, he'd have seen John's tracks emerging from the marsh, and he
hadn't.

It was conceivable—barely—that in a few weeks John could have
reached Belmarie on horseback. But there had been no word of him
in the countryside between. And even such a turn of cross-country
speed didn't explain why he'd come here, of all places, before going to
Bel and being arrested, sentenced to death, and rescued ... by another dragon, according to Morkeleb.

So what had he been doing here?

Visiting the Demon Queen? Jealousy stirred in Jenny's heart like
steam on a winter bog. For months now her dreams had been a torment of fantasies of John's infidelity, of John lying in the Demon
Queen's arms. . . .

The mirror stood silent where last Jenny had seen it, its glass painted over black. Framed by the pinkish-blue alien metal of a thunderstone, the long glass itself—a pane some six feet tall by a foot and a half wide, three times the size of any that Bel's craftsmen could produce nowadays—seemed enigmatic under its coating of black enamel, a shut door through which it was possible only to guess at sounds. In the bright light of the hothwais it looked harmless enough. By lantern light it had seemed to smoke or steam. A piece of paper, charred nearly to illegibility, still clung to the matte glass: the sigil Miss Mab had made for John, by which he had passed through into Hell.

Jenny shivered, remembering the silver marks on his flesh, the burn at the pit of his throat. The Queen had marked him, as if claiming him as her own. Deeper still was the shadow that lurked in the back of his eyes

Curious, Jenny thought, stepping close to the glass. She had never actually seen the Queen, though she felt as if she knew her well. Now she realized that the image she had of her—tall and black-haired, slender and coldly beautiful—she had only from her own dreams, in which John and the Queen lay together and giggled their derision of Jenny herself. At one time those dreams had been so real, she had been unable to separate them from reality, and had hated John for the pictures that arose out of her own mind.

Perhaps the hatred had sprung in part from the Demon Queen taking Jenny's own demon Amayon away, to torture forever behind the Mirror.

She put out her hand to the black glass, not daring to touch, and thought, *He is THERE.*

And remembered again how it had felt, to love Amayon.

All those things the demon had whispered to her—his love for her, his need for her, the trust and dependence he placed on her love ... Even as they rang false and absurd in her mind, her heart pinched with the poison of that clinging, childlike profession of absolute love.

She turned her head and saw Morkeleb, falcon-sized in the darkness of the round chamber, hanging close to her shoulder with wings spread like a hawk in the air. The hothwais of light made him sparkle, as if carved by a master-craftsman of jet. His eyes caught the light, and the jewel-like bobs on the ends of his antennae flickered in the dark.

The touch of his mind on hers was warm as the comforting pressure of a hand.

Why is it so hard to believe that demons lie? she asked him. *It is their nature to lie.*

It is their nature to be believed, replied the dragon. And he called on a spell of light, blazing to fill all the chamber. On the other side of the room, a door showed up, which the shadows had hidden before.

Jenny crossed the room to it, walking wide around the mirror. Everywhere she felt the malice of demons. She had assumed—she did not know why—that the circular chamber in which the Burning Mirror stood was the farthest it was possible to penetrate into the hill. When she had gone there with John to pay his teind, and turn over to the Demon Queen the demons they had extracted from the minds of the possessed mages, her powers had already burned away. The door was bricked shut, the lintels remaining but the bricks painted like the rest of the wall. Only magelight would have shown it up, or a mage's ability to see in the dark.

Morkeleb shifted in size, as a shadow alters with the retreat of light. But his claws and muscle were no shadow. He tore the brickwork as if it had been dry wattle. Jenny flinched at the noise of rubble and mortar crashing to the floor and she glanced back at the mirror as if she expected something to come forth angry. *Absurd,* she thought. *If it has held them all these years, why expect they could emerge now?* Behind the broken wall a stair ascended, narrow and deeply worn. The sandstone was pitted, and stained black in great pools and dribbles. Walls and stair were charred, as if swept with fire.

They tried this first, she thought, quite calmly, standing at the foot of the stair. *The wizards who sought to defeat Isychros's dragons and demons.* Rubble blocked the ascent no more than a few yards above her. *Only after the Arch-Seer—whoever he was—failed to destroy the mirror did they call on the Sea-wights for help. They, or those of their friends who survived them.*

This she knew as if she had heard their ghosts telling of their hopeless attack in the dark of the stair.

She stepped through the crack Morkeleb had made, and held the hothwais up, to shed its unveiled light in every corner and cranny.

Just where the lowest step and the wall came together a silver bottle was wedged. Shadow would hide it when torches were borne down the stairs, or carried in from the mirror crypt itself. *After the Arch-Seer and his mages attacked Isychros here,* she thought, *Isychros must have had little leisure to ascend to the library. And after Isychros's defeat the two daughters of the King who succeeded their father must only have wished to have the whole place sealed, with everything inside.*

A *catch-bottle,* the demons had called the thing Folcalor sought. Surely the same object that Caerdinn had told her of, the trap inscribed with the true name of its intended victim, woven with certain spells. It would draw the soul into it like smoke.

She picked the bottle up. It was just larger than the hollow of her hand, and very light. The silvery bulb of it was a globe, the thin neck stoppered tight with something that looked like a crystal, embedded in a petaled rose of hard crimson wax.

We know she was never trapped in it. The name within it will still be the same. The spells will be waiting.

Her heart pounded in her chest, so that she could scarcely breathe.

Aohila.

The Demon Queen.

The dream of her returned, snake-like and sinuous in John's arms. Laughing at Jenny, and making him laugh at her. Saying things like *old,* and *ugly,* and *spent.* Heat rose in Jenny's flesh, the heat and the nausea and the wavering shadows of migraine reminding her that the Demon Queen was right.

It was only a dream, she reminded herself. *Only a dream, and MY dream at that.* But every time she thought of the silvery serpent whorls and spirals of power on John's flesh, which showed up when the angle of the moonlight was right, every time she thought of the scar in the pit of his throat, as if a white-hot jewel had been pressed between the small points of his collarbone, she remembered those jealous dreams. He had never said so, but Jenny guessed that Aohila spoke to him in dreams, as Amayon sometimes spoke to her.

She knew what it was that Amayon said. Knew the dreams that Amayon sent.

And Folcalor is coming, she thought. Coming with spells of new power, to open the mirror. To trap the Demon Queen and devour her, as Adromelech, his own master, had for untold ages devoured and re-gurgitated him. Folcalor would eat her power before turning upon Adromelech to become the Sea-wights' lord. And from there, to hold sway over all the Realms of humankind, turning them into their hunting-ground and larder.

And woe to any, thought Jenny, who were in the way when the demons fought their war of vengeance and power and pain.

She untied her sash and knotted a loop of it around the silver bottle's neck, not sure exactly what she would do. As long as Aohila was within the Burning Mirror she was safe, from Jenny at least. Whether Folcalor would be able to pursue her into her own Hell, Jenny did not know.

She went back into the mirror chamber and stood before the black-painted glass.

Amayon is in there, she thought again.

And then, with a sudden flinch of horror, *JOHN may be in there.* Morkeleb had spoken of the rumors in Bel, that the demons had sent a dragon to save him from the stake. Aohila had controlled dragons before, a thousand years ago. Was it inconceivable that she could ex-ercise that power again? True, Jenny had seen no trace in the corridor of anyone coming or going after John's second visit, but would there be other ways into the Hell behind the Mirror? The urge over-whelmed her to call out Aohila's name, to demand . . .

What?

It is the nature of demons to lie.

She closed her eyes for a time, silently praying only, *Let him not be dead.*

Give us another chance.

Then she drew her plaid close about her, and walked from the mirror chamber, Morkeleb drifting behind her like a shadow out into the light.

*T*he Lords of Ylferdun Deep established watch posts throughout these *northeastern foothills,* Morkeleb said, *at the very fringe of their realm.*

Whatever might become of the roads of men, the gnomes do not per-
mit their tunnels to decay. If Folcalor comes to Ernine, it will be through
one of these. Especially if, as we suspect, he now wears the guise of a
gnome.

The dragon found a cave in the foothills that had been carved
out as a stable for a villa whose very foundations had crumbled away.
Snow lay thick outside, but the place was protected from wind and
the hothwais of warmth quickly filled the smallest of the surviving
rooms. Morkeleb glided away, like a great raven among the trees to
hunt, and Jenny scouted for squirrel hordes and cattail roots, and for
enough dried bracken, buried beneath the snow of the thickets, to
make a bed and a fire.

She knew better than to treat with demons in any fashion, neither to bargain with them nor listen to anything they said. The silver
bottle nudged her hip bone whenever she bent or moved, reminding
her again and again of its presence. It was still as cold as it had been
when she picked it up, for it would not warm with the warmth of her
body. She could not rid her mind of the image of the Burning Mirror,
could not rid her thoughts of the impression that when she had stood
before it, with the silver bottle at her belt, that behind the mirror, Aohila had looked out at her.

And said . . . what?

And thought . . . what?

She cooked and ate the rabbit Morkeleb caught, and lay down
to sleep, exhausted. Miss Mab's spells had saved her life, and to some
extent healed her body, but exertion and cold still took their toll
on her far more quickly than she was used to. She slept like a dead
woman, and the darkness of the mirror chamber followed her into her
dreams.

She was back there again, watching as John set out the things he
had been ordered to bring back for the Moon of the King's Sacrifice. A
dragon's tears, contained in a bottle wrought of glass and alabaster
that the tears would dissolve before they could be used. The softly
shining hothwais that held the light of a star, rather than the iron
thunderstone that the Queen had mistakenly thought was a piece of
a star. An arrowhead stained with blood.

And like a thirteenth doughnut or a flower seller's gift-posy,
John had added to his tithe smaller bottles, or stones, or shells, sealed

with red wax. Eight glass spikes filled with something silver that moved like mercury in the wavering light of the lantern. Though the night had been silent, when Jenny had sat there in truth, in her dream she could hear the demons inside screaming. They knew what they were going to.

Amayon's sobs especially rang in her mind. *I never meant to harm you, Jenny my darling! Not you, not anyone! You don't understand what they do to you—Folcalor, and Adromelech....*

If anyone could have saved me, it would have been you, my Jenny, my beloved.

And by that wavery glow John's face was grim and quiet, the smudges of sleeplessness very dark under his eyes.

It's the Moon of Sacrifice, love, he said to the mirror. *And here I am.*

In Jenny's dream the mirror wasn't black, but showed the Hell beyond. A suggestion of pillars in darkness, a whisper of marble and gold. Instead of John's reflection, Jenny saw the Demon Queen, quietly beautiful, combing her long black hair. Meeting John's eyes and smiling, complicit as a lover. *And you, beloved?* she said, in a voice like roses and smoke.

John came back here after leaving the North. Why?

He had walked into the Wraithmire on foot, and three weeks later, in the worst season for traveling, had emerged in Ernine, not a hundred feet from the Mirror of Isychros. When he was in trouble, a dragon—or something that looked like a dragon—saved his life.

In her dream, Jenny turned and fled the room. But it didn't keep her from seeing him still. He walked slowly toward the mirror, pressed his palms to the glass. On her side the Demon Queen did likewise, palms pressing. Lips pressing. Jenny ran down the corridor, endlessly long now, desperate with grief. The pounding of her heart sounded louder in her ears, but still she could see John standing against the mirror, and still she could hear the Queen's deep syrup-dark voice, murmuring words of love. Lightning flashed in the mouth of the tunnel, and Jenny ran toward that light, heart and mind bleeding-raw.

She had been a dragon and had returned to mortal humanity for John's sake. She had had the form and the magic of those beautiful alien creatures, and had said to Morkeleb, *Return me to being what I was.*

Nothing can ever return to being what it was, had been his reply.

And then he had asked her—had asked another being, for the first time in his life—*Is this what you truly want?*

From that asking, he had not been able to return, either.

He was walking away from her, flying away through the columns of the clouds, through the flare of the lightning. Jenny ran down the miles of corridor with its painted gazelles, gasping for breath, desperate to catch him, her heart pounding louder and louder, or perhaps it was the crash of the thunder.

But when she opened her mouth to cry out, she cried, *John . . . !*
JENNY . . . !

Light speared her eyes and she woke. Lightning outlined the mouth of the cave—*in wintertime?* Then darkness, but as she fumbled for the hothwais under the bracken another white glare illuminated the whole wall of snow-clotted bramble that fronted the cave and outlined Morkeleb's bony black shape in the tunnel he'd dug through it. Jenny scrambled to her feet, nearly fell when her sore hip protested, and limped to the dragon's side.

"Folcalor . . ."

It must be, I think.

She pulled her plaid closer around her, followed the dragon out through the snowy bracken, into the dark of the woods. Red light drenched the night's darkness, wildfire burning in Ernine. Morkeleb caught Jenny up in his claws, flattened his wings to his sides, and glided like some strange curving snake through and among the bare trees. There was a sort of bench of land above the valley in which the old city lay, just clearing the tops of the trees below, and from there Jenny looked across the dark lacework of bare crowns and snowy earth to the Temple of the Moon. Fires roared in the leafless trees around that tall knee of rock. Against the crazy orange glare Jenny could see broken columns, shattered walls, and it seemed to her that the shape of the hill itself had altered. The sky had been clear when she had lain down to sleep, marked with the fat pale crescent of a sinking day-moon. Now a pall of cloud roofed it to the horizon, split by lightning again and again, levin-fire that struck always at the same place.

Smoke-wisp shrieks whirled away on the wind. Her hand closed around one of Morkeleb's spines.

Nothing came down from the watch posts nearby, the dragon said. *That I will swear.*

And Jenny saw the flicker of his memory, of lying in the cave-mouth while she herself slept. Listening, with the starlight-fine net of his dragon-senses spread over the whole of the mountainside. She saw through his eyes that first flare of lightning from Ernine, heard that first crash of thunder. Felt the searing unheard cacophony of demon magic and demon rage.

"The gnomes could have had some old way, straight into the Citadel of Ernine."

Men were more trusting in those days, then.

Her mind on her own jealous dreams, Jenny replied softly, "Even so."

And she heard/saw in Morkeleb's mind the memories of other Deeps, delved before Ylferdun: the Great Droon and the Lesser Droon, tunnels reaching everywhere, turrets on the mountainsides not too far from Ernine. Miss Mab had led John to this place by those hidden roads, when first he sought the Demon Queen. There were any number of gates.

A whirlwind rose up, trees creaking as their roots were pulled about in the earth. Fragments of twig and branch smote her out of the dark. Lightning blasted once more, and she saw that the whole side of the hill, where the Temple of Syn had stood, was split as though with a monstrous ax; fire spouted up through the cleft, sparks rivering into the wind. Shadows thrashed among the sparks, dissolved in smoke. Demons? Manifestations of some other sort of power? Voices yammered, a howling very different from the screams of before, and in Jenny's mind she made words of them, from the memories of when Amayon had dwelled within her, and understood those sounds.

Terrible words, curses and evil laughter, hatred and pain. Spells that made her want to cover her ears, pull her mind away. She felt Morkeleb's disgust, like a dark ripple of anger, and the spines of his joints bristled like the hair of an angry dog.

A booming crash, rocks and earth and fragments of masonry bounding out in a cloud of earth as the hillside split again. The glare made Jenny cover her eyes, and blink blinded for moments after. Dark shapes outlined in fire circled the city, moving like a whirlwind: She saw them in yellows and greens against her shut eyelids for a time as she crouched against the dragon's side, his invisible shadow covering them both. Near them a tree exploded into flame, showering her with burning fragments. When she opened her eyes again the first thing she saw was the stumps of pillars uprooted and hurled into the air, dragging hunks of foundation on their feet. All the clouds that swirled so thick about the city were rimmed in thin, deadly blue. In the heart of that chaos the whirlwind gathered itself, a dense column of red-shot smoke. It revolved slowly, burning shapes—souls? ghosts? demons?—visible in the circling wall of smoke, even at that distance, clear and small as if she still dreamed.

Slowly at first, then faster, the cyclone moved away toward the east. The ground steamed where it tore through the snow. Jenny clung to Morkeleb, watching it pass through the wooded bottomlands, spreading fire through the bare ice-locked trees. Deer fled crazily before it across the snow. The burning crown of it re-mained in sight for a long time, stretching up to join the red-lit lour of cloud.

Trembling, Jenny crouched against the dragon's dark body. The silence that lay upon the city was dreadful after the crashing and the shrieks. Smoke from the burning trees mixed with the steam from puddles of snowmelt, until everything blurred in a shifting cauldron of fog and through it she thought she heard voices still.

Magic hung in the air. Not dissipating with the passing of the whirlwind but, it seemed to her, growing stronger. She passed this thought, this question, without even forming it into words into Morkeleb's mind, and the dragon's reply came to her: *No. It is not over.*

Something was still in Ernine.

Some terrible malevolence beaded like water from the wet choke of the air. Darkness waiting, watching as the firelight sank to embers and died.

Blue light flickered on the brow of the broken hill.

She is here. Jenny's hand went to the catch-bottle at her belt.

She is here. And if she survived that attack by Folcalor, she will be at her weakest.

She cast her mind out over the hillside, the dragon's senses twin-
ing with hers until she could not have said whether she heard with
her own ears or his. She breathed, scenting like a beast for the smell
of demons, a stink like scalded iron and blood. She smelled the
burned flesh and hair of animals trapped by the fire, rabbits roasted
sleeping in their holes and squirrels burned up in their nests; smelled
the vast gritty stench of smoldering trees.

But she did not smell demons, or hear their whispering laughter.

Only that thin light that wasn't really light burned purplish on
the hill's savaged crest. She followed the cliff's edge to the path that
led to the hill where the palace had stood. Morkeleb followed without
a sound. The Demon Queen was there, and she was alone.

The whole of the hill's top, where first the palace with its
diamond-windowed library had stood and later the Temple of Syn,
was sheared off and charred as if sliced by a monstrous blade. Pillars,
walls, trees thicker than a man's body, all swept away into heaps
of smoking rubble on the hill's flanks. What was left of the dead
grass and wiry leafless ivy had burned under the snow, and the
whole of the hilltop glistened with smoking patches of water, with
smoldering sheets of ash and cracked paving-blocks tilted and
thrown about on their sides. Vapors rose from the gaping clefts in the
hill itself, and against that fume the Demon Queen burned with a
sicklied light.

She looked human, precisely as she had appeared in Jenny's jealous dreams. Tall and slender and heartrendingly beautiful, with her
long black hair lifting around her as if she floated in water rather than
in air. She had marked the ground all around her with charred circles
of fire, embers still flickering in the sigils of power she had laid down,
and the air was marked, too, in pale rising rings of blue-burning light.
Beyond the circles the earth was dotted with gray shards of what
Jenny at first thought was broken glass, burned nuggets of ash. Only
when she picked one up and saw the rough facets of fire-scored crystal did she understand.

The heat that filled her was more terrible than the worst the
change of her womanhood could do. She recalled the family she had
rescued from slave-dealers in the woods of the North only weeks ago,
Dal and Lyra from Rushmeath Farm, and their children: people she

knew, children she had helped to birth. Saw the faces of the crippled Layla Gorge and her frail niece, Ana, whose family had wanted gnomes' silver more than it had wanted them.

The Demon Queen still gazed east. Only mageborn eyes could still have distinguished the red flicker of the retreating whirlwind. Her attention was focused there, and toward that diminishing light she made the gestures and passes of power, as if summoning great events infinitely far away.

She hid from Folcalor, thought Jenny, trembling still with anger. *Hid and waited until he went east. Only thus could she summon power from a distance without him trapping her through her own spells.* All this went through her mind in a single word, knowledge like a drop of molten glass, and she crept forward, the red wax stopper of the catch-bottle cold even through the leather of her glove. She moved silent, fearing that the Queen would hear the beating of her heart. Fearing that the waves of her rage would heat the very air around her, and warn Aohila of her presence.

But the Demon Queen only traced signs in the air, over and over, and they hung smoking in the cold for a few moments before dissolving. Like her hair, her garments drifted about her, thin veils of what sometimes appeared to be fire, sometimes smoke. But her white feet pressed the ground. They were large, the feet of a tall woman. Jenny saw the nails were curved and black like Morkeleb's claws.

She is calling all her power, Jenny thought. *Calling it, and directing it on Folcalor.* Like a small cat hunting she shifted herself up the hillside through the steaming puddles, the burned and perished gems. Her hand around the catch-bottle grew cramped and cold, and exhaustion gnawed at her bones. The longer she waited, the more Folcalor in his turn, wherever he was, would be weakened. Her whole being concentrated upon stillness, as she had in those days when she was only a Winterlands hedge-witch, relying on her slender powers to keep herself safe from bandits and the Iceriders who came down in bad winters from the North. She smelled rain, though there was no rain in the sky; sometimes also the burning tang of desert dust. Then these things were gone, and all she smelled was burning and death.

At last Aohila lowered her arms. She stood straight and tall, staring into the east, her dark hair floating about her like kelp. Only a rim of embers outlined the riven hill. Huge stillness covered the silent ruin of the city. Overhead the clouds broke, and stars gleamed coldly through.

Jenny brought the catch-bottle from the folds of her plaid and, as if even at that distance, Aohila had heard the rustle of her clothing, the Demon Queen turned. Her gold eyes widened, and she raised her hand, and in that instant Jenny pulled the stopper from the bottle.

Chapter 7

"My children," said the King, "the plague is ended." He raised his hands, palms out, as if instead of making an announcement he was himself bestowing this healing on the shocked and ravaged city. To those who saw the tall, broad-shouldered figure standing in the turret of lacework stone—the King's traditional pulpit above the market square—it was easy to believe.

Five years of rumor and speculation, of fragmentary tales handed out by palace servants concerning His Majesty's "indisposition," five years of an inexperienced Regency, high taxes, and murmurs of revolt—all these seemed sponged away by the sight of that grave gold-bearded face, and the ringing clarity of the beautiful voice that had always been one of Uriens II's greatest gifts.

For nearly five years, since the year of the dragon, little had been seen of the King. Even when he'd been under the influence of the witch Zyerne, Uriens had made his appearances at festivals, had led the torchlight dawn processions to the Temple of the Red God of War, and had spoken to the people from this turret beside the door of the town's great indoor market. When the doctors said Zyerne's spells had affected his mind, a thousand contradictory tales had fleeted through the city's cobbled streets. The Regent Gareth was shy, and too many people had seen him hanging on the fringes of the mob of overdressed younger courtiers to take him really seriously. There had been many in the city who'd sided with the King's niece Rocklys, Commander of the Northern Garrisons, when she'd made her bid to take the throne, simply because she looked like she knew what she was doing.

So the murmur that ran through the crowd in the square was one of relief.

The King was himself again. The jaw under the golden beard jutted as of old, and the blue eyes that swept the crowd had their old hawk-bright glitter. The big hands rested firmly on the pierced stone of the turret's railing, and no longer fussed and picked like a child's. The tall, powerful body was clothed in decent mourning, for all the hundreds who had died of the mysterious fever that had swept the city, but it was a mourning of majesty, the restrained grief of a man who understands that there is work to do.

"We have found the men responsible for it, the men whose evil machinations, whose bargaining with demons, brought all this to pass. They have been punished." His booming voice carried clearly over the heads of the crowd and rang on the tall stone houses that bordered the square, and he struck his purple-gloved fist into his palm. "It grieves me to reveal to you, my friends, that they had allies in this city, in every neighborhood. But the traitors have been induced to name those who did their bidding, those who spread the plague among their neighbors in the hopes of weakening our Realm and leaving us prey to the rebels in Imperteng and the Marches. Those men—aye, and women, too—will be sought out and taken, however cleverly they think they have covered their foul tracks. *They shall not escape justice!*"

A cheer went up from the crowd standing shoulder to shoulder, where three days a week in summertime farmers set up barrows of fruit and milk and cheeses. Men and women forgot the cold slush underfoot and the colder wind, and raised their hands in salute to their reborn King. But near the corner of the market hall, where the Avenue of Kings ran back up the hill to the main palace gates, a woman covered her face with her veil and sobbed. Another, stout and tightly laced into the black of mourning, muttered under the din, "The plague may be done, but what about the killers in the streets, eh? What about those who wander in the night, without torches and seeing in the dark like cats, and kill those they meet? Yes, and climb over walls, to kill even those who think themselves safe in their own gardens! What about my daughter, then, that was found torn to pieces in her own house? Have you got the men who did that, Mr. Justice-Giving King?"

And the beggar beside her in a coat of black and white goatskins cocked his stubbled head and asked, "Have the city guards all died off, then, ma'am?"

A yard away a man in the crowd turned his head sharply: a yellow-skinned southerner in a traveler's leather tunic and hood, his face blue from hairline to lips with scrollwork tattoos. But though his eyes narrowed at the words, he said nothing, and made no approach, and the bereaved mother laughed, a barking sound like wood being chopped. "City guards! A man was killed behind my house—down in the Dockmarket we live—and half my neighbors say it was city guards who did it, and left the body bleeding in the street. Where have *you* been, Four-Eyes, that you don't know what's happening in this city? The plague isn't the worst of it by a long chalk."

"Those that spread the plague are the ones that're doing the killing, Mae," protested a prosperous-looking man standing near, his cloak pulled up tight against the cold. "You heard the King. It's the rebels from Imperteng that started it, the rebels that slew General Rocklys, when she would have come down and restored order. That's when this all began. Thank the gods the King's recovered, and in time!"

"Aye, now he'll take a hand," agreed a fat man in a master gold-smith's apron and smock. "And not a moment too soon! We'd have had the gnomes running all of us out of business before long, friendly as the Regent got with them. Not that I've aught to say against the boy, of course, but boy is all he is—"

"And too friendly with the Master of Halnath, for my taste. The Masters were always trouble. Changing things and making machines—I wouldn't be surprised to hear the plague started with some of their meddling. . . . What does Master Polycarp know of the plague, eh?"

"What indeed?" John Aversin murmured, and slipped back from the crowd and along the cobbled street toward the palace gate. Behind him Uriens's voice sounded above the heads of the crowd like a gorgeous bronze bell, chiming out encouragement and hope:

". . . peace shall be reestablished, and prosperity return . . ."

Thin sunlight gleamed through the clouds, silver on the garbage-boltered snow.

The palace of the Kings of Bel—the House of Uwanë—stood on a low hill south of the river; the Avenue of Kings led to its newer front gate, brave with banners and gilt. The former processional way, the Queen's Lane, curved around south to the older precincts dominated by the big dungeon tower, and the gate that was now used primarily by petitioners for the King's grace. There weren't many of these today, with the King clearly occupied elsewhere, and the porter who generally sat in the lodge beside the open gate had retreated, like a sensible man, to the fireside of his inner chamber: John could smell coffee beans roasting as he walked quietly past into the court.

Having seen the vision of Amayon as Trey speaking with the demon-ridden King, John hadn't been surprised to find the man back in apparent possession of his reason and command of the Realm. In fact, during Rocklys's rebellion, Uriens had led his own armies into battle and had done quite well as long as he had advisers to tell him where to dispose his troops. The erosion of mind and spirit that Zyerne had caused had not affected his courage or his sense of duty as King.

Still, it had made John's flesh creep to see him, knowing what he knew.

When John and Jenny first came south to deal with Morkeleb the Black—who had descended on the Deep of Ylferdun, driven out the gnomes, and made a lair for himself on their stolen gold—the witch Zyerne had been in power, and Uriens had refused to see them for many days. During those days of kicking his heels at Court, John had rambled a great deal about the palace, talking to servants and stable boys, insatiably curious about everything from the drainage system of the palace pig-yard to the distillation of perfumes in the stillrooms behind the kitchens.

This curiosity stood him in good stead now. He knew where the door opened from the petitioners' court into the pages' room—vacant now, like the gatekeeper's lodge, with the absence of any petitioners—and how to get from there to the servants' wing. Though not a hairy man, John had grown enough of a beard in the twelve days since his capture so that he didn't look simply unshaven: At the inn outside the city walls, where he'd spent last night, he'd dyed the stubble black and trimmed it close. He'd also dyed his hair, what there was left of it, and his eyebrows, and once he'd located the pages' storeroom and borrowed a footman's crimson hose and tunic, he pocketed his oddly particolored spectacles as well.

His own clothes he rolled in a bundle, and stowed in one of the wicker baskets that servants used to bring garments from the wardrobe stores to their masters when they dressed in the morning.

There was no telling when he might have to stop looking like a foot-man in a hurry. Hooking one arm through the basket's handle, he lis-tened at the storeroom door to make sure the courtyard outside was empty, then slipped out and crossed to where a line of newly cleaned chamber pots sat neatly ranged on a bench to be taken back to their respective apartments. With one in either hand, his thumbs hold-ing the lids in place, if anyone did meet him it was unlikely they'd demand that he stop.

And in fact he encountered no one as he ascended the back-stairs that he knew led to the former Regent's quarters.

People disappearing. People being slaughtered wantonly, with-out reason, as he had seen a young girl with pink-dyed hair slashed to pieces in that other world where he'd found Corvin hiding: slain while those who heard her cries feared too much to even open their windows to see who was dying.

The cancer of mistrust, that was one of the several horrors of de-mon incursion into the world of humankind.

Everyone gathered in the muddy market square to hear the King's words was desperate with hope that all would be well again, that the wounded world would heal itself. And John knew that if in fact Folcalor managed to break the Henge at Prokep, what had gone before would seem laughably mild compared to the world where demons roved at large.

Jenny didn't remember stoppering the catch-bottle. But she must have, she thought. For it was stoppered, and in her hands.

She was no longer cold.

That was the first thing she knew, through the shock of disorien-tation: almost before she understood that she was no longer on the hilltop in Ernine, no longer with Morkeleb. In tales and legends they spoke of someone being transported elsewhere "in the twinkling of an eye," but she'd never had experience with such a thing, and neither, apparently, had the makers of tales and legends. None of them spoke of the breathless confusion of such a transportation, of the sinking sensation of the belly, of how the heart pounded and the brain swam with the change of light, the change of smells, the change of air.

She felt panic and sickness and giddiness and terror and not the slightest particle of surprise. She didn't think there was so much as a half-second in which she wasn't aware of where she was, or what had happened to her.

She was in the catch-bottle herself.

There was no other place that she could be. Though there was no visible source of light, still she could see the dim quicksilver curve of the walls, ascending in the shape of the bottle upward to the round shadow, like a closed circular window, of its neck, high in the domed ceiling above her head. She knelt on the concave nadir of a silvery sphere perhaps fifty feet in diameter, with the catch-bottle itself—the metal hot now, as if warmed from within—cradled in her cupped palms.

Jenny did what John would have done in the circumstances. She said, "Bugger."

And looked at the bottle in her hands.

"You will have to let me out, you know." Aohila's voice came, not from the bottle in Jenny's hands, but from overhead, from the window/neck of the bottle in which she was imprisoned. She recognized the voice, too, from her dreams. The Demon Queen spoke softly, but her voice echoed in the dim quicksilver sphere, and Jenny saw in her mind the image of that dark-haired beautiful woman holding the bottle in *her* hands, bending red lips to the red-stoppered neck, to speak to Jenny, trapped inside. "I certainly won't release you until you do."

"*Can* you release me?" Jenny didn't know whether to address the ceiling or the neck of the bottle in her own hands. Sometimes the Queen's voice seemed to be coming out of it, sometimes from above her.

"Of course."

Demons lie.

"The moment you release me."

"Never." But Jenny's heart went absolutely cold as she said it. When you deal with demons, the word *never* takes on a terrifyingly literal meaning. Jenny recalled vividly her recent imprisonment in the green demon-crystal. She had felt no hunger there nor thirst, no weariness beyond that horrifying exhaustion of the spirit. No physical sensation or discomfort at all. She wondered if her physical body was imprisoned here or merely her spirit—Caerdinn had spoken of devices that worked either way—and pinched the back of her hand. It definitely hurt. But what did *that* mean?

Can you really stay here FOREVER, with no one to speak to but the Demon Queen?

Do not treat with demons. There wasn't a book in John's library on the subject that did not begin and end with that admonition, and all spoke with absolute truth. First, last, and eternally—*DO NOT treat with demons.*

Dread was a lump of ice in her belly.

"Never? And never get word to Gareth, that his wife is not his wife?"

Don't answer her, thought Jenny grimly. *Don't reply. They take you, not through your magic, but through your speaking with them. They draw you closer, coax you into a net of lies.* "Morkeleb will tell him."

"You think so, dearest?" Her voice was that of a stylish woman confronted with a blond friend's determination to wear purple. "He may be interested in humankind these days—which quite frankly surprises me—but I think you know he's far more interested in you. I consider it likelier by far that he'll spend days—or weeks—tearing what's left of Ernine to pieces searching for you, or for some trace of this bottle, then fly east after Folcalor and his wights. As far as Morkeleb is concerned, Gareth is only slightly less worthy of notice than a squeaking wormling just out of the egg."

The only thing worse than a demon telling you lies, reflected Jenny, *is a demon telling you the truth.*

"I will not let you out into the world of men."

"Oh, Jenny," sighed the Queen patiently. "Listen to me. A thousand years ago, when the Star-Juggler made this trap, it made sense for him to be imprisoned here with me for eternity. He understood the principle on which the trap works, he had fitted his mind for the task, and there were other Masters in Prokep who would carry on the fight against Isychros. At the time, I was the most deadly threat against the world they wished to save. But that is not the case now. Folcalor is your enemy, as he is mine."

"The fact that you and I share an enemy," replied Jenny, "does not make us friends."

And if she says that an enemy is not all that we share . . .

But the Demon Queen said nothing. And Jenny thought again, *Those were MY dreams. Not John's.*

What does John dream when he hears the sound of Morkeleb's wings?

She drew a deep breath and let it out, trying to expel her jealousy with it. Trying to master her fear.

"Where is John?"

"My darling, would you believe anything that I told you?"

"Is he behind the mirror?"

"If I told you he was not, you would think, *The hag lies, as all demons lie.* And if I say, *Yes, he is,* you will think, *She only says that so I will let her go, to keep him from being skinned alive in her absence by the demons that remain in her realm.* For were he there I would be his only protection, you know."

"Is he there?" demanded Jenny, her voice trembling.

"No."

"Then where is he?"

"My dear Jenny, let's not start that again. In this bottle how would I know anyway? He may be Folcalor's prisoner by this time."

"And naturally you'll help me rescue him, if I let you out?"

"Naturally."

Jenny was silent, shaking with anger. Anger at the Demon Queen, and anger at herself for entering speech with her at all. She found herself again that awkward, half-magic witch-child in a village of children who taunted her, who told her tales about sprites they'd seen in the woods only to follow her as she rushed to those places, grinning behind their hands.

In time she drew another deep breath to steady herself. "And where has Folcalor gone?"

"To Prokep," Aohila answered promptly. "Where the gate into Adromelech's Hell of the Sea-wights stands, prisoned in a Maze of magic and a Henge of ensorcelled stones. It is why Folcalor has been gathering the souls of dead humans, you know—to source enough power to break the Henge. Such death-spells work best in the full of the moon, and the next full moon—the Moon of Winds—will be the last in which the Dragonstar will be in the sky. If Folcalor does not break the Henge then—and devour Adromelech's power, and mine if he can get it—the final setting of the Dragonstar will reduce him to being a minor wight of little power, hiding in swamps and puddles for another thousand years."

Her rich voice was almost gossipy, as if she were about to pass a plate of cream cakes. "Of course, Adromelech has agents in this world gathering soul-gems, too—I think you encountered some of them in the North. They'll be on hand in Prokep, too, at the full of the moon. Whether Folcalor wins that fight, or Adromelech swallows him, from what little I understand of human needs and human hearts and human flesh, I don't think any of your race is going to like what happens next."

Jenny was silent, seeing again the slow-spinning column of blackness and flame moving away over the lands, and the ground behind it strewn with cracked lifeless crystals.

"Not that anything I'm telling you will do anyone the slightest bit of good," added the Queen, "if you choose to spend the rest of conscious eternity here with me in boredom. Do you like games?"

Games about where John might be, and what would be happening to him? Games about Amayon?

Other games Jenny couldn't for the moment imagine, with Aohila placidly drinking in every flash of rage or grief or panic that kindled in her heart? Forever? "And if you're lying?"

"Of course I'm lying, dearest—I'm a demon, aren't I? But only about some things. And you'll never know which, will you, if you stay here, grimly keeping an eye on me. So it scarcely matters, does it?"

Jenny lay down on the curved bowl of the floor, and wrapped her plaid about her. She felt sick with exhaustion and dread. Could the Demon Queen see her, in this hollow sphere where there wasn't even a wall against which to prop her back? The Star-Juggler of ancient times, whoever he had been—the Arch-Seer the demons had spoken of—had been ready to spend the rest of an undying eternity here, rather than let Aohila roam at large in the realms of mortalkind.

Can I be less willing than that?

No one lasted long in the Winterlands who did not have a fairly good sense of direction. John knew which way he had to turn to get to the discreet passage that serviced the royal rooms. Gareth's chambers lay farther along the wing than Trey's, and his one fear as he slipped through the narrow doorway and up the short flight of dim-lit steps was that he'd open the wrong door and walk slap into Trey herself. Amayon would see straight through his simple disguise, and then the game would be over indeed.

Because Corvin was absolutely right, reflected John, putting his makeshift spectacles on again to count chamber doors. *I am a fool.*

The dragon had called him one again—with multiple variations of metaphor and emphasis—when he'd left him, at sunrise yesterday, in the Magloshaldon woods, where the River Clae ran down out of the foothills and turned toward the city walls. John had subsequently had a long, cold walk into Bel, but not a difficult one. The road wound through the woods that fringed the riverbank, ice-locked and silent at this season of the year. Through the trees John had occasionally glimpsed the rustically elegant hunting lodges built by the great families, and with winter and plague both gripping the land, the few caretakers came out no more than they had to. It had been a pleasure only to see trees again, and to read the signs of familiar beasts, deer and foxes and hares, in the snow. After a week in the desert's terrible silence even the winter-hushed woods had seemed lively.

Toward sunset he'd reached the shabby cluster of inns, orchards, vegetable farms, and laborers' cottages that clumped like colonies of barnacles around the city's eastern gate. It had been good beyond speaking to sleep in a real bed again. People were still talking about his rescue by the black and silver dragon—not that they recognized in the ragged stranger the Demon Queen's knight who had supposedly been so instrumental in the Realm's recent woes—and John had experienced considerable qualms about passing through the city gate again that morning.

But I can't leave Gar, if there's a hope of gettin' him clear.

I can't leave his daughter, who'll be the next target of these things if they haven't got her already.

And the part of him that was his father's son, the part of him that for twenty-three years had been Thane of the Winterlands dispensing the justice of an absent King, added: *I can't leave the Realm.*

The passage by which footmen brought breakfast, wash-water, and the day's wardrobe selection—and carried away night soil—for their betters was barely a yard wide and illuminated only through an occasional window high in the left-hand wall. These were of oiled linen, not glass, and the light they admitted was dingy at best. Without the plaster or paneling that finished the bedchambers and sitting rooms, the narrow space picked up sounds like a cave. John heard the steady scrape of a broom in Trey's quarters—*Good, she's out and like to stay that way*—and a woman say, "It isn't the poetry I mind so much, but he gave her the same poem with her name written in. . . ."

Then, from somewhere far off, he heard a cry, a sharp sob of exhaustion mingled with agony, desperately protesting and fading suddenly in despair. He stopped in his tracks, listening, trying to trace the direction of the sound, but only knew that it came from somewhere ahead of him rather than somewhere behind. When he listened again, it was gone.

But he knew what it was, and the shorn hair on his nape prickled with rage and fear.

Trey, he thought. Or another demon. Amayon and whatever Hellspawn it was that now inhabited the body of the poor old King likely weren't the only ones in the palace.

Like the demon who'd taken over the body—and the fortune—of the Otherworld millionaire Wan ThirtyoneFourtyFour, Amayon would have a secret room, where she could feast and drink the pain of human prisoners uninterrupted. In that endless city where John had found Corvin, he'd seen how demons amused themselves: seen over and over in nightmares the bloodied walls, the crawling lines of ants, the crusted straps and fragments of skin and hair. Wan ThirtyoneFourtyFour, the first man to come back from the dead, had been wealthy enough to hire men who didn't care what he did so long as he paid them well. Presumably such men existed in this world, too. Though, at a guess, given the smaller community and chattier servants of Bel, John suspected Amayon's henchmen would be demons like herself.

Any one of whom might easily recognize him.

Cautiously he moved on, barely able to breathe with anger.

Behind a door a girl was singing. A tiny girl, probably no older than his daughter, Maggie. He set down his chamber pots and his basket, and pushed on the panel such as all rooms had, doors concealed, not for any nefarious purpose but simply so that a servant could come and go without any chance of forcing a guest—or a member of the family—to confront the realities of the lower classes having access to their dirty underclothes and breakfast-leavings.

Through the crack in the panel he saw a child who had to be Gareth's daughter, a solemn toddler of three, seated on a footstool singing to her doll. Millença was small and dark, as Trey had been, but with the gray eyes characteristic of the House of Uwanë. She, like the King, her grandfather, wore the somber purples and blacks of half-mourning, in sorrow for the griefs of the city. John had not seen her since he and Jenny had come south for her naming-feast, but her resemblance to Trey was striking, and he recognized the nurse who sat nearby on a low chair. Danis, or Danae, her name was ... the widowed daughter of one of the great noble houses, with a round, cheerful face and eyes creased about with smiling.

She was not smiling now, but had set down the smock she was making to watch the child with an expression of mingled grief and love. A girl who was almost certainly her daughter sat on the floor beside Millença's footstool—same pug nose, same sturdy build, the long braid hanging beneath her embroidered cap of the same strawberry-blond hue as the wisps visible beneath the nurse's starched linen coif. That child stated matter-of-factly, "That's enough. If Dolly had the plague she's dead by now."

"She's not." Millença drew herself up with dignity. "Dolly was dead and then came back to life."

"Don't have it be that," objected the child-in-waiting. "If she came back to life—"

"Branwen," said the nurse warningly, and her daughter turned her head protestingly.

"But when people come back to life they're mean. Struval came back to life and he killed Bria's kitten."

"Dolly won't be mean when she comes back," Millença said, and hugged her bisque-headed rag-baby close.

"Yes, she will. And if *you* die, and come back, *you'll* be—"

"Branwen!"

John eased the panel shut. Voices sounded in the next chamber, Gareth's bedchamber, if John remembered how the royal rooms were disposed. "Is there no hope for her?" Gareth asked, and a gentle, rather prissy tenor replied.

"Not through medicine, no."

"But she looks—"

"It is the nature of this malady that the child does not appear to be ill, my lord. That is the—the terrible tragedy of it. Only last week, I witnessed a woman walking in the Street of Lanterns, holding her little boy by the hand. The child turned pale, and then crimson; he cried out, and blood poured suddenly from his mouth and nose."

John pushed the door, very gently, holding his breath, for he recognized the voice. He saw Prince Gareth sitting on the padded velvet lid of the chest at the end of the curtained bed, looking up into his visitor's face with ravaged eyes. In the young man's shock and despair John could see all his own weary pain of early in the winter, when he himself had searched desperately through every volume in his own library, looking for some hope, some guidance in dealing with the darkness of soul that had come close to destroying his son Ian. And then again later he had searched for any reference to the demon plague that Aohila had threatened to call down on the people of the Winterlands, if John did not undertake the quest for the man she sought.

"Of course I rushed over and did what I could," the visitor went on. "But when the malady advances so far as to actually strike, it is far too late to save the patient's life." His lined, gentle face was sad, framed in the close-fitting velvet cap of an old scholar, and the hands that clasped before the breast of his blue velvet robe were thin and stained with ink and decoctions of herbs. *An old fuddy-duddy, I'd have said, seeing him on the street,* John thought.

Maybe a year ago I'd have been right.

And a year ago he himself would have kicked through the doorway in the paneling and yelled, *That's a lie and you know it....*

In all his researches into plague and disease, he had never found anything remotely like what the fussy old gentleman described.

Of the seven mages whom Folcalor's demons had possessed in the summertime—the mages of Caradoc's corps that had come so close to conquering the Realm of Belmarie in the name of Gareth's cousin Rocklys—only three now survived. *At least,* John prayed, *Ian and Jenny survive....*

And Bliaud of Greenhythe, whom Rocklys had lured north out of quiet obscurity. He looked much the same as he'd looked the first time John had seen him, in the courtyard of Caer Corflyn with his two sons, checking and double-checking everything in the baggage train and scribbling cantrips and sigils on all the packs, to the obvious disquiet of the guards. And it had been all an act, too, John thought. By that time Bliaud's soul and self were trapped in a shard of amethyst and the thing imitating his finicking mannerisms for the sake of his sons—Tundal and Abellus, their names were, he re-called, a stuffy merchant and a dandy in plumed hats—was a thing that later drew the entrails of captured soldiers like a housewife draw-ing chickens....

Well, not quite like, since most housewives killed the chickens first.

After the demons had been driven forth, and sent to amuse Ao-hila behind the Burning Mirror, John had encountered Bliaud again. And like Ian and Jenny, in the wake of exorcism, when John had met the old man in the fog-shrouded ruins of Ernine, Bliaud had seemed lost in some desperate inner grief.

Even at the time, John had thought, *At least Ian and Jen have each other.* Maybe each was sunk in darkness too thick to admit any word of comfort, but each would at least know that the other had walked that road, too.

Bliaud had been alone. Every night, listening to Folcalor whisper little rhymes in his dreams.

I don't ever listen, the old man had said.

And John knew even then that he lied.

There was a look in the eyes of the possessed, a look John had come to know hideously well. He'd seen it in his wife's eyes, and his son's. A kind of silvery glitter, and a way of looking around any room they were in, as if tracking the movement of invisible things.

"The doctors will tell you there is no such ailment," Bliaud's voice went on, as if trying to hold steady in the face of terrible grief. "And indeed, I have never been able to ascertain whether it is a malady, or a spell. But its mark is on your daughter. She has very little time, my lord. Let me take her to my house—and I assure Your High-ness it will be done in all discretion, in all secrecy—and let me see what I can do for her. There are spells, very long spells, very subtle, that can work wonders in cases like these."

I'll just bet they can, thought John, fury sweeping him again like storm-wind over a field of barley. *And when she comes back—and her nurse, too, I'll bet—you'll spend the rest of your life wondering what was changed about her.*

Or what's left of your life until they get you, too.

Gareth made no reply, only sat looking down at his big, awkward hands, and turning a ruby ring round and round on his thumb. Bliaud, who had had his back to John most of the time, now turned, and John drew the panel shut. He heard the mage's light steps cross the room to the communicating door—*Am I going to have to take him on now, to keep him off the girl? Smash him over the head with a chamber pot? That'll work.*—and his voice, addressing the nurse:

"Send for me immediately, at once, at the slightest sign of fever or trembling." And in a softer voice, presumably turning back to Gareth, "Not that there ever is. But please, if there is any change at all, let me know."

The Prince said nothing. The mage's footsteps retreated. John pushed open the panel a crack, to see Gareth lying stretched across the top of the chest where he had been sitting, his face hidden in the crook of his arm. He had taken his spectacles off, and they dangled from his fingers by one silver temple-piece, catching the light of the windows as he wept without a sound.

Chapter 8

*O*nce entered into the world of men, demons have two goals: to cause pain and death for sport, and to open gates for others of their kind.

Jenny couldn't remember which of John's crumbling old books those words had come out of. He had a scholar's magpie memory, and would argue for hours about who said what and where he'd read it—and whether the Gantering Pellus who wrote the *Encyclopedia* was the same one who'd written *A Treatise Upon Brewing,* and why he didn't think this was likely—if he could find anyone to discuss such matters with him.

She closed her eyes, smiling at the recollection of her erratic spouse trading old lore and granny-rhymes with the dotards of every village within riding distance, or getting herself and everything in the Alyn Hold kitchen covered in soot while trying to design a better drawing chimney.

What *had* he been doing in Ernine?

How had he come there, and when?

Where was he now?

Was he trapped behind the mirror, a prisoner in the terrible, shifting Hell there without the Demon Queen's protection?

Was he, as Aohila had said, Folcalor's prisoner, tortured and enslaved to force his help in trapping Ian? Folcalor had enslaved, and presumably could control, dragons, too. The thoughts went through Jenny like the cold scorch of the arrow poison, bringing sweat to her whole body and images that she could not force from her mind.

She opened her eyes. It didn't matter whether they were open or shut. There was nothing to see. Only the silver walls of the catchbottle, curving up to the dark, sealed neck overhead.

Would Aohila let her out if she unstoppered the bottle she still held in her hand? Would she be freed automatically? Did the bottle somehow work by magic drawn from *her?*

The fact that she was no threat to the Demon Queen—once she'd opened the bottle and dispelled the geas that had drawn Aohila into it—wouldn't matter, of course. The Demon Queen was perfectly capable of keeping her sealed in simply to torment her—and to gain leverage over John. John had first entered the Hell behind the Mirror—had first put his soul in pawn to the Queen who ruled it—to save Jenny.

It is the whole aim and purpose of the Hellspawn to find in the world of the living a servant who will be theirs....

Would he do that again? Now, after what had happened in between then and now? Always supposing he wasn't a prisoner there already, always supposing he hadn't already had his soul enslaved....

Always supposing he wasn't dead.

She didn't know. She thought of the white shell into which Amayon had been magically drawn, sealed with red wax. Remembered it lying in the midst of the dark-glittering power circle in the mirror chamber at Ernine. Remembered Amayon screaming.

Closed her eyes. Opened them.

If I don't get out of here I can never beg John's pardon, for turning from him in the depths of my own pain.

He would never know. Gareth, and those in Bel who might save the Prince, would never know about the souls of the slaves, their deaths imprisoned in the crystals. How many more would be killed, with Trey's mind and body inhabited by a demon?

And demons were haunting the Deep. Gareth needed to be told of that, as well.

There is no lawful reason for humankind to touch, or speak to, or have traffic with the Hellspawnkind. Rather should that man perish, and suffer his wife, or his son, or his goods all to perish utterly, than that demons be given a gate into this world.

Jenny leaned her head on her arm, stared at the curve of the wall, her heart pounding. The catch-bottle felt heavy now in her hand, and hot. What was Aohila thinking of, remembering?

What had she thought of, all those years behind the mirror?

The Star-Juggler, Aohila had spoken the name casually, as one who knew him well. Perhaps she had. Whoever he had been, he had learned somewhere the Demon Queen's secret name, the shape of the true essence of her secret self. That argued acquaintance.

And knowing her that well, he had been ready to give up the remainder of his life to his empty, living Hell.

Had given up his life, trying to rush the mirror chamber. Had he written down that name somewhere, so that it could be reapplied to the bottle...?

Reappplied? If what? If I open it now ... and she for whatever reason opens hers, and lets me free?

Why would she do that?

So she can use me as she tried to enslave John?

To share an enemy does not make of her a friend.

More memories. The Winterlands in summer, when the twilights dwindled endless and unextinguished and Jenny would lie on the thick turf below the harsh black rock of Frost Fell's north face, watching birds dart above the pools of the moor. Ian when he was a small child, a thin little black-haired boy following her about the herb garden, breaking off leaves and crushing them in slender fingers, ecstasy in his face at the scents. The way Adric's tongue protruded from the side of his mouth when he was concentrating on his shooting with that bow that was almost too big for a nine-year-old boy. Red-haired, black-eyed, silent Mag, sitting by a mouse-hole for hours, waiting for the mouse to emerge ...

A rush of anger filled her, the mad desire to lurch to her feet, to pace ... but the spurt of energy was no more real, or physical, than hunger would have been in that place, and she remained where she was.

Do you like games?

Was this all a game? Jenny had feared the Demon Queen's taunting, but did not know what to make of her silence.

Is she waiting for me to say something stupid like, "Do you promise you'll let me out...?"

Or is she that certain that I will not have the strength to endure?

The power that holds her in the bottle is being sourced from me. From my memory, from my anger, from my fear, from my jealousy ... from my love for John and for my children.

Maybe from my life alone, like the power sourced from the gems by the demons.

Did Folcalor destroy the demon mirror, and devour the other denizens of Aohila's Hell? Was John there when he did it? Is she alone now, an exiled Queen in flight from her enemies?

Would it make any difference to me if she was?

Only silence. Jenny closed her eyes, imagining the Winterlands again, and Morkeleb's skeletal black silhouette high and tiny in the twilight sky. Dragons sang of past joys, resonating them through refined gold and drinking in the joy a thousandfold forever. She wondered if doing that would pass the time here.

If I go mad here in the silence, will she laugh?

Laugh forever?

Past and present and yet to come, this thou art.

Jenny got to her feet, drew a deep breath, and with a quick motion, pulled the stopper from the bottle.

John was pushing open the panel into Gareth's room when a shadow appeared in the curtained chamber door. He stepped back quickly, pulled the panel nearly to. It was the nurse, her face troubled in the frame of coif and wimple. Millença pushed past her and ran to her father, holding out her arms. Gareth sat up and caught her to him, her face pressed to the fanciful trapunto of his blue-and-black velvet doublet, his fingers stroking the thick pearl-twined braid of her hair. His gray eyes, naked and vulnerable without the spectacles, blinked in the direction of the nurse with a kind of desperation, as if asking her to make what Bliaud had said be untrue.

In an almost inaudible voice the Prince asked, "Where's her mother, Danae?"

Gaw, no, don't send for Trey....

"I don't know, lord." There was a world of private doubt and fear in that carefully expressionless voice.

"Dolly died of the plague, but the doctor brought her back to life," Millença informed her father, holding up the lace-trimmed poppet in her arms. "See? He said she's not going to die ever again."

"That's good." Gareth pushed back the doll's raw-silk hair, peered into the exquisitely painted face. "Yes, I can see she's going to be alive forever now. And she'll always be just as beautiful as she is now. As beautiful as you."

"Silly," said Millença gravely. "Dolls aren't alive. She just isn't dead anymore."

Gareth kissed his daughter, then lifted her down from his skinny knee and looked around for his spectacles, which had dropped from his fingers when Danae and the child had come into the room. They lay on the floor beside the cushioned chest, within inches of his foot. In his situation John wouldn't have been able to see them, either. The young man bent down, groping, and Millença said, "Warmer, Papa," in the voice of one playing a familiar game. Gareth smiled in spite of his red-rimmed, swollen eyes, and began to hunt all around him in places that were obviously absurd: under his cloak, on the bed, in the bed curtains, with his daughter giving him hints. "Warmer—colder—warmer . . ." until he found them and put them on again.

"And now I can see my princess," he said, and kissed her again. "Do you feel all right today?"

She nodded. "I just didn't feel good yesterday, but I'm better, like Dolly."

And Gareth's eyes met the nurse's, over the child's head. "That's good," he said. "And we'll . . . we'll make you all better, like Dolly, so you'll never die ever."

As the nurse led the child from the room, Gareth settled again on his cushioned bench, looking after them with desperate longing in his face. Thinking back over the days just past—the long horror of the night in the prison, the stake and the fire and the despair in the desert—John reflected, *Of the two of us, I've had the easier time. I didn't have to make a decision. I didn't have to try to figure out where I was bein' lied to by those I love, with their lives at the stake if I guessed wrong.*

But he said gently, as he pushed opened the panel in the wall, "It's only demons that don't die ever, Gar."

Gareth turned his head. He didn't even seem surprised—not at John's survival, not at his return—and it crossed John's mind belatedly to wonder what Trey—and doubtless others—had told him over the past eight days.

If he screams for the guards, I'm a dead man.

But the young man said nothing, only averted his face quickly, though not quickly enough to conceal his tears. John stepped over to him and took him in his arms, as simply as he would have taken one of his own sons. With a dry sob, Gareth turned in his grip and clung to him, his whole beanpole body shaking with grief. Weeping in desperation and in fear, for perhaps the first time since Trey's death.

John held him for a long time, saying nothing, his head bowed over Gareth's. The long curtains drawn over the doors drowned the room in shadow—now and then voices filtered in from the terrace, and the Long Garden outside. By the look of it the young man had spent hours here alone: The floor around the bed, and the coverlet itself, were littered with the books and scrolls that John knew were Gareth's primary joy. Cups, dishes, writing tablets strewed the small marquetry table, the seat of the chair. There was no sign of Trey's presence, not even of a visit. John wondered how soon after her "resurrection" Gareth had ceased to seek her company and her bed.

"You have to get out of here," he said gently, when Gareth's sobs ceased and the young man only held to him, rocking a little in his arms. "You know Trey isn't Trey anymore."

He felt the young man struggle to form the words *I don't believe you*, and let them trickle away unsaid. The realization must have been growing on him for a week, desperately shoved aside.

At least I was able to get Jenny back. At the cost of dealing with demons—of putting my soul in pawn and endangering God knows how many others . . .

But I did get her back.

And then like an imbecile lost her . . .

Trey, he knew, would not be coming back.

"They said you were possessed." Gareth sat up and fumbled his spectacles straight, then took them off again to wipe his eyes. "That you're in league with demons."

"D'you think that's true?"

"A dragon rescued you."

"A dragon rescued *you*, me hero, once upon a time. I begged this one not to—said I could never hold me head up as a dragonsbane again if he did. . . . Have you caught Trey at anything?"

Gareth didn't ask, *At what?* By the look in his eyes he knew exactly what John was talking about. That was answer in itself.

After a time he said, "Not really. Only I found . . . this sounds stupid. To suspect Trey . . . to suspect my *wife* . . ." He shook his head and dug around in the purse that hung at his belt for a kerchief to wipe his eyes.

"You know how gentle Trey is, how considerate. You remember when first you came here she lent Jenny a dress, so she wouldn't be mocked by Zyerne and her ladies, even though Zyerne would never have let Trey hear the end of it if she'd found out. But now she'll say things to me, cruel things, things that hurt. Even perfectly normal things for someone else. She'll watch me out of the corners of her eyes, as if she's laughing."

His jaw clenched hard and he made a business of wiping the tear spots and smudges from his spectacle lenses so as not to meet John's compassionate eyes. He was twenty-four and looked forty, a thousand times worse than he had, John thought, only nine days ago, when he'd come to the prison.

"She disappears for hours at a time, I don't know where she goes. Some of the servants ... I've heard rumors ... they can't be true. This whole city is a cesspit of rumors now, about this person or that person seen running mad, or being caught drinking blood or running through the streets with dead cats or dead rats strung around their necks like amulets. Trey keeps telling me it isn't true, that she loves me, that I have to trust her, and I keep thinking, *I don't know this person. I've never met this woman before in my life.*"

His hand tightened frantically on John's sleeve, his shortsighted gray eyes pleading. "But if I don't trust her, what are we? What has our love meant?"

"Your love meant that you were one of the lucky ones in this world," said John quietly. "Lucky to find love at all, and to know enough not to bugger it up when you did. But it's gone, Gar. Trey is gone. What was it you found?"

Gareth was silent for a long time, his mouth working a little with distaste. Then he said, "The wings of insects. Flies—we had some warm days here, and spring is close. Roaches. The legs of crickets. All laid out along the windowsill in her room. From the garden I'd seen her sitting in the window only a few minutes earlier, and there had been no one else in the room. I found one of the flies, too, crawling around...." He shuddered.

"You have to get out," repeated John. Under his hands the young Regent's shoulder bones felt like velvet-covered sticks. "Get out before the thing that's livin' in her body gets you, too."

"Her child—"

"There is no child. That child died when Trey died. The thing she'll birth will be a demon like herself."

"No." Gareth's gray eyes turned bleak and moved aside. "You

can't know that. You're only guessing. A child is innocent. I felt her baby move this morning, I felt—"

John put his fingers to the young man's lips. "D'you really believe that?"

Footsteps sounded in the anteroom. John reached the servants' door in one panicky bound and flattened himself into the corridor beyond. Voices murmured on the other side of the painted and gilded paneling, Gareth said, "No, nothing, thank you."

"You father wishes to see you after dinner, sir. I must say, his reassurances to the people were well received." The chamberlain Badegamus sounded both tired and relieved. "He's ordered a celebration—free wine in every public square. That should cheer the people, help them forget." His voice had the ring in it of a man trying to convince himself. "I venture to say things will be better now that he's himself again, sir. And I never thought to see that day—never thought to see it at all. You could have heard the cheering in Halnath. Not that *you* haven't done wonderful work, sir," added the chamberlain hastily. "How you've kept the Realm together . . ."

"Thank you, Badegamus," said Gareth. "Tell my father I'll be there. But now I just need to rest."

"Of course, sir. While you're at dinner, shall I have someone tidy up here a little? I understand how you'll have needed to rest, after all the terrible things that have gone on. . . ."

John wondered, hearing the faint jingling of shoe-bells retreat, whether the stout, meticulously correct chamberlain also had "died" and been resurrected by Bliaud's magic. Once Amayon/Trey came into the palace, such things could have taken place in the dead of night, without a soul knowing.

As they would, beyond the smallest doubt, if Millença went to stay at Bliaud's house.

"You have to get out of here." John stepped back through the hidden door after silence returned to the room.

"And go where?" Gareth's voice was listless, worn out with struggling, as if it were simpler just to die. John understood the feeling, but wanted to take him by the neck and shake him, anyway. "Flee to Halnath, as I did before? Polycarp urged me to. He—he tried to tell me that Bliaud was in league with demons, that Trey—" He shook his head and looked down at his hands again, turning the ruby ring around his thumb as if it were some complex rite demanding all of his attention. "I couldn't listen. I suppose I should have. I ordered him out of my sight, out of the city. Now they tell me that the Master was in league with the gnomes, kidnapping people and selling them to them. . . ."

"If the Master was doin' that he'd be here at Court swearin' loyalty to your father an' tellin' Trey how pretty she is," said John bluntly. "What's this about the gnomes, then? Are there demons in the Deep as well as here?"

"I don't know. No one knows." Gareth gestured helplessly. "One hears all kinds of things, terrible things. There was a riot in the Dockmarket, and people marched on the Deep of Ylferdun, but the gnomes turned them back. People were killed. My father's meeting with a representative of the King today to—"

More voices, this time on the terrace. Though the curtains were shut, John made a lunge back to the panel and stood close beside it, ready to vanish again, until they passed.

"Here." Gareth got to his feet, seeming to suddenly piece together John's disguise, his shorn hair, and the circumstances under which they'd spoken last. "You can't stay. They'll kill you if you're seen. I saved the things you asked me to, the bone-and-silver box, and the silver bottle—your spectacles, too, and your sword." He led the way into the anteroom where the children and their nurse had been, and through it to his library. This chamber, too, was cluttered thick with parchments, books, lamps, and all the paraphernalia of scholarship, pumice and pounce and uncut quills in a crystal vase, untidy in spite of servants' ministrations. Here, too, the curtains were drawn, as if Gareth's battered spirit could no longer tolerate light. At least here the dishes had been taken away.

The spoils of John's adventurings through Hell—duplicate box and bottle, notes and sword—were where John had glimpsed them through Corvin's rememberings, concealed behind the books on a high shelf. Gareth brought a ladder over to get to them, and handed them down one by one. "This wasn't open when I brought it here," he said worriedly, turning in his hand the box that the un-wizard Shamble had made for John in that stuffy and bug-ridden apartment in the

79th District. The chip of dragonbone on which Shamble had written the Rune of the Gate was still there, but cracked through and charred nearly black.

"Don't worry about it." John took the box, stuffed his packet of much-crossed and overwritten notes into his servant's red doublet, and looked around the library. One of the small panes of the window out onto the terrace was recently repaired, its frame bright with new putty. "Was that broken, then?" That would be where Corvin pushed through. Tiny, as he'd seen Morkeleb shrink himself to the size of a cat. . . .

Gareth nodded. "I don't remember—when Trey was . . . was ill, I think, or just after she . . . she got better. It's all right. I mean, Badegamus tells me nothing was taken." He handed him down the sword Shamble had wrought, covered with runes that had no virtue in the world where the League of the White Black Bird were condemned to live and die. Runes for the murder of demons, handed down through generations of sterile magery and rote repetition. Not being a mage himself, John hadn't the faintest idea whether they'd work or not, but the sword balanced well in his hand. He put his own spectacles on and blinked gratefully. Maybe the headache he'd had for days now would go away.

He tuned and regarded his friend for a quiet moment, then asked, "What about Jen?"

The bruised-looking gray eyes avoided his. "I—I don't know. She was here—I spoke to her—the day Trey . . . Trey was so ill. I was so tired. I hadn't slept, I was half-distracted. . . ." A quiver ran through him, and he bowed his head, as if expecting anger or blows. After a moment he looked up and went on: "I know I told Badegamus to prepare a room for her, and he told me she went there. But someone said they saw her, that evening, in the First Hall of the Gnomes' Deep, just as the gnomes were closing up the gates. No one has seen her since."

She is dying . . . the Demon Queen had said. Dying in the Deep . . .

So the part about her being in the Deep at least hadn't been a lie.

And Corvin, bad cess to him, had only blinked up from his bed of gold: *I cannot see her; I have tried. . . .*

If she had no more magic in her, the dragon should have been able to find her.... Unless she was in some place that was scry-warded. Was the Deep? Or parts of the Deep?

Only ten minutes ago he had said to Gareth, *It's only demons that don't ever die.*

Why couldn't his heart accept that she was gone?

He glanced at the angle of the sunlight through the slit in the curtains, heard the tread of the guards on the terrace, the creak of battle-harness and mail. Badegamus had come here from the King, who must be back from the market square. That meant more guards about the palace, more servants tending to their duties, more people who were likely to recognize him, spectacles or no spectacles, dye or no dye ...

The King would be going in to dinner soon, and bidding his son to his side.

"Meet me at moonrise where the road goes into the woods along the Clae," said John, forcing the image of Jenny from his mind. *First things first.* "Bring Millença, and as much money as you can scrape up without callin' attention to yourself. We can hire a nurse in the countryside, where there won't be tattlin' tongues. Have you a place you can go? Not one of the royal manors—Trey and your dad'll have word of it, and find some damn good reason for bringin' you back, an' then you'll never get out...."

"I won't leave the baby. Trey's baby," Gareth added, seeing the blank look momentarily in John's eyes. "Trey will be brought to bed in a few weeks. After that I can—"

"That baby's dead." John hated the words as they came out of his mouth, hated the way those too-soft gray eyes hardened with anger. But there was nothing else that he could say to make Gareth understand. "When Trey gives birth it'll be to a demon like the demon that's livin' in her flesh now. The demon that you see when you look into her eyes."

Gareth's gaze flinched away. "I can't.... If the child is human when she bears it, I can't leave it in her care, to be ... to be taken that way. Millença and Danae, I'll move to a different establishment, one under my control—"

"And what good's that like to do you ... ?"

A voice boomed on the terrace, deep and melodious and unmistakable: "... keep the feast with us, my lord Goffyer. Tomorrow you and I can speak about this rumor of slave-buying, which I doubt not was begun by those whose intention has always been to cause confusion and strife in the Realm. Maybe later you and I can have a quiet talk together. Perhaps I can show you some things here that would amuse you...."

John bolted through into the bedroom, Gareth at his heels; nipped through the concealed door into the servants' passage again. "Tonight," he breathed. "Moonrise. At least bring Millença to me."

Gareth opened his mouth, shut it again, helpless uncertainty in his eyes.

"And when you've a minute," John added grimly, leaning around the panel, "search about the palace for the special room Trey asked for, the 'secret boudoir' or 'meditation chapel' or whatever it was...."

"How do you know she asked for a meditation room?" The young man stared at him, amazed.

John tapped the side of his nose, an ironic twist to his lips. "It's what demons do," he said. "Search for it and have a look inside—if you can do it without her knowin' of it."

"My son?" The King's voice raised in jovial cry, and one of the terrace doors opened in the next room. "Don't worry, Badegamus," he added, "I should think I know my son's rooms...."

"My darling?" A woman's voice, lilting and sweet. "Lord Goffyer is here, sent by King Balgub of the Deep...."

Amayon.

John's blood turned cold and he closed the door, barely breathing, wondering if the pair of demons could hear the pounding of his heart, or the smell of his blood or the fear-sweat that poured down his face. But Gareth's feet retreated from the wall and John heard the former Regent's light voice, "I'm here, Father." If John had ever doubted Gareth's courage he had proof of it now, for there wasn't a trace of fear in his speech. "Badegamus tells me you've made festival in the streets."

John moved away from the door, trembling a little with panic and fright. *Dear God, did I remember to take away the old specs...?*

He groped in his doublet pocket, then found them, exhaled.

And the dragonbone box, and the silver bottle, and the sword belted at his waist.

Voices in the other room, the King's and the lovely trained

mellifluousness of Badegamus, interrupted now and then by the cautious gruff alto of a gnome. Though his hands were shaking so he could barely fumble the door-catch, John pushed the door far enough to glimpse the King through the connecting archway of the anteroom. Uriens had clearly just come from the pulpit above the market square, still clothed in the somber hues of half-mourning, his body framed in an aureole of wired and stiffened Court mantlings that set their wearer off as if against a private backdrop of color and movement.

Trey had gone to clasp Gareth's hand, dainty as a roe deer in blue velvet and garnets—how could anyone not see Amayon in the way she titled her head, in the ironic smile? Badegamus, stouter than ever with his enormous, waxed, and wired golden mustache, kept glancing at her as if he'd heard some rumor about her that he didn't wish to believe.

Beside him—and only a little shorter than the tubby Chamberlain— was a gnome John vaguely recognized. Barrel-chested and harsh-featured, Goffyer wore the usual gnomish profusion of jewelry, his long hair of faded pink wound up in silver pins and the familiar demon glitter in his eyes.

So they're in the Deep as well, John thought, and drew the door closed again. *Where have I seen that one? Goffyer* ... He couldn't recall a gnome named Goffyer among those his gnome friends had introduced to him in Ylferdun Deep. Not that Goffyer was his actual name, of course, any more than Miss Mab's real name was Miss Mab: Taseldwyn, she was called among her own people, and by those humans not too lazy to deal with gnomish names.

He moved off a few yards, then halted, listening. Trying to get his bearings, to locate if he could the woman who had cried out in despair and pain. With the King and Trey back, not to speak of a hundred servants who'd recognize him from his amiable habit of talking with anyone he met, he knew the danger of remaining, but he couldn't leave her without searching.

The door at the far end of the corridor was locked, barred from the other side. It butted, he knew, onto the old palace, a logical place for Trey to have her "meditation chapel": There were courtyards, and gardens, and pavilions in that rambling stone warren that hadn't been entered or used in years.

If he recalled correctly, he thought, backtracking through the service passage toward the main laundry and scullery, he could get to the old palace through a small courtyard that had once served the Queen's Wing. A small gate opened onto a minor street called the Cooksway at the foot of the palace hill, which would serve for a quick getaway if necessary. The gate was bolted from the inside, without a more modern key, and the courtyard was used to store fuel these days. Nobody went there. . . .

But as he descended the enclosed stair to that small court, the stone walls around him picked up voices. Ahead of him, and, a moment later, behind as well. The voices behind him were accompanied by the ominous creak of sword belts and the clank of weapons. John removed his spectacles, shifted the wicker basket into both hands, assumed the rather haughty mein of a servant going about the business of his betters, and strode down the stair, praying nobody was going to ask him what business he had transporting laundry around an area of the palace generally given over to baskets of charcoal and cords of wood.

Nobody asked, for very good reason. When John stepped through the arch at the bottom of the stair he found half a dozen men just coming into the wood-court through the little Cooksway gate, men who wore the sable robes and black mail of the scholar-soldiers of the Master of Halnath. One of them he was almost certain—by the way he stood, and his height, though a hood covered his head—was in fact Polycarp of Halnath, but John didn't dare stop for a closer look. He knew Polycarp quite well, and the Master knew him, and had been one of the votes cast in favor of his execution: Given what John knew about demons, he didn't blame him one bit for it. It was a struggle not to break into a run, but he only passed across the corner of the court, and not a man of them turned to observe him. . . .

Mostly because a squad of guards emerged from the stairway a few paces behind him, coming into the court as John barely made it through a gateway at the other side.

"Lord Polycarp?" demanded a harsh voice—*Guessed right,* thought John, and sneaked his spectacles back on as he turned and flattened himself behind the nearest buttress. "You and your companions are to come with me."

Polycarp turned with truly commendable presence of mind and pulled open the postern-door that led back out into the Cooksway. He stopped and fell back as several more armed men came through it wearing, like the first group, the crimson leather cuirasses and gold plumes of the House of Uwanë. Their halberds were leveled within inches of his breast. Polycarp turned back to the original guards, asked, "By whose authority, Captain Leodograce?" His voice was light, like Gareth's; husky and rather high. "I came here to speak with the Prince...."

"You came here to murder the Prince," retorted the commander of the guards, and though John was too far away—and at the wrong angle—to see the man's eyes, he heard something in the tone of his voice that made him think, *He's one of 'em.* "Having sent him messages to lure him here...."

"That's ridiculous." It was, too: Polycarp, Master of Halnath, had been Gareth's friend and counselor for years.

"Then why send him a note to meet you in this place, far from help? Take them!"

Polycarp drew his sword, but the conclusion was foregone. He and his companions were outnumbered, their swords outreached by the longer weapons of the guards. Watching the brief struggle among the stacked cords of wood, John was almost confirmed in his guess that Captain Leodograce was possessed—he didn't fight like a man who had the slightest concern about either wounds or death, not even taking elementary precautions—and probably three others among the guards were demons as well. Two of Polycarp's men were killed outright, the rest, and the Master himself, disarmed and bound, and dragged back up the covered stair by which John and later the guards had originally come. Polycarp said, "I demand to speak to the Prince," and Leodograce struck him across the face with the back of his hand, knocking him against the wall.

John stood for a few moments in the concealment of the little inner gateway, watching them go and wondering what he should do now. Try to return to Gareth and let him know of Polycarp's arrest? If he could make it back that far, the Prince would almost certainly be with the King—or with Trey. Leave a message in his rooms via the service corridor?

Would Amayon be able to sense John's presence in Bel by touching the paper? Quite possibly. In any case, he'd speak to Gareth tonight, on the edge of the woods, if Gareth brought his daughter. . . .

If he brought his daughter.

And if he didn't . . .

"Lord Aversin?"

John turned—and cursed himself as he turned—to find himself looking at the tattooed southern merchant who'd stared at him in the square.

Chapter 9

Cords of wood heaped the first ten feet of the little walkway in which John stood and he didn't hesitate for so much as a second. He caught up a billet from the top of the nearest one, flung it straight and hard at the southerner's head, and bolted back across the wood-court without even waiting to see whether it reached its target. The incoming guards who'd stopped Polycarp in the outer gate hadn't closed it behind them. John shot through like a startled hare, fled down the Cooksway, dodged into the first turning he saw.

This part of Bel, around behind the old palace, was a dilapidated neighborhood where the town houses of the nobility of a century ago had been largely abandoned for more spacious and showy quarters on the other side of the palace hill. Merchants had bought the town houses, and turned the great halls into warehouses and shops. Artisans rented the upper floors, and pigs and chickens dwelt in the stables and courtyards. The great Temple of the Purple Goddess of the Hearth had fallen into decay and lingerie sellers had set up barrows in its forecourt. It was a quarter of narrow streets and small squares that at one time had been private gardens. John dodged around as many corners as he could, ducked into a shop selling wool and leather and out by another door, took refuge in a carriageway leading back into a courtyard where laundry was being boiled in a cauldron long enough to drag his baggy, striped trousers and goatskin jacket from the wicker hamper and pull them on over the crimson tunic and hose.

Not that that'll get me much, he thought. *He's seen me in this as well....*

"Here, what you doing?" the laundress demanded, coming down the carriageway with her stirring-paddle leveled like a lance. "You can't change clothes here."

John returned to the street, looked quickly around, and saw, at the next turning, the southerner talking to a man whose yellow cloak and extravagant plumed hat John recognized as belonging to the wizard Bliaud's younger son, Abellus. John turned, fast, and headed the other way, discarding the wicker basket down the first cellar he passed. The neighborhood with its back-looping streets was confusing, but it was small, and John worked his way out to the city wall, and along it to one of the cramped and squalid streets of the Dockmarket, where weavers and day laborers lived two families to a room, and where every corner boasted a tavern or an establishment that dealt in old clothes. He had little money—most of the gems in the red velvet robe Corvin had given him had turned out to be glass and paste—*Of course no dragon would give away real gems, you nit,* he'd reflected bitterly when the moneylender had broken this news to him—and couldn't spare any of it, but bought himself a thirdhand coat of green wool, anyway, and left the goatskins behind. Then he found a tavern, and settled himself in the darkest corner of its ordinary, to wait for the search to pass to other quarters.

He wasn't sure whether Amayon would be able to locate him once the demon knew he was in Bel, but it was critical, now, that he get himself, and Gareth, and Gareth's daughter out of the city at once.

And after that, he reflected, keeping as wary an eye on the tavern door as was possible without putting on his spectacles, *the Old God's grandmother only knows how we're going to deal with the demons here, let alone what's going to happen if Folcalor breaks the Henge at Prokep.*

In time, the line of pale winter sunlight visible through the doors rose up the faces of the gray narrow buildings across the lane. It was time to get out of there and see if he couldn't get himself out the gate and back to the Silver Cricket Inn without being arrested. If Gareth was to meet him at moonrise—some two hours after midnight—he had to make arrangements for horses and food with what little money he had....

He'd also pledged Gowla and Grobe, owners of the Silver Cricket, that he'd help serving ale in the ordinary tonight to pay for his lodging.

Thus it was that John Aversin was crossing the fountain square by the Dockmarket gate just before sunset of a chill and cloudy afternoon. Wind rose cold again off the sea, and ravens quarreled with pigs over garbage in the lanes. The farmers who'd brought chickens and milk into the city were leaving now, and the lane before the eastern gate was a choke of jostling backs and baying asses. Torches were being lit around the gate, and the air was gritty with the smoke of suppers cooking. Despite the King's asseveration that all the city was in festival, there was little laughter or song. A few butts of wine had been broached before the Temple of Mallena, but the voices of those who came to dip into them were harsh and uneasy as the ravens. Men still in mourning shouted, now and then, standard praises of the King. Women haggard with hunger or grief carried water back to their rooms. Sometimes one would speak to John from a doorway, or give him a painted smile.

Everyone seemed to be watching one another, or watching their own backs.

It's turning into the Winterlands, thought John as he hurried through the wintry dusk.

It's turning into the city in the Otherworld, where no one trusts, and everyone hurries and fears.

It's turning into a world without law.

A woman passed through the square in front of him, and the sight of her stopped John in his tracks. She was gone before he got a better look at her, but his impression was that she was far too well dressed for this disreputable neighborhood. His impression, too, was that none of the beggars, whores, and laborers in the square so much as looked at her, as if she did not really exist.

But she existed. And he knew her: the tall, almost serpentine build, the melon-heavy breasts, the black hair coiled and glittering with jeweled chains. He hadn't seen her eyes and was glad they hadn't been turned his way. He knew—he was positive, as one is positive of things in dreams—that they would be yellow, with horizontal rectangular pupils, like a goat's.

She's out from behind the mirror, he thought, almost queasy with shock.

Walking the streets of the city in a woman's guise, she who was not a woman at all.

The Demon Queen.

The impact of cold, and of brittle afternoon light striking her eyes, was so sharp that Jenny staggered, catching herself against the rough-timbered wall of a house. The smell of privies, of wood smoke, of horses and mud dumped itself over her like water from a bucket, and someone said close by, "Narh, Marbel, I know what he *says*, but what's he actually *done* besides sit in the taverns talkin' to his friends and makin' *you* pay the rent?" Jenny blinked and saw a couple of market-women walk past her, their faded gaudy layers of skirts tucked into sashes and their head scarves and veils tied this way and that to give information about neighborhood and marital status.

There was no mistake. She was in Bel.

She looked down at her hands. She still held the catch-bottle in one, the stopper in the other. At her feet lay the notched staff she'd carried underground. Her hip hurt her, as it hadn't, she realized, dur-ing the time—days? hours? weeks?—she'd been in the bottle. The gnomish trousers she wore were still damp at the knees, from kneel-ing in the snow at Ernine.

She was definitely in Bel. In the Claekith district, near the river, the smell was unmistakable. Not far from the Dockmarket, in fact. She could see the roofs of Mallena's temple over the houses. Old snow heaped the sides of the lane, mingled with dirty straw and garbage. It was late afternoon—*of what day?*—and storekeepers were taking in their wares. A smell of garlic and stew from a nearby tavern puffed over her and reminded her that she was ravenously hungry.

Jenny knotted the neck of the catch-bottle back into her sash, and made sure that the hothwais of light, and of warmth, were still wrapped and in her pockets. Then she stooped and picked up her stick. In a poor neighborhood like this one there were enough women who'd had their heads shorn for one crime or another that she wouldn't be much stared at, but she drew up a fold of her plaid over her head, anyway.

Trey is a demon, she thought. And John could be anywhere, alive or dead or in chains in Hell.... *First things first,* she told herself. *As John always says.* And though it wasn't likely the Regent's wife would be anywhere in this neighborhood, Morkeleb had told her that demons roved the streets, particularly at night. It would only take one recognizing her, to raise a hue and cry.

So though her hip barely twinged her now, Jenny bowed her back and leaned exaggeratedly on her staff as she limped toward the wider street along the river that would lead her to the city walls. In the days she had been gone from Bel, the plague seemed to have abated, though she saw marks of its aftermath everywhere. A few yellow paper seals still clung half-scraped to the doors of some of the buildings she passed, and many people she saw wore mourning, their hair newly cropped.

But the smoke that filled the air now bore on it the smell of nothing more sinister than cooking, and though this riverside neighborhood was a crowded one, she saw no doors that bore fresh seals. Vendors had returned to the narrow lanes, selling crullers or head scarves, or cups of steaming coffee dispensed from little stoves. A girl drove a donkey past, laden with baskets of last year's dried apples. A small dog barked in a fifth-floor window.

The city was coming back to life.

Jenny reached out with her thoughts. Someone asked a woman selling steamed buns if she was doing well. Yes, she said, she was getting over it, though her husband's death had near broken her heart. . . .

Her friend said, "Darling, I know . . . you tried the wine yet? The King's men set up a cask near the Green God's temple."

"D'you think he was right? The King? About the plague being done?"

"Cragget knows. I wouldn't ha' thought any man could say that for certain, but then I'd have bet money against the King coming back to himself. My niece works in the palace kitchens, and she said he was like a child."

The King recovered? Jenny shivered as she rounded a corner out of earshot, guessing what had to have happened. And that being the case—if a demon now ruled in Uriens's form—what had become of Gareth? Had he, too, "died," to be returned to life with some other consciousness looking out from behind his eyes? Polycarp of Halnath had sent her to find Miss Mab in the Deep to begin with: What had become of him? Had he escaped from Bel in time?

"I swear I'm still afraid to go out of the house," said a young girl to her friend as they both scraped buckets full of the least-filthy snow in the lane, "once the sun's out of the sky."

"It's the plague," said her friend, "that drives folk mad. . . ."

No, thought Jenny, struggling not to quicken her stride as she hobbled toward the flagged embankment of the river. *Not the plague. Demons.*

And I released the Demon Queen, when I could have kept her out of the world for good.

I have to get word to Gareth. See him, see who and what I'm dealing with. Or is Folcalor only waiting for that?

What, then? Flee from the city? Search for John? Return to the Winterlands? *And how long until the demons come there in force, instead of in ones and twos?*

How long until they go after Ian? If they're not attacking the Hold already?

The next moon will be the last that the Dragonstar is in the sky, Aohila had said. The Moon of Winds, which would start growing, if Jenny's reckoning was in, within a few days. By what the Demon Queen had said it sounded like the extraordinary power of Folcalor and Adromelech would wane after that—that they were somehow bound to the comet. But even if that was the case, thought Jenny—and the Demon Queen may well have been lying, to give her one more reason to feel that she must get free of the catch-bottle—what mages now remained to fight even the weakened demons that would come forth from the place where Adromelech and his devils had been trapped these thousand years?

One mage at least had to have returned to the demons' power, the "great doctor" Gareth had brought in to "resurrect" Trey. The only mage Jenny knew of still alive in the South was Bliaud. All the others had been taken over by Caradoc, and most of them were dead.

That left Ian, and Miss Mab. And Miss Mab, to all intents, was a prisoner.

Ian . . .

Folcalor nearly destroyed him. I can't let him face him again.

But she knew she might have no choice.

Before anything, she thought, *eat. Whatever else is happening, you'll be able to think more clearly on a full stomach.*

She felt in her pockets for coin and of course there was none. When Morkeleb had brought her from the North she had gone straight to the palace, and Gareth's chamberlain had food sent to her immediately, as an honored guest.

She shook her head at herself and sighed. After a lifetime of being known as a sorceress and healer, it was too easy to forget that people weren't going to simply hand her bread and cheese. She knew she could earn the wherewithal to fill her belly by washing dishes or sweeping up the kitchen at an inn, if she found one where the innkeeper was friendly. Keeping away from sight of possible demon-ridden patrons would be trickier, but with her shorn head she could come up with a story that accounted for a desire to remain out of sight.

There was no shortage of inns in Bel, especially in the Dock-market, but the crowded streets made her nervous. There were tav-erns, she knew, outside the gates as well, where she would not run the risk of being trapped inside the city walls, if recognized and pur-sued. Thus she joined the straggle of home-going farmers and dairy-maids, making herself as small and old as possible as she passed the disinterested guards. All about her in the crowded lane the talk was of the King's recovery, and of the free wine being given out in the public squares—she'd passed several barrels and any number of drunkards already. She guessed, piecing bits of conversation together, that she hadn't been in the catch-bottle long.

Her soul cringed at the recollection. She had had the Demon Queen at her mercy, and had let her go. Turned her loose in a world already facing demon war.

Morkeleb, she thought, but knew that the dragon would find her soon. As Aohila had said, he'd be scrying for her, seeking her.

And John.

Gareth might know something of John, she thought—if Gareth was still himself. She'd have to find some way of reconnoitering, to see whether it was safe to approach him. Miss Mab was still in the Deep, awaiting the arrival of a gnome who might very well be pos-sessed by Folcalor himself.

Once outside the Dockmarket gate, Jenny felt safer, calmer. She picked the smallest of the several inns that served the cluster of market-gardens near there, turned down a muddy lane that ran be-side its stable wall. There was a bare orchard across the track, the trees still beehived in straw, and a gaggle of empty pig-yards by the stable gate. The kitchen door stood open, firelight an amber blessing in an afternoon darkening to indigo cold: A servant in shirtsleeves was scraping leftovers down for the household dogs. Jenny pushed back the plaid from her head and said, "Excuse me," and the servant straightened up and looked at her.

It was John.

The stillness in the yard lasted for what felt like five minutes; Jenny thought later it was probably only thirty seconds or so. It surprised her, when she thought about it later, that she recognized him at all, for his hair was cropped to a stubble and it, and his grubby whiskers, had been dyed with lampblack. He still had on the spectacles she'd long ago enchanted against breakage or loss, and wore the shabby clothes of a shepherd or a bumpkin. Only when she came closer to him did she see, in the open neck of his shirt, the burned mark that the Demon Queen had left, and a savage half-healed gouge in his left cheek.

He took a step toward her, then hesitated—hating her? Jenny wondered, though curiously without fear. Angry? *He has a right to be....*

She stepped toward him, and it seemed then that without any intervening thought or action they were suddenly together in the middle of the yard in each other's arms.

"Gaw, love, how'd you get here?" He pulled back from that first kiss, his hand stroking her cheek, her hair, her shoulder; his eyes—so bright behind the lenses—looking down into her face. "Are you all right? Love, I'm sorry, I'm sorry...."

She dragged his mouth down to hers again, tears running down her face. She thought the strength of his arm around her ribs as he lifted her off her feet would drive the breath from her lungs.

"Hey, lad!" yelled a voice from the kitchen. "You canoodle on your own time, eh? We got customers...."

"God save 'em," muttered John. The dogs he'd been feeding—an immense brindled mastiff and a slightly smaller black bitch—snuffed warily at Jenny's boots when John set her down, then tried to lick her hands. "I got pots to wash if I'm to eat tonight...."

"Split your dinner with me and I'll help."

"You've got a bargain, love. Are your hands all right, though?" He took one in both of his, strong fingers probing at the scarred joints that a month ago had been stiff and crooked as wood. Jenny bent and flexed them, to show him; he raised them gently to his lips. "She told me you were dead," said John softly. "The Demon Queen. I'm glad that you're not." Their fingers laced together, he led her into the scullery—bowls and platters, steam, garbage, and mice, and the kitchen's amber light roaring through the archway at the side.

Grobe, the landlord of the Silver Cricket, only rolled his eyes when John informed him that this was his wife ("Oh, aye, right . . ."), but shrugged at her offer of help. "Long as I've got cups to put the ale in when I need 'em, you can split the leavings with whom you choose. We're near out of punch, though—"

"I'll get some started."

"*I'll* get some started," corrected Jenny, who had experience with John's erratic attention span when it came to cooking. She found a scarf and tied it over her head: Gnomish trousers were disregarded among farm women, but a woman with her head uncovered would get unwelcome stares. "You bring me in some kindling." As Grobe's wife had quite enough to do serving in the ordinary itself, Jenny was welcome in the kitchen, carving slices from the roast on the blackened stone hearth and loading platters with ducks, poults, beef, and fish stew. "I've missed you," she said, meeting John in the scullery door with a basket of dirty ale-mugs on her hip. "John, I never—"

He put a hand on her shoulder and looked down into her eyes. "Another apology and I'll beat you." He drew her to him again, kissed her, his mouth tasting of honey mulled with cinnamon. "If we start in like that we'll both be sayin' we're sorry for the rest of the night, if not the rest of our lives—or I will be, anyway. Ian's all right, you know. He was doin' better when I rode out—"

"I've seen him. We rode together to Eldsbouch—"

"We've got three wanting duck," called out Mistress Gowla through the kitchen door, and John took the ale-cups and disappeared into the scullery while Jenny went to serve up scorched birds and plum sauce.

Only when the supper customers were done and Grobe brought in the last of the platters ("What with the killings in the streets, there's not many will walk after dark.") were John and Jenny able to retreat to a corner of the kitchen for a meal of meat drippings and bread pudding, honey and ale, the dogs watching every bite with mournful intensity from the warmth of the hearth. "I told Gar to meet me at moonrise, where the east road runs into the trees." John poured out ale for them both from a boiled leather pitcher. Whatever Mistress Gowla's virtues as a homemaker, Jenny reflected, as an alewife she left a great deal to be desired: The brew was muddy and cloyingly sweet. No wonder the place hadn't many customers once dinner was done. "I don't know if he will. He's that set on not 'deserting' the baby Trey's carryin'.... God's granny knows what we'll do about that, because you know it's a demon."

"I know." Jenny looked wonderingly across at him, thin and unshaven and haggard-looking, as if he'd been living on jackrabbit for a week, which apparently he had. In the firelight she could make out bruises, too, fading almost to nothing now. She had come so near to losing him, she reflected wonderingly. Had come so near to losing herself. "Everywhere the dead are walking: Pelannor of Palmorgin in the North, and Trey here ... even Caradoc, the real Caradoc, took a corpse to dwell in, and I fear will be haunting the woods near Alyn, trying to trap Ian."

"Ah." He nodded, as if putting together two accounts of the same event. "That's what that was, then. I had a—a vision of it. Of somethin' lurkin' about outside the Hold, tryin' to get in. Sendin' evil dreams. As I had a vision of you, love, hurt an' in the Deep, an' of the old King an' Trey."

"Ian knows to be on his guard," said Jenny, her mouth full of duck scraps. "Muffle put the whole of the village on the alert, that there would be some attempt on him."

"Good for Muffle! And for you, love." He touched her hand again, as he had a dozen times during supper—as her foot had sought his, her knee had pressed his knee, beneath the table, craving and delighting in merely the warmth of his flesh and his bones. "Gar has to be warned. Not just about Trey, but ... Jen, the Demon Queen's got out from behind the mirror."

"I know." Jenny felt her face get hot with shame. "John, I—I let her out. I had her trapped—in this"—she held up the silver catchbottle—"and I let her out."

His eyes held hers for a long time in the low orange glare of the hearth. Then he sighed and shook his head and said, "First time I've ever seen her properly dressed, all kitted out in black velvet with yellow stripes to her skirt.... I wonder where she got it? Not that she couldn't go about this neighborhood wearin' only that sort of veil thing she does, but she'd be stopped with offers every ten feet, and not so much as a purse on her to put the money in. And then I came in here, and almost convinced meself it wasn't her after all, maybe for that reason. But it was her, walkin' through the square like she'd leased a house here—which I wouldn't put past her."

Chin on palm, John listened to Jenny's account of her injury in the mines of Ylferdun, and what she had heard in the tunnels there, and all that it had led to, listened with the firelight glare touching glints in the half-seen silvery marks on his face and throat. The light slipped and flickered as his jaw muscles tightened, but he said calmly, "She was right, you know, love. About it bein' more important for you to come back here and warn us than to keep her tied down in that bit of a jar. We're already hip-deep in demons, anyway. I'm surprised you found the bottle, given that Folcalor thought he'd need spells an' that to get past whatever glamours the Queen kept on the place."

"I knew where to look," said Jenny. "I guessed where it had to be. And I had a hothwais, to give proper light. Though now that you mention it, it does sound odd. This Star-Juggler must have gone in through the back way, through the old library—probably smuggled in by loyalists within the old High King's Court—and been killed on the threshhold of the mirror chamber. He could easily have been trapped on the stairs. When the chamber was bricked up—"

"Aye," said John softly. "But the thing is, that catch-bottle wasn't Folcalor's first weapon of choice, was it? You said you heard the demon in the mines ask, *Any luck with the dragon?*"

"I think—I'm not sure—that I was shot with a poisoned arrow, rather than being killed outright, to lure Morkeleb down into the mines." Jenny tore off another piece of bread and drizzled honey over it. She had been in the catch-bottle, she estimated, about a day and a half, and had watched through most of the previous day in Ernine with only the few rabbits Morkeleb had killed. "They set off an explosion of blasting powder to trap him there. Maybe to kill him, maybe as a way to maneuver him into using his magic, either to save himself or to save me, so that the demons in the mines could take him. They've lost the dragons that they had—Centhwevir and Nymr and the others. And Morkeleb is the most ancient of all, a mage among them and a loremaster. The lore and spells in his mind would give them power over her."

"That it would," agreed John, and spun the catch-bottle on its round end, like a top, among the muddle of gravy-soaked trenchers and dribbles of honey on the table. Beside the fire the dog-mastiff gave a muffled snore in his sleep. "But it might not have been Morkeleb they spoke of, though he'd be that miffed if he heard me say he wasn't foremost in their thoughts. I was sent to Hell and back— two or three times, in fact—to fetch a man named Corvin, who turned out to be a dragon: who turned out to be a dragon in whose mind Ao-hila had established herself, as Amayon established himself in yours. And far as I can tell, he considers *himself* the most ancient mage an' loremaster of 'em all an' a scientist to boot, so there! You've said as how you understand the demon-speech because Amayon left a shadow of himself—like a footprint, or fruit peels in a corner—in your mind. D'you know Amayon's true name?"

Jenny blinked at him and said, "Yes." It was not something she had thought of before, but the question brought it forward in her mind. An ugly name, not music like a dragon's name, but a wicked lit-tle cluster of barbed glass hatreds that it fouled her even to con-sider.... But his name. Its name. And she understood with disgusting intimacy every one of those hates, and wondered how she could ever have loved or pitied him.

"I think the dragon they spoke of was Corvin, not Morkeleb," said John. "And I think Aohila sent me to fetch him, not from hate or vengeance, but just to keep him out of the way of Folcalor's goons. So that they couldn't trap him, and prise Aohila's true name out of his mind. Failin' that—since he was in Prokep with me—they hit Ernine, tryin' to find the catch-bottle, or to take Aohila by main strength, which obviously didn't work. Did they get the mirror?"

"I don't know."

"It'd pay us to go to Ernine and check. Is Morkeleb nearby?"

"Not that I know of. I think he will be soon. He'll be scrying for me, searching for me...."

John opened his mouth to ask something, then closed it. Re-membering that John's anger at her during the darkness that fol-lowed her release from the demon had taken the form of jealousy of Morkeleb, Jenny inquired matter-of-factly, "Is this dragon Corvin nearby?"

John shook his head. "Gone off to the Skerries of Light." He threw the remains of the trenchers to the mastiffs and carried the cups into the scullery. Worrying still about his feelings, Jenny dipped a jar full of what hot water was left from the copper by the fire, and followed. It was freezing cold in the scullery and dark: she took a rushlight from the box and stuck it into the holder near the sink, and kindled it with a glance. But when John spoke, it was in his usual tone. "Corvin knows the danger he'll be in if Folcalor does break the Henge—he, and the other dragons who were possessed before. They don't miss the demons, as humans do. . . ."

He paused apologetically, and Jenny made a resigned gesture and a wry smile, not pretending that she hadn't missed Amayon nearly to the point of madness. A rueful glance passed between them, like a mutual head shake and shrug: *Goose and gander, love.*

"But the demons know their names, which for creatures of magic is dangerous in a different way than it is for us." He sopped the rag in the hot water, washing the ale-cups while Jenny scooped sand from the bucket to scour the last of the pots. "He's got until the full moon, if Dotys's account of the comet is to be trusted. Say just over two weeks."

"It is," said Jenny. "At least, Aohila told me much the same in the catch-bottle, if she was telling the truth. She said the spells work best in the full of the moon. Since they destroyed so many of their soul-crystals attacking the mirror in Ernine, I'm guessing they'll wait until the full moon to try again. It's cutting it close for them, with the Dragonstar growing fainter each night."

"Damn them." John hurled his washrag into the basin, the murky light of the dip flashing off his specs. "Brâk warned me about that in the summer. Brâk was the leader of the escaped human slaves who were hidin' out in the Tralchet mines, you remember, when I went callin' on the gnomes up there. Brâk warned me about Goffyer, too—the Lord of the Twelfth Deep, an' a mage who was obviously in league with the demons long before Folcalor took him over bodily. Brâk didn't know what was afoot, but he warned me to fight to the death if Goffyer came at me with opals in his hand."

"He had a bowl of jewels in my dream." Jenny shook the scouring sand into a second bucket and wiped out the pots. "Folcalor was driven from Caradoc's body in the sea. He could have used any water as a gate, to get to Goffyer. You say the mages of Prokep were astronomers, who used their own knowledge of the Dragonstar to trap the demons. Some of that knowledge may have remained in the library at Halnath. But if, as you say, the Master has been taken . . ."

"We'll have to do somethin' about that, yes," said John. He dried his hands, his eyes bright with a faraway gleam. "But as it happens, we don't need to go up to Halnath to learn about the Dragonstar's nature. I've got notes about the whole thing—what it is, what it's made of, how it works—in me jacket."

They banked the fire, turned the mastiffs into the yard, and went out themselves, barring the kitchen door behind them. The Dragonstar stood barely visible above the black line of the stable roof, so clear that each of its multiple tails stood out like an infinitely tiny thread of fire. Through Jenny's glove, John's gloved fingers were strong and warm, steadying and reassuring, as if he could support her through flood and fire and world's end. She felt as if she'd come home.

Ridiculous, given the peril they stood in and the horror she was certain they'd have to face. But she wanted to laugh and dance.

"First thing to do is make sure Gar is safe," said John as they stepped out into the inky lane. "Gar and his daughter, and get Polycarp away from the dungeons . . . they can't just murder the Master of Halnath in his cell without a major war breakin' out, and I don't think Folcalor's willin' to risk that until he's had a crack at the Henge in Prokep. Though with demons it's hard to tell what they'll do. But those things done—"

"I like the way you say that."

He shoved her, like a schoolboy nudging a mate, and she shoved him back.

"Those things done, we can see what we can do about finding Corvin, and putting Aohila's name back into your little catch-bottle."

"If it's Aohila we need most to trap," said Jenny thoughtfully.

"Who else did you have in mind, love?"

"Folcalor."

"And wherever are we to get . . . ?" He thought about it a moment, and said, "Oh, aye. Yes." That was, Jenny reflected, one of the things she loved most, and had missed most, about John. You didn't need to explain much.

They walked for a time in silence down the lane, the stars of springtide glittering sharp through breaking clouds. "I was afraid for you," said John out of the dark. "I missed you something desperate, I wanted you ... an' you'd have been gie interested in the Hells I saw, an' the Otherworld.... But all the time I kept hopin' you'd be all right. That you'd ... that you'd forgive me. Because I did act like a right bastard."

"You acted like a man who was afraid," said Jenny softly.

"Afraid? I was dissolvin'! What I don't understand is ... and you can tell me this is none of my business if you want to ... you said you took on dragon form again, of yourself, with Ian's help, when the demons attacked the Hold." He stopped in the alley along the stable wall, holding her hands in his. Moonlight glimmered a little on the dirty snow, made silver rounds of his spectacle lenses and diamonds of his breath. "What I don't understand is, why did you come back after that? After what I said, and what I did ..."

Jenny put her fingers to his lips. "When I made my choice five years ago—when Morkeleb first offered me the power of dragon form—my choice was a real one. I knew that to be human is to have what humans have, which is the near-certainty of occasional pain. And that there is a kind of pain that comes from loving, that doesn't come from any other thing in the living world. I chose to be human, John, something very few people can truly choose."

He shook his head and said, "No, love. We all choose it, sooner or late."

"Maybe," said Jenny. "But having chosen, I would no more have called on Morkeleb to change me back—to run away from pain—than you would have called on the Demon Queen when you were at the stake. It is not what I am."

"And what are you, love?"

And she smiled. "What I am."

Then as they turned to go, Jenny paused in her stride, something catching at her mind, half-remembered like a dropped glove. Something she'd left in the kitchen ... done in the kitchen ...

She looked straight across the lane at the bare ground of the orchard, at a wisp of the straw someone had unwrapped from around the first of the pear trees and left in a corner in the snow. The straw burst into flames, causing John, a half-pace ahead of her, to whip around, sword in his hand like a conjurer's penny. He looked at the burning straw, looked at her, as she turned her eyes to the yellow flag of fire again and quenched it. Even above the moss-smell and the dung-smell and the piss-smell of the neighborhood, the wisp of fresh smoke was a touch of perfume.

John said, "Ah, love," and, sheathing his sword, put his two hands on the sides of her face and kissed her again, gentle and deep as the stir of spring beneath winter's ice.

Chapter 10

"There's someone there," whispered Jenny, in the breath-soft murmur of hunters in the Winterlands, whose life depends upon not being heard. Under the sigh of the wind in the pine trees, and the distant sursurrance of the unseen river, this wasn't difficult. She strained her ears, extended her senses toward the dark blot against the dark of the trees. "A woman . . ."

She made her own heart quiet, listened beneath the soughing of the boughs. Putting aside the voice of the river, and each sound of the still winter night. Scenting the cloaked forms as a fox scents rabbits. "Herbed soap, no perfume. A child is with her, sleeping. Two children." And whimpering with cold and fear in their sleep.

"The nurse." John's voice was no more than a thread in a mingled skein of tree rustlings. "Danae. And at a bet the nurse's child. Anything else?"

Meaning, Jenny knew, any demons watching the place. She half-shut her eyes, closing out the sea roar of the wind in the trees and the leathery creak of the branches. Closing out the scents of coming rain, of wet vegetation, of smoke and sewage discernible even at five miles' distance from the city itself. Demons could wait in perfect silence, but the human bodies they wore would breathe, and their boots would creak and their clothing rustle. She heard none of these things. Moreover, the nurse's breathing, though the tense breath of wakefulness, was reasonably deep, not shallow with panic.

"I don't think so."

"Well, I'll scream and point at you if you're wrong."

He whistled softly twice, just loud enough to sound over the wind, and walked toward the inky huddle of cloaked forms against the snow. Jenny heard him call out softly, "Danae," and saw the pale oval of the woman's face against the ruffles of her hood. A knife glinted. She'd been holding it out of sight beneath the cloak. But she didn't attack, only held it ready, watching John with her whole body tense. "Where's the Prince?"

"I don't know, my lord." Her voice trembled with the cold, but she spoke as evenly as she apparently could. "I waited for him as long as I dared. But when I saw the Lady Trey returning from supper, I thought it best ... I could not help overhearing ..." She looked quickly aside, and shifted the knife in her gloved hands. Struggling, Jenny guessed, against speaking ill of the mistress who had for years been her dear friend.

In a quieter voice she said, "He asked me if I thought she had changed. Trey—the Lady Trey, I mean." And her other arm tightened protectively around the children sleeping within the all-blanketing cloak.

Jenny remembered Danae from Millença's naming-feast, almost three years ago. A cousin of both Gareth's and Trey's, she was of the country nobility, barely a step above the wealthy yeomen farmers whose wide manors in districts like Nearhythe and Istmark were little kingdoms in themselves. She'd been married to one of the palace guards, a younger son of one of the lesser houses; her daughter Branwen had been barely six months old when he had died, in the fighting when the witch Zyerne had been trying to break the Citadel of Halnath.

Without her elaborately starched coif, Danae looked younger, though now her shoulders had a weary stoop to them even when she straightened up, like one who has carried too heavy a load for too long. Her voice, deep for a woman's and with the slight accent of the West, was tired. "And she *has* changed, lord. Since her illness—or since she recovered, I should say, for when she was very bad, when we all thought we would lose her, she was ... she was still ... still herself, if you know what I mean."

"Aye," murmured John. "Aye, I know exactly what you mean."

"It isn't that she isn't pleasant with me," Danae hastened to add. "Afterward, I mean. Nor concerned for the child, especially now that the poor thing's started having these ... these little sick spells. But she's short with the maids. Try as she will, she can't help that it angers her, that the children have taken against her. Not just poor little Milla, that might be expected, with this sickness they now say she has, but Branwen, too."

"And you?" John asked softly.

Jenny saw Danae turn her face from him again. With the rising moon still tangled in the thick of the trees, and clouds coming in, the nurse must be struggling even to make out sight of him. Then Danae put away her knife and stood, John sheathing his sword to help her, for she was cramped with long sitting in the cold. There was a whisper of metal sliding, and a glimmer of yellow lantern light. By the thready glow of her lantern Danae studied John's face, not reassuring, Jenny thought, with his black beard and the savage half-healed wound on his cheekbone. Then she asked, "Is it . . . do you know if it's a catching sickness, that the child has, lord?"

"Nay," said John, "I don't know. I don't think so." He reached down to touch the child Branwen's round face. "D'you have a horse?"

Danae shook her head. "I thought it better . . . Prince Gareth said to take the girls out without being seen, and wait for him—and for you—here. There's a hunting-box that belonged to his mother—Queen Lyris—about four miles from here, where the river bends. The keeper's cottage is kept stocked with wood and food, though there hasn't been a keeper there this winter. I was afraid one of the grooms would send Trey word if I took out a horse so late, after the gates of the palace were shut."

"Likely they would. I'm just glad you were able to get out the city gates."

Danae shook her head and said, "If you have money, or a jeweled ring, that isn't hard."

"You didn't really send the plague, did you?" asked the girl Branwen, when John took the lantern and held it close to Millença's face. Jenny saw the child move, and she must have opened her eyes: John looked at her long and steadily. Whatever he saw in the child's sleepy eyes must have reassured him, for he moved more easily as he looked into Branwen's face, then Danae's. Then he straightened up and snapped his fingers twice, once at shoulder height and once at waist height, an old signal that he and Jenny had used for years between them when patrolling the Winterlands, to say at a distance that all was well.

Branwen followed these proceedings with curiosity, then willingly accepted the lantern John handed her as he drew his sword and gently lifted Millença into his other arm. "Prince Gareth said you didn't."

"I'm glad he believes in me," remarked John, glancing around him at the woods as Danae gathered up the small bundle of the girls' belongings. "Nobody else seems to. And I did get a bit worried when they were tyin' me to that stake."

"If you didn't send the plague," Branwen persisted, "why did the demons send the dragon to save you? I watched from the South Tower balcony. Mother told me not to, and I had to stay in my room afterward. But I'm glad I saw the dragon."

"Not near as glad as I was, believe me."

Jenny followed at a distance as the little party moved off into the woods, sometimes keeping in sight of the bobbing firefly of lantern light, sometimes tracking them only by the sound of the nurse's boots in the crust of snow between the trees. The wind blew harder and the cold deepened, piercing Jenny's sheepskin jacket and plaids like a thousand burning needles, until her body ached with it and her fingers grew numb in her gloves. Once Branwen said, "I'm cold, Mother," but Milla, wrapped tight under John's decrepit cloak, never complained. Never said a word.

What did she think, wondered Jenny, about the mother she had lost? About the woman who came to her one day wearing her mother's face and her mother's garments and her mother's hands, whom she knew was not her mother? Who looked at her with demon eyes?

Jenny shivered at the wary silence of that child who had already learned so young not to trust. Her own daughter, Mag, was a year younger. Silent, too, but her silence had a different quality: She'd learned already that to find out things it was sometimes necessary only to keep completely still and wait.

Three or four times, while Jenny lay in Miss Mab's small warm enclave in the mines, she had asked Morkeleb to scry the Hold, to tell her if all things were well there with Ian and Adric and Mag. She remembered the fire again, blazing out of the straw at her calling, and wondered if, when next she gazed into standing water, she would be able to see her children herself?

What of all the children in the city, she thought, who had had the same thing happen to them? To pass through the grief at a parent's illness, helpless witnesses to a mother's or a father's helpless prayers for a dying spouse—and then to see that dying parent come back to life and to KNOW something had changed.

She thought of what a demon-parent would do to a child—would do to the survivor spouse, who hoped against frantic hope that all would be well with the beloved one—and her stubbly hair prickled on her head with rage. She understood demons now and understood what they did, to amuse themselves. Tears were a different entertainment than blood. Many demons preferred them.

Do you like games? the Queen's voice whispered again in her mind.

"... said he would speak to Lord Bliaud about the matter." Danae's soft voice flickered back to Jenny on the raw whip of the wind. "But when I looked out into the court, I saw Lord Bliaud among those around Lady Trey, and no sign of Prince Gareth. It's true that since his father's recovery he has kept more to his own rooms, and I refuse to believe those who say it's jealousy. My lord Gareth hasn't an envious bone in his body, and so many times I've heard him speak of his father's illness. He'd never begrudge his return, to being the man he was. . . ."

And John, his sword in hand, watched and listened to the darkness around them, above and past that murmuring voice, and the thrashing snarl of the winds. Jenny, whose ears were sharper, listened farther, and detected nothing but the bitter sounds of the night.

All was darkness and cold at the hunting-box, a rustic longhouse built of logs and decorated with elaborate peasant-style carving after the fashion popular among the very rich. John remained with Danae and the children at the foot of its front stair while Jenny flitted through the single shadowy hall of the downstairs, the myriad attic chambers above, then across the stable-yard to the keeper's cottage and the stables themselves. There was no sign of demons, no smell or whisper of them anywhere, not even in the covered well in the center of the yard. Jenny marked the corners of the buildings and the rails of their galleries with sigils of protection and inconspicuousness, still not at all certain that she had the power within her to make them work, though afterward she felt the familiar exhaustion of having called power.

But it was unfamiliar power, and could have been only her imagining, and the cold. She incorporated, too, for the first time in her spells a sigil of sourcing from the Dragonstar comet itself, weaving its little signs of iron and ice, of two tails and dual nature—details John had given her on the long walk from the city walls—like an improvisatory rill on her harp. "Why does it take so LONG?" demanded Branwen, when Danae and the children walked past her to the keeper's cottage. Danae shook her daughter by the shoulder in horror at this lapse of manners, but Jenny laughed.

"It's like a great lady applying face-paint," she explained, standing back from the light of the lantern as they passed her. "One cannot hurry."

The child halted to look up at her and sighed with grown-up exasperation. "I know. Mother always tells me that when I use her paints."

Jenny would have liked to go into the cottage with them, for the night was icy. Instead, she crossed to the gallery that circled the main longhouse, and sheltered there from the wind, the hothwais of heat cradled in her hands. Watching the woods, and scenting the night. She would have liked to sit still, eyes shut, and let her mind drift, seeking Morkeleb's awareness as she guessed he sought hers. She had had no time, since she had emerged from the catch-bottle, to hunt for him so. In the city she had not dared take her attention from watchfulness, wariness. And when she had left the city, she had found John.

Morkeleb would be seeking her, she knew, and would find her in time. The danger of demons was still too great to take her attention from each separate moan of the night-wind, each individual scent. She thought, *I am here, my friend,* and his image came to her mind briefly, shearing his way through the blackness of the clouds, or rising above them, through the billowing columns of moon-edged vapor, silver light flashing on his wings.

In time, John emerged from the cottage door, crossed through the yard to her, leaning hard on the wind. He stopped to scan the gallery, though in the pitch-black darkness it was a wonder he could see even the outline of the longhouse; Jenny spoke the words of light, hesitantly, in her mind, and was rewarded with a thin blue radiance that flickered along the gallery's carved railing from ward to ward, then at once died.

John's boots made barely a sound on the halved logs that made up the steps.

"It's no gie wonder a great realm like Ernine fell to pieces and couldn't defend itself against foes that were no more than the Icerider tribes are to us." He groped his way along the gallery, and Jenny threw an end of her plaid around his shoulders as he joined her on the rustic bench on which she'd been sitting, and crouched close over the hothwais. He wore a coat of green wool, like a merchant's, and an assortment of scarves tucked around his neck, under a sorry hand-me-down cloak that smelled of dogs. "It's clear to me we need to send someone out here to keep guard over 'em, an' everyone I think of I think, *What if they're a demon these days?*"

He passed her a substantial chunk of cheese wrapped around in a couple of hot griddle cakes, and a handful of dried apricots. Despite the supper they had shared a few hours ago, the cold and the walk and the setting of the ward-signs had left Jenny ravenous.

"I don't even trust those little girls, though Danae swears she's kept 'em both at her side since first Milla started havin' her sick fits . . . which'll be no more than a pinch of dried tansy in her food. Branwen says, *I'm cold, Mama,* an' I think, *Is that the kind of thing a little girl would say when she's cold? Why doesn't Milla complain of the cold? This all looks very suspicious to me.* It's enough to send you barkin' mad."

"And it did," Jenny said softly, and their eyes met with the same ruefulness of shared folly, of disaster somehow survived.

"Aye, well," said John. "That it did. But accordin' to Danae, Gar's been missin' since he said he'd go speak to Bliaud, who I'll swear is demon-ridden these days. . . ."

"He is," said Jenny. "He's the one who's been raising the dead in the town." She pulled her coat tighter about her, thinking of the long walk back to the city in the predawn's icy cold. "But I think Danae and the girls are safer here than either of us would be if you or I tried to go back to Bel to look for Gareth alone."

On the walk back to Bel, with the slow gray of winter dawn creeping between leafless wind-combed trees, John asked Jenny for more details of all that had happened that winter: How close had Folcalor's baskets of jewels lain to the inhabited Warrens of the Deep; how many of the burned-out husks of them had scattered the split and smoking hillslope in Ernine? Was she sure it was Caradoc she and Ian had spoken with on the crumbling breakwater at Eldsbouch, and not a demon?

"It was Caradoc," said Jenny. "Squidslayer and the Whalemages brought me Caradoc's staff—do you remember it? A demon's head carved in wood, with a moonstone in its mouth. Caradoc's soul was imprisoned in that moonstone. When I took the staff from the ocean it burst into flames, soaking wet as it was, and I let it fall again. Presumably it fell into the corpse of a drowned sailor—there had been a shipwreck only days before on those rocks—and with the moonstone inside it, that sailor's corpse first tried to drown Ian, then escaped into the wastes."

Jenny kept her voice even, but the recollection of the sailor's rotting eyes disturbed her profoundly, the memory of how the worms had moved beneath his wet clothes. "I spoke to him. It was Caradoc."

"He'll have his work cut out for him, dodgin' wolves." John tucked his gloved hands into his armpits. "An' him doin' that good an imitation of carrion. What do we do if we can't find the jewel containin' Bliaud's soul anywhere in his house? Always supposin' we make it that far. He was rid of one demon, an' let another in of his own free will, remember."

"You don't understand what it's like." Jenny hugged close to John under the shared wrap of her plaid. "I'm not saying that to mitigate what Bliaud did, or to argue that we give him clemency beyond reason. But . . . when you've had a demon within you, there's a part of you that wants it back. I'm fairly sure that I would, but I can't be absolutely positive that I'd turn Amayon away if he took me unawares."

"Meanin' if we find a jewel in Bliaud's house, an' somehow manage to force the current demon out of him . . . he might still take on the next one he meets, even after the Dragonstar's gone from the sky. They'll no longer be able to force their way in past a mage's wardspells then, but that doesn't mean they can't seduce a mage the way they seduced Caradoc."

"They need our bodies," Jenny said quietly. "Magic is partly a thing of the mind, but a good deal of its essence lies in human flesh, and in the flesh of some more than others. Now that Rocklys is defeated, and her corps of mages and dragons is broken up, there are fewer mages than ever for demons to seek. Sometimes when I slept in the Deep, after I was wounded, I would dream of Ian in danger, dreadful dreams."

"It's a two-edged weapon," said John, and they paused to rest in the lee side of a house near the road, until the barking of the dogs in the farmyard drove them on. "Magic, I mean. If it isn't demons comin' after a mage for his power, it'll be a King, you know. Or a friend. Or the part of your soul that thinks it's entitled to whatever fate's denyin' you that week. You can only do what you can."

Maybe Morkeleb had the right idea, reflected Jenny, *when he'd surrendered his power, and moved on to something else.*

For his part, John told Jenny more of the Hells through which he had traveled on errantry for the Demon Queen: Hells that looked like Paradise, where the butterflies spat poison and the milkweed-puffs sowed twisting hookworms into human flesh; Hells where gales scoured barren cliffs and flames burned in ravines forever; Hells where the voices of the dead cried from the darkness. Hells where shining things roved, that devoured human and demons alike. And beyond those Hells, a world of human beings where the dragon Corvin had hidden himself for unimaginable years, masquerading as a scientist and shifting from identity to identity as the people around him aged, and he did not. "There's no magic there, but there's this thing called ether, this sort of ... of power that made lights in the darkness for everyone, an' hot water to bathe in, an' computers an' Personal Ambient Sound Systems that're enough to drive you screamin'...."

"What are computers?"

"I dunno, really," said John. "It was all in writin', which I didn't understand, of course—nor the language, bar what was spoken to me. Everyone there seemed to set great store by 'em, though, an' it was out of one that I found out all that guff about what the Dragonstar's actually made out of. I took notes...." He patted the front of his ragged coat, which bulged with his customary wad of drawings and jottings, and tried to keep his cloak from tangling his feet in the wind. "I'll be years figurin' 'em out. I copied things you'd want to know of, too, love—the sigils of the gates from world to world, an' what was writ on the silver bottles an' boxes that Aohila used for a soul-trap. Some of it's demon magic, but other things you might be able to make work. It'll come in gie handy," he added, "when you and I go back there together to have a look about."

They entered the city with the farmers who brought dried apples and thin winter milk to the markets. The day was a foul one, and spits of sleet stung Jenny's face; there would be little, she guessed, for anyone to sell or buy. She and John divided as they neared the gate, and passed through this crowd some thirty feet apart, watching each other's backs. Now and then Jenny would see a face in the streets that made her flinch inside, demon-eyes burning in a human countenance.

Could there be people who did not know, who could not see? Apparently—Jenny had to remind herself that most people did not have her gruesome wealth of experience. Even after the King's reassurances of yesterday, the men and women in the streets looked frightened and cold, and clumped to whisper outside the doors of the shops. When she reached out to touch their conversations, Jenny heard muttering about people who had disappeared, or tales of random murders. Everywhere she felt the fear and mistrust, and the panic smoke-whiff of rumor. A child had killed both her parents, in the neighborhood of the Temple of Cragget, and afterward threw herself in the icy river. A woman had gone to the palace to petition the King, and had not been seen again. People whispered of demons, of who was in league with them, and who was not, or probably was not. . . .

Being a member of the old Greenhythe nobility, the wizard Bliaud had a town house in the quiet districts south of the river. Dwellings there stood in their own walled grounds, and even the shops had trees growing beside them, to shade their doors in summer. Jenny asked a girl hawking hot pies in one of the mews that ran behind the great houses; the girl looked at her strangely and said, "Don't go to him, sweetheart. I went—I paid him everything I had, to bring my boy back from the plague. But when they come back, they ain't the same. Death takes whom She wills, and I've learned now it's best to let Her be the judge of it, not me. When they come back, they ain't the same."

"Aye," whispered John, when he and Jenny reunited briefly in an alleyway. "And we want to be careful, because I suspect at least one of Bliaud's sons is demon-ridden, too, or in league with 'em, anyway.

Abellus, the one with all the hats. Anyroad, he was with this tattooed southern feller who tried to catch me in the palace. I didn't go up and look close, but watch out."

They divided again, making their way around two sides of a quiet square where an enormously tall fountain stood bearded fantastically in icicles. Their goal was the alley that backed the stables of several town villas, Bliaud's among them. While still in the nearly empty shopping arcade that fronted all four sides of the square, Jenny heard the measured tread of feet in the nearby lane: chair-bearers, and the armed footmen who habitually protected the rich from those who were desperate and poor. Looking back, she saw a covered chair emerge from the Avenue of Limes that led toward the palace precincts, borne by eight gnomes and guarded by eight more in mail that bristled with spikes. She glanced across the square and caught John's eye for the fleetest moment as he melted out of the shadows of the opposite arcade; they both hastened their steps.

Jenny didn't think for a moment that either of them doubted what gnome would be visiting whom at this early hour of the day.

Or why.

As she passed a woman bundled in a red coat selling coffee from an urn on her back, Jenny overheard her mutter to a customer, "You can't tell me they don't have men working in their mines. My cousin's husband claims my cousin died of the plague, but I've heard they're buying slaves. . . ."

The alley was puddled with dirty snow and slick with dropped straw and frozen horse dung. She and John counted back gates. Most of the servants would be turned out to prepare for visitors in the front part of the house. Another time, Jenny thought, she'd have to try operating the gate's bolt by magic, as she'd used to do, but wasn't sure enough of her powers, or of how great a strain she'd have to put on them in the immediate future, or of what Bliaud could detect. She listened at the stable gate until she heard the voices dim away toward the kitchen, then John boosted her over as if they were children going to thieve apples. She slipped the bolt, and let him inside.

Like most of the great town villas, this one was separated from its stables by the snow-covered square of a kitchen garden, onto which looked the kitchen, laundry, stillroom, dovecote, and offices. A strip of orchard lay beyond, and greenhouses for forcing grapes.

Jenny's scalp prickled at the disorder she saw in the stables and in the garden as she and John ducked and crept from hedge to hedge, freezing into hiding as servants emerged to hurry along the paths toward the house. The dirt everywhere, the stinks of garbage and of stalls weeks uncleaned, were more than the slovenliness of a household in upheaval. Being deathless, and having no care for the humans they rode, demons are careless. They are lazy, shrugging away the tedious chores that hold starvation and sickness and sores and bugs at bay. Why keep a body from being consumed with festering flea bites if one can always possess another? Why take time to grow food to eat, or to clean away stable waste? If the horse stumbles from thrush, well, there are other horses.

Around the dovecote a dozen birds lay dead. At first glance Jenny might have attributed this to rats or a dog, except that their heads had all been wrung from their bodies, the snow pink with blood.

The house was rank with demons.

And there was neither cat, nor dog, nor even evidence of mice and rats to be seen.

Servants were carrying trays of sweetmeats and wine to the main block of the house, three storeys of tall-ceilinged reception chambers, of glass windows warm with candlelight in the gray bluster of the overcast morning. A dilapidated wing stretched back from it, half-timbered wood rather than stone, and isolated by overgrown trees from both the outer world and from the servants' portion of the property. From the unkempt orchard Jenny reached with her thoughts into that wing, calling on the power that she had felt all night taking shape inside her.

Nothing. In the main house, shadows crossed back and forth over the windows, and she could now and then catch fragments of voices. A human voice, and a gnome's, but speaking in the tongue of the demons. No sound in the long, narrow wing; no sound but a single sleeper's stertorous breath.

A small door looked out into the shaggy wilderness of bushy hedges: John slipped his knife under the bolt. Once Jenny heard what she thought was the crunch of a footfall in the orchard behind them, but looking back saw only a servant hunting for last autumn's windfalls. One of the few, she guessed, unpossessed by demons in that house. She wondered what sort of rumors the girl passed among the neighbors. The smell of the wing struck her like that of a shambles, a stink of blood and filth, of old smoke and chamber pots either uncleaned or unused.... The place was freezing cold, too.

The room they entered from the garden was clearly Bliaud's workroom, the smallest chamber at the end of the wing. Windows on three sides admitted clear snowy light that bathed the paraphernalia of a scholar and a naturalist. Flowers pressed or dried strewed the long tables under the windows, reminding her of John's study at the Hold. Bunches of herbs hung on strings close by the hearth where the rising warmth would desiccate them, and jars containing the embryos of birds or pigs, preserved in brandy or honey, stood on shelves. Cupboards of books. Pestles and mortars and sieves of hair or bolting-cloth; bone knives; pots of gum or charcoal; a green glass jar of quills.

But all of it dusty and disused. The specimen jars were broken or opened, the curiosities within them rotting in the air. Jars of various types of poisons stood open on one worktable, with a scatter of packing-straw. Beyond that, little looked as if it had been used for months. Directly beneath the room's central lamp stood a small table, a chair thrust back from it with such violence that it had tipped on its side, never picked up. On the table a porcelain bowl held blood, clotted with exposure to air but still fairly fresh. Jenny recalled a vision she had had—when? Back at her home in Frost Fell, during those hellish winter weeks of sickness and grief and self-pity?

A vision of a man's hand, dipping into a basin of blood and bringing out the little glass shells in which the Sea-wights hid themselves.

Blood in the bowl, peace in your soul.

She had heard the demon Folcalor whisper that simple, logical-sounding rhyme.

Blood in the bowl, all will be whole.

"He may have meant it for the best," she breathed, looking up into John's impassive face. "Bliaud, I mean. He may have seen the plague break out, and have thought that he could make a bargain with Folcalor, to obtain the power to fight it."

"Aye." John's expression did not change. It was for precisely that reason, Jenny recalled, he had twice treated with the Demon Queen.

And what had Caradoc thought when he first opened the demon-gate? What rhyme had Folcalor sung to him?

Gareth lay in the room beyond.

Chapter 11

The chamber had been a bedroom once. There was still an old bedstead there, a canopy-ring depending from the faded red-and-blue stampwork of the ceiling. Gareth lay on the bare ropes, his hands and feet manacled to the wooden bedframe. Jenny heard his breathing change as they came into the room, and the thin, desperate sound that came from his throat. He twisted his head around, as if he could see them through the blindfold that covered his eyes. He was gagged, too, but he struggled to pull away from them as he heard their footsteps approach. Jenny knelt beside him, pushed the blindfold up as John bent to examine the chains.

"Bugger it, we'll have to cut your hands and feet off, lad."

Gareth gasped, "Do it if you have to," though he'd heard the jest in John's voice. His shortsighted gray eyes were wide with terror and shock. "Millença—"

"Is safe." John was already looking around the room for something to pry the chain links with. "How's your lock-foxin', love?"

Jenny ran her fingers over the wristlets. "I can try. These aren't spell-warded."

"Gie sloppy of somebody."

"John, there's a lot I can't . . ." She raised her head sharply at the far-off closing of a door. Voices . . .

". . . Sindestray will preside. But I'll give a lot to be there when our boy here confirms the sentence."

Jenny's eyes cut to John, saw his face blank, uncomprehending. Demon voices, speaking demon speech. Gareth gasped, "Don't leave me!" frantic as John caught Jenny's wrist and pulled her to her feet. The feet were near, and the guttural foulness of a demon's gloating laugh nearer still. John dragged Jenny behind the great cascade of rotting silk that dangled from the canopy ring to the floor behind the bed, instants before the door opened and the wizard Bliaud entered, followed by a hard-faced, pink-haired gnome.

Jenny recognized the gnome at once, though she had never seen him before. In a way even the seamed face was familiar. A vision, she thought, a dream she had had while in her dragon form. She remembered the twist of his heavy lips, the thick-jeweled rings that studded his fingers. Fingers she'd seen turning over and over the blue jewel in her dream, the jewel in which Ian's soul had been imprisoned.

Folcalor. She knew it. As she had known John, with his dyed hair and scruffy beard in the inn-yard. There was no chance of mistake.

"Well, it's a clever boy, is it?" Bliaud had dropped all the fussy mannerisms he'd imitated to fool those who'd known him as a diffident little gentleman whose only use for magic was to keep his gray hair from thinning, and to chase the aphids from his roses. There was no one present but Folcalor to see them, Folcalor who had known this demon—whoever he was—from eternity. His eyes glittered with the horrible demon-light as he prodded the gag and the blindfold with the tip of his knife, then jestingly poked it at Gareth's eyes.

"And did anyone come? No? Oh, too bad . . . I hoped they would. Is that a little teardrop?" He scraped at the tear, of fright and shock, with the tip of the knife. "Your precious confidant Danae, maybe, to sing you a song while you waited here for us? To listen to your troubles, like she's been doing—" he added another crude suggestion, then laughed derisively—"or pretty Milla, to give her daddy kisses . . . like she gives the guards in the barracks at night—"

"That isn't true!" screamed Gareth, and Bliaud roared with laughter.

"Oh, I promise you she does it well! As you'll find out, once we've taken care of you . . . what do you think, m'lord?" he called to the gnome Folcalor—Goffyer, John had said, and Jenny hoped desperately Miss Mab was keeping on her guard—as the gnome passed into the workroom beyond. "You think the poor sods in those crystals know what's happening?"

"Of course they do." Folcalor reappeared in the doorway, flipping a chunk of pale blue topaz in his hand. In the shadows of the storm-dark morning the jewel flickered palely, like his burning eyes. "They even feel it when we ride a whore in their bodies, or get that nice warm thrill from blood on our hands." He met Gareth's eyes and smiled nastily, and Jenny felt rage wash over her, remembering that smile on Caradoc's face. "I like to put my ear to the stone, and hear them scream. Or sigh," he added with a grin, "as the case may be. As you'll see, when we get your daughter here, and that fat-titted nurse—"

"It isn't true!" shouted Gareth again. Tears were running down his haggard face and he lunged against the manacles. "You're lying! Devils—monsters—"

Folcalor came out of the workshop, one hand red to the elbow with sticky blood from the basin. With his stubby fingers he was wiping the blood off something—a delicate glass shell, Jenny saw, such as the Sea-wights wore to travel through the lesser gates they convinced human wizards to make. It gleamed through the blood, and she could see something silver shift viscously inside.

"They're putting your cousin to the question today," he said. "Quietly, of course. It would never do for the King to admit that he had the Master of Halnath put in the Boot or the Rack like a common felon. But Ector of Sindestray insisted. Nothing's too much, he said, for a man who's sold himself to demons. Think how your cousin Polycarp will appreciate seeing you there; maybe even you holding some of the irons."

His fist crunched on the glass thing within it. Through his fingers the silver demon oozed, and fell to the floor with a sticky plop. Gareth shrank back on the bare ropes of the bed, thrashing and bucking. The silver thing whipped along the floor tiles like a gleaming snake, slithered up onto the bedstead, while Bliaud stepped forward with the knife in one hand, the blue topaz in the other. "Now, open your mouth," he said, holding up the jewel, and the silvery demon crawled up onto Gareth's thigh, looked at him with tiny, black, jet-bead eyes.

John stabbed, straight through the curtain and up under Bliaud's ribs. The demon wizard spun, eyes bulging, and screamed, a sound Jenny had never heard from human or Hellspawn before. And fell forward across the bed.

The silver demon darted off the bed, flicked across the floor, at the same moment Folcalor whipped from his side one of the short jeweled swords of the gnomes. He sprang at John as a blinding dazzle of light exploded in the air between them—John was expecting it, and fell back, parrying and lashing out with one foot to trip the gnome, on whom he had a good half-yard of reach. Folcalor fell, rolled, sprang back. Jenny, tearing the keys from Bliaud's belt, saw John wince and stagger, as if blinding pain had struck him somewhere, but he caught the demon's next strike handily on the knife he'd scooped from Bliaud's nerveless hand, driving in with his greater height.

Boots thundered in the hallway. Jenny twisted the keys in the manacle locks, dragged Gareth to his feet, and was turning to look for a chair to smash over Folcalor's head when three of the gnome guards entered, halberds in hand. They saw John and Folcalor but didn't see Jenny, who struck with the chair and snatched the halberd from the nearest gnome's grip. The gnome dragged out his sword and lunged at her, but the halberd was Jenny's favored weapon, suited to a woman's smaller stature. She slashed her attacker across the chest and sprang back from the explosion of blood. The gnome grinned at her, a horrible demon grin, and came on, the body dying but the demon driving it forward nonetheless. Gareth seized the chair and bashed another of the gnome guards away from John, who was being driven into a corner. Folcalor had darted back to where Bliaud still lay beside the bed, thrashing and gasping with blood streaming from his mouth.

Jenny heard Folcalor shout, "Belior!" which must have been the name of Bliaud's demon. "Belior, damn you . . . !"

"I don't . . . ," choked the demon, and Jenny heard in the demon speech the gasp of utter uncomprehending terror. She hacked again at the gnome who was slashing at her, the longer reach of the halberd keeping his sword at a distance, but he came in on her, taking the cuts, caring nothing. She severed one of his arms, and he only bent to pick up the sword with the other, driving her to the wall. And still she heard Folcalor cry, "Belior!" in a strange voice, disbelieving and horrified.

John turned and took Jenny's gnome in the back with his sword. The gnome cried out, fell to his knees. Past John's shoulder Jenny saw another of the demon gnomes on the floor, bleeding, unmoving, head half-severed. John's clothes were splashed with blood. He sprang over the downed gnome, driving at Folcalor, and the demon sprang to his feet and bolted through the workshop door. He slammed it in John's face, and Jenny heard the bolt shoot. John lunged to the outside door into the garden, then turned back: "He's gone."

He walked to the gnome guards, all three of them sprawled on the floor.

Gareth said, in a strange voice, "They're dead."

By the way they were lying they had clearly been demons. Had clearly driven in on taller opponents, secure in the knowledge that killing the bodies they rode would not stop them.

Bliaud's eyes were jammed wide open, staring at the ceiling as if viewing some unsuspected ghastliness descending suddenly on him from the dense shadows beneath the plasterwork ceiling. John turned his sword over in his hand, studying it: Jenny saw that the blade and hilt both were written over with runes in a kind of spidery blue light, runes that faded even as she watched. She wondered if these were even visible to John.

"I'll be buggered." He knelt to clean the blade on Bliaud's clothing. "Either the blade drove them straight out of the bodies they'd taken . . . or it killed them. I think it killed them."

Jenny said, with a kind of rich and bitter satisfaction in her voice, "They must have been surprised."

"Near as surprised as I am," said John. "The man who forged this sword is a mage, livin' in a world where magic doesn't exist, God bless him. I only wish there were a way I could thank him, and tell him that the spells of ruin he laid on demons there work here like bloody heroes."

"He'll go to the palace." Gareth straightened up—he'd gathered every weapon he could lay hands on and looked like a second-rate squire. "Goffyer, I mean. My father . . . my father and Trey . . ." His voice faltered, and the muscles of his jaw stood out tight in his silence.

"Is Ector a demon?" John pulled down a handful of bed curtain to wipe the blood off his boots. His trousers and the red doublet— palace livery, Jenny saw—were splashed with it, his own blood as well as that of his attackers. Jenny ripped Bliaud's shirt for a bandage, to tie up the thin slash on John's arm.

Gareth swallowed, thought a moment, and shook his head. "That's Ector's strength," he said. "He really believes what he's doing is right, and that carries the Council. Most of its members are—are still themselves. And they're meeting at the fourth hour. . . ."

"And it's gie near the second now, and winter at that. I'm well, love, we haven't time," John added, to Jenny, who was trying to get him to hold still long enough for her to bandage his bleeding arm. "Look through the workroom, would you, Gar, and see if you can find a jewel in a box. I couldn't."

"It won't be here." Jenny thrust John down onto the edge of the bedstead. "You stay there," she added, and followed Gareth into the workroom, John at her heels. As she'd suspected, when the demon Belior had taken over Bliaud's body he hadn't troubled himself with the healing powders the old wizard had stored in the cabinet. They were still there in their porcelain pots, neatly labeled and smelling sweetly wholesome when Jenny stirred them. John's arm was cut in two places, and he'd taken a shallow slash across the chest. None of the wounds were deep, but they bled freely. Jenny could detect no poison in the wounds, nor smell of demon curses, but the general filthiness in which demons lived and operated made alcohol and slippery elm a must.

"Folcalor wouldn't let another demon have charge of a weapon as powerful as a wizard's soul," she added. "*Will* you sit down? He's a traitor himself." She poured some of the drinking water from the workroom pitcher into a dish taken from an upper shelf, mixed in astringents and salts. "Is there brandy in that...? Yes, thank you, Gar...." John jerked and flinched at the sting of the healing poultice.

"Honestly, it doesn't hurt *that* much.... Some dragonsbane you are. Folcalor would know how tempting it is to a demon who possesses such a tool to focus and extend his own magic—especially to a demon inhabiting the body of a mage to begin with. He kept the talisman jewels with him last time. It's on him, believe me, if it still exists at all."

"It certainly isn't here." Gareth came back to the bench where John sat. All around them the big house was silent. If the Otherworld swordblade could indeed kill demons, thought Jenny, it was no wonder they fled. She wondered where they went. "What Bliaud said about ... about Millença ..."

"Is a lie, pure and simple," said John. "I left her and Danae and Branwen—who's a pert little minx and needs a good spankin', by the way—at your mother's old huntin' lodge in the woods. She waited for you last night ... ow! That bloody stings, woman!"

"It stings because the infection is leaving it."

"That's what you always say."

"I always say it because it's always true. It would sting a lot more if it turned purple and fell off."

"I . . . I couldn't leave without being sure," Gareth said, and ran an awkward-jointed hand over his face. "I knew Bliaud was coming to the palace last night. I thought, while he was gone, I could have a look around here. If he was a demon, there was bound to be something. Mages—wizards—we do need them, need them against the plague. I've been keeping Ector off of him for weeks. I had to be sure." He shook his head, and put a gingerly hand to the back of his skull. "I don't remember. . . ." He looked around him vaguely—Jenny finished tying the last bandage and got up to fetch the spectacles lying under the workbench. The gold frame was bent, the right lens cracked. Gareth winced as he carefully replaced them on his head.

"Where'll they have Polycarp?" John asked, pulling his slashed and bloody jacket back on and looking around for his cloak. "If we can get him away to Halnath and get a stronghold for ourselves, we might have a chance of driving the demons out of Bel. As it is, God knows how we're to do it. We can't even get into the palace, and the Captain of the Guards is a demon as well, and who knows how many others."

"They'll have Polycarp in the old Tower prison where they held you." Gareth pulled a hooded cloak from a hook behind the door, threw it to John to cover his bloodstained clothing. "The Chamber of the Question is there, too, on the other side of the watchroom."

Jenny slung her plaids around herself and followed the two men down the broken brick pathway through the orchard, and across the kitchen garden. Still, not a guardsman, not a servant did any of them see, and listening around her Jenny heard no sound in the empty kitchen buildings, and only the painful nickerings of thirsty horses in the stables.

"Even if we get him away—even if we get to Halnath," Gareth continued, "what can we do about the demons then? They've taken root here, they can't be exorcised—"

"They can't be exorcised *now*," said Jenny. She strode fast, keeping up with the Prince's longer legs, the cold wind billowing in her plaids. "After the Moon of Winds, their power will lessen. Spells of exorcism will work again. . . ."

"There won't be a Realm left by the Moon of Winds!" said Gareth desperately. "My father ... there's trouble with the Prince of Imperteng again, and if Polycarp is killed, the whole March is going to split away. People are beginning to flee the city, even at this season. There was a riot yesterday in Deeping, and if the gnomes turn against us—"

"I've a theory about how the demons here can be dealt with." John glanced right and left as they crossed the square, then headed for the quiet back-streets that led around toward the palace. "It isn't only to cause pain and grief that demons take on human bodies—they need 'em for protection in certain places as well, an' I think Prokep is one of 'em. If that's the case, just count up who goes missin' at the Moon of Winds."

"And I tell you we may not have until then," the Prince said grimly. "And if the Realm holds together through that, what happens after Folcalor frees Adromelech from his prison? You say their power will be weaker, but they'll be everywhere, fighting one another, if what you've told me is true. And you know as well as I do that there will always be men who'll ally with demons, out of greed or malice. What then?"

Gareth and Jenny both halted in the quiet back-lane to look at John, who pushed up his spectacles with one bloodstained grubby finger and scratched his nose. "Aye, well," he agreed. "I'll have to give that part of me plan a bit more work."

There were guards stationed all around the Palace Hill. Had the market square been crowded, as it customarily was at this time of the morning, the men stationed in the arcade might have been inconspicuous enough, but in the stormy weather their crimson cloaks stood out even in the shadows, like splashes of blood.

"I count twelve," John whispered, drawing back into the shelter of Wellspring Lane and peering around the corner of a house painted with mermaids and flowers.

"There's another one at the end of this lane," whispered Jenny. She pulled Thane and Prince by their cloaks into the nearest turning. Eyes half-closed, she listened for the creak of swordbelts, for the faint squeak of armor-buckles and the clink of metal on the plaster of house walls.

The neighborhood between market and palace was deathly

quiet. It wasn't only the sneer of the wind around turnings and over
the moss-greened tiles of the roofs that kept people indoors, or the
flecks of sleet in the air. Like the zone of stillness in the Winterlands
woods, which hinted to Jenny of the presence of bandits hiding in the
thickets, she could hear in the silence the fear that emanated from
the waiting guards.

"For a short little gnome, Goffyer made gie good time to the
palace," murmured John as they stepped back into the tightly shuttered doorway of one of the district's numerous chocolate shops to re-
connoiter. "Think you can get us past, love?"

"They're my father's guards," Gareth protested, indignant. "I can
order them—"

"I wouldn't try it, me hero."

A small squad of soldiers in the blue and white livery of Lord Ector of Sindestray's private company strode past the end of the street,
heading for the fashionable district where Bliaud's house lay. Jenny
said, "Who do you think will speak for you if both Trey and your father claim that you've been 'acting queerly'? If in your absence a bowl
of blood, or a mirror painted with demon signs, were found in your
chamber?"

The Prince opened his mouth in shock, and closed it again, and
a look of gray weariness passed across his face. He had, thought
Jenny, lost his wife, and his unborn child, less than a fortnight ago;
had undergone not only that grief, but the added agony of renewed
hope, eaten away by the acid of doubt and still more dreadful grief.
He had been Regent, virtually King of Bel, and had fought for his father's realm against betrayal by a cousin he had trusted. Then the
Realm, too, had been taken from him, and the father he had cared for
and loved, while at his feet opened the dark threat of still more terrible days to come.

He was fighting still, as wounded men will when their blood is
up. But his heart and his soul had been hurt, perhaps mortally. Jenny
could see it in his eyes. She touched his arm again, and he made a
smile, and covered her hand briefly with his bare, cold-reddened fingers, then dug out a handkerchief and blew his nose. "Badegamus will
let us in," he said, his voice steadier than Jenny had thought it might
be. "He can still be trusted. Or he could as of last night, anyway. We
can send him a message. . . ."

"They'll be watchin' for that lad," said John. "Let's see what things look like round the kitchen quarters."

The whole of the palace district was alive with guards, moving among the tall gray-stone houses like red-shelled ants. Jenny wrought a cautious glamour about herself, John, and Gareth, but she had little confidence as yet in these new abilities, and did not know their strength or their extent. It was even possible that this faint whisper of magic would draw the attention of demons. The stakes were far too high to risk capture.

"One thing I don't understand," Gareth whispered, once when they stopped in a gateway, to let the swift clump of booted feet stride by in the turning ahead of them. "Why did Polycarp come back? They said they had him.... Or was Goffyer only saying that to hurt me? Like Bliaud talking about Milla and ... and Danae. Polycarp left Bel the day after Trey ... Trey died. Went back to the Citadel at my command. I can't imagine why he'd have returned...."

"He returned to warn you, son," John murmured, and glanced back over his shoulder at the younger man. "He sent you word asking you to meet him in the wood-court that opens onto the Cooksway, and of course Trey intercepted the message. He was taken yesterday, just after I talked to you."

Like hunters in the Winterlands, they probed down the narrow streets behind the palace, made cautious expeditions along mews. They followed the distant line, glimpsed beyond turnings, of the old palace's tall, moss-smeared wall. Intermittent flurries of sleet kept them from meeting anyone, but at the same time made them conspicuous to whatever guards might glance their way. Jenny's hip ached, from the night's long walk, and sleepiness chewed at her bones. She wondered where Morkeleb might be, and what was happening to Ian and Adric in the north. Fleeting thoughts, fleetingly put aside.

Then she would look ahead of her at John's familiar wide shoulders and the way he turned his cropped bristly head, and her heart would turn over in her breast.

In Bliaud's workshop she could have kissed the flesh of his arm, when she bared it to daub on the poultice, and the memory of his kiss in the alley behind the Silver Cricket's stable-yard was a sunrise, through all the morning's blustery, brutal cold.

Whatever happens, she thought, *I have that kiss. And I was able to tell him I love him. That even at my worst, I was doing the best that I could.*

They were in the slightly shabby district behind the old palace, with its little shops and ateliers, its lines of laundry hung between the projecting fronts of those splendid decrepit town houses. All around them lay that silence still. Sometimes a woman would pass them on her way to a fountain, or a man carrying a delivery would go by in the lane. But no vendors' cries sounded in the street, no singsong wails of *Apple-pie, penny a pie, sweet as summer honey* . . .

"There's a man watching the end of the lane." She touched John's shoulder, halting him. "Not a guard." She listened, getting her bearings: The palace wall lay past a line of houses to their left, and she knew there were guards at the petitioners' gate, about a hundred feet down the Queen's Lane from where they stood. The Cooksway cornered around a tower to join the Queen's Lane, and as far as she could tell there was no one near the wood-yard gate, save for that single man standing just out of sight where the cramped lane turned into the wider way. The Cooksway was, of course, the main one into the kitchen quarters. She could smell the dung churned into the snow, and over the gray wall the warm scents of baking and brewing.

"Bugger." John slipped the sword from its sheathe beneath his cloak. "Whereabouts . . . ? I see him." He nodded toward the end of the lane, where a cart had been unharnessed and left to stand by the corner of the wall. "Can I circle back and around?"

"Yes—no." Jenny listened hard. Her concentration wasn't what it had been twelve hours ago, but still she was able to sift out the muted babble of servants' voices—scullery maids, wood-haulers, watermen—from the palace itself. She heard the wind groan around the corner of the alleyway a few yards behind them, heard a woman in one of the houses say to her child, "All the little birds will be back in the spring. . . ."

"Someone's just past the turning behind us," she breathed. "Two of them . . ." A boot crunched in the frozen muck as someone shifted his weight.

"Not a guard, either. At least he's not wearing a guard's armor or harness." She half-shut her eyes, breathing deep. The last time she had slept, she realized with a kind of wonderment, had been in the snow-cave in Ernine, with Morkeleb crouching outside the door. She had dreamed of the mirror chamber. Dreamed of Amayon crying to her from his prison.

And the time before that, she had slept in the Deep, to be waked by demon voices whispering of slaves.

"I'm sorry. I can't ..."

"It's all right, love, you're doing champion." John touched a hand to her shoulder, then slipped away. She wondered where and when he'd last rested. The man behind the cart in the lane continued to watch the gate. Somewhere in the Dockmarket a clock struck the hour, answered by the bronze chime of the palace carillon, and Gareth's breath hissed. The fourth hour of the morning.

"All Ector will need is someone accusing Polycarp of collusion with demons," the young man whispered desperately. "His father was a traitor—he was brought up a hostage in the palace, with me and Rocklys. All winter there's been unrest in the Citadel, and in the Marches it rules. We can't let them kill him—put him to the Question ..."

Jenny lifted her hand for silence, hearing John's feet stop. There was a quick scrunch—feet moving in snow?—and John said, "Don't try it. Put that down where I can see it."

And a deep voice said, "Lord Aversin?"

Chapter 12

"You won't recognize me." The voice at the end of the lane was so soft, Jenny could tell, glancing sidelong at Gareth, that he heard nothing but a murmur. But to her ears, the accent of the South was strong.

"I do, though," said John's voice, and Jenny heard the metallic hiss of his sword being sheathed. "You'll be Brâk, won't you? You didn't ever walk all the way from the mountains of Tralchet here by yourself?"

There was the whisper of a deep bass laugh. "We cannot all ride flying machines, lord."

Brâk, thought Jenny. Chief of the escaped slaves in the Tralchet mines, to whom John had given poppy powder from Jenny's medicine bag to knock out the guards at the outer gates. Later John had left maps of the territory between the Tralchet mines and the northern-most of the King's small Winterlands garrisons, so that the southerner could lead the escaped slaves to safety.

They had never seen one another's' faces, but knew one another's voices, from the speech they had exchanged in the dark.

John stepped briefly from the shadow to snap his fingers twice, signaling Gareth and Jenny to come. Behind them, Jenny heard boots in the mud and turned to see the other watcher emerge into the lane as well. His drab clothing caught in the wind to reveal a flash of exquisite lace at sleeves and throat. Even as he came near she recognized Bliaud's younger son, Abellus, no demon glint in his somewhat mild brown eyes but a grimness to his mouth that hadn't been there when he and his older brother, Tundal, had parted company from their father at the fortress of Caer Corflyn in the summer.

"My family is a powerful one among the merchant guilds of the South," Brâk was saying as Jenny, Gareth, and Abellus came close. In the shadowy slot between the buildings the dark lines of his facial tattoos formed a mask through which his eyes glinted like a beast's in darkness. "I was all the summer making my way south to them again. Then this winter I heard rumor concerning you, Lord Aversin, and concerning the gnomes buying or stealing human slaves, even from the Far South where they no longer dwell. I came to Bel with my uncle's next shipment of coffee and silk, and since I have been here I have seen evil things."

"What, evil things comin' in an' out of the kitchen gate of the palace?" John gestured down the Cooksway, to where the gate of the wood-court could be just seen, in a sort of turret in the palace wall. "Don't tell me their cook is possessed as well."

Brâk chuckled again, the unvoiced breath of one who has lived for years in fear of making a sound. Jenny guessed he was in his forties, with the first brush of frost on the long black braids, and beneath the line of the tattoos, a mouth both sensual and firm. He was well dressed against the cold, in quilted wool, and his boots were unobtrusively expensive.

"This is me lady Jenny Waynest," John said, taking her hand and presenting her to the merchant, who salaamed deeply and made a motion as if to lift and kiss the hem of a nonexistent skirt. "And this's me lord Gareth, Prince of Bel, who was Regent for the old King."

"My lord." The merchant bowed again, though not so deeply, and pressed his fist to his brow. "We heard you had gone to the mage Bliaud's house—"

"Who's 'we'?" asked John, and Gareth said, "What's happening? They're trying the Master of Halnath this morning. . . ."

"It is why we're here." Brâk glanced up the lane as Abellus salaamed first to Jenny, then, deeply, to the Prince.

"Everyone's always complaining how servants gossip," said the wizard's son. "Well, they might be servants, but they ain't stupid—fact is, my valet's a dashed sight more brainy than I am, not that that's praising him to the stars. . . . Never was one of the clever sorts, you know." He tapped his temple and shook his head. Like Gareth, he dyed his curled lovelocks—the two that escaped his velvet hood were a lively green. "The aunts always said I was the fool of the family— well, me and Papa, anyway. But nobody ever said you had to be able to run up double-column accounts to see when someone you know isn't someone you know anymore. 'Specially now. Papa"—he paused— "where was I? Oh, the servants."

"There are those—in the palace and out," said Brâk, "who, if you will forgive my saying so, my lord prince, never trusted this 'recovery' of your father's. Or that of your poor lady wife. And the things that have been rumored about her, and about what servants have witnessed in the palace and especially in this private quarter she has lately had set aside for her, sound too much like other rumors concerning those who, like her, suffered death from the plague, and later . . . came back." His dark eyes met Gareth's. "She died," he asked softly, "did she not?"

Gareth looked aside. Then, after a moment's silence, he drew a deep breath and returned the merchant's compassionate gaze. "Yes. I . . . did a foolish thing. I should have known better."

Brâk held up his hand, and shook his head. "There are many in the city," he said, "who could not accept, and who made the choice you made. Who among us who loves would not do the same? Many in the city have come to the conclusion that you did since then. And many still fight that conclusion with all that is in them, not wanting to understand what they know in their hearts to be true."

"That my wife is a demon?"

"That *all* those who return are demons. I don't know how many I've spoken to in the streets who say, 'It may be true that *some* are, but *my* beloved is one of the *true* resurrections. . . .' And there have been no true resurrections. Only more careful demons."

He glanced across the lane at the gate to the wood-court. It opened a crack, and a white cloth waved twice, as if a servant shook out a rag. Then it closed, but Jenny could see that it did not close all the way.

"So." Brâk touched the short-sword he wore beneath his quilted cloak. "Where can we find you, my lord, after we come out—if we come out?"

"You can find me in my father's hall," Gareth said quietly, and fell into step with Brâk as he moved down the lane toward the little door. "Or my father's prison."

"She said her illness had made her think about how she had used her life, and what she owed to the gods," recounted Gareth as Brâk closed the postern behind them. They were a goodly company by that time, for while Brâk spoke nearly a dozen men and women had melted like ghosts from the surrounding lanes, grim-faced and quiet and armed with the weapons of their trades, butcher knives and hammers and knots of lead. There were hasty introductions, clumsy salaams among the wood-piles, the whispered names of husbands or children or wives vanished or killed. Gareth's hands were kissed and John's shoulders slapped encouragingly.

"We were in the market square, lord, a fortnight ago, but there were too many guards for us to rush the stake...."

"Just as well, as it turned out," said John. "Though I didn't think so at the time." Inside the court another dozen servants waited, and nearly a score of the Palace Guard, led by the dark-browed Captain Tourneval who'd arrested John on his return to Bel, and whom later Gareth had spoken of as a loyal man. He bowed to John—Jenny saw no trace of the demon in his eyes.

Only a man doing as he was ordered, she thought, and loyal to his King.

Gareth led the way, up an enclosed stair and then right, through a pillared gallery beneath a hall and thence into a cloistered garden, snow glimmering wanly among uneven mats of neglected hedge and mounds of overgrown vine. "She asked for the whole of the old Queen's tower, the keys to all its doors and rooms, because it was closed off from the storerooms. Even the servants never come." There was a gateway of wrought-iron openwork, locked, leading into a second, smaller garden. One of the town conspirators was a blacksmith who'd brought tools.

"She didn't know much about the ways of servants, then," Brâk remarked dryly as the blacksmith forced open the gate. "Nor did the demon who took her know a great deal of how humans will take advantage of any place where they can meet their lovers, or hide stolen tablecloths, or take a few minutes to rest between scouring pans and carrying wood." A couple of the red-liveried servants traded glances and embarrassed grins.

"I'm sorry no one came to you before this, m'lord," added a man in the rough garb of a stable-hand, speaking to Gareth. "Seems like everybody whispered about the sounds we'd hear, coming from the old Queen's chapel, but nobody'd talk about it out loud. Nobody'd admit of being there, for fear she'd hear—"

"She showed you a gentle face, lord," Tourneval said, striding beside Gareth, his sword drawn.

"She was gentle," Gareth said softly. His voice cracked a little, then steadied. "Gentle and loving and kind. And kindness ... isn't something that can be counterfeited. Not even when the one you're deceiving desperately wants to see it."

"We only feared that in your indignation, you'd speak of it to her. Or to one who might get word back to her."

They crossed the second garden, still more overgrown. The day's intermittent flurries of sleet had blurred away any tracks from the unkempt mounds and hummocks of snow in its center, but where the surrounding colonnade sheltered a long crescent of old snow Jenny saw a woman's tracks, small feet in the tall-soled shoes fashionable at Court, and mingled with them the heavier tracks of a man. Man and woman had come and gone this way many times since the snow first fell, tracks over one another, and always those same two. In one place the snow was rucked up and stained brownish with old blood, as if someone had knelt there and used it to wash her hands.

Gareth halted, looking down at the scraped muck. From the door opposite, decorated with exquisite carvings of the Twelve Gods, came the foetor of old blood, the lingering pungence of charred meat. Jenny, standing among the group of servants and guards, met John's eyes. All her own horrendous memories passed in a nightmare stream through her mind. She tried the door, and it was locked. John would have drawn Gareth away, but the young man said, "No. I need to see." The blacksmith—his name was Dor—came forward again with his tools.

The Chapel of the Twelve was dark, and not very large. Pendant vaulting, delicate as lace, lost itself in blackness overhead. Only the extreme cold kept the air even remotely breathable. In summer, the place would have been a hell of flies. Jenny looked at the chains, and the bloodstains, and the things all laid out on what had been the altar-table of the Twelve, implements uncleaned after their last use and ready for their next. There were a few crystals left, flawed topazes, and a number of low-grade opals in a dish. Jenny's own eyes were mageborn, and she hoped the dense shadows hid at least some of this from Gareth, but looking up into his face she couldn't tell, in the sickened light, what he felt or thought. There was a smell, too, of turned earth, coming from a small door half-hidden behind the altar: turned earth and rot. Behind her, one of the guards flinched aside, gagging.

Before she could stop him, Gareth walked past her into the desecrated chamber, and Jenny hurried at his heels. "You don't need to see that."

"I need to see all," he said, his voice quite calm. "I'll need to charge her with it." But she sensed that what he sought was enough anger to turn him against one who looked so much like Trey.

From that half-open door by the altar a stair no wider than a man's shoulders led down to what had been a crypt. Tourneval and Brâk had lanterns. The grubby light showed a floor dug up, tiles thrown carelessly in heaps along the walls, with no attempt at tidiness or thought to replace them. Mixed with the tiles were clots of dirt, smelling of mold and worms and worse things. Whatever was buried there hadn't been buried deep. From the wet black earth hands stuck out, and here and there parts of skulls. One of them still trailed long black gore-clotted hair.

Behind her on the stair Jenny heard the shocked whispers as guards and servants passed word back of what they saw, or struggled to come forward to see, or back to seek the outer air.

"So this is how they make the crystals you spoke of?" Gareth asked her, still in that voice of unnatural calm. "With magic raised from deaths like these?"

"I think so, yes," said Jenny. "But were there no need for them to raise such power, I think they would still kill thus, for sport."

When they came up the crypt steps and out of the chapel into the raw cold of the garden, Gareth said to Brâk, "Of the others in the city, the other women who were resurrected by demons, were any with child? Have any given birth, since their resurrection?"

And Brâk shook his head. "None that I've heard of, Prince." He looked around him, at the servants, and the rabble of artisans and laborers and merchants whose beloveds had died and returned. But they all shook their heads, men and women both.

The young dandy Abellus said, "M'father went to see women who were with child, I know that, but none so far advanced as . . . as your lady was."

Gareth pushed up his spectacles and rubbed tiredly at his eyes. "Come, then," he said. "I've seen what I needed to see. They'll have Polycarp in the council chamber. We can charge them with this there."

When they reached the King's council chamber, however, they found the room empty, and not even pages in the antechamber to tell them what was happening. "That doesn't look good," John remarked, ambling into the vaulted and tapestried round room with his air of deceptive laziness, his hands tucked into his belt. "When the servants are keepin' their distance you know there's trouble. They expected to try him here this mornin', though—" and he nodded at the logs and kindling laid ready in the clean-swept fireplace, the long-legged silver braziers standing behind the chairs and the cloths laid over the tables. "Which means Goffyer reached 'em with word—"

"Guards," Jenny interrupted, hearing the swift tramp of boots in the stair behind them. John and Brâk and Tourneval's guardsmen all drew their swords, but Gareth held up his hand and stepped into the council room's antechamber as a small squad came in from the corridor, some clothed in the crimson tunics of the royal house, others in Sindstray blue. The captain was the big fair freckled man who'd taken Polycarp yesterday, a demon glitter in his eye.

"Captain Leodograce." Gareth stepped forward even as the man began to speak, cutting off whatever it was he would have said. "Where is my father, and where have they taken the council meeting concerning my cousin Polycarp?"

"Polycarp, m'lord?" The Captain shook his head. "I've heard nothing of the Master of Halnath—this is the first I've heard he's still in the city. And your father is hunting today. But before he left he heard rumors—lies, I'm sure—about some that say you've had traffic with demons, and with those that caused the plague. For that reason you're to come with us, to wait on his pleasure—"

"You've a gie short memory," remarked John, emerging from the crowd at Gareth's side. "Seein' as how it was you who took Polycarp yesterday, an' killed two of his men. Their blood's still on the snow of the wood-court."

Leodograce's lip went up to show his teeth like a dog's. "You believe this man . . . ?" He turned to his squad. "Take them." His gesture took in servants, artisans, guards. "Bring the Prince. Kill the rest."

John strode toward the red-cloaked captain, raising his sword, and Jenny saw the captain and one other guardsman flinch back as if they'd been burned. Leodograce cried, "You! Take him, men!" and backed away fast as his soldiers came forward, and Gareth said, "Touch me on pain of treason."

The soldiers hesitated, looking at one another and at Tourneval, all except for the one other demon soldier, who had retreated to the back of the group. Gareth, tall and stooped and surprisingly kingly despite the rumpled clothing and broken spectacles, looked at one of the crimson guardsmen and said, "Where is my father?"

The man hesitated, then said, "He's gone to the prison tower, lord."

"Dog!" Leodograce whipped his sword from its sheathe and lunged at Gareth. But when confronted with actual fear of death, the demon had no courage, and would not step near. When John lunged at him, only brandishing his sword, the captain broke and fled from the room, the other demon soldier at his heels. There was clamor in the hallway, the crash of a man being thrown against the wall, and footfalls retreating; the men of the squad stared at the door in astonishment and considerable confusion.

"Who among you is for the Prince?" demanded Tourneval of Leodograce's confused squadron.

One of the blue-clothed Sindestray guards ventured, "Those who traffic with demons—"

"... lie about those who do not," Tourneval replied, and stepped aside to let Gareth stride ahead of them out of the anteroom and down the hall.

So it was at the head of a good fifty armed men and women— some of whom didn't look any too sure about whether they wanted to be allies or jailers—that Gareth entered the prison tower. The original guards, both Tourneval's squadron and Leodograce's, had been joined by others still as they passed swiftly down the great staircase of the new palace and along the galleries leading to the prison tower in the old. More servants joined the company, too, some bearing kitchen knives and others clubs or rakes. Even the fat, elderly Badegamus appeared, toddling anxiously at Gareth's side and saying, "Please don't hurt him, Prince. I mean, please make very, very sure of what you're doing. . . ."

But Jenny noticed that he carried his beribboned staff of office like a war-hammer rather than a cane.

The gate that led from the gardens of the new palace into the great central courtyard of the old was barred. An ancient portcullis, amber with rust, had been let down in what had been the original stronghold's main gatehouse: "Oh, for pity's sake," snapped Tourneval. "Do they think we can't get through the Long Gallery upstairs? Everybody—"

"Don't do that, guv'nor," said a groom. "That's the way everybody goes. They'll be up there with bows in the minstrel gallery, sure as check. But the wine cellars connect up, too, and the backstairs passages. You will go easy on my lord, won't you?" he added, to Gareth. "I mean, he may just not be in his right mind. . . ."

Jenny scouted ahead listening, when the servants led them down through the wine vaults, but evidently the demons had had little use for servants, and had possessed none who could have told them of this way through. "Leave 'em guarding the Long Gallery, if that's what they want to do," remarked John as they all edged between the massive kegs of Somanthus vintage and southern sherry wine. And Jenny held up her hand for silence, listening.

Far ahead, echoing in the stone vaults of the prison tower, she heard a confusion of voices cursing, and the splintery crunch of axes on wood. Someone shouted, "Bring him out!" and another, "Got him, my lord!" "Are you satisfied, my little traitor?" asked the King's voice, more softly. "Barricading oneself into one's cell isn't exactly the act of an innocent man."

Jenny said, "Hurry," and began to run, up the stair from the cellar into a deserted watchroom that had been the old kitchen, John and Gareth like hounds upon her heels.

"That way." Gareth pointed down a stair, and ahead of her Jenny saw in the torchlit corridor at its base the blue-clothed soldiers of Ector of Sindestray's private guard crowded together, a wall of azure backs.

"It's the act of a man who knows he'll get no justice from demons," retorted Polycarp's voice, and there was the meaty thwack of a blow, and the jangle of chains.

"Bring him to the watchroom." Trey's voice was cold as silver, and at the same moment that Gareth checked his stride, face gray with shock and grief, Jenny felt the piercing knife of recognition.

John had told her already that it was Amayon who had taken over Trey's body.

Her own words came back to her: *I can't be absolutely positive I'd turn Amayon away....*

Words spoken so casually, in the certainty that she would, in fact, not react to the sound of his voice.

She was aware of John watching her, not warily, but with compassion in his eyes. "You want to wait back in the wine cellar?" he asked, under cover of curses and blows farther along the corridor. "Some of the lads'll stay with you...."

Jenny shook her head.

"It could be dangerous," he said. "Now your magic's comin' back, an' all."

"No," she replied. "I'm in no danger from that." At the same time, unexpected and unbidden and against her own will and better sense, she felt screaming anger at Amayon, as if he'd betrayed her by taking on another woman's body—*Mine wasn't good enough, with my magic gone? Or is it just because I'm old....*

What on EARTH are you thinking? her saner mind demanded instants later. But the anger remained, bitter as gall.

And under it, disgusting her, still lay that unbidden yearning for the demon who had whispered to her how she was the only human he had ever truly loved.

The others meanwhile surged past them, streaming along the cramped corridor. Jenny shook her head, appalled at her own thoughts, and, shifting her grip on her halberd, hurried on their heels. John strode at her side, sword in hand. "You leave if you need to," he said. "And only you know if and how that'll be."

"I'll be all right." But she didn't know if she would be. The thoughts demons put in human minds are not rational thoughts, and she knew their strength.

Shouting ahead of them, and the clash of chains as Polycarp was thrown against the wall or to the floor: "I think the actions of your co-conspirators this morning have abrogated your right to a hearing," said the King. Through the watchroom doorway as she reached it,

Jenny glimpsed his golden hair in the light of the two torches, above a crowd of backs. "The murder of Lord Bliaud—"

Then shouting, as the first of Gareth's insurgents bulled into the watchroom before her.

Steel clanged; the stink of blood lashed hot into the damp, cold air. Trey screamed, a theatrical shriek of feigned terror, and Ector's rather high voice yapped, "How DARE you draw steel against your King?" John released Jenny's arm and surged forward into the maelstrom as the guards and servants clashed and locked in struggle.

"Kill him!" the King shouted to the men who held Polycarp against the far wall. The Master of Halnath tripped one of them and smote the other with the hank of chain that joined his wrists, flattened back against the wall and scooped up a wooden bench to shield himself. By the bruises on his temples and mouth and hands, Jenny could see that in the day of his imprisonment he had been subjected already to what was euphemistically referred to as "the Question." One of the palace cooks stepped in with an iron skillet and smote the guard who would have stabbed Polycarp through the cracks in the bench; then the melee closed around them again.

Jenny slashed with her halberd, trying to stop Lord Ector from fleeing, but one of his guards struck at her and the councilor slipped by, shouting for more guards. The torchlit watchroom was a cul-de-sac. If Ector was clean of possession, at least some of the men he would fetch would not be. Tourneval shouted, led four or five guards and servants back into the passageway to intercept the attack that would come. The King had scooped up a fallen guard's halberd and was striking out all around him, crying, "Traitors! Traitors!" while Trey, at his side, wailed, "Oh, dear gods, save me! My husband has gone mad!"

Guards ranged before them; at Gareth's shout, his insurgent force fell back.

"Those of you who think I've gone mad," the Prince panted, "go out to the old Queen's garden in the East Tower. Look in the chapel there—the door's unlocked. Ask anyone, who it was who had me give her the key to that wing of the palace. Ask who has gone to 'meditate' in that place every night since her so-called resurrection. . . ."

And Trey stared at him, with terrified wild doe eyes. "Oh, my lord," she whispered, her little white hand stealing to her lips. "Oh, my lord, how *can* you? I begged you—how many times I begged you!—not to do those things in that place." She pressed her hands on the swelling of her belly, beneath her gown of yellow velvet and sable fur. "That you would choose my own rooms, my own chapel, for your terrible rites. . . ."

The guards around the King looked at one another, uncertain in the flaring orange glare.

"Yes, go," snapped the King to them, with a bark of laughter. "Go all the way to the other end of the palace, like he says—I'll be fine here with his armed troops and his demon-possessed friends till you get back." He turned a scornful sea-blue eye on his son, and added, "Why don't you tell them their boots are untied and be done with it, boy? You can't even lay a ruse properly." Even in his illness, after the witch Zyerne had drained away his mind and his personality, he had been a kingly figure, as tall as his son and broader, stronger, far more handsome, with hair still thick and golden as Gareth's had prematurely faded and thinned. *How easy,* thought Jenny as she glanced from father to son, *for men to trust that strong bluff competence above a gawky, stoop-shouldered young man who would throw up for hours after a battle.*

And Polycarp, lowering the bench that shielded him, said reasonably, "Send one man, then, one whom you all trust. Send Lord Ector. And bid him look whose footprints he sees on the snow in the garden."

Trey struck like a cat—Amayon struck like a cat—whipping a dagger from her belt and lunging at the Master. He caught her wrist, but Jenny could see he would not strike a pregnant woman as he would strike a man, even a woman whom he knew to be a demon: It was not in him. She saw in his face, too, the love he had borne for Trey.

Trey slashed Polycarp's hand open and bolted for the doorway, but John stepped in front of her, sword held ready, and she stopped, staring, dark eyes huge.

And in that frozen second Jenny sprang forward and caught her arm and twisted it behind her.

Trey screamed, fought, breaking the arm—she didn't care and pain was nothing to a demon—but years in the Winterlands, cutting her own wood and carrying water daily to her own kitchen, had given Jenny a grip like a blacksmith's. Trey was taller and younger, and with the strength that the possessed have, and had she fought as a demon she would have overpowered Jenny easily. But instead she appealed to the men, screaming, "Oh, my lords, she will kill me!"

And Gareth looked straight at John and said, "Do it."

John met Trey's eye and smiled, and then lunged in with his sword.

Trey's eyes rolled back in her head and her mouth opened, and instead of a scream, there issued from it the silvery gleaming whip-snake of the demon. It rolled down Trey's breast like spilling vomit and whipped across the floor, the shocked men leaping aside lest it touch them. Before John could turn to cut at it a second demon poured itself out of Trey's mouth, fell to the floor with a wet little slap, and bolted like a fleeing roach to the door, and Trey's body collapsed, limp, unbloodied—untouched by the blade—dead in Jenny's arms.

John was already turning toward the door after the two demons, the men around him—the King's and Gareth's—dumb with shock and confusion. Jenny saw Gareth lurch away, hand over his mouth and eyes shut, as she lowered Trey's body to the flagstoned floor. Even as she did so four men burst into the room, Ector's guards in blue, and Ector shouted from the passageway outside, "Don't let him speak! Don't let any of them speak!" and John sprang back, barely parrying a halberd and taking a cut from another across his shoulder.

Gareth cried, "No!" and his voice was drowned out. The King bellowed, "They have murdered the Lady Trey! The Prince is mad!" and catching up his own halberd, lunged from his guards straight at John. John parried, driven back by the longer weapon and the King's greater height and unexhausted strength. The King continued to shout, "Murderers! Hellspawn!" and someone in the corridor screamed.

And screamed again.

Ector of Sindestray fell into the watchroom, collapsed on his knees, eyes jammed open with purest terror. There was a stench, a horror of grave-stink and corpse-stink and the reek of blood-soaked earth, and then the Thing burst into the watchroom, a reeling monstrosity of bones and worms and graveyard mold, animate with malice that burned from the holes in the black-tressed skull that was its head.

John fell back, turned to meet it, and the King cut at his back with the halberd, the blade opening a glancing gash across his scalp where the back of his neck had been a moment before. The graveyard thing–the corpse-wight, the horror, whatever it was–smashed John aside with a force that hurled him into the stone wall like a rag doll, and fell upon the King, razoring him open, flinging him down in a fountain of gore before a man in the room could move.

John sprang at it, stumbling as he got to his feet–he had walked all through the night that Jenny knew of and fought once already at Bliaud's, and goodness knew what else before they'd met in the inn-yard–and Jenny caught up her halberd and leaped at the corpse-wight from the other side. Men were shouting around her; she struck fast, and the monster swatted at her with the arms of the corpses dragged up out of Trey's burial vault. The heads of corpses embedded in the monster's body shrieked lungless, throatless strangled gasps at her, and in the long black hair of its topmost head, the red worms stood up and hissed. The halberd blade bit into the dead flesh and the dead hands seized the shaft, wrenched and twisted it from Jenny's grip, and spun to strike John with the handle across the body.

He caught the handle, wrenched it down and aside, parried the knives the thing had in its hands, the knives that had been on the chapel table–torture-knives, skinning-knives. He lunged in again among the blades, the thing caught him by arms and throat and shoulders. John wrenched at its grip, trying to bring up the demon-killer blade in time, and there was a blazing flash of light, a billow of unspeakable stench, and a scream such as no one in that room had ever heard. Every torch in the watchroom dimmed and belched smoke, and Jenny saw something like a dark cloud, or a winged limber shade flopping in the light. . . .

Then her eyes cleared and the torchlight returned, and she saw the monster collapsed in a heap on the ground, the size of a small horse, dead and spewing filth and fluids onto the flagstones of the watchroom floor. John was on his knees between it and the dead King's sprawled body, slime and blood dripping from his clothing and hair.

It was Ector of Sindestray who first moved. He stumbled to John's side, gray brows and gray beard standing out almost black against a face pale with shock. He held out his hand. "My lord," he whispered. "Oh, my lord . . ."

John raised his head and brought up his free hand to wipe some of the goo off his spectacle lenses. "I am definitely," he said, "gettin' too bloody old for this kind of thing."

Chapter 13

Uriens II was laid out in state in the great hall of the palace of Belmarie, the twelfth King of the House of Uwanë to lie thus. By sunset of the day of his death word went out to all the city of Bel that the King had been slain protecting the Lady Trey from the very demons against which he had warned the people the day before.

Even before the horrified Palace Guard brought in hurdles to carry away the corpse-wight that had slain the King, and the bier for the King himself, Gareth of Belmarie gave the order for the arrest of every man, woman, and child who had been resurrected by the mage Bliaud, or whose death had been attested by their families and who had later proved to be alive. This order given, he knelt for a long time on the watchroom floor beside his father's body, and by the lifeless, untouched corpse of his wife, Trey. While Tourneval and his guards departed to carry out this command, the southern merchant Brâk and Bliaud's son Abellus spread their cloaks over the King's body, and Jenny Waynest sent various servants running for water and dressings for the wounded.

"My lord Thane." Ector of Sindestray stood before the bench where John sat, as Jenny washed the wounds on his back and scalp. It was the first time the white-haired treasurer had given Aversin his proper title: In his uncouth peasant breeches and dirty jacket, blood and slime and hair dye trickling through two weeks' worth of scrubby black beard, he looked like some kind of wight himself.

"Forgive me," the councilor said. "I was deceived by the ... the demons that possessed Her Ladyship." He could barely bring out the words, but too many people had seen the demons slither out from between Trey's lips. He himself had seen them whip past him in the corridor, and slither through the cracks in the stone wall. "I did you a terrible wrong, my lord, and would have done you a greater one had you not escaped. I can only plead that you will forgive an old man for putting the safety of the Realm, as he understood it, before the rights of any single man."

It said a good deal, Jenny reflected, for Ector that he would make this apology in front of his own men.

"Gaw, no," said John cheerfully. "You were doin' your duty an' doin' it damn well. I'd've done the same thing meself, if it wasn't me." And he looked hugely embarrassed, when the white-haired Treasurer knelt before him and kissed his hand.

Badegamus returned with more servants and two biers, and palls of velvet and brocade. Gareth kissed his father's hands, and the lips of the dark-haired girl who had been his wife. Then he wiped his eyes and put his spectacles back on, and stood beside the Master of Halnath as servants bore the bodies away.

Only later, when John and Jenny were at last alone in the rooms to which Badegamus escorted them overlooking the Long Garden, did John say, "What the *hell* was that thing, Jen?"

"*Did* you kill it?" Servants had brought water for the bath, and made up the fires in the hypocaust beneath the green marble bath chamber. The whole suite smelled of soap and oils, the warmth of steam languorous on the air.

"No. I don't think so. I don't know." John sat on the chest at the end of the bed, gingerly working his boots off. He'd rinsed the gore from his face and Jenny, as she knelt to help him—for his wounds were stiffening—saw in the curtained chamber's lamplight how his ribs stood out under his flesh, and how small round scars marked his arms, that had not been there before. When she shed her plaids, and began to unlace her bodice, he asked, "Would you like a hand? Or would you like just to be alone, to have a bath and a rest?"

Her eyes met his, knowing what he was asking. And she smiled. "I'd like company in the bath, if you feel up to it."

His answering smile, and the way his shoulders relaxed, told her his thoughts better than words could. He said, "Mind you, between one thing and another I can't promise you anythin' except that I'll soap your back for you...."

Rising, she put her hands on either side of his face and kissed his shorn forehead. "All this winter long," she said, "I have thought how I would trade all the treasures of the gnomes and the spices of the South, only to have you soap my back."

* * *

"That thing that killed the King, now." John poured out the herbed tisane that a servant had brought, coffee being one of those things that was put aside during mourning. Under gray morning light the Long Garden outside looked wet and cold under a patchy blanket of pocked, half-melted snow, and Jenny could dimly hear the slow tolling of the death-knell for the passing of the King. Through the wrinkled panes of the window's glass, servants and guards visible on the terrace across the garden all wore the black of mourning.

She turned back from the window, and drew around her the robe and the shawl that had come from the palace stores.

John handed her the steaming porcelain cup. "It had me, Jen. I thrust up at it at the last second, but I was stabbin' blind, for it was right on top of me. But I'll take oath it was fallin' already when I stabbed it. That it was dead before it fell."

"I saw a thing. . . ." Jenny hesitated. By the light it was the third hour of the morning, and even after the hot bath last night her muscles were board-stiff and ached. John had a whole new set of bruises to go with the old. She couldn't even remember the last time she'd fought full-out with a halberd as she had yesterday—probably not since the siege of Palmorgin in the summer, if then. "A flying shadow, that showed up against that flare of light. I thought at the time it was the demon leaving the King's body."

"No," John said decisively. "I saw that one, a silver salamander like the others, whippin' away covered in blood from where the corpse-wight threw him. Could the wight have been called by Goffyer, d'you think, to distract me—an' everyone else in the room—an' keep the King's Demon from bein' killed?"

"Maybe," Jenny said slowly. "Though I'd say it was likelier called into being by Adromelech, to break Folcalor's power in Bel by destroying the tool he was using."

"Could Adromelech have done that? At this distance, an' trapped in the Henge as he is?" John lifted the silver lid from a tray of pastries: Mourning also forbade jams and confits, but there was, at least, butter and honey, which he attacked like a starving man. "An' if that's the case, why not do it earlier? Why just yesterday? Why take the risk when I was there with the demonkiller blade?"

Jenny only shook her head. "I don't know what Adromelech

knows," she said. "Or how he knows it. He's intelligent," she said thoughtfully, remembering the gross shining thing as Amayon remembered him, the Lord of Hell who had both loved and tortured Folcalor. "Presumably he has agents in Folcalor's camp, demons who are loyal to him playing lip service to Folcalor as well as those who are openly arrayed against him."

"I dunno," John said, licking melted butter off his wrist. In the North, most cows were dry at this time of year; butter in the wintertime, even plainly molded and without its customary southern decoration of flowers, was a delight and a treat. "There's somethin' about that whole fight that just felt ... odd. As if what was goin' on wasn't quite what was goin' on. Not," he added, offering her a piece of cinnamon bread, "that I plan to share me suspicions with Ector, or anyone who's likely to talk to him. It's a change not to worry about which way I'm to run if someone speaks my name."

They dressed in the somber garments that the servants had brought, Jenny remembering with a pang of grief how Trey had lent her a black and white gown the first night she had dined with the Court, lest she be mocked by Zyerne. John, who could look extremely respectable when he tried, washed the last of the lampblack out of his hair and shaved off his beard, and together they made their way to the great hall, to pay their respects to the King whose law John had all his life served.

"The people will be admitted at noon." Gareth rose from the cushion where he'd knelt, according to custom, all night: Jenny couldn't imagine he would have slept much, anyway. The great hall—the only portion of the original palace still incorporated into the new—was curtained now in sable hangings, and the warm yellow honeycomb tiles of its floors covered with rush-matting dyed black. Badegamus and the servants must have been busy as squirrels in autumn, thought Jenny, to have accomplished all this since noon yesterday. She would have to seek the old chamberlain out and compliment him on the deep respect his efforts showed to the King he had served for so many years. The chamberlain and the King had been boys together, and Badegamus had loved the King, she knew, very much.

"They're gathering already before the gates. They're very quiet...."

"My lord?" Danae appeared at the doorway to the left of the dais where the twin biers lay. She, too, was dressed in mourning, her fair hair loosed over her shoulders as was the custom, and only half-hidden by a mourning veil. When she saw John and Jenny she salaamed and made to go, but Gareth signed her to remain, and led the way toward the doorway where she stood.

"The people are very quiet," said Gareth again. "Those whom Tourneval and the guards went out to arrest yesterday? They're dead."

"What?" Jenny hadn't expected that, though, she reflected, she should have. "All of them?"

"All the women, and such of the men as weren't warriors. The men have simply disappeared."

"Oh, that'll make me sleep better at night," John remarked dryly, and Gareth nodded.

"Brâk and Abellus are checking, speaking to everyone who might know of someone who was resurrected. But it seems to have been a clean sweep. In some cases the disappearances were inexplicable—from rooms that had no other way out, that sort of thing. The people don't know what to make of it."

"And what are you tellin' 'em?"

Gareth's pale face colored a little, and he grinned. "Abellus and Polycarp are putting it about that the resurrection spells caused madness in men, and simply failed in others. That the missing men have simply run away, and will be sought. That we'll do the best we can for them...."

"But I venture to guess," remarked Jenny, "that the prognosis isn't good."

"Abellus's brother, Tundal, was one of the men who died," said Gareth, more quietly. "As was his wife. Abellus is with their children now—he got them out of the household as soon as he began to suspect there was something amiss about the resurrections. They're all right."

In the withdrawing chamber to the right of the dais, Danae had brought coffee and plain rolls for Gareth, and she watched him with a combination of motherliness and worry while he ate. She did not appear to have slept herself, and when Gareth asked her only said, "I will. I didn't like to leave Milla, as long as she was awake. But now she's sleeping I'll take some rest. My lord." She knelt to John and kissed his hand. "Thank you for taking us out of the city. I don't know what might have happened to Milla last night, if we hadn't gone."

"She was lucky to have a friend to care for her."

When the woman had gone, John asked, "Any news of old Goffyer?"

"The man I sent to the Deep yesterday hasn't returned. It's several hours' ride."

Hesitantly, Jenny took one of the shallow porcelain cups from the tray Danae had brought and, filling it with clean water from the pitcher in the niche near the door, retired with it to a corner. It felt odd to try to summon power now, as if it were shaped differently within her than it had been before. Gareth's voice and John's faded from her mind. She found herself looking into darkness, as if the cup were filled with ink instead of water, ink that gleamed with pinpoints of flame.

Miss Mab smiled at her, and said, "Child?"

Her eyes were wise and bright and as they had ever been. She was in her usual chambers on the Ninth Level; Jenny could see past her to the terraces above the subterranean waterfalls where she meditated, and a table refulgent with lamps and scattered thick with scrolls. "Are you all right?"

"Thinkst thou a demon could trick an old gnome-wife into folly? We gnomes are like the stone that gives us birth, child—our memories are long. This Folcalor came in the guise of poor Goffyer and treated with Sevacandrozanus our King, telling all manner of tales of demons in Bel. But our King is wary of demons. How not, when he has had me imprisoned all this time, and under watch, just for aiding thy husband in his search for the Mirror of Ernine? When it was suggested by the Patriarch of my family that Goffyer be likewise incarcerated, and Rogmadoscibar his brother also who has been helping him here, both fled after slaying many warriors of the King's guard. There is argument still, and those who have made money from the demons are spreading rumors about what has taken place in Bel, but I do not think thy little Prince need fear that in the end the gnomes will do anything but what they have always done: wait."

When Jenny relayed this information to Gareth, he looked deeply relieved. "I've sent messengers also to Prince Tinán of Imperteng, asking his presence here in twenty days, to swear allegiance at my crowning. After his defeat in the summer there has been trouble there again, the mountaineers rising in rebellion." He shook his head, and John asked something about the status of the disputed farmlands since last summer. Behind her Jenny heard their voices drift into talk of the rebels' cause, and which clans in the Trammel Hills had gone to fighting with what hill-tribes, and to what end.

While they spoke, Jenny turned her attention back to the water bowl, and called to mind her elder son's thin face, and the way his thick black hair fell over his forehead, and the bright lobelia-blue of his eyes.

Ian, she called. *Ian ...*

Conjuring into her mind the ash-gray stone of Alyn Hold's walls, against the white of the snow. The amber brightness of the kitchen fire in that huge stone hearth, black iron pokers and hooks and chains arrayed like weapons in an armory, and everyone sitting at the long oak table: John's aunts and cousins and Sergeant Muffle. The howl of the wind around the walls. Ian ...

But there was nothing. Her head began to ache, and she wondered if she had overextended already her slight powers. Or was there some other reason, some other danger ...?

"If he doesn't come to the crowning," Gareth was saying, "it will be a declaration of war."

"Aye, well," replied John cheerfully, "if we haven't settled Folcalor's accounts in twenty days, I promise you a war with Imperteng isn't going to be your biggest problem, anyway."

Ector entered, and Badegamus, and other lords. John took Jenny's hand and led her back to the hall, where the members of the Great Houses of the Realm were already being admitted, to walk past the biers of the King and the Lady Trey. Trey's handsome brother was being led away, weeping: Jenny knew that the girl had been everything to him, as she had been to Gareth. He was not the only one to shed tears. What further rumors of yesterday's events had gone about the city Jenny did not know, but the nobles of the Realm all salaamed profoundly as she and John took their places in the line, and afterward this nobleman or that spoke to them, people they had met when they had come south to free the land of the dragon, and who had later entertained them in the feastings that surrounded Millença's naming.

Some were missing, represented by anxious wives or brothers who spoke long to Polycarp in the corner. They left looking troubled still, but comforted. Abellus was there, too, pale-lipped in gorgeously cut black mantlings that seemed incongruous against the weary grimness of his eyes; without being obvious about it, Jenny went to him and looked long into the eyes of the two boys with him, but saw no trace of demons there.

"What will we do?" she asked softly as she and John walked the length of the somberly draped hall with the black-dyed rushes crunching softly underfoot. Between the sable curtains the windows showed only a gray light, and despite the fire that burned on the dais hearth, the huge chamber was icy as a cave. "It is sixteen days, until the Moon of Winds."

"Sixteen days should be enough," said John, "if all goes well." And, when Jenny looked at him in surprise, he tapped the side of his nose and said, "I've got a plan."

On the steps of the hall a man stood, slim and small with his black garments billowing around him in the wind, his long gray hair a spidery cloud. Diamond eyes went first to Jenny's hand, locked in John's, and then to her face, and she felt that he could see there the afterglow of last night's loving, brazen as a love-bite.

Wizard-woman, said his voice in her mind, *I did not think ever that I would say so—or feel so. Yet I rejoice with you.*

He held out his hand to her, black gloves masking the curved black claws.

She greeted him, *Dragonshadow.* The word itself the reminder to her that he, too, had moved through the crossroad of possibilities they had shared, and into open country beyond.

"Dreamweaver." He turned the kaleidoscope gaze upon John, who met his eyes, trusting as no other of humankind did. "I have heard ill report of you from the Black-and-Silver One, who has gone into hiding in the Skerries of Light. He says that you are an insolent mortal and without regard for the greatest mage and loremaster among dragonkind."

"Made it there safe, did he?" John propped his spectacles with his forefinger, without releasing Jenny's hand. "He has to know—the other drakes have to be warned—that in time the Hellspawn will come after them again. Human magic can defend against 'em, or will be able to, once the Dragonstar sets for the last time, but to be honest I don't know about dragon magic. Dragons *are* magic, it's the stuff of their bodies an' bones. It'll make 'em a target, once the demons start fightin' amongst 'emselves. The great drakes, the old drakes, might be able to shut 'em out, but what about the young ones, that aren't ... aren't what they'll later become? You'd know about that. I don't."

"Nor do I, Dreamweaver," the Dragonshadow said quietly. "Nor what danger those star-drakes will be in, who were possessed in the summer: Centhwevir, and Nymr, and young Mellyn, and the rest. For all Corvin's claims of learning in the other world—about these crystals through which he channeled ether-magic, and about how comets are made, and these great all-knowing *computers* that he speaks of so frequently"—sarcasm curled in his voice—"still he knows no other answer than flight, and that answer, only for himself."

"Well, it has the virtue of workin', anyway," remarked John. "Trouble is, when it stops workin' you've still got your problem right there up your nose again. Let me get my notes, an' Jen her catch-bottle—an' I wish I'd had time to make a copy of the notes for Poly-carp, but there's pages an' pages of 'em, an' I'll be years puttin' 'em straight ... an' then, if you would, I think it's best we got back to the Hold as quick as we can. There's someone there I need to talk to before the first thaw hits."

First they journeyed to Ernine, on the far side of the Nast Wall, among the burned and ravaged woods. The savage explosions, and unquenchable fire, of Folcalor's attack on the mirror chamber four nights previously had utterly destroyed the stair that had for over a thousand years ascended from the stream-bank to the Hill of the Moon: amid a sodden desolation of burned trees and frozen mud even the doorway that had led into Isychros's chambers had been obliterated, so that Morkeleb had to descend like a black silk kite down through the cleft that had riven the hill above.

The mirror chamber was empty. Walls, floor, and what was left of the ceiling were black with fire, the golden constellations and the many-tailed comet smashed to rubble. Under a thin muck of snow, burned-out talisman jewels crunched beneath Jenny's boots as she and John surveyed the devastated room.

Of the bricked-up archway behind which Jenny had found the

catch-bottle, only a heap of broken stone remained. John knelt to
scrape in the frozen slush with his fingers; this he did in two or three
places before straightening his back and wiping the muddied fingers
of his glove on his doublet's leather sleeve.

"No glass," he said thoughtfully. "They said the mirror bein'
made of thunderstone would keep it from destruction, an' it looks
like they were right. It was too strong for Folcalor, anyway. Looks like
he's carried it off whole, to smash when he's taken Adromelech's powers into himself."

"Leaving only Aohila herself," Jenny said softly, "at large in the
world."

John raised his eyebrows. In the sickly snow-light the silver
curves of Aohila's spell-lines glinted on his throat. "God knows that's
trouble enough."

They slept the night in an empty manor house in Farhythe, not because Morkeleb was at all weary of flight but because in the high
sooty roil of cloud the cold and wet were too bitter to be borne by his
two passengers. Whether the inhabitants of the manor had gone to
Bel for the assembly of the King's Council, or had fled because of the
plague, Jenny did not know. The beds had been stripped from the
bedsteads and the windows were fitted over with wooden shutters in
place of the expensive glass; it hadn't been precipitate flight. Wood
lay cut ready in the shed behind the kitchen, and John made up fires;
they ate the remains of the palace luncheon that John—ever mindful
from long years of Winterlands patrols—had wrapped up and tucked
into the bundles of their clothes. In a bedroom Jenny found a small
harp swathed in velvet. It had been untuned to spare the frame, and
she could find no key for its pegs. But her hands, a few months ago
stiff and twisted claws, flexed almost easily as she ran them over the
inlaid pearwood of the soundbox; she met John's eyes and smiled.

On the borrowed sheets she dreamed again of her children, and
waking, stole softly out of doors. Fog from the Snakewater and the
marshes covered the whole of the land, making the night black as
pitch, and even Jenny's mageborn sight had trouble penetrating it.
From the cloister that looked out upon the kitchen garden she could
see only the dim outlines of first bare hedges, but a voice in her
thoughts said, *Keep your feet dry, Wizard-woman, and stay where it is*

warm. In the darkness she saw the diamond glint of eyes, and the moving flicker of the jewels on the ends of his antennae. *What brings you from your bed?*

In the music of his thoughts she would have heard jealousy or sarcasm, had there been any; anger that she shared that bed with a mortal man, when she could have been the dragon consort of a dragon.

There was none. His joy for her reunion with John had been real.

My friend, she said. And then, *I dreamed of my children, and my power is not such that I can see yet into the North. Can you listen so far, to see if all is well in the North Country?*

Wizard-woman, I can listen unto the ends of the earth, if so be I dream deeply enough, and long enough. When all this trouble with demons is done with, and the world sleeps in peace once more, I will teach you how this is done. For I think that having once been a dragon, you are capable still of dragon dreams. Their secret is this: that you do not think, 'I will seek the sounds of bandits, that I may learn if my husband's hold is in danger,' or, 'Where do the rabbits feed, that I may know if demons are near?' To dream as a dragon dreams is not to seek, and not to expect. It is merely to observe all, with no one grass blade more important than any other grass blade, nor any meaning attached to anything. Only being, throughout the whole of the universe and all of time.

Jenny thought about this, about the stillness of the fog-shrouded night, and the invisible friend hidden in the darkness.

She said, *You are not of this world, are you? The dragons. You came from one of those other worlds, that John traveled to, lying somewhere beyond beyond. You traversed Hells, and realms that have no existence beneath the sun and the stars that I know; perhaps you came from one of the many Hells, and not a true world at all.*

All worlds are true worlds, my Jenny, said the dragonshadow.

And the Dragonshadows, who have outgrown their bodies and their magic ... what are they?

Morkeleb said, *I do not know.*

Even though you are one? When you crossed over into that being, did they not tell you?

He said, *No. Since I became a dragonshadow I have spoken to no other of my kind, and before, when they still inhabited the Birdless Isle, I*

*thought I knew what they were, and did not ask. It is no unusual thing
for them to be gone for a time, though they have been gone now longer
than ever I can remember before. I can only be as I am, until upon their
return I can ask them what they are.*

Are they gods? she asked, and again he said, *I do not know. But as
for your children …*

And in her mind Jenny saw as if in a dream the stumpy tower of
Alyn Hold, sticking up on its hill above the grubby ring of its dilapidated walls. The wind scoured the walls with snow in the darkness,
and no light shone, but Jenny was aware of the repaired thatch on the
kitchens and stables, the new plaster over the places where Balgodorus and his slave-trading bandits had burned, earlier in the winter.

Impossibly, above the screaming of the wind, she heard the
breathing of the sleepers within those walls: Ian and Adric, huddled
together in their tower bedroom; little Maggie in her cot beside
Cousin Dilly, who acted as her nurse. Sour grim Aunt Jane in her
cramped room off the kitchen, and Aunt Rowe in the trundle bed beside hers, as if the two sisters of old Lord Aver were young girls still
glaring around the corners at their brother's unwanted beautiful
witch-wife mistress. For a few moments—or a few hours—Jenny was
conscious of every sleeper within those walls, of Bill the yardman and
his wife, Betne, of Peg the gatekeeper and her children, of old Cowan
in the stables and Sergeant Muffle in the room he'd taken with his
wife and children behind the forge. Of scullerymaids and grooms and
the half-dozen militiamen dossing on the hall floor around the firepit
among straw and rushes that smelled of month-old smoke and dogs.
A kind of gentle glow, like the embers of a banked fire, rose to Jenny
from their dreams.

And as Morkeleb's consciousness widened, she became aware of
the sleeping village outside the walls. Of Father Hiero the priest in the
attic loft above the broken-down and disregarded village Temple. Of
her own younger sister, Sparrow, and Sparrow's husband and children,
and all those other families near whom Jenny had grown up. Of the
cows in the byres and the horses in the stalls, and all those near and
far whose holdings and families were under the protection of the
Thane of the Winterlands, who looked to John Aversin to protect
them and be answerable for them, even at the cost of his life.

Farther off she was aware of the bleak woods, deep in snow and thrashing beneath the flail of the wind. Of muskrats in their holes and squirrels rolled tight in the hollows of trees, surrounded by the plunder of the autumn on which they'd been living for months. Of deer in the thickets and fish sleeping in the darkness of the frozen streams, of turtles in the mud and bandits far off in the ruined huts and manors that they'd made into hideouts, scratching fleas and snuffling in drunken sleep. Of the degraded Meewinks in the marshes picking over the bones of the travelers they'd killed, and even the whisperers peeping to one another in the slick-frozen ice of the haunted Wraithmire, frozen themselves and singing keening songs of the comet that hung low and smoldering somewhere beyond the hammering storm.

And in all that dark and storm and sleep, gradually Jenny saw, and heard, and felt something moving, something that crept among the torn-up snow of the woods. She felt the rabbits in their holes startle hammer-hearted from sleep at its smell, and curl down tight into the darkness until it went past. Felt the deer grow still in the thickets, ears pricked forward at the staggering, crashing stride. Like a clumsy shadow it moved, frozen flesh tearing unheeded on broken twigs. A fox sniffed at the drip of black fluid that came away on the spearpoint shards, and hastened the other way.

In the village stables a cow flung up her head and lowed in fright. Behind the church, Father Hiero's dog threw himself to the limit of his chain and barked.

The thing did not enter the byre, nor attempt to come near the church. It had no need of warmth in this bitter night. But Jenny dreamed of it circling the walls of the Hold, circling patiently, and now and then coming close enough to scratch at the gates and at the stones.

She woke, losing her balance and stumbling against the doorframe of the old manor house where she stood. Her feet were numb within her boots. Across the bare kitchen-garden in the fog, Morkeleb, a shadow himself, lay invisible between the bare, invisible orchard trees.

Your children sleep safe, my Jenny. In the dragon's speaking she felt his odd tenderness, and his quest as to what her love was, and why the destinies of these three children—and of all who slept in and about the Hold—drove her so. Since surrendering his magic he had become, she knew, curious about all manner of things that were not things of dragons. *But as you see, all is not well in the Winterlands.*

They reached Alyn Hold the following day at noon. Morkeleb descended, unseen, through the rending howl of the storm winds to the lane before the Hold's main gate, but had he come down in all his glittering midnight splendor Jenny doubted there would have been anyone outside their houses to see. It was last night of the Moon of Ice, the time of year when even bandits and Iceriders lay low. Every one of the fifty or so families of Alyn Village would be huddled around their hearths in kitchens crammed with wood, whittling or sewing or mending harness or chairs, doing all those things for which there was little time in the short gorgeous Winterlands summers. Every shutter in the village was bolted tight, and John had to pound on the gate and shout before Peg put her head out the window above it to see who was there.

"All the dear gods, where did you spring from?" gasped the gate-keeper, hanging hard onto the postern door to keep it from being slammed out of her grip by the wind. "How did you get here, in all this storm? You must be that frozen! Where are your horses?"

"Never you mind. We're back now, safe and mostly sound...." John shook back the hood from his head and looked past Jenny out into the sleety rain, but in the gray half-visible whirl of the village street, no sign of Morkeleb was to be seen.

Chapter 14

Mag, Ian, and Adric fell on their parents like savages as they entered the kitchen. In the Hold, as in the smallest village hut, for most of the winter the life of the household centered around the cooking fires. Sergeant Muffle, sweat-soaked in shirtsleeves, strode in from the forge where he'd been making nails, at the summons of his wife, Blossom, who'd been helping Aunt Jane and the kitchen girls with dinner. Cowan, Bill, and Betne appeared all swaddled up in sheepskins and dripping hay from the stalls they'd been cleaning, with the stable dogs Bannock and Snuff trailing at their heels. It was just as well there was a storm, Jenny reflected. Otherwise the whole village would have put in an appearance as well.

"Aye, we've seen it," said Muffle grimly, once all the exclamations and shouting were done and Aunt Rowe had ladled hot cider from the cauldron for the homecomers, and Cousin Dilly had stopped three-year-old Mag six or seven times from unraveling both their bundles and strewing the contents underfoot. "Or seen its tracks, anyway. At first I thought it was some poor traveler that'd been seized and stripped by bandits even of his boots."

The blacksmith sipped his own horn of cider, a big man, four or five years older than his brother and the burly, red-haired image of old Lord Aver, but with a pleasanter expression. His mother, Hollyberry, had been the village blacksmith's wife at the time of her liaison with the old Thane, and she was still to be found, four days out of seven, at the Hold: It was a miracle she wasn't in the kitchen this afternoon as well.

Muffle went on, "But next day I found more tracks skirtin' the village, when any man in that state would have gone to one of those houses for help. Mol Bucket said as how her dogs have woke her two nights this week, barkin'—you know what brutes they are, livin' as she does out at the village's end. And she told me she's been havin' queer dreams. Peg has, too."

Peg nodded, in the act of slicing up an onion into a fry-pan, to make more dressing to add to dinner.

"It's Caradoc, isn't it, Mother?" At thirteen, Ian was too old to crowd onto the bench between his parents to snuggle in their warmth, as Mag was unashamedly doing—or even to sit squeezed in at his father's side like Adric, though Adric was being careful not to hang on to John's arm as he clearly wanted to. But Ian's large blue eyes spoke more clearly than shouted whoops of joy, to see his mother and his father sit together on the bench by the kitchen table as they used to. To see the way John's glance touched Jenny when she spoke, and Jenny's close-lipped sidelong smile.

Oh, my children, thought Jenny, looking from that suddenly-tall, rail-thin boy to his burly red brother and little sloe-eyed Mag. *Oh, my children, how could my grief have been such, that it took me away from you?*

Whether Ian saw in Jenny's quiet calm what Morkeleb had seen, when the dragon began addressing her as *Wizard-woman* again, Jenny wasn't sure. It was something to be talked over with her eldest-born when they were together alone. In the days of her bereavement she had spoken to Ian of magic, not instructing him as she formerly had, but reflecting on what it meant and how it changed her perception of the world. She felt, now, that this boy, fine boned like all the Waynests of the village in contrast to Adric's rufous height and bulk, was hardly her son at all, but something closer: another mage, and a mage who like her had come through the harrowing nightmare of demonic possession and the unexpectedly worse horror of its aftermath.

The stories, she reflected, *never talked about what happened, once a demon was driven out.*

"I think it's Caradoc, yes," she replied. "I trust you've all been watching one another's backs?"

"Like wolves watching sheep." Adric slapped the hilt of his sword. It wasn't the boy's weapon John had given him last spring, Jenny saw, but a man's short stabbing-sword pilfered from the armory. At just-turned-nine, Adric was almost tall enough, and certainly strong enough, to wield it as a man, and his face was snow-burned as if Skaff Gradley and the other local militia captains had been letting him ride out with them on patrol.

"I came on tracks just the day before this latest storm, on the other side of Toadback Hill, and tried to get Bill to follow them with me. They led into the bog. I was out with Bill, none of us ever goes out alone. And when he said we shouldn't, but should get help from here, I even went, even if I knew nothing would get done that day and there was sure to be a storm the next. And there was," he added, aggrieved.

"You have my eternal gratitude, Bill," Jenny said feelingly, and the yardman grinned.

"And good on you, son," added John, "for rememberin' your orders an' not goin' off on your own. Your old father's had enough gray hairs for one year. What'd Mol dream, Muffle? I didn't think she ever dreamed of anythin' but"—he caught Aunt Jane's warning glare and glanced at the two younger children, and altered his undoubtedly rude first thought to—"gettin' her corn-patch plowed," and Jenny kicked him, hard, under the table.

"It's a dream others have been havin'." Muffle scratched his unshaven chin. It had been less than a month since Jenny and Morkeleb had left the half-burned Hold, to carry the news south that the demons were dealing in slaves with the gnomes and raising the dead. But by the tired lines on the blacksmith's face it looked to have been as exhausting a time here as any that Jenny and John had faced. Roofs burned by Balgodorus Blacknife's outlaws had had to be rebuilt, quickly, the snows and winds that hampered repairs making those repairs all the more desperately urgent, and many of the men and women injured in the defense of the Hold had not been able to lend a hand. Jenny was only glad that her transformation into dragon form, to drive away the attackers, had come before they'd managed to burn the stored grain and seed-corn. That would, perhaps, have tilted the balance for many from survival to death.

But the big blacksmith had rallied the village, and even the little she'd seen of the Hold spoke worlds of the efforts of them all. Had Muffle's mother not been married at the time of his birth, he would probably have been acknowledged as Lord Aver's son and raised as a warrior—a job he fulfilled, anyway, two winters out of three, when the Iceriders came down from the North. Possibly he would have been made Thane, for he was nearer what the old lord had sought in a son than the bookish John.

John would have been happier, reflected Jenny, looking across the table at her husband, who was gesturing with a bannock as he talked and getting honey on his sleeve. He hated riding the summer circuit of courts of justice and making hard decisions about local crimes and squabbles, hated the hours of training required to maintain a warrior's muscle and reflexes. In his childhood, Muffle had been his sparring-partner, a young and angry Muffle who resented the boy who'd supplanted him.

Yet had Muffle been Thane there was a good chance that no one in the village would have survived the subsequent years, or the coming of the Golden Dragon to the North fifteen years ago. The blacksmith simply did not have John's wits, or John's ruthlessness.

It was enough to make one wonder, thought Jenny, about the ultimate intentions of the gods.

"Not the identical dream, of course," Muffle was saying now. "But along the same lines. Mol dreamed as how she'd lost a necklace she valued—those pearls that fool Gosbosom bought her from that trader. . . ."

"Why'd Farmer Gosbosom buy Mol Bucket a pearl necklace?" Adric wanted to know, and Aunt Jane said darkly, "Never you mind."

"In her dream, Ian found the necklace for her, deep in the woods near the Queen's Beck. But in her dream, Mol said, Ian couldn't find it if anyone but her was there. He said—or somebody said to her—*the spells won't show, if any's there to know.*" He frowned, cogitating on the matter for a time, then said, "But you see, two days later the necklace *did* go missin', an' she hasn't found it yet. I've told her as how you've said"—his glance went to Jenny—"not to go off like that in the woods, 'specially with Ian, but she's spoke to him of it. She spoke to him yesterday."

Ordinarily, of course, an invitation to go off into the woods with Mol Bucket involved neither dreams, spells, nor disappearing pearl necklaces—at least, unless one was the besotted Farmer Gosbosom. But Jenny said nothing, turning the matter over in her mind.

"When Dan Darrow dreamed that dream," Muffle went on after a moment, "it was his best heifer as was lost—that black one he calls Madame, with the white star on her forehead? And she was strayed away, next day, only of course Dan has more sense than to obey what someone whispers at him in a dream."

"I dreamed Roth would come back," said Peg, coming to the table with her bowl of stale bread crumbs in her hands. "My husband, you know, the goddess bless him wherever he is. Would come knockin' at the gate by the half-moon's light, in the tenth hour of the night, when all's pitch-dark an' cold." Her dark eyes were wistful, and in the hearth-glow her long brown braids gleamed with silver, which had been bright as a bay colt when Roth had started off across the hills to visit his sister in Far West Riding one autumn day.

"First I dreamed I went downstairs with Nin"—she named her youngest daughter, ten years old now—"and poor Roth held out his hand cryin', an' disappeared into the dark. That woke me, and when I slept again I dreamed again, and in my dream I got up and ran and fetched Muffle, like he'd told me to. But when we came to the gate all I saw of Roth was him fadin' back into the storm, cryin' my name."

The others at the table were silent. By their faces Jenny saw they'd heard the tale before, but it troubled them still. Ten years ago at the time of Roth's disappearance John had searched the Winterlands for weeks, for some sign of either his body or his desertion—for Roth the Gatekeeper had always been a lighthearted and light-minded man—and had found nothing.

"Well," said Peg, "on the night of the half-moon someone *did* come knock on the gate, in the tenth hour of the night, an' the night dead still an' calm. And I swear to you I didn't dare to even open the window, Jen. Just lay in the bed listenin'. Though the night was so still, no one cried out below. And after a while the knockin' stopped."

There was silence, and the weeping of the widowed winds against the shutters. Jenny reached back and put her hand over Peg's wrist. The gatekeeper gave her a tight cockeyed smile, like a child daring a chum to top *that* for a ghost story.

"Were there tracks?" John asked at last.

"You better believe there were tracks, an' none Roth would have made, neither, not with *his* narrow little feet." She turned back to the hearth, where Aunt Jane waited impatiently for the bread crumbs: no ghost tales for *her*.

"Did Farmer Darrow get Madame back?" Adric wanted to know.

"Oh, aye," Muffle said cheerily. "Found next day, over near the Wolf Hills, and it's a wonder the wolves didn't have the poor thing. I went down to the Queen's Beck after Mol told me of her dream, and found these tracks there, too. Barefoot tracks, staggerin' like as if him what made 'em was drunk or sick—or dyin' of cold, most like—but they went off into the glen straight enough. That was three days ago."

Jenny rose, as the talk turned onto other matters: the repairing of the stables, the prospects of the harvest's stored corn lasting until spring. Everyone, as usual, had to have his or her word and John talking nineteen to the dozen with them all as usual. Few noticed as Jenny picked up one of the sheepskin coats left to hang in the turret stair, and slung her plaids about her, and climbed the twisting stone flight to the walkway that circled the Hold's outer wall. The storm dragged at her skirts, shoved and thrust her about on the narrow battlement. Looking out over the wall, she could see only a blurred desolation of moorlands and heath, the village fields obscured by snow, the walls barely dark lines in the grayish white. Crescents of blowing ice skimmed the ground, the gauzy tracks of the wind.

She thought of her house on Frost Fell, and the solitary peace she had had there for so many years, alone with the winds, and her herbs, and her cats.

What are you? John had asked her, and she had replied, *What I am.*

Miss Mab had said, *The magic comes from what thou art, and all that thou art.*

The good and the bad. The dragon and the demon and the woman who had turned aside from them both.

She saw Morkeleb, a skeleton shadow silhouetted in the mealy sleet, and grieved for a moment that she could not be two beings, and have two futures. But that, she understood now, was the essence of humankind. To have only one, and to choose.

She held out her hands: *my friend.*

Wizard-woman. He hung in the air, obscured by the blowing twilight but untouched, beautiful with the lean, thorny beauty of the dragon-kind, and his voice in her mind was the velvet essence of dreaming. *Your Dreamweaver has said that he saw the Demon Queen, walking abroad in the sunlight of the streets; therefore must I go. She knows you have the catch-bottle still. She will journey to the Skerries of Light, lest others arrive there first and wrest from Corvin the secret of her name. Beware, Wizard-woman. This they will try to do, the servants of Folcalor and the servants of Adromelech and whoever Aohila finds to serve her—or tricks into doing her will—once they know the bottle is in your possession as well.*

I will beware, she said. *Can you not, Dragonshadow, warn Corvin in dreams, that fly swifter even than the flight of dragons to the islands of the west?*

And she felt the ripple of annoyance and scorn. Whatever else Morkeleb had laid aside, when he had laid aside his magic, there was still evidently the matter between Corvin and himself of which dragon was still the greatest loremaster and sorcerer of all of dragon-kind.

If I warned him in dreaming of fire raining from the sky in the next hour, still he would but turn over in his sleep. And if I warned others—Centhwevir and Yrsgendl and Enismirdal—I am not sure they would understand. It is not a thing of dragons, to band together, save in our flights between the stars. I must go myself, and see what I can accomplish.

Are you not, as Dragonshadow, able to convince Corvin of his danger? Or lead the others?

The Dragonshadows . . . He hesitated, as if not certain that she would understand. And she heard in her mind the music of the Dragonshadows, felt the spirit-light and the warmth of them, dazzling and simple yet incomprehensible—even to the dragons, never understood.

And she remembered saying to John, *What I am . . .*

The Dragonshadows did not lead us, he said at length. *We came here, and they followed. I suspect—but I do not know—they followed because they loved us.*

Yes, thought Jenny, feeling, understanding, that this was true. *Yes.*

But I did not understand this at the time, because I did not understand what it was to love.

Once you said to me, Wizard-woman, that the key to magic is to be found in magic, and the key to love, in love. The love that I learned of you was indeed my bane as a dragon. But like all true banes, all death, it proved to be a gate through which I passed into an unknown country. As for the Dragonshadows, they are very old, and have observed many things, and dreamed upon what they have seen. Yet most dragons never ask them why dragons exist, and what it means that we have the abilities that we have. Much less have they queried about the things that dwell on all the various worlds that we have seen. And now that I have passed that gate myself, and become a Dragonshadow, and seek the answers to these questions, they are gone.

Things are as they are, Wizard-woman. And things being as they are, the only thing that I can do is go to the Skerries of Light to warn my nestmates—it was the first time she had heard him speak of relationship, or comradeship, with the others of his kind—*of the danger they are in, and speak to them of your Dreamweaver's plan. I will return in a fortnight, to bear you and your Dreamweaver south again, time and to spare to be there ere the demons come to that place.*

Blessings ... And the word could not encompass all that she wished for him, the shining glory of fortune and hope that she poured into his mind. It surprised him—she could feel it—as the understanding of love had once surprised him.

And blessings on your nestmates, Centhwevir Blue-and-Golden, and Nymr the Blue, on my lovely green-and-gold Mellyn and Enismirdal and Yrsgendl and the others that were saved from the demons.

Morkeleb said, *Blessings upon you and yours,* and she felt the hesitancy of his musical thoughts, and knew that he had never blessed anyone before.

His blessing was like a double-handful of chiming stars.

He turned upon the wind, and flew away through the dark afternoon toward the west.

"How long's this storm been blowin'?" John was asking as Jenny came back into the kitchen. Several more people had arrived, Blossom and Aunt Hol and Muffle's daughter Cobweb and old Granny Brown, all of them talking at once and offering advice to Peg about what belonged in the pie.

"This's the second day," Aunt Rowe said, without even a pause at her loom.

"Anyone else had any dreams?"

"If they have," said Muffle, "they're keepin' it to themselves."

John nodded thoughtfully, and glanced at Jenny across Mag's bent red head. "Someone will," he said.

The someone was Aunt Jane.

She had always disliked Jenny, having seen what loving a witch-wife had done to her brother. During the weeks of Jenny's estrangement from John, Jane had said cruel things about Jenny, both to John and to Ian, and to other women in the village as well. So Jenny was surprised, the next day, when she and Ian were sorting dried herbs in the loft above the kitchen, to hear Jane's heavy step creak on the ladder, and the woman's deep voice call out, "Mistress Jenny?"

Jenny and Ian worked in near-darkness—night-sighted as mages are—but as Jane's red coif appeared above the trapdoor, Jenny kindled the wicks of the two iron lamps that hung on the wall near the great warm column of the kitchen chimney. "Thank you," said Jane, as Ian came to help her—unnecessarily but politely—up the last few rungs. "Might I speak to your mother a bit alone, sweeting?" And she turned to Jenny, her square, heavy face uncomfortable in the wavery glow. The worst of the storm had abated during the night, but winds still scoured across the heath, and the day was very cold. This room, and the kitchen beneath it, were some of the few in the Hold that were genuinely warm, and shirts and petticoats were hung here to dry beneath rafter-loads of smoked meats and cheeses, fare on which the Hold folk lived most of the winter. The vast, dim attic smelled of rosemary and onions and clean linen, and smoke from the kitchen below.

"I think I've had the dream you spoke of in the kitchen yesterday afternoon," Jane said. "The dream of taking Ian out somewhere away from the Hold, into the woods."

"To find something only he could find?" Jenny brought over a firkin of raisins for her to sit on, and settled herself beside one of the smooth-scrubbed marble slabs where apples were dried in the fall.

"In a manner of speaking." Jane folded her big brown hands. "I dreamed there was a woman, a—a lady, hurt by bandits and needing help, but fearing to let any grown woman or man come near to her. It didn't feel like it had aught to do with stupid ruses, like Mol Bucket's necklace—not that those were real pearls, any more real than the kisses Gosbosom bought with them. But I saw this hurt lady plain, a sweet, decent woman, and needing healing, huddled out there in the storm. And I knew—and I think this is what made me know this was a sent dream after all—I knew that our John would fall in love with her. I saw them together, and him holding her hands, and looking at her with the eyes of love. And that was when I woke, and knew this was telling me what . . . what I wanted to hear."

Jenny was silent, looking into the older woman's apologetic dark eyes. Downstairs she dimly heard the thump of Aunt Rowe's loom, and Dilly's voice telling Mag a story in the kitchen. John was at the castle forge, engaged on a project with Muffle that even before breakfast had covered both men with soot and grime and the dust from the vaults beneath the Hold, where John had unearthed the debris of some curious old projects of his own. John had burned his workroom, before riding forth on his errantry for the Demon Queen. The things he had dragged out to work on with Muffle were years old, covered with mildew and rust.

In any case, Jenny reflected, Jane would not have spoken to John about that dream. Not to Muffle, certainly, nor to any other in the Hold. "Thank you," she said simply. "That was clever of you, to read the deception in something that . . . that unobvious."

Jane sniffed, and got to her feet. "I may not be clever like my nephew," she said, with her wry toothy smile, "but I've lived long enough to know that a man who holds out candy in one hand usually has a rope in the other." She added grudgingly, "And I know John'll never love any but you."

And you know a woman would understand that dream, thought Jenny, *and a man, not—or not in this way.* She said, "Where was this woman lying hurt?"

"In your old house," she said. "On Frost Fell."

Ian rode out to Frost Fell alone the following morning, when the winds finally sank away. From the attic of the small stone house, where she had watched John vanish into winter's first snowfall, Jenny listened for her son, sitting beside the hole where the steep stair ascended. She had scried the storm's ending just before dawn, and had taken the road over the crest of Toadback Hill under cover of the final flurries of blowing sleet. As the wind calmed, snow began to fall, a thin dusting that covered her tracks. Just after that, Bill and Sergeant Muffle went out to cut brush in the cranberry bog, which, John pointed out, was actually the logical place to ambush someone bound for Frost Fell. Between the bog and the Fell itself, there was no cover.

So the ambush would have to be here in the house.

Jenny smelled Caradoc when he entered, coming in through the old stable where Ian would not see his tracks. Her nape prickled. It was here, in early summer, that the demon-possessed wizard had waited for Ian. All those months ago—a lifetime, it felt like. And to this house Ian's dreams of despair had driven him after the loss of his demon, when he feared Folcalor's will would bend him to open a demon gate, as Bliaud had been bent. Even without Folcalor dwelling in his mind anymore, Caradoc would remember this place, as Jenny remembered the Sea-wights' Hell.

Fool, she thought, listening to the faint, squelching thumps in the kitchen below. The stench of rotting flesh drifted up to her despite the afternoon's bitter cold. When he had taken the corpse of a dead sailor for his body, Caradoc had spoken of bargaining with Folcalor, of "making what he could" of the situation and of his knowledge. *Is this your idea of rescue?* he had demanded.

Trapped in the moonstone, Caradoc had some power, weak and attenuated but possibly, Jenny reflected, almost as strong as her own small gifts were now. What he would do, or might do, with the greater powers that were Ian's, if he should kill the boy and use a demon spell to enter his body, she could only imagine.

Years ago the man had been trapped by Folcalor through his vanity, his lust for greater powers than he had. And it was only a matter of time, thought Jenny, before he was trapped so again. It was clear to her he had not changed his belief in his own cleverness.

Silence below, a waiting silence. Jenny, crouched close to the top of the attic stair, waited also. And touched, at her belt beneath the thick sheepskins of her coat, the silver catch-bottle that had held, for a short time, the Demon Queen. This never left her. Folcalor had too many agents in this world.

Had the rebellious demon seized the Burning Mirror, as John had said in the ruins of the mirror chamber in Ernine? Jenny had watched Aohila from almost the moment of Folcalor's departure, until she'd trapped her. She didn't think the Demon Queen had had the opportunity to move the mirror herself.

And where was she now? What would she do, with the ten days

until the setting of the Dragonstar returned the powers of the demons to what they had been for the past thousand years?

Would she go to the Skerries of Light, as Morkeleb feared? Would the Dragonshadow encounter her there, in that solitary world of rocks and birds and shining water? And would he encounter her before she could destroy Corvin, or seize him as she had seized him before?

Below her Jenny heard stealthy creaking, as if Caradoc leaned his weight on one of the bent-willow chairs for support. Her quick ears picked up the crunch of hooves on the frozen road up the Fell. She didn't move—didn't dare. If he was able, within his borrowed body, to send out dreams, he had sufficient use of the corpse's senses to detect her movements in the attic. She could not count on his being distracted by his prey's coming. Her sore hip was stiff from sitting in one position and her back ached. She hoped she wouldn't stumble when it came time to leap down the stair.

John's right, she thought wryly. *We're both getting too old for this.*

The light squeak of snow as Ian dismounted. His soft, husky alto: "Is anyone there?"

"Here!" gasped a reply, startlingly woman-like, hushed and pleading. "Dear gods . . ."

The squeak of the iron door hinges. Ian's boots on the flagstoned passage floor. "Where are you? Are you all right?"

"Here! Kitchen . . . oh, please . . . I am dying. . . ."

"Smells to me like you're gie dead already," said John, from the kitchen door.

Jenny was on her feet and down the stair, halberd in hand, as Caradoc whirled. She lashed out with a counterspell that completely failed to block whatever Word of pain and confusion he laid on John— John gasped, staggered, and Jenny cursed at her own weak uncertain powers, and stepping forward, whacked Caradoc hard behind the knees as he tried to rush John in the kitchen doorway. The wizard collapsed with a grunt and struck the floor, and from beneath the ragged gown he wore gusted a still fouler graveyard stench.

"Bitch!" Caradoc gasped, struggling to stand and clearly unable to do so. "Damn you black, you whore-hag!" A line of brownish fluid trickled from under the hem of the robes, and Caradoc raised a face that was bloated, discolored, sunken with rot. The eyes remained to him, and the tongue, though it was swollen so that his speech was distorted. The hair that surrounded the horrible visage was brown, what little was left of it, so Jenny knew he'd transferred the talisman moonstone at least once, from the original blond sailor's corpse to another, and who knew how many besides? "You see what you've done?"

"Little enough, given what you deserve," John remarked, and pulled up a bench—warily—to sit. He still looked a trifle gray around the lips with the shock of whatever pain-spell Caradoc had thrown at him, but he had his sword in hand, and Jenny was willing to bet he could carve the animate corpse to collops before another such spell could be laid.

"What *I* deserve?" Caradoc's glottal voice was thick with genuine indignation, rage, and self-pity. "For being enslaved by demons—for only trying to preserve my life ... ?"

"For bein' bone-stupid enough to call on Folcalor in the first place." John propped his spectacles with the back of one mailed knuckle. "Without which piece of poor judgment we wouldn't none of us be in the fix we're in now. Not to mention what you've tried to do to me son. You all right, Ian?" He raised his voice to a yell.

"I'm fine." Ian appeared in the doorway, and drew back with a wince at the horror on the floor between his parents.

"Stay back for now," ordered Jenny. "Watch the front of the house."

"You can't blame me for trying to save my own life," repeated Caradoc sulkily.

"But you aren't trying to save your life," pointed out Jenny, still holding her weapon ready. "Your life is perfectly preserved, within that moonstone. And at least a residuum of your powers. You are trying to steal my son's powers—and to murder him, to take his place in his body."

"That's preposterous."

"It's also beside the point," remarked John. "Because you're not goin' to be able to do it, even if it is why you did all that shadow-show with the dreams an' tryin' to get folk to open the Hold gates an' all. You know it's only a matter of time before Folcalor finds you, or one of the demons workin' for Adromelech, or Aohila for that matter—you know she's out from behind the mirror? I thought not. Or till wolves catch up with you, or a warm spell brings on maggots to finish you off an' you spend the next couple centuries trapped in that moonstone under a dead tree somewhere, tryin' to talk some bandit into killin' a traveler an' haulin' the corpse to where you can use it, which'll be a pretty complicated set of instructions to get across in a dream. Now I have a bargain for you, if you like."

"Piss on you."

"Bit cold in here, isn't it, love?" He glanced over at Jenny. "Shall I build a fire here in the stove? Thaw things out a bit?"

And he flinched, as if at the stab of migraine.

"All we have to do is wait, Caradoc," pointed out Jenny. "Folcalor *will* find you. Don't tell me you don't believe that he can, or that you're cleverer than he. He *can't* let you remain free. He wants the talisman jewel that contains your soul, so that he can use it as a weapon against Adromelech: fodder for his spells against the Henge, as I would have been, and Ian. As all those other poor souls have been, that he's been buying from the gnomes."

"If you know that," said Caradoc petulantly, "you can't blame me for—"

"You've known that from the start," Jenny cut him off. "And you can't bargain with him. You know his name, his true name, the inner heart of him. You had him living within your brain. You are the only mage who can trap him." She took the catch-bottle from her belt, held it up, gleaming in the gray-blue morning light from the kitchen door. "In this."

Caradoc's eyes seemed to bulge at the sight of the bottle; his lips parted and he reached out with one sticky, crumbling hand. "Where did you get that?"

"Do you know it?"

He nodded, making his head lurch sickeningly to one side— he did not appear to be able to straighten it afterward. "*He* knew it. He was seeking it. The Star-Juggler made it, in the deeps of time. The Arch-Seer, who knew more of demons than any of the rest. Folcalor bade me go to Ernine in search of it, but after he ... after I ..." He waved a hand dismissively, still not able to admit how he had been tricked and betrayed, and with a twist of his mouth brushed aside the

end of the sentence like a cobweb. "In the end, even with the protection of a human body upon him, and that body a mage, he feared to
go too near the mirror."

"Smarter than I thought," remarked John.

"Now that you have it, he will do anything, pay you anything."

"The trap's been sprung," said Jenny. "And it must be set again.
Not for Aohila this time, but for Folcalor. You understand why
Folcalor can not, will not permit you to live."

"Botched it up, eh?" The dead eyes glittered nastily. "Trust a
woman to fumble a simple act like getting the cork out of a bottle and
then back in again. Or did the bitch talk you into letting her go?"

Jenny said nothing, but John folded his arms and commented,
"Well, we all know how good demons are at talkin' even perfectly intelligent wizards into doin' daft things, don't we?"

"He didn't talk me into anything," insisted Caradoc petulantly.
"He took me at a disadvantage, unfairly . . . and what's in it for me, if I
help you? And don't spew me bilgewater about the holy peacefulness
of death. There's not much I can do to prevent you from smashing
the talisman jewel once I've given you what you want, is there? And it
isn't likely you'll hand your son over to me. I'm sure there's some nice
fresh corpses around, but do you know, my dear, I'm a little tired of
surviving this way. So what can you offer me, really?"

John leaned back against the stone wall and crossed his ankles,
"A body that'll stay fresh and won't rot," he said.

The bulging, discolored eyes swiveled his way. Studied him,
while the fluids trickled from whatever had burst or ruptured under
those ragged robes when he fell. "Go on."

"Back in the days when I was first learnin' how gears an' pulleys
worked, I made a lot of metal limbs that worked by 'em. Even made a
metal hand, with all these little joints an' wheels an' cables. Me dad
wore me out with a strap, when he found what I'd been sneakin' off to
the forge to do, instead of gettin' on with learnin' to ride an' shoot an'
kill people. Now, I saw in this movie . . ."

He paused, clearly trying to rearrange an explanation of what
a *movie* was—he'd told Jenny, who had been fascinated, and the two
of them had spent hours discussing how moving pictures such as
he had seen in the Otherworld might have been brought about.

He amended, "I heard a tale of a bloke who made a man out

of bits of metal like this, an' brought it to life, an' it walked about an' did all sorts of things. Talked, too, I think. But if you can make dead muscle an' dead cartilage pull an' twist an' balance, why not wire an' wheels?" He pushed his spectacles up onto the bridge of his nose again. "Beats hidin' in the woods waitin' for a thaw, anyway."

Chapter 15

*D*o *you trust this wizard?* asked Morkeleb, three days later when Jenny rode out again to Frost Fell in the clear cold westering light. The wind that had set over from the sea on the morning of Ian's visit to the stone house on the Fell had blown, chill but steady, driving back the storms from the North: Last night Jenny had guessed what it meant. In dreams she'd seen them, beautiful shapes like silk and bones, skimming over the beryl ocean, and in her mind she'd heard the music that was their names.

Centhwevir Blue-and-Golden, had said the old list, which had made no sense at the time, and with the list, the gay brilliant threnody of a tune; *Nymr is blue, violet-crowned . . .*

Other music, which she'd learned in her days of possession, in her days of union with the demons that had ridden these creatures, these star-drakes, these magical wanderers through space and time. The curious bass sonorities of the true name of Yrsgendl White-and-Scarlet, the minor twirls and twists of pink-and-green Hagginarshildim, the beautiful soaring dance of Mellyn. When she had saved these creatures, these souls, from the grasp of the demons, she had seen what no one in all John's lore or all the tales of the Line of Herne had ever spoken of: how all these airs blended together, into a single entity a thousand thousand years long and more.

And they were coming here.

An hour after noon she saddled Moon Horse, and rode out to the Fell alone.

And there she saw them, winging down from the pale cloud-streaked sky, like a V of butterflies but flying fast, a bright-colored arrow whose tip was silver and black. They broke formation and hovered, flowers floating on the clear air. Their voices reached down to her, unearthly music in her mind. *Dragonfriend . . . dragonfriend . . .* silver bells and falling water and blue crystal chimes deep as night. *Well with you . . . well. . . .*

She held up her hands to them: *Blessing,* she said. *Blessing.*

They settled to the ground. Seven of them she knew, even the rainbow-colored youngling whose name had only begun to form—Byrs, she thought it was—he had had no name in the days of the demons, though that was only six months ago. The eighth, black and silver with eyes like green opal, settled a little apart, and she said to him, *Corvin NinetyfiveFifty?* And heard in her mind the light voice, human-sounding like Morkeleb's was.

This was the name I was called, in the Otherworld. And you will be the Lady Jenny, Lord Aversin's wife.

Yes, said Jenny. *I am John's wife. Thank you beyond what I can say, for saving his life.*

She had known Morkeleb was among them, invisible, when she first saw them flying, and indeed he melted into being, like a razor-armored snake wrought of shadows: he touched her mind and smiled.

Do you trust this wizard? he asked.

He has no reason to lie, she said, and hoped that Caradoc, lying in a guarded tower frozen now in buckets of snow, could not cast his mind this far, to hear their words. *Betraying us would put him back into the hands of those who would use his soul for kindling-wood, if nothing worse.* She must ask Centhwevir, she thought, if his mind was linked with Caradoc's still in dreams. Ask Yrsgendl whether Bliaud had ever tried to speak to him with the remnants of the demon-forged link. Their answers might tell her how much danger Corvin stood in, of being retaken by Aohila.

Mellyn, who had been her own dragon, reached out a shy thought to her, like a cat bumping her nape from the back of a chair. The young jere-drake—a female who had not yet taken on the characteristics of a bearing matron—did not form her thoughts into human words, having not been in the practice of taking human form, but their music made Jenny want to dance.

He knows what Folcalor would do with him, with the moonstone that holds his soul, should he gain possession of it. He knows that his only hope is to trap Folcalor, and work for his defeat. Beyond that, no.

And she shivered, drawing her plaid close about her, thinking about the stench of Caradoc's current corpse as Bill and Muffle had dragged it by sledge from Frost Fell to the Hold. About the way those sticky, bulging eyes had followed her, when she'd drawn the protective circle around it in the disused dungeon beneath the southeast tower. John and the others had hauled in buckets of snow for three days now to dump over the corpse, in the unheated stone chamber ("There was this vid I saw in the Otherworld, about this creature that they kept frozen in ice like this, till some chap threw a magic blanket over it and it all melted. . . .").

I trust your son is nowhere within those walls.

My son sleeps in the house of my sister in the village; his brother and sister with him. It had cost John and Jenny both a good deal of uneasiness, deciding whether to keep their children where they themselves could defend them—but where Caradoc would almost certainly know their whereabouts—or to conceal them at a distance, trusting in Ian's skill of dealing with emergencies. Jenny guessed that in the ghoul-mage's weakened condition he could not spread out his awareness to the village, but she wasn't sure. Every villager and every inhabitant of the Hold had been instructed not to speak the children's true names ("Have everyone call me Alkmar Thunderhand," requested Adric breathlessly); Jenny hoped that this would serve.

At least I trust Adric is still there, she added drily. *Though he begged to see this thing that John and Muffle are creating, this "robot" as John speaks of it.* This had been not the least of the reasons for the final decision.

Robot, sniffed Corvin, the dark ripple of his scorn slapping like a little wave against her mind. *Pah.*

As for Caradoc, I think he still believes himself smarter than either Folcalor or Adromelech, capable of double tricking them, of playing off one against another to his own ends. This vanity above all else makes him a perilous ally; this arrogant belief that he understands all things about the situation, and is more clever than everyone else involved.

They are amazing creatures, humans. The black dragon shifted his weight on his haunches, and all his bristling scales sparkled with the fading afternoon light. *How much greater is their variety than among dragons; how astonishing the beliefs they convince themselves are true. CAN he summon the Hellspawn, in the state that he is in?*

That I do not know, for I do not know how much magic remains to him in the decaying flesh of a non-mage's corpse. Yet I do not doubt Folcalor listens for him, and also whatever demon agents Adromelech commands who walk this world. And as she spoke the warring demons' names, she felt the whisper of uneasiness among the drag- ons, handing the shared memories of their possessions back and forth among them, a deadly sound in Jenny's mind, like the hissing of tide over rocks. *Perhaps we should ask, can he conceal himself from them, and for how long? Did you see the Demon Queen near the Skerries of Light?*

The dragon Corvin bristled at her name, and in the music of his anger Jenny heard, despite himself, the winding threnody of fear.

I saw a thing that hung above the waters like blue mist shot with lightning, said Morkeleb. *Yet when I turned my eyes upon it, it dissolved and fled away. Birds fled from certain of the isles, where we later found a stench and the marks of strange tracks, and some among us heard the whispering of her voice in dreams.* He glanced sidelong at the black- and-silver dragon, who lashed his tail uneasily.

Jenny guessed that Corvin had discovered what John had learned: that once the Demon Queen marked a man—or a dragon— with her silvery signs, she had access to his dreams wherever he fled.

We must travel on, said Morkeleb. *The winds of the winter are strong. We cannot hold them at bay forever, and we have far to go. Have you read through your Dreamweaver's notes, concerning all he has learned of the demons? For these are things that we must know, if we are to escape their notice and their power.*

I have read through what he has written, said Jenny, and indeed, for three days, while John and Muffle worked at putting the "robot" together and testing its cables and joints, she had done little else. The notes were made on every kind of paper imaginable, on scraps of vel- lum purchased from Father Hiero in the village and the papyrus-reed paper brought north by the last trader to the King's garrison at Caer Corflyn two years ago, and sheet after sheet of something John called plast, which he'd acquired in the Otherworld, and all of it in John's cramped tiny bookhand, which fortunately Jenny had learned, too, from the same sour old hedge-wizard who had taught John.

The notes spoke of marvels, of Hells and worlds unimaginable; of gates and traps and monsters. Sketch after sketch in John's cock- eyed scribble: carry-beasts and demonettes and things like wheels of fire. Doorways in rock, wells hidden in canyons of stone; runes and sigils and the tracks of nameless beasts. Things that had to be computers, and long lines of the symbols in which they spoke. Charts of ether-crystal relays. Facts about not only the Dragonstar, but other stars of Heaven as well.

Sketches of faces—the friends who had looked after him in that alien Otherworld. An old man with a mole on his nose. A fat, bearded man with something that looked like spectacles wrapped around his face. A rangy, slightly potbellied woman with kindly eyes, combing her long hair.

Jenny felt Morkeleb's mind enter hers, touching and drinking all that she had read, in one great brilliant draught. Thus it was, she understood, that dragons passed lore on to one another, like great single pictures or tapestries, to be recalled and told over in detail later, over the course of months or years. And in his taking from her, she glimpsed the endless, bottomless, starless wells of the old dragon's lore, roads going back and back into time beyond the world, tales learned and never forgotten, spells mastered and compared and put aside. Visions and dreams and fragments of memory clear as jewels emerging from that darkness, so that all John's journeyings, all John's notes, were swallowed up in the dragon's greater journeyings like a drop in the sea.

She stared, wonderingly, into that vista of dark treasure-rooms, and from its midst Morkeleb looked back at her, as if from the threshold he held out his hand.

It was beyond human comprehension.

Turning away from dragon form, she had turned away from this.

And for a moment they regarded each other, in understanding and regret.

Then Morkeleb said, *Thank you, Wizard-woman. What you have given me is something I do not think a dragon would have seen or understood. As for the rest, there will be time for us to trade lore, you and I.*

I am what I am, thought Jenny, watching as the dragons lifted from the Fell and circled like brilliant birds in the evening light. *I could not choose other than what I chose.* Yet she felt the regret, a little, as she raised her hand to them, understanding that in her short human span she could not absorb a hundredth of Morkeleb's lore, not even if she lived to deep old age.

But we all are what we are.

She returned to the stable of the little stone house, where she had left Moon Horse in her usual stall. The west wind had failed, and the storm clouds were scudding gray from the north by the time Jenny reached the Hold again.

In the blacksmith's shop off the main courtyard, John and Muffle were fitting the central gear-box onto John's robot, a sort of iron basket that would hold Caradoc's moonstone talisman and, joined to it by silver wires, the smallest of the succession of gears that would power the machine's six limbs.

"In the movie the robot was made to look like a human bein'," said John, spectacles glaring back the flame of the forge. John had explained that the spell of tongues that Aohila had laid upon him in the Otherworld had only worked with direct human speech, not whatever caused sound to come from the animate pictures alternately called movies and vids—he'd had to guess a great deal of what was happening and why. "God knows why they made it look human. There wasn't a hope of foolin' anybody about what it was. But I tried that, too, back when I first tried to build a mechanical man when I was twelve, and the thing wouldn't even balance, let alone walk, always supposin' I could have powered it somehow."

He tapped the robot with one booted foot. "I never did get that right in later attempts. This'll at least move about."

And it probably would, thought Jenny uneasily.

Even as dragons stayed aloft in flight by the magic of their minds, rather than by any physical manipulation of wings and air, so the robot was supported by a pair of wood-and-iron wheels that held up, at the end of a short stake, the egg-shaped iron basket that housed the gear-relays and the moonstone that held Caradoc's soul. A knot of pulleys and gears multiplied whatever force the magic of the moonstone would generate to the limbs, which were hollow steel, the lightest and strongest alloy John had been able to obtain over years of trading with the gnomes.

Familiar with John's experiments, Jenny remembered these limbs. They'd originally been part of a system of ballistas that John had alleged would hurl stones from the highest castle turrets without danger to those who operated them. Their pulleys and springs had been rearranged, and they'd been fitted with round wooden feet, padded in leather to give them traction on the stones of the floor. A fifth limb supported John's youthful masterpiece, the five-fingered steel hand whose wheels and pulleys mimicked the arrangement of human tendons and joints. A sixth limb, also projecting upward, sported a simple iron pincer: Jenny had seen John and Muffle working on it the previous day.

"We figured he'd need more than one hand," Muffle explained. He and John were like a couple of soot-black devils, unshaven, half-naked in the shop's dense heat and streaky with sweat. Jenny was hugely reminded of Ian and Adric, when the boys were engaged in one of their messier pranks. Both men were grinning like schoolboys let loose in a candy shop. Jenny knew neither had had more than a modicum of food or sleep in days and knew that neither cared.

"The thing takes a deal of oilin', see," added John. "The hand, especially, just about every time it moves. The pincer'll do to daub goose-grease on it, an' work a polishin' cloth."

"A lot depends on how much weight Caradoc's able to shift just by magic from within the moonstone," put in Muffle, pointing with his pliers. "How much friction he can push against. D'you have any idea, Jen?"

She shook her head. "How much of magic lies in the flesh, and how much in the mind, I don't know," she said. "I don't think anyone does. Nor do I know how strong Caradoc's powers actually were, when it was just his own mind in his flesh; nor whether his long possession by Folcalor increased his abilities or lessened them."

"Well, he couldn't have had much magic as a human, could he?" John turned back to crimp the clamps that held the basket among the nest of gears. Firelight gleamed on the Demon Queen's marks, traced on his bare shoulders and arms. "You've said that's what Folcalor tempted him with, wasn't it? More power?"

"But that doesn't mean Caradoc's power was weak." Jenny smiled with wry understanding. "There isn't a mage in the world who wouldn't risk his soul—or her soul—trying to secure more. We're stupid that way."

And John looked down at her and grinned, and wiped the sweat from his face, leaving a long streak of grime. He'd risked his own life too many times hunting for rare books not to understand. "Could you see, Jen, when you were inside the talisman? See an' hear?"

"After a fashion." Jenny perched herself on the corner of the saw-bench, and shrugged out of her sheepskin jacket, for the low vaults of the ceiling trapped the heat like an oven and with the failure of the daylight a dozen torches had been kindled around the walls. She frowned, trying to remember the weird timelessness of her green crystal prison, of feeling her body and being unable to control it. Of feeling Amayon dwelling in her mind.

She tried to separate those memories from the exhilaration of power, from the deadly sweetness of Amayon's constant presence, the whispering voice that assured her of his love even when he made her do hideous things. Some memories were still hard to sift: Was it her own delight that she remembered, in being utterly without responsibilities, without consequences to any action she took? Or was that, like the recollection of his name, only something he'd left behind?

She shook her head, pulling away from the shame and despair she'd felt in the wintertime, healing now but still close beneath the surface of her mind.

"It wasn't exactly sight, or precisely hearing," she said. "But I did know what was going on around me. But then, I saw and heard through my own eyes and ears as well. In the talisman I could feel sensations of the body from which I was separated. What it would be like once the body is dead, I don't know."

"Seems like a gie lot of trouble to me." Muffle knelt, holding up a water-filled glass lantern to throw magnified light into the egg-shaped seat so that he could hook up the twisted wire cables. "Can't be that painful to die, can it? I mean, within the talisman."

He spoke jestingly, but the glance he gave her from under his sparse reddish eyebrows was serious, and Jenny spoke seriously in reply.

"That also I don't know," she said. "I have no idea what Caradoc felt when I speared his body beneath the sea, when the demon went out of it and ceased to keep it alive. The Whalemages sent fish to devour the body, with him alive still in the moonstone talisman. He was there, he must have seen it, as well as felt it. It's no wonder," she added thoughtfully, "he won't forgive me that. But I think he fears death for the same reason that the demons do: because it is a state that he cannot control, and he cannot be *in* control. No more than any of us does he know what lies beyond. He does not and will not surrender his power over himself."

"Is that such a bad thing?" inquired Muffle, after a little silence and a few scatological comments addressed to the pulleys. "It's what kept you alive in the talisman, isn't it? What kept our Johnny alive in the Hell behind the Mirror."

"I suppose it depends on the lengths you'll go to, to stay alive."

Cousin Dilly came in, sleet beading her long dark braids, to tell them supper was ready in the kitchen: All three said, "We'll be there in a few minutes," and immediately forgot all about eating as they started hooking up, and testing again, the final adjustments on the pulleys and cables.

For days now Jenny had watched the thing take shape, her deep misgivings alternating with excitement and interest at this bizarre and curious machine. Years of watching John tinker with mechanical clocks, with flying machines, with self-propelling sleds and steam-opening doors had given her some familiarity with the workings of such devices, but she had never seen anything remotely like this.

She saw, too, how John's journeyings through another world had sharpened his judgment of mechanical efficiency, and wondered what direction—if they survived the next week—his future experiments would take.

In the ice-cold deeps of the night they dragged the sled bearing Caradoc, propped in one of the kitchen chairs from the Frost Fell house, across the courtyard from the old stable to the forge. Ice-winds were well and truly blowing down from the north by then, and after the heat of the forge the southeast tower dungeon, and the courtyard in between, were like frozen marble.

Stiff-frozen and barely smelling at all now, Caradoc's eyes could not even narrow as he studied the insect-like robot, with its round tiny body and its mismatched limbs. On top, between the two arms, John had set a bulbous wooden sounding-box made from portions of two mandolins, covered with tuning-keys to stretch and adjust the strings of catgut and wire within. "It'll take you a while to learn to sound 'em," said John apologetically. "It's the best we could do at short notice, understand. But it won't rot, an' you won't have to keep on goin' from body to body."

The muscles of the dead face twitched against the ice that held them. Jenny could almost hear him thinking, *I would not have to keep going from body to body if I could have the body of a mage....*

But even that, she thought, might not be true. There were few enough mageborn, whose human magic could animate the flesh of a corpse and keep it from rotting once death occurred. And none that she knew of who could displace a living mage from his body, and take his place.

But she did not know how to say so to Caradoc without offense. And, in any case, she thought, looking at those glinting, angry eyes, she doubted that he would believe her. He would rather believe the world was conspiring to victimize him, when he'd made only a reasonable request.

They dragged him into the storeroom beside the blacksmith shop, where the cold still gripped, to ensorcel the catch-bottle. Jenny set candles around the Circle of Power, and the outer Circle of Ward, as the animate corpse clasped its dead hands around the silver bottle, and bent frozen lips to whisper Folcalor's secret name into its neck.

But the wizard spoke nothing aloud. Within the circles Jenny had drawn, Caradoc drew others, though he was barely able to command his decomposed muscles, and fell and staggered like a drunken man. He marked these circles with sigils she recognized as demonic, and the power she felt in the still cold air of the room seemed to creep along her skin. From the Ward-Circle she had drawn around herself and John she watched the wizard sway, clinging to the back of the chair, and the candle flames burned blue, the darkness creeping in between them. More than ever, now, she was glad she had kept Ian out of the ghoul-wizard's sight. She wished for her son's power, and for the knowledge he had of demons, to check what she could not of Caradoc's sorceries. But not at the cost of the risk she sensed he would run, to be in the same room—or even the same fortress wall—with this unstable and unnatural thing.

At last, Caradoc set the bottle down, and made passes with his hands over it. Then he beckoned her forward. "It is accomplished," he whispered. He seemed to melt into the chair, and let Jenny unmake the circles, and call back the Limitations and Boundaries of the spells. She could hear a horrible gurgling sound from him, though he did not breathe, and once he turned to her and snapped, "Oh, for the love of the gods, woman, hurry up!"

"So the trap is set." John stepped carefully from the unmade Circle of Ward, and crossed to pick up the bottle as Muffle peeked cautiously around the door.

"It should fetch him, if he can be fetched." Caradoc's voice was little more than a gluey slur. The spells had clearly drained him of what energy and power he possessed—energy and power that kept the corpse moving in a semblance of life. "And I warn you both, there's a curse upon my death, a curse sourced *in* my death. Curse . . . the one who destroys the moonstone." He mumbled like a drunken man, head jerking on the dissolving muscles of the neck.

"Where'd you get the thing, Jenny? . . . old magic, old power . . . Star-Juggler was the greatest of them all. Only needed the name . . . Once you seal him in it, what then, eh? Folcalor . . . he's powerful—tricky. Bottle . . . needs power—constant source. He escapes, you'll be in trouble." He cocked an eye up at John mockingly. "Or had you thought?"

John's glance crossed Jenny's, and in his eyes she saw her own thought: *He's heard of the catch-bottle, but he doesn't know how it works. Doesn't know it's a double trap.*

That means Folcalor doesn't know, either.

And if Folcalor doesn't know, neither does Adromelech.

Both drew a long breath, and let it out, words unsaid.

"Bargain wisely," muttered Caradoc as the Muffle came forward and together the brothers prepared to drag the sledge back through the door to the forge's heat. "Can't hold him yourself . . . have to sell it . . . Adromelech. Bargain wisely, and after, you'd better run fast."

They sent Muffle away, though Jenny, listening, could hear his breath and the beating of his heart in the wood-store just the other side of the smithy. She drew the signs of ward and guard all around the corpse on its sledge, and the spider-like robot in the corner of the smithy; set marks of Limitation in the corners, marks of ritual cleansing to keep ill influences away during the transfer of the moonstone talisman from the body of the corpse into the egg-shaped chamber in the robot's heart. As she laboriously drew out the lines defining what the spells could not do, aligning and focusing the powers of the heavens and the earth with the unexplored magic of her altered body, the corpse on its chair moved its head a little and mumbled. Caradoc's powers were too depleted—or his vehicle too far gone—to be understood clearly, but she heard anger and impatience, and once she caught the words "—needless palaver ... wasting time ..."

She went on as if she had not heard. But her heart misgave her, that any wizard would disregard the spells that kept magic within its proper bounds, only for his own convenience. With full darkness the storm-winds had risen in earnest, and she felt as if the shop were a bubble of light, adrift in hammering blackness, a tiny hell in which John, and she, and Caradoc of Somanthus were forever trapped. Sitting on a milking stool within Caradoc's circle, arms folded around his drawn-up knees, John watched Jenny work in silence. Now and then the firelight would flash on his spectacles as he turned his head to watch the door or to look at the robot, as if wondering whether he should be party to the extension of Caradoc's life. As always it was difficult to read his face.

But he had made a bargain, and when Jenny said, "I have done. The room is as clean and as safe as I can make it," he stood up and matter-of-factly took up the butchering knife he'd brought in with him. Caradoc watched his approach with cynical calm, and in Jenny's mind she heard a whisper:

Remember, my girl, a curse is on the one who smashes the moonstone. A curse of ill fate and dying, and all his loved ones dying with him. You know how strong a source is the death of a mage. And I assure you, if the moonstone ends up buried or locked in a strongbox or thrown in the sea, believe me I'll scream for Folcalor to come fetch me.

And Jenny said to him, *It takes a traitor to fear treachery everywhere he looks.*

In her mind, Caradoc laughed. *Gods save me from a good man doing what he thinks is his duty, girl. There's no treachery he'll stick at.*

John and Jenny had both assisted at enough pig slaughterings and deer hunts to find the moonstone within the corpse quickly and easily. If Caradoc felt anything, or thought anything, when they dug through the frozen flesh, he gave no sign of it; Jenny wondered if he had withdrawn that portion of his senses, or whether the dead meat was simply too cold to be anything but numb. John washed the stone in a pail of herbed well-water before seating it in the egg-shaped chamber among the pulleys and wheels that controlled the robot's limbs, and closed the tiny latches.

Then he and Jenny rinsed their hands and arms, shivering in the water's cold, and John dragged sledge and corpse and chair into the storeroom next door again. A coffin and winding-sheet waited there, to make the poor remains fit for burial once spring warmth thawed the ground. Afterward he came back and stood by the forge's outer door, listening to the howling winds of the night as Jenny called back the power from the corners of the room and dispersed the magic of the wards. The thick tallow work-candles had burned low in their sockets by then, amid brown winding-sheets of dribbled wax. Shadow clung around the massive trusses of the roof-beams like cobweb, and loomed across the rough-cast plaster of the walls in distorted echoes of anvil, saw, and hanging racks of tools.

In the midst of it all, in the cleared space beyond the forge, the robot sat, a curious and monstrous shape, like a great insect. The pincers and the hand, rising up out of its center, extended stiff as the arms of a corpse. On top of the egg-shaped talisman chamber the voice-box with its many tuning-pegs gleamed dully of polished wood, mute and sinister. Between the chinks of the talisman chamber's lattice, the moonstone glinted, like a malignant eye.

But all was silent. After his effort at charging the trap-bottle with Folcalor's name, Caradoc was too weary, his powers too drained, to make the fine-balanced wheels turn or to set in motion the pulleys and pistons of the robot limbs. Wrapping herself in her plaid for the dash across the snow-choked court to the kitchen, Jenny turned back to regard the thing, remembering her own days of imprisonment, helpless within a jewel.

Remembering the shattered crystal fragments that had littered the temple hill in Ernine.

At least she had known, in the time of her imprisonment, that her body still lived. That there was hope to return to it, even a desperate hope against terrible odds.

Her hand slid into John's, and felt the flesh of his strong fingers icy cold. "I never said thank you," she whispered. "For saving me as you did. For driving the demon out. For letting me return to my body again, even ravaged as it was. For doing all you did."

He pushed her plaid back, to ruffle her barely grown hair and kiss her forehead. "They never do say, in the legend, whether the Sleepin' Princess wanted to be waked from her dreams or not, love. Maybe they were better dreams than her life had been, an' the first thing she did comin' out of 'em was to slap Prince Charmin's handsome face for him."

"As I did?" Jenny put up her hand and laid it along his cheek, bristly with the fine, rusty stubble that was beginning to powder gray.

"We all do as we must, love." His lips brushed hers. "I'm just glad you're back. I'll keep this," he added, more loudly, holding up the silver bottle on the end of the red ribbon he'd tied around its neck, and closed the door between them and the thing in the forge. "It's a sennight yet, till the Moon of Winds," he said more quietly. "If Morkeleb comes in the next day or two, we should be in Prokep well in time. One way or another we'll get this into Adromelech's hands, though Caradoc's right: It'll take some gie wise bargainin' not to come to grief ourselves."

Jenny would have spoken. But John laid a hand on her lips and, pulling his doublet close around him, opened the door into the whirling night. "Aunt Rowe said she'd have a bath sent up to our room for us," he said. "I think we deserve it. Let's hope the water's still hot."

With an end of her plaid wrapped over John's shoulders, they leaned and groped and stumbled their way across the courtyard to the lights of the kitchen, barely to be seen in the mealy scour of the snow. But Jenny could not rid her mind of the black spiky shape of the robot, crouching in the dark blacksmith shop. After bathing, and washing John's back, and lying together in the curtained warm dark of the bed, she dreamed of it: dreamed that the white moonstone eye watched her still.

Chapter 16

Before John was awake, Jenny rose. The bedchamber was nearly as dark as the night before, though the innate sense of time that wizards must develop—if they are to source power from where the sun stands in the sky and from the phases of the moon—told her it was morning, an hour when a month ago the sky would have been pitchy black.

The wind still groaned, that frigid northern storm-wind that flailed the Winterlands six months out of twelve: wind which had, two centuries ago, transformed the sweet-blooming heart of the Realm to a wasted backwoods province that not even the Kings thought it worthwhile to hold. The small stone room, its walls covered in smoke-darkened winter hangings that stirred uneasily with the drafts, was warm near the hearth and no place else. The bath and towels and jars of soap and oils remained before the banked embers, and on her way downstairs Jenny put her head in at the kitchen, to ask Aunt Rowe to get Bill to carry them away.

Then she wrapped her plaids around her again, and crossed to the smithy.

Generally the big doors of the workshop stood open, or were only latched against the wind. But when John and Muffle had started work on the robot, John had had a bolt added, and had looked out one of the padlocks his father had traded for from the gnomes. At Jenny's touch it opened, and she slid back the iron bolt.

The low-vaulted stone room was dark. Its shuttered windows held in the heat, and admitted only grayish slits of light. Around the iron fire-bell the ashes in the forge radiated a dense white warmth. Last night when they'd passed Muffle in the kitchen—the blacksmith trying to pretend he'd been sitting there since they'd sent him away, and not keeping unobtrusive guard in the woodshed—John had warned him not to enter the smithy until Jenny had seen the place first. On this icy morning the big man was probably having a comfortable lie-in with Blossom.

Jenny stepped quickly through the door and closed it behind her. She did not need light to see the robot. It seemed to her that shadow lay thicker about it, that the heat of the forge did not penetrate into that end of the room.

"Caradoc?"

The robot moved.

Laboriously, painfully, one of the legs flexed. The cables creaked as they drew through pulleys, pistons grated as they rose. The wheels squealed, a horrible sound. The high knee-joint lifted, then fell as the limb straightened; then the next, and the next. Testingly, as a man will test broken fingers when they first come out of splints. From the gut strings of the voice-box came a deep humming, that scaled abruptly up into a furious insectile whine.

The metal hand—twice the span of a human one—curled in a clumsy half-fist, then spread out wide. The pincers touched the tips of their metal crescent, and gaped with a brittle screech of ungreased rivets.

Then with a mad, buzzing snarl of voicebox strings the robot lunged at her. It jounced across the uneven brick floor with the horrible speed and gruesome, scuttling motion of a bug, wooden feet scrabbling and knocking. Jenny leaped back and out the door, slammed it after her and sent the bolt crashing into place. She heard the robot smash into the thick oak planks, heard the squishy leathern squeak of its feet as it backed for another run, then the rattling, squeaking cacophony of attack again. The whine of its artificial voice boomed eerily from the soundbox, inarticulate, roaring, and at the same time Jenny heard Caradoc's voice shouting at her, shouting in her mind, like the voice in a dream.

Bitch! Cheat! Hellspawn whore! The planks of the door started at the impact of hundreds of pounds of iron, and there was a crashing sound, as if a bench had been kicked or flipped against the nearest wall.

Cheated me! Cheated me! Put me in prison! Bitch, bitch, you and your dunghill bullyboy pimp!

Caradoc, she shouted at him, *Caradoc ...!*

But he was beyond listening, beyond framing words. The bolt

jumped and jiggled as she slipped the padlock's crooked arm through
the hasp. Spells of pain, of sickness, of blindness, of cramp flapped
against her, ineffectual as moths on a glazed window, and the screams
of the trapped wizard's rage redoubled in her mind as she flicked
those crazed spells aside. Jenny pressed against the door, hearing the
crash and clawing within, while over her consciousness sluiced the
raw sewage of wrath and indignation and self-pity.

*Cheat, cheat, may you both die! Would that Folcalor had used my
hands to choke you to death!*

More helpless whifflings of pain and ill luck, which whirled into
the air and dissipated like a flatulent stink. She felt spells paw at the
lock, but it held. Even had it not, she doubted the heavy iron could
have been maneuvered out of the hasp that held the bolt. Jenny
thought, *It takes all the magic that he's capable of mustering, only to
move his limbs.*

And maybe even that isn't enough.

You call this a bargain? he screamed at her, trapped mind shrieking into hers. *You call this LIFE, that you're offering me? Mute, nearly
blind ... I've been trying all night to reach out into the rest of the Hold,
to hear, to sense, to know what's going on. Mumbling, confusion, clam-
oring far off ... Is this what you think I'm worth? Is this the reward you
give me, for putting Folcalor into your hands? Is this all you rate me,
ME, Caradoc of Somanthus?*

What would you have, then, Caradoc of Somanthus? Jenny pressed
her thoughts against the red raging stream of his fury. In her mind
she could almost see him, for she had been where he was now, conscious of the iridescent lattices of the moonstone around him, as if he
stood in a chamber of crystal, seeing the consciousnesses of others
outside. *Another corpse, and another, to stagger about in the snow until
you rot? How long do you think you could keep that up, before your
powers failed you utterly or Folcalor's servants found you? What John
gave you was the best he had to give....*

*Your pitiful fancy-man cheated me, as I'm told he cheated the De-
mon Queen herself! Best forsooth! The best he had to give is his son, his
son's body and his son's magic ... yes, and why not? What has that
worthless brat ever done of his own volition? What good could he be?
Aversin owed me—still owes me! After what I've done ...*

What you've done you did knowing exactly what you were offered.

Faugh! There was another crash in the smithy, and the hard crash of metal striking stone. The anvil going over, Jenny guessed. Muffle would be furious. *I knew nothing!* Through the closed oak door Jenny heard the roaring boom of the voice-box that Caradoc had not yet learned to control. *This—this THING is a deadweight, a useless chunk of iron! The human body, even dead, has some magic, some vibration, ever in its marrowbones. This thing is not human, never was human. It has no eyes to see, nor ears to hear....*

You're aware enough of where I stood to spring at me, returned Jenny. *I notice you have no trouble finding things to knock over.*

Bitch! He screamed at her again, and more iron crashed against the door. *Hag! Slut! You owe me! You all owe me! I deserve more than this!*

The soft tread of boots in the sheltered porch—audible to Jenny's ears, even above the moaning of the winds—made her turn her head, though she recognized John's stride. He'd shaved, and wore one of Aunt Rowe's knitted tunics under his much-battered black leather doublet, a brown-and-white winter plaid wrapped around him for added warmth. "Caradoc," she answered the lift of his eyebrow, though it was quite obvious what was going on. "He says he deserves more than you have given him."

"We all deserve more than the bodies that trap us, Caradoc," said John, raising his voice to carry through the door. "We all deserve more than a hundredweight and a half of meat that has to be fed and kept warm; that drives us to do the damn-all stupidest things when it needs to seed itself, and tells us we're more special than the next man when there's not enough of somethin' to go around. And when all's said in the end none of it does any good, for it's still gonna die on us, no matter who we kill or what we do to prevent it. An' those around us are gonna die, too."

"He isn't listening, John," Jenny said quietly, information that was scarcely necessary in the face of the roars, the crash of breaking benches and bins of charcoal hurled and smashed, the vicious clatter of iron limbs against the door. In her mind she could hear Caradoc shouting,

Don't fob me off with your puling philosophy, you bumpkin nitwit! I've read everything worth reading on the subject and know more than you even imagine exists!

And the crashing continued, like the fist of an enraged child.

"Can he set fire to the building?" Jenny asked softly.

John thought about it a moment, then shook his head. "Muffle banked the fire pretty good, after we were finished," he said. "To get it goin' again needs a fine touch with kindlin', an' gentle blowin'. If Caradoc pulls down the forge itself it'll just go out. He hasn't lungs, an' if he did have, that hand isn't near as mobile as a human one, for all it was as fine as I could make it."

Jenny flinched, remembering her own rage and sorrow at summer's end, immediately after she had slain Caradoc's body, and the scarring from the steam-burns had crippled her hands.

I was the lord of the dragons corps! Caradoc screamed in her mind. *I mastered them, through life and death! I rode in triumph at the head of the most feared force in the world. I subdued and defeated every mage in the west of the world....*

No, thought Jenny, though she did not project the thought into the maddened wizard's mind. *No, you're forgetting. That was Folcalor who did and was all those things. Using your body, as you wish to use my son's.*

"I'm that sorry for him," John went on. "I really am. I think he expected it would be sort of like the robots in the movies I saw. That it'd have balance, an' deftness—all those other things it takes a human mind five or seven or ten years to work up to, when it's born into a little lump of pink flesh called a baby—that it'd have 'em right away. It's got to be hard."

Only now, under the influence of the gentle magic of Ian and Miss Mab, was Jenny beginning to regain mobility in her fingers, and their joints still ached. Still, she had found she could weave a cat's cradle in play with her daughter Mag last night, and manipulate the tiny seed-pods of poppy and flax. Last night, while John had drowsed in the bath, she had taken her harp from the corner of the bedroom, tuned its strings, and played a simple air—played it very badly indeed. Still, it had given her joy.

"He still wants Ian, more now than ever."

"Well, he won't have him. The children are safe enough with Sparrow, and I'm gie glad for this storm—not that I thought I'd ever say I was glad of any storm—because if anything could keep Adric away from comin' up here, it's that. I'll go in and have a word with Caradoc later, after he calms down some. Not that I think it'll do a twilkin' bit of good." And he fingered the silver catch-bottle, strung on its red ribbon around his neck. He wore it, Jenny saw, outside his doublet, as if he wanted it to be seen, and it gleamed like far-off ice in the cold storm-light that leaked in under the smithy's porch.

"He's got what he wanted, anyway," Jenny said as John double-checked the door and the bolt, and the hinges as well, before putting an arm around her shoulders to lead her back to the kitchen to break-fast. "He is immortal—and probably indestructible, in that iron body. How long will he be able to keep it moving, do you know?"

John shook his head. "He'll have to grease himself up pretty often—that's what I want to tell him, among other things—but there's a lot of weight to contend with. In damp weather like this, the friction'll build up fast. God knows how the folks in the other world kept their robots from rustin'. It was damp there as a swamp, you know, an' now that I think on it I don't think I saw much rust any-where, not even down the dead subway tunnels." And he frowned, puzzling this over.

Jenny said, "Without the residual magic he was able to glean from his corpses, Caradoc may very well lose any ability to move the robot's limbs at all."

"Leavin' him exactly where he was." John bent his head, hunched his shoulders against the slashing wind as they struggled across the court. "Just in a bigger moonstone, that's all."

For a few minutes neither spoke, breathless with cold, until they fetched up in the kitchen. Aunt Jane was just taking the day's first bread out of the oven, and the whole long room smelled of it, and of the herbed ointment Cousin Dilly was daubing on the blisters Muffle had acquired during the construction of the robot. Snuff and Bannock thumped their tails and rolled on their backs, like small shaggy horses wanting their tummies scratched, which John obligingly knelt to do.

"So what do we do," asked Jenny, unwinding her sleet-flecked plaids, "if this is the case? What do we do when he realizes this?"

John glanced up from tussling with Snuff, and smiled. "We watch him."

The storm lasted another two days. Like John, Jenny could only be thankful for the hammering winds and sleet—like John, she knew their second son too well to think he'd be kept away from anything as fascinating as a robot by any lesser force. Her one fear was that the iron monster would, if it succeeded in escaping the smithy, make its way to the village in search of the boys, and she went to the smithy door a dozen times that first day, listening for the scrabble of wooden feet on the stone floor, the squeal of the pulleys and wheels.

Sometimes she heard the angry clanging of Muffle's tools as they were thrown or kicked about.

Sometimes she heard the buzzing of the voice-box, now loud, now soft, ranging up and down from shrill squeals to bass drones without ever coming into semblance of words.

Sometimes she heard nothing.

If there was punishment for the mage who had touched off the whole circle of horror, she thought—from the kidnapping of Ian through the possession of the wizards by demons, and so to the nightmare in Bel of the walking dead—this was close to what she might have envisioned. She wondered what was in Caradoc's mind now, and if he still thought he could bargain or think his way back to the true power he had always craved.

She did not know, for after that first morning he made no further attempt to put words or thoughts into her mind, or to communicate with her in any way. Sometimes, when she stood next to the door, listening to the scrapings and draggings within, she would feel a sharp stab of cramp in her sore hip, or get a blurring glitter of migraine in the corners of her sight. She could always tell when these were Caradoc's doing, and was easily able to brush them off her like dust. Muffle sometimes came with her, asking worried questions about how much damage the robot could cause to his tools:

"Anything else I can mend, mind, but if he breaks the anvil we're all in a fix." He winced at the dull crack of charcoal or stones flung at the door. "And mind you, I'm not looking forward to putting the forge back together again."

In the nights Jenny would listen, bending her thoughts toward the courtyard and the forge, trying to hear under and through the shriek of the wind. By day she would talk to Ian, through the medium of a scrying-crystal and the mirror her sister's husband had bought from a trader, and her son reported one or two disquieting dreams that might have come from Caradoc: dreams of Jenny's death at the hands of demons, or of terrible misfortune falling upon the Hold.

"Last night I dreamed of magic," the boy told her on the second day. "Like when Black-Knife attacked the Hold: fires breaking out in the thatch and the wood-room, and people's clothing catching fire, and the animals going crazy in their stalls. I woke up positive that this was actually taking place, because in the dream there was the wind howling around the walls, and I knew the only way any of you could be saved was by me going up there right then."

He grinned, sidelong and shy and heartstoppingly reminiscent of John. He was sitting in the kitchen of Sparrow's house, which had belonged to Sparrow and Jenny's mother before. Firelight flickered over his face, and Jenny could almost smell her sister's cooking. "He always overdoes it," he said. "Caradoc. Because of course I scried the Hold and everything was fine. But you watch out for him, Mother. He's up to something."

During this time also Jenny tried to communicate with the Whalemages, sinking deep into meditation in the small, thickly curtained cubbyhole that was her own library and workroom off the bedchamber she shared with John. She reached out with her mind over the windblasted miles of the Winterlands, across the bare black of the rock and the scoured white of snow, to where the snow piled the brown margins of the sea and the foam pounded bleak miles of empty coastline. Reached into the waves opaque as obsidian, down into dark water, calling on those great gentle weightless lords in their murmuring kingdom, asking for news.

She thought once Squidslayer answered her, though her power was not strong enough to make out such word-thoughts as the whales used. She had a glimpse of endless dreamy songs in which years and centuries blurred and it was impossible to determine whether one had come in at the beginning or not. She thought she recognized, as in a dream, the black rocks of those deep abysses that lay west of the Seven Isles of Belmarie, where Folcalor and his demons had concealed themselves for centuries in what appeared to be caverns but were in fact a separate Hell, an enclave in which they'd taken refuge a thousand years ago, separated from the real world by a gate they could not pass unless summoned by name.

She wondered, even as she saw this place, whether it was her own vision she saw or Caradoc's. She had killed him hereabouts, pinned his body to a rock with a harpoon in billowing clouds of scalding steam. If it was Caradoc's vision, what she saw might not be the truth. She saw where the demon gate had been, that Folcalor and his band of demons had come through, ostensibly to begin the process of rescuing Adromelech and opening the gate of their true home, their great Hell. It was blocked now, sealed with the stones that Squidslayer and the other Whalemages had driven into it. Even the glowing demon fishes seemed to have gone.

And as she drifted out of the vision, she thought, *They have gone to wherever Folcalor is keeping the dead men of Bel, until it is time for them to go to Prokep.*

They will come there at the Moon of Winds, as Aohila said, to break the Henge.

Chapter 17

On the third morning there was only silence. Outside the barred door of the smithy, Jenny listened beneath the steady hoon of the western wind for some sound within. But if there was no trace of residual magic in the metal body of the robot, neither was there the life that tells a mage of human presence. No breathing, either quick or slow. Neither the rustle of clothing, nor creak of belt or boot leather. Inert, the robot would make no more noise than Muffle's anvil.

There was nothing to tell her whether the creature was there at all.

She fetched Muffle and John before going in to check, Muffle disgruntled at being barred from his forge for yet another day: "It ain't like we haven't plows to sharpen and the harrow-chains to fix, with spring on its way." This was an optimistic pronouncement, for snow lay ankle-deep in the main courtyard, but the smith liked to be beforehand with his work so he could hunt for wild strawberries in the spring woods. Jenny herself was worried, for only five nights remained until the night of the Moon of Winds, and John was quietly preparing the things he would need to go to Prokep. The cloud-clearing wind blowing out of the west signaled, they both knew, the dragon's return.

In the back of Jenny's mind, too, was fear for her children. She and John had intended to walk down to the village that morning, to see them before departure, and she had a lively fear that Adric would either slip away and come up to the Hold by himself today, or, even worse, do so after they were gone.

The silver bottle glinted on John's neck on the end of its long red ribbon among the jumble of scarves and plaids. Jenny remembered the shining chamber within, and prayed that that part of the plan, at least, would go off without a hitch.

Do you like games?

She had no doubt that they would find Folcalor, when the demon came to the haunted city at the full of the moon. But as John had said, they wouldn't know how to hand the bottle off to Adromelech until they got there, and Jenny flinched from the knowledge that one or the other of them might, in the final chaos, have to operate the trap instead. She had not spoken of this to John, nor he to her, for there was much they dared not speak of with Caradoc so near, but it was in his glance sometimes.

Jenny pushed open the smithy door. The room was dark and deathly cold, for as John had predicted, the ashes had long ago gone out. The thick oak benches were smashed to matchwood, and the flagstoned floor was strewn with lumps of charcoal and twisted rods of iron. A shovel had been broken by being hammered on the wall, and the anvil—mercifully undamaged—lay in a corner: The dents and holes in the wall showed where it had been shoved or slid repeatedly against the stone. The forge itself had been pulled apart, and the stones scattered the floor.

In the midst of all this the robot stood inert. A broken pot of goose-grease lay against the wall in one place, a brush in another. Blots of grease gelled on the floor beneath the thing's joints. Jenny wondered whether, as the room cooled, moisture had condensed on the steel of the pulleys, crippling it.

Caradoc?

There was no reply.

For three days Jenny had listened, too, for any sign, any whisper that in his fury Caradoc would call on Folcalor or Adromelech—madness, given what they would do with a talisman stone of a wizard's soul, but it was not beyond possibility that Caradoc was mad, or close to it. And his vanity, she knew, was strong.

She had heard nothing, but did not know whether she would be able to hear such a summons. Her own powers were too new, too unfamiliar, and she had never had the ability of demons and dragons to read human dreams.

They could only keep silent, and wait.

John came in, fingering the silver catch-bottle. He glanced from Jenny to the robot, and raised an eyebrow. "He isn't dead?" His breath was a cloud of white in the icy gloom.

"I don't know." Jenny walked over—cautiously—to the robot, but when she crouched to examine it more closely she kept her skirts gathered tight around her, lest she have to spring away fast. "I don't think it's possible to die within the talisman . . . I certainly can't imagine how one would do it. Though of course, having been so close to Folcalor's mind, Caradoc may know something I don't."

"I don't think Folcalor would know, either," murmured John. "Demons don't. They know about killin', but they know nothin' of death. You saw them in Bel. It terrifies them blind even to think of dying. They'll go through a thousand tortures rather than let go."

Like Caradoc, Jenny thought, and backed warily out of the room.

John lingered for a moment behind her, then followed. "Morkeleb should be here by tomorrow," he said. "If nothing further happens, we'll have to leave for Prokep the day after, come what may. We're cuttin' it close as it is, if we mean to have all in place before Folcalor and his lot arrive."

"And if they're there already?"

"I doubt they will be, by what Corvin said." John's voice sounded calm, but she could feel the tension where his shoulder touched hers. "It's an uncanny place. Given the way they attacked Corvin an' me there—a fast frontal assault with all they had, no sneakin' around beforehand—I'm guessin' he was right when he said there was traps there that they don't want to deal with. But we won't know a thing, really, till we arrive."

He paused, to work the bolt back into place and snap closed the lock, chilblained hands clumsy in his gloves. For all the relative warmth of the day, it would still be a long time till spring.

"The least we can do is get this thing out of the forge, before poor Muffle gives birth from frettin'. But when we lock it into the southeast tower dungeon again I'm going to disjoint the legs and take the hand off it, and I still don't feel right, about leavin' it here. God knows how I'll keep Adric away from it, till we get back."

Jenny glanced up at him, questioning, anxious. She had read all John's notes, two and three times now, and understood how he planned to cope with Adromelech breaking out of the Henge and Folcalor swallowing him up—or vice versa.

And still she thought, *What if it doesn't succeed?*

She—and John—would be standing smack on the doorstep of Hell when the demons poured out.

Her thoughts were in her eyes.

John put an arm around her shoulders, smiled down at her, "You're not doubtin' my plan, are you, love?"

"Yes."

He sighed, crestfallen. "I was afraid you'd say that." And then, more gently, "Don't fash yourself, love. It's got to be done—*somethin's* got to be done—and this is the best we can do. We'll manage. See if we don't."

Jenny wished she could believe him.

The robot stood motionless all that day, and all the next. Toward sunset the next day even the western wind faded into stillness, and from the observation platform where John and Jenny had watched for the comet's coming, many years ago, they saw Morkeleb circle down out of the primrose sky.

All is in readiness, said the dragon, *and in accordance with your notes, though Corvin will still have it that flight is possible, and conceal-ment is possible.* He perched on the battlement of the tower, like an angular bird, wings spread for balance and seventeen feet of spiny tail hanging down over the wall, switching like a cat's. *I have myself ob-served this Dragonstar, and it is as you say, wrought of ice and iron. The sigils that have been sourced upon it should hold against the magic of the demons. Whether that will be enough to weave their complete ruin, I cannot say.*

"And the Demon Queen?" asked John.

The bobs of Morkeleb's antennae flickered, small and cold as the comet itself burning in the twilight above the bleak eastern hills. *Since she was glimpsed in the Skerries of Light, I have not seen her, and in Prokep there was no sign of her, or of any other of the Hellspawnkind. Yet as I flew back I felt her presence, as if she were always behind my head, visible from the corner of my eye.*

John nodded, familiar with the sensation.

For the rest, Prokep is silent, as it has always been silent: If the demonkind came there before us, they fell prey to the dangers of the place ere we arrived. Yet as the moon waxes full so the power of the de-mons' talismans waxes, the power of their stored deaths. It will not be long before they can tread its sands with impunity, at least for a time.

"We'll be ready to leave in the mornin'," said John. "Did you have a look about you, at those places I marked on my map that felt odd to me? Or that had strange tracks comin' an' goin' from 'em but didn't seem to be gates?"

I did, replied the dragon. *Two of them are places where magic will not work, blind spots in the fabric of the world. The place between the red pillars, and the space to the north of the palace platform. There is a chamber, too, in that platform, where magic will also not work, but it is difficult to come to.*

And Jenny felt, and saw in her mind, the visions that the dragon showed to John, adding to the man's own perceptions and memories of the vanished city, like new colors painted onto a map. To Jenny, it meant little, only fragments of awareness, but she saw John's eyes widen behind his spectacle lenses, and he said, "That's gie brilliant, better than computers, even. Is that a thing of dragons, or somethin' only the Dragonshadows can do?"

It is a thing of ME, replied Morkeleb. *And as to the Dragonshadows ... I know nothing of them. Not what they can do, not where they are, not whether they are aware of us or not. Nothing.* And he was silent for a time, the diamond gaze that could trap and hold the human mind like shining quicksand turned outward upon the darkening horizon, and his own half-seen shape fading slowly into the night.

Then he glanced back down at John and added, as he flickered back into visibility, *But I will say, Dreamweaver, that the dragons do not entirely trust you, and Corvin least of all.*

"Aye, well," sighed John, "that puts 'em in company with about three-quarters of the population of Bel." He shrugged his sheepskin coat closer about him, the tip of his long nose red with cold. "I wish I could tell 'em everything'll be well, because I'd love to believe it meself. But that's somethin' we'll all have to see."

In the deep of the night Jenny was wakened by a change in the note of the wind.

Her first thought, still cloudy with sleep, was that despite Morkeleb's efforts the storm was rising again: 'Spring is coming' forsooth. She had dreamed of him, dreamed of him calling out to her as black winds swept him off the tower, drove him far north of the Hold, above the bleak tundra that in this season was like frozen marble beneath the inky darkness. Dreamed of him surrounded by demon voices and demon magic, trying to return.

But his voice was drowned by the happy singing of birds, and she sat in a garden with the demon Amayon, holding Amayon's hand. He looked as he had always looked to her, like a boy in his mid-teens, dark curls clustering around a beautiful face, wide-set eyes of deep speedwell blue that looked at her with an expression of trust and utter love. She felt protective of him and of that love, as if he were a child: felt his reverent love, the half-awed first love of a boy for an older woman, drawn by her wisdom and her beauty through a gate of delight into a new and different world.

She was, he had told her, the only mortal woman he had ever loved. It was an astonishingly potent fantasy, and it made sense in her heart, even as the seductive little songs that Folcalor sang in people's dreams made sense. Only he understood that she, Jenny, had had no responsibility for the dreadful things she had done. Only through his love could she be utterly free. He would take vengeance for her upon the world for the hardships of her life.

Why was Morkeleb calling to her, out in the hammering tempest? *Wind,* he called out to her, and something else. . . .

Amayon put his hands around her face—over her ears—and kissed her. "I love you, Jenny. . . ."

And still in her mind she heard the dragon's voice: *Wake up!* . . .

She woke up. The wind had changed. Coming from all directions, it beat now one side of the tower, now another, like the blizzard winds of deep winter. For the first instant, hearing by his breathing that John, too, was awake, she felt shame, as if he had waked because he had dreamed of her with Amayon in the garden, even as she had so often dreamed of him lying with the Demon Queen.

But he whispered, "You hear it? Smell it?"

Yes. There was a different note to the storm's howling, a kind of thin scream. A smell that was not the scent of snow.

"It sounds as it did in Prokep, when Folcalor came to get Corvin." The ropes creaked beneath the bed ticks as John rolled to his feet: the harsh slice of cold on her flesh. "Smells the same, too." The creak of John's boots, and the soft whump of her skirts and plaids tossed onto the bed where she could get them easily. "I'll fetch the lads."

Jenny dragged on her skirt, latched up her bodice. Ran down the tower stairs behind him. One twist of the pitch-dark steps put her at the threshhold of the open door of her sons' room; she saw the dark loom of the big bed and thought, *Dear gods, what if the demons are in the village after all?*

There was no way of knowing, no way of telling, what Caradoc could and couldn't hear, how far he could cast the probing tendrils of his mind. He had cried out in his rage that he couldn't hear, couldn't see, and yet John had maintained the silence—both in the Hold and the village—concerning the children and anything to do with them ... Had that been enough? Would Adromelech's demons—they had to be Adromelech's—guess where Ian was, despite all precautions? (*Dear gods,* she thought in panic, *did Adric do something silly ...?*)

No, she thought, flying down the dark stair as the red reflections of torchlight flashed across the walls far beneath her. Whatever happened, the children were safer in the village than they would be here—if anything Caradoc would assume Ian was staying at her old house on Frost Fell. About Adric and Mag, she doubted he gave so much as a thought.

Another twist of the stair and she was in the hall. Someone had stirred up the central fire and the men of the household—Bill and Cowan and Blunder, and Tabble the kitchen-boy and Ams Puggle and the half-dozen villagers whose week this was for Hold duty—were pulling on their clothes while Bannock and Snuff stalked among them with the hackles dark upon their backs. John was giving orders in a quiet, decisive voice as Jenny darted through, all sounds muffled by the thick hangings that covered the walls and were supposed to absorb some of the drafts and noise and never did, quite. Underfoot the matting of woven straw whispered limply, giving back its smell of dirt and dog-piss; Jenny thought, *Spring can't come too soon, to take this out and burn it....*

If we're here, in spring.

In the kitchen Aunt Jane opened the door of her little room, in the shadows between the banked hearth and Aunt Rowe's loom: "What is it?"

"Demons," said Jenny.

"It's that thing in the smithy, isn't it? It called them." This was something Aunt Jane generally said about any misfortune—she'd ascribed the increased numbers of mice three years ago to Jenny's teaching Ian to ensorcel herbs for healing—but in this case, she was absolutely right. Jenny pulled her plaid and her sheepskin coat tighter about her, and caught up her halberd from the corner near the door before stepping out into the bricked porch. The wind hit her like a swung plank.

It was hard to hear anything, hard to see, as if dark hands pawed to cover her eyes. She called, *MORKELEB!* into the wind and got no reply.

He was out there somewhere, impervious to the demon spells that sought to seize him through the magic that he had surrendered. Had they clogged his eyes and his wings with snow, as John had spoken of them trying to overwhelm the dragon Corvin with gold-dust? No chance, now, of a fortuitous thunderstorm to wash the air. . . .

Fortuitous? Her mind snagged on the thought as she stretched her senses out toward the smithy, around the walls of the stable court. But the thought was driven from her by the effort of reaching, of listening, of trying to hear anything over the wind.

It was useless. She could not even touch his mind in the hammering blindness of storm and magic that surrounded the Hold. Jenny cursed, and worked her way a little distance along the wall, trying to get close enough to see the smithy door. She couldn't, and waited until the men came out. The robot was an unknown quantity, as far as strength went, but she had seen its speed. Only when Muffle and Cowan were at her back did she struggle to the smithy porch, and see the door standing open. The hinges had been wrenched free, and Muffle, after a quick look around the smithy by the feeble glare of the lantern he bore, shouted, "The axle of the harrow's gone! It used it as a lever—seven-foot bar of iron. . . ."

So much, Jenny thought, looking at the splintered oak planking, the torn-out bolts, *for guessing the robot's strength.*

The screaming of the wind had covered the sound.

"It's gone to the gate!" she shouted, and the three of them fought their way across the court, Jenny driven to her knees by the gale, so that her two bulky escorts had to hold on to her arms, to keep her from being thrown back across the courtyard and against the kitchen wall. The cold made her gasp.

And all the time she was thinking, *Amayon. Amayon is here.*

She could feel him, sense him. Rage rushed over her like heat, at the longings that spun in her mind.

There were spells of confusion in the wind, like turning hands in blindman's bluff. She could feel them tug at her consciousness, and Muffle turned and tried to drag her down the passageway to the cowbyres. "This way!" she yelled, and he yelled back, "What? No. You're mixed up, Jen," and dragged her, hard, the wind pounding them both and the flecks of flying snow obscuring everything into a tangle of blackness and walls. Cowan had already vanished—Jenny thought, *He'll freeze....*

"*You're* mixed up!" she called back, and Muffle yelled, "What?"

"This way!"

She could never have hauled the massive blacksmith if he hadn't trusted her, but he did. He said, "Jen, we're gonna end up in the armory!" but he followed her all the same, and the wind that smote them grew less. Voices clamored dimly, echoing somewhere in the darkness—nowhere near the gate, anyway. Jenny felt overwhelmed by the momentary conviction that the gates lay to her right—where the storerooms were—and fought it aside, and sure enough, a few moments later the squat archway loomed above their heads, and the stone walls echoed with the crash of iron striking stone.

Spells of confusion, to divert help to the other side of the Hold until it was too late, even as the demon winds had swept Morkeleb away.

Someone shouted, "Johnny!" and there was the clash as if buckets of chain had been hurled down the stairs. Jenny saw, through her unnatural blindness, the spider-like shape of the robot tangling and fighting against the chains that Ams Puggle and Peg the Gatekeeper had thrown over it like a net. Beyond the robot Jenny saw that the portcullis had been raised, and the tarred brown-black wall of the gates was raked and scored with slits, as if struck by axes from the other side. The robot stood between John and the capstan-wheel that held the portcullis chains; a heavy bar stretched across both leaves of the gate, but to get it, the robot would have to cease guarding the portcullis chains. John struck at it with the six-foot wooden beam he held in his hands like a single-stick; the robot got its legs clear of the chains and lunged at him again, swinging the iron axle it held as a weapon.

Clearly a halberd would be of little use. Jenny looked around and caught up one of the buckets of gravel that had been brought to the gatehouse last fall to mend a pothole in the court. In the dark at the end of the passageway crashing and splintering resounded, as something struck the gates again—axes, hammers, maybe only the forces of malignant magic. John lunged with the beam, trying to trip the robot, and the robot swung at him again. Jenny sprang in and emptied the gravel over the thing's center, pebbles and grit bouncing. The robot did not turn, did not need to, only sprang at her, its pincer biting into the flesh of her arm with terrifying violence, ripping through sheepskin, chemise, and flesh as she pulled free. At the same instant it stabbed at John with the axle again, trying to pin him to the wall as with a spear. He slipped past, struck at its feet, then, when it sprang at Jenny, he dropped the beam and went for the capstan.

The robot was on him, like a cat on a mouse, catching his plaids as he tried to duck past. John slithered out of them, threw the yards of dull-striped wool over the center of the thing, where the moonstone was. While the pincer and the hand groped and thrashed at the fabric he yanked on the capstan, yelled something about the gate, gasping against the wind....

It was too late. With a booming crash the gate's thick planks burst inward, forms crawled and wriggled through. Puggle and Muffle ran forward with their halberds and their flails, but the attackers—gnomes, Jenny saw, at least a score of them—were armed with maces and spears. In the same instant, the robot caught John by the back of the neck, like a cat catching a mouse. Jenny's breath jammed in her throat, knowing the strength of those pincers and knowing, too, that she could not, dare not, use magic to save him....

But John turned in its grip before it could shake him, caught the pincer in both hands, and did something to it that broke its grip—literally broke its grip, for Jenny saw the hinged crescent jammed open, unable to shut. He dropped to the ground, but before he could jump clear the robot struck him with a foreleg, smashing him against the wall. It made to spring at him, but one of its leg-joints jammed. Jenny heard the furious whine of the voice-box, the robot struggling to go forward—more than one of its joints frozen by the grit locked in them.

The next second the gnomes were around John with halberds ready, like hunters on a speared boar. Amayon's voice—unmistakable—shouted, "Get back! Get back or he dies!"

Muffle, Puggle, and Jenny stopped where they were. Amayon—the only human of the attackers, maybe not human at all, Jenny could not tell—stood over John, looking as he had always looked to her: a slim boy in his teens, curly-haired, blue-eyed, seductive, smiling. Though the air was bitterly cold in the passage and snow whirled through the hole in the gate the boy wore only a short tunic of quilted black velvet sewn with garnets, black hose, and slippers. Neither the gnomes nor Amayon breathed—in the glare of the cressets that lit the passageway, Jenny could see John's panting breath.

The demon's blue eyes, dark as mulberries, met Jenny's, and he smiled. "Well, darling?" he said softly. "What will you pay me for his life?"

He reached down to take the catch-bottle and the ribbon from John's neck, and John's sword suddenly glinted in the firelight. Amayon sprang back as if he'd been burned.

"I'll pay for me own life," John said, using the stones of the wall behind him to get himself grimly to his feet. "Thank you very much." By the way he moved, Jenny guessed the robot had cracked some of his ribs.

The wind ceased. In the cressets' iron baskets the fire flared suddenly, and the next moment sank, as if life itself had been drained from the wood. Through thickening darkness Jenny saw something in the splintered hole in the gate, something that seemed to pour through rather than crawl. Something she could not look at, try as she would. She smelled mold and dust, and the chill breath of wet stone, and without intending to, her eyes flinched away.

When she looked back there was nothing there. But a shadow hovered in the corner near John, the shadow of something tall and stooped; veiled in darkness, it seemed to be, though to her mageborn sight other things were still clear. In a thin cold voice that seemed to come from a great distance away, it said, *This man was in Prokep with the dragon.*

The gnomes pressed close around John, their halberds a glinting ring of steel.

"Get the woman," Amayon said, and Muffle struck the hand off the gnome who stepped forward to seize Jenny—the gnome merely looked at him, mildly surprised, and picked up the sword in his other hand while his heart's blood poured out into the churn of mud and snow.

"Leave her be." In the torchlight, John's eyebrows stood out black against ashen skin.

One of the demon's butterfly eyebrows quirked. "Will we have heroics here? Don't tell me she's got back enough of her enchantments to beguile you still? After deceiving you with half the cavalry corps—"

"I said leave her be." He lifted his sword, though the halberds had reach on him. In the lantern light the silvery lines on his skin burned as if reflecting the light of an unseen moon. "What'd Caradoc offer to sell you? This?" He held out the catch-bottle.

Amayon's smile broadened, and he extended his hand. But John said, "Not this time," and stepped quickly past the gnomes to hand the bottle to the gray thing, the thing unseen in the shadows beside him. When he stepped back to grope for the support of the wall again, Jenny could see his hand was unsteady with shock at what he had seen or almost seen.

"Now I said, leave her be. Leave us be."

The chill, distant voice said, "Bring him. And the woman. We must talk about Prokep, you and I."

Amayon smiled, and moved toward Jenny again—*He knows I'll use magic to save him,* she thought dizzily. *Or to save myself. I can't, I won't . . .*

John brought up his sword and glanced, with deliberate calculation, at the gnomes around him, as if marking whom he would kill first, and who next. The gnomes backed nervously away.

"It's naught to me what demons do to demons," John said, in his toughest back-country bumpkin voice, "so be that you let me and mine alone. What is it you'd know about Prokep?"

Morkeleb, thought Jenny, *where is Morkeleb . . . ?*

The cold-voiced thing said, "The way into the Maze. And the way through."

"Give me a scrap of aught to draw on and a chalk and I'll draw it," said John. "It's like them Hells Amayon took me through—"

"It is not, precisely," replied that chill voice out of the darkness, "but leave it so. It would be best, Dragonsbane, did you journey there with us."

Me! The gut-strings within the sounding-box raged like swarming wasps, but no articulate sound came forth. With a great squeaking of joints the robot dragged itself forward, and Caradoc's voice screamed in Jenny's mind. *You promised me the boy. He is in this place somewhere, he must be! Hiding ... Or else he is in the house on the Fell! Give me the boy!*

And like the deep thrumming of the wind, the strings of the box formed up the word "... oy...."

"Leave the boy," said John. "That's me price, me alone, and I'll take you through the Maze at Prokep."

Out of the shadows the thing regarded him, barely discernible darkness within dark. "Do not think to play the fool with us, Dragonsbane." Eyeless and without sound of breath, the voice, like that of the robot, seeming almost to be mechanically produced, like the deceptive whistling of wind through long-bleached bone. "We will know if you delay us in the city, so that its traps may entangle us, or if you slow your steps in the Maze. And we will have no mercy."

"You haven't any mercy, anyway, that I've ever seen," retorted John. "So what's that to me? Just leave me family alone, and I'm yours."

Adromelech promised me the boy, insisted Caradoc, and the sounding-strings groaned again, "... oy ..." *To let you into the Hold, to give you the trap for Folcalor.*

"But *you* did not give us the trap," taunted Amayon, "did you?"

You cannot leave me thus! The robot, creaking and shuddering, flung itself at the demon, and Amayon stepped back with a look of surprise, like the gnome whose hand Muffle had cut off. He moved lightly aside from the great iron insect, and in the shadows the gray thing stretched out a finger, white bone gleaming in the dark.

There was a small explosion, and white light speared out between the lattices of the robot's heart. A cracking sound, like glass left in a fire, and, in Jenny's mind, a failing shriek of despair and rage and terror. When she blinked the after-glare of brightness from her eyes, it was to see the robot standing frozen on its wheels, thin smoke trailing up from its metal heart. Inside the moonstone was broken into fragments, as if struck by a hammer. The pieces had the burned, blackened look that the soul-crystals had had, on the hill above the Temple at Ernine.

Of Amayon, and the gnomes, and the shadow-thing, and John Aversin, there remained no sign.

Afterward it took three men to remove the pieces of the robot from the gate-passage and lug them back to the storeroom behind the forge, when Muffle dismantled it. But this Jenny only heard at secondhand.

For within an hour she was sitting between the razor-tipped spines of Morkeleb's back, flying through the cold still darkness toward Prokep.

And all around her in the night, she heard the silken shearing of dragon wings.

Chapter 18

On the occasion of his previous journey through Hell in company with a demon, John had asked whether the road they traveled was a standard path: Did one who sought the horrors of Paradise first have to pass through the Hell of Winds, for instance, if his starting point was the world that John knew as reality?

This had seemed to him a reasonable question, but Amayon wouldn't answer, not that John had expected the demon would tell the truth in any case. He had therefore made careful notes of the sigils that marked the doors opening between one Hell and the next, and leading from the Hells into the worlds that they abutted: It was all he could do. Those sigils, as far as he was able to tell, were written on the doors through which he and the demons with whom he now traveled passed on the way to Prokep.

He had no time now to make notes. The demons drove him mercilessly through a Hell whose air clogged wet and almost unbreathably thick in his lungs, as if he were perpetually drowning; where all things seemed to glow greasily in half-twilight and where balls of light swam like schools of fish in the air and fled the sight of the demon band—"Fat lot of good to rush, isn't it?" he inquired of Amayon as he stumbled through knee-deep muck whose composition he could only guess in the dim blue light. "We're going to come out in Prokep pretty much the same time we went in at Alyn, aren't we? I mean, we'll still have three days before the Moon of Winds."

The demon said, "You know nothing about it," and kept walking—lightly, on top of the sucking odiferous ooze, moving as if neither it nor the gluey air touched him.

John retorted, "Of course I know nuthin' about it, you silly oic! If I did I wouldn't be askin' you!" But later he guessed the reason. Though time did not alter in Hell—and travelers emerged, as he had noted, at pretty much the same time in the real world as they went in—the corpses of the gnomes that the demon escort rode continued to decay. The flesh of their faces discolored, sagging and puffing up grotesquely beneath moldering beards; the demons seemed to take delight in the growing stink of the flesh, like boys holding farting matches to offend adults. Amayon—presumably a senior in the infernal ranks—treated their behavior with amused contempt, but like them he never offered John any threat. As for the gray thing, it was always in shadow, never clearly glimpsed, gone whenever John turned his head. But he could feel it, always behind him, a cold presence he never forgot.

They passed again through the Hell of the Shining Things, marching for what felt like days along one of the black-rock river-cuts through those desolate red highlands under a scarlet sky. John was stumbling from thirst and hunger, and from the exhaustion of pushing through the Blue Hell, but the demons forced him on. They were afraid here, watching and listening, pushing forward in visible dread. Even before those flaming wheels of light and eyes appeared, John was confirmed in his suspicion: The Shining Things had the power to kill demons. When one appeared on the cliff-top above them in a glitter of ozone and lightning, Amayon and the gnomes and even the gray thing took cover. John himself collapsed onto a silver-flecked rock, desperate only for rest, his drawn sword across his knees. He watched the thing warily, but it ignored him. Instead, it flushed one of the gnomes and pursued it down the gully, the gnome racing in panic and then, when the dead flesh would flee no faster, the demon shucking clear of it, escaping in a long glowing serpent through the mouth and growing legs to run. The glowing wheel overtook it, though—the Shining Things could travel heartstoppingly fast—and ripped it to shreds. John could hear it screaming from where he sat.

A creature belonging to the Lord of this Hell—if this Hell had a Lord? Or was it like a dragon, an independent being, with thoughts and intentions of its own?

If he walked up to it and tried to open a conversation, would he be glad or sorry thirty seconds later?

He leaned his head back against the rock, shut his eyes. It might save him some effort.

A hand fell on his shoulder, gone when he turned his head. "Let us be gone," said a cold, distant voice, from somewhere behind him. "The Moon of Winds is on us. The stars move to their appointed places."

"We'll still have three days when we get out, won't we?" he inquired interestedly, but the voice only said, "Come."

Five or six gnomes emerged from the thorn-bushes, filthy now with clotted blood stringing out of their slashed and perforated flesh, and thrust at him with their halberds, forcing him to his feet. They passed the motionless corpse of the gnome whose demon the Shining Thing had slain, and even the demons who would happily play games with the entrails of their victims walked gingerly around the spot. They pressed on along the watercourse as quickly as John could be driven to march. The huge, leathery carry-beasts raised their heads from the watercourse at the bottom of the gorge like obese birds, watching them pass. Even had John been ignorant enough to drink those rusty waters he suspected the gray shadow would not have let him.

They needed him in Prokep. Otherwise, of course, Amayon would have derived considerable amusement from getting him to drink the water in Hell, trapping him there forever.

There was a gate beneath a shelf of black rock, halfway up a cliff. Two of the gnomes fell in the climb, shattering their bodies on the rocks below the perilous thread of trail. Pressed to the rockface himself, John glimpsed them crawling frantically to their hands and knees again—most of their bones were broken—and dragging themselves toward the trailhead to get away from the Shining Things, which appeared on the hillslope below. Before John could see the demons taken the gray thing drew him through the gate.

Then they were in Prokep.

The baroque pearl of the moon was much as it had been when last he'd glimpsed it between the Winterlands storms, clipped like a debased coin. Its silvery light edged the dark block of the palace foundation, silhouetted the irregular shapes of broken pillars against pewter sand. Dust fraying from the dune-tops caught the wan light, ghosts fleeing in the emptiness. The air was bitterly cold.

"Where is the Henge?" Though the voice that hissed behind him generally had no expression, John felt now that he was being accused of putting it in his pocket the last time he was here.

"What does it matter?" he replied. "It's three days yet till the moon comes full." The Dragonstar was barely to be seen above the far-off ridge of hills, a blurry dot no brighter than some of the stars called Seven Sisters (though there were actually over a dozen of them, when John had viewed them through a telescope—*They brought their maids,* he'd explained to Ian). He looked around him and pulled his gloves from his belt, glad he'd had them on when the gnomes had dragged him through the gate in the blinding glare of light.

Amayon, who had walked off a step or two to view the city in its shallow basin before them, said something in the tongue of the demons, and John thought he caught the name of Folcalor.

"He'll be here already, you know," he commented casually, and felt the cold grip close on his arm from behind, far stronger than that thin, bodiless voice would give one cause to think. "Maybe not in the city, but in the desert, watchin'."

"If you have betrayed us to him—"

"And what good would that have done me?" retorted John. "Both lots of you are much of a muchness, y'know. But if you think Caradoc didn't, I've got the Crown Jewels of Bel here in me pocket that I'd be glad to sell you ... an' stop doin' that!" he added, for he had turned around, instinctively, to face the thing he spoke to, and of course there was nothing there.

"What do you know of it?" Amayon planted himself in his path.

"I know Caradoc," said John simply. Filthy, ravenous, and trembling with fatigue, he was in no mood for the demon's mocking remarks. "You think, as close as his mind was to Folcalor's, that he didn't scream out his name as you blew his soul into eternity?"

Amayon's blue eyes went to some point just beyond John's shoulder, as if meeting the gaze of whatever it was that stood there smelling of dust and grave-clothes.

"An hour before the sun rises," said John, "a gate'll open into a place called the Garden of Winds. We can stay there safe until the moon waxes full. I can get you from there into the Maze, an' thus to the Henge. I hope one of you's brought water an' food, because I'm clemmed."

Of course they hadn't. So John led them down the dunes, their boots sinking into the sliding black crystalline sand, and by a circuitous route toward the foundation of the palace, where, he hoped, the last of the dried meat Corvin had left stored for him would still be moderately edible. If, as he guessed, they had emerged from the gate in the same hour that they went into Hell, even flying at top speed Morkeleb could not bring Jenny here in under a day. He prayed he wasn't far wrong in that calculation. If Folcalor or any of his minions awaited them already, they gave no sign of it.

Nevertheless, the demons were nervous, holding close together and scattering in panic at the sight of every dust-devil. Even Amayon was on edge, and left off his needling references to Jenny to lapse into watchful silence. One of the gnomes who strayed from the group did vanish, and by the way the others muttered amongst themselves, John didn't think the demon had simply fled.

They gathered the two jars of water and the few scraps of rather leathery mutton that John had hung down the coldest well in the crypts; returning through the dark windy desolation he led them across one of the places Morkeleb had identified for him—a square of about thirty feet in the midst of the city, close beside a pair of crumbling pillars of red sandstone—where magic would not work at all. Two of the gnome bodies collapsed, the demons emerging from them in a whisper of silvery smoke. John himself, who'd taken the precaution of carrying the water jars, made sure he jumped like a startled deer, then went straight to where Amayon and the surviving gnomes stood—they'd walked spread out and he'd only managed to maneuver two into the Blind Spot.

"I told you no tricks!" The bony pressure of a hand crushed his shoulder, and all over his body his skin began to itch, and then to burn.

"You think if I knew of traps here I wouldn't pick a better one than that?" he protested, and forced himself to stand still while the searing heat grew. "If I'd wanted 'em dead, believe me, I've got a sword that'll kill quicker." He didn't add that whittling down the odds with his sword would have brought them all down on him, aside from making it obvious what he was doing; he did his best to sound like Adric when accused of borrowing the boar-spears. The smell of charred flesh breathed for a moment in his nostrils, then subsided. The moon's cold light shone on thin ghosts of dust blowing over the empty city. The shadow did not reply.

Shoving and glowering at each other, the dis-bodied demons rematerialized and returned to the fallen corpses, pawing at the necks and bringing out from behind the mildewed beards small sacks of leather on strings. But their hands couldn't grasp the material objects easily, and one fell, scattering its contents: queer-gleaming jewels, the sight of which brought John's shorn hair bristling on his nape. Talisman gems. Stolen souls.

Deaths.

Aohila was right, John reflected as the dead gnomes scooped up the jewels, when she told Jenny that Adromelech would be collecting these soul-gems, too. That pointed to treason in Folcalor's ranks, because if he recalled correctly it had been Folcalor's original idea, to betray his master the Hell-Lord by imprisoning and keeping the souls of the wizards they took.

Guesswork on the Demon Queen's part? *Like goose, like gander*... Or was she in fact allied with one or the other?

The possibility made him shiver. *Now, that's REALLY all I'd need....*

"Hurry," snapped the cold voice behind him. "We must be out of here, in concealment, before Folcalor comes."

"He's one up on you, anyway, if he's got a gnome mage's power to work with." John turned to survey the desolation with leisurely interest that he was far from feeling. Something caught his eye, a gleam of light on the corner of the palace foundation that loomed behind them, that had not been there three weeks ago. "How many hid out with him under Somanthus Isle, when the Gate of the Sea-Hell was closed? Or has he been recruitin' little wights an' pooks out of the swamps, all these years?"

"Do not jest, Dragonsbane." The voice sounded colder and yet more distant; the lesser demons seemed to be trying to look around them, in all directions at once. Two materialized extra eyes to assist in that effort—there was no more jocularity about stinks and throwing rotting ears and toes. "The traitor Folcalor has not forgiven you for enlisting the Hell-Queen's aid against him. It will go ill for you indeed if he prevails. And for all those you hold dear. Remember that, when you are tempted to betray us."

They passed through the invisible gate—whose location John had meticulously noted on his previous stay—and into the place Morkeleb had called the Garden of Winds. They were in hiding there for three days.

As Morkeleb had shown him, in that brief, dazzling vision of the map of Prokep spread out in strange pools and corridors of awareness in his mind, the Garden of Winds was the desert itself. John turned the moment they came through the gate and triangulated on the distant landmarks as he did in the Winterlands, rather than physically marking the spot with stones. Though Amayon and the shadow appeared to appreciate the fact that they needed John's guidance to reach the Henge, the rest of the demons would probably think it an enormous joke to move whatever markers he placed. He wasn't entirely sure that the demons couldn't see the gate from this side, or perceive something about it that he could not.

It was best, he had found, when dealing with demons, to assume that anything they could tamper with, they would, sheerly because they could not help doing so.

Still, three days was a long time, to remain in the wilderness with demons.

It helped that what lay beyond the gate was nothing but open desert. From the midst of the ruins of Prokep, the gate opened straight into endless wasteland. The sand was red, not blackish, and even the rocks of the hills nearby did not seem to be of the same composition. When John walked to those hills, laboring under the weight of the water jars, from the summit he saw nothing but more emptiness, limitless plains of rocks stained black by years in the sun. He spent most of the ensuing days in the small cave that he found, keeping an eye on the water. There wasn't much else to do, and though he was not able to sleep much, between the night cold and the demons and the dreams the demons sent, the rest was welcome.

The demons, once they found they could not disconcert him by whatever hideous or lascivious forms they took, scattered over the sand to pursue other amusements by tormenting one another, for there were not even animals in this blasted land. From the cave-mouth John watched the dust-devils chase one another, and wondered how many of those Hellspawned wights followed the gray shadow willingly.

Always, when he turned back to the cave's darkness, he glimpsed that tall, silent form out of the corner of his eye. It never left him, even when he stood outside in the noon sun. He could not see it, but he smelled the cold breath of stone and mold.

Which was good, he thought. There was less chance it would be anywhere near the gate, when Morkeleb and Jenny reached Prokep.

In the Garden of Winds, John ate and drank as little as he could; slept as little as he could, lying on the sandy cave-floor with the demon sword beneath him, shivering in his Winterlands clothes. There were not even scorpions here, or snakes; nothing but sand and arid rock. The days were hot; the nights, cold enough to freeze the water in the jars.

Amayon, in various guises both female and male, ceased trying to seduce him when he discovered John was taking notes of his ploys. The demons who remained in the decomposing bodies of the gnomes would come into the cave now and then, but after dealing with Caradoc and the corpse-wight in Bel, John was not impressed, and said so. As long as he had the demon-killer sword, they would not come too near. In the bitter nights he watched the stars, observing that the Dragonstar was no longer even visible above the horizon, and wondered if Jenny and Morkeleb had reached the enchanted city in safety, and whether in hiding there they spoke of other worlds. If they were in greater peril in Prokep's haunted Mazes, at least they had company, and there was much to be said for that. He found he missed them both.

The silver marks traced on his skin gleamed permanently now, even shining faintly phosphorescent in the dark.

The moon waxed, and the eternal wind blew winter-cold. But whether this place was in the same year or the same lifetime as the ruins of Prokep where Adromelech waited in the Henge within the Maze, John could not tell.

He lived in the silence of wind thrumming over stone, and waited, hoping to goodness Jenny and Morkeleb would figure out from his tracks what he'd done and where he was, and arrange their plans accordingly.

Just after midnight of the second night, John drank the rest of the water in the jar and started for the gate. Amayon walked beside him, in his usual guise of a beautiful boy of about fifteen. The remains of the gnomes, perhaps eight strong, followed, amid a rabble of unbodied demons whispering and shoving and glowing like fungus in the dark.

Would they rather, he wondered, have remained in this desolation, without even animals to torture, rather than risk torment and being devoured themselves? Or did they care, not knowing any other way to exist?

They all seemed to be present, however—John counted them, as undoubtedly the gray thing did as well. The gnomes were in bad shape, each trudging along in a humming column of flies, the only life John had seen since coming to the Garden of Winds. Presumably the corpses had been fly-blown long before their arrival here. Each still bore his small sack of talisman jewels, which troubled John far more than the presence of half-seen shadows or animate corpses. The moon had set, and the sky overhead seemed filmed, though there was no trace of cloud to be seen. The light sickened, as if the desert stars were in eclipse. Wind brushed chill over the silent land.

In the predawn hush beside the gate, Amayon whispered something in the demon tongue, and again John heard Folcalor's name.

"There's two ways into the Maze," John said over his shoulder to the shadow. "It's a gie long way across the city to the first one, that opens at sunrise. The second doesn't open till noon, but if Folcalor is lurkin' about, he's gonna have his goons to back him up. Your lads don't look in any too good shape. An' don't tell me to keep me voice down," he added, as Amayon opened his mouth to do so. "Folcalor can smell your friends better than he can hear me, that's for certain. We may not make that gate by sunrise as it is, y'know."

In the event they did not. John said, "Curse," as the brightening light found them still hurrying along the edge of the palace foundation, their steps slowed by duned sand. Though he strode fast, his longer legs far outdistancing the stumbling gnomes, he knew the likelihood of finding the gate still in existence was slim. Amayon flitted beside him, weightless and tireless as he had been in the Blue Hell: "Can't you go faster? No wonder Jenny deceives you with every man she meets. You have no more strength than a dotard."

"I'm gie glad she does," replied John, trying hard not to pant, "for she always comes back to me with wonderful tales of 'em all . . . you, too, come to think on it, you and Folcalor—"

"Shut up!"

John didn't flatter himself that he'd annoyed the demon—he, too, saw movement among the broken pillars, men striding toward them through the dust, and the glitter of swords in the rising light.

Folcalor's men, here at last.

"Ticked at you, is he?" he inquired conversationally, seeing the fresh-faced demon's uncertainty. On the high corner of the palace foundation John glimpsed again the spark of crystal, catching the morning light with an inner fire. "Vowed to be his vassal, or somethin' of the sort?"

"You know nothing of it," snapped Amayon.

"I know you were Folcalor's little pal over the winter," said John. He leaned against a broken corner of a wall, thrusting up through the sand, and noted that a sigil had been recently burned into a stone. The charring was fresh; it hadn't been there three weeks ago. "Jenny's told me of the pair of you, back in the days when you were helpin' him put together the dragon corps to put Rocklys, poor fool, on the throne of Bel as his pawn. How much that means among demons I don't know, of course—"

"It means among demons what it means among men," said the shadow's cold voice behind him. "One cannot always be watching one's back."

"I was always Adromelech's vassal," Amayon insisted, a trifle loudly, looking like he wanted to transform into a wisp of smoke and fly to the gate. "Can't you go faster? Or is this, too, a trick . . . ?"

"Aye, I just can't wait to cut loose from Peek-a-Boo back there and throw meself into Folcalor's arms. Curse it, we're never gonna—"

One of the gnomes seized him, thrust him behind a pillar as an arrow sliced past, missing him by inches. The gnome's hand left a sticky brown blot on John's sleeve. Men came running at them from one of the doorways in the palace foundation, men in the garb of common ruffians in Bel, or the leathers and furs of the Winterlands bandits. John hadn't realized quite how many of them there were, resurrected to demon life.

The next instant a stab of blinding pain went through his skull, almost dropping him to his knees, overwhelming and instantly abated: spell and counterspell, he guessed, angry at having his very flesh turned into a chess-piece in the demon war. He caught at the wall for support, fighting not to vomit; a foot away one of the gnomes struck a demon-ridden bandit with an ax, splitting its skull. As it collapsed, Amayon seized it, paying no attention whatsoever to the knife it thrust into him; grotesquely, the bleeding body straightened up, struggling with the remains of the head flopping back and forth.

Amayon opened his mouth, inhumanly wide, absurdly wide, jaw disjointing, like a grotesque puppet's in a play. The demon boy inhaled, and something silvery pulled out of the bandit's face, something that whipped wildly from side to side—

Amayon caught it with his teeth, grinning horribly, then took another breath, drawing it into himself. With the screaming thing still lashing back and forth against his chin, he glanced over at John, and winked as he sucked it in.

Elsewhere one of the dead gnomes was down, sliced to pieces by the men of Bel. Two others were chopping up one of the attackers, their own brown bones sticking out of their shredding flesh. Two of the men of Bel seized on a disembodied wight, devoured it as Amayon had done; John heard it shriek as it pulled apart. Flies roared and hummed. A dust-devil laced with fire swirled toward John across the sand and he pulled out his sword, but before it reached him the whirlwind shattered, flying apart in a rain of pebbles and silvery fragments. The cold skeletal hand of the shadow took him by the arm from behind, and he nearly jumped out of his skin.

"The place where the gnomes fell the first day," said the demon voice in his ear. "The place where magic will not work—"

"Good thinking," said John. "Follow me."

He supposed the Blind Spot had been a room in some mage's house. It seemed to have those dimensions, though its enclosing walls were long gone. The dead gnomes still lay there, alive with maggots, marking the spot—*Saves me the trouble of triangulating, anyway.* And incidentally would have saved Morkeleb and Jenny the trouble of searching the dust for his tracks, to figure out whether he'd gone to the Gate of Winds or not and how many demons were with him when he did. Amayon and the other demons, who whirled along beside them now in the shape of dust-devils or ghosts, dove at and struggled with the attackers, clawing and screaming. Only one gnome remained and he was clawed half to pieces, bone showing through the flesh; before they reached the Blind Spot he, too, was devoured. Talisman crystals scattered the sand, trampled into the dust.

Just as they reached the spot, two of Folcalor's men sprang from behind the red pillars with spears. John saw them coming—human bodies on the whole slowed demons down. His first slash cut halfway through one attacker's neck; as he disengaged for a sidelong chop through the body, he saw the other one turn suddenly, at no visible threat, and vanish in a flash of silver fire with a cry. Since slaying individual demons was no part of his plan with the dragons he guessed it was one of the traps set within the city—in any event, that, or the dying shriek of the attacker he'd struck, swept away further assault. He collapsed to his knees in the Blind Spot, darkness swirling into his vision:

Don't faint. Whatever you do, don't pass out now.

"Where lies the Maze?" the shadow's voice hissed in his ear. "Show me, now, in case you can't lead us later."

You've got to be joking. John rolled over, but it was nowhere to be seen. He could only feel the chill of it, smell it just beside him, behind him.

At least most of the time Aohila looked like something, even if she did have snakes in her hair.

Snakes in her hair . . .

The image snagged in his mind, almost reminding him of something, but it was driven out again when the shadow urged, "If you are killed—"

"Hard cheese to you." John shut his eyes, waves of dizziness making the desert sway around him as if he clung to a raft at sea.

The gray thing was saying something about Jenny and the children, but all John could do for a time was cling to the cold sand. *Aohila,* he thought, not knowing why the Demon Queen's image returned to his mind so strongly now. *It's the full of the moon, the last day of the Dragonstar's influence, Folcalor and his goons are here, Adromelech is readying himself to come forth. . . .*

So where is she?

His sight cleared. The first thing he saw was Amayon, drawing a sigil in the dust with one finger and putting talisman crystals around it, weaving a pattern of sacrificial deaths.

Noon was five hours off. Moonrise, twelve or so.

Jenny me love, he thought, *I hope you're somewhere near.*

Chapter 19

The sun stood three-quarters of the way to noon. Heat rippled in waves from the sand. Dust crusted on his skin, in his mouth, in his nose, on his spectacles, John forced himself to stand. The ribs Caradoc had cracked in the gatehouse fight gouged him like knives, and he felt eighty years old.

Curiously, he noted that through everything his spectacles were intact. Whatever else could be said about Jenny's magic, he reflected, that was one spell that worked like a champion. Gingerly, clumsily, he tore strips from what was left of his shirtsleeves and bandaged a cut arm and the lacerated fingers of his right hand: Amayon jeered, "Did we get a boo-boo?" as if to a child, but a shadowy hand slipped around John's shoulder to steady the rag as he tied the knot. But for the presence of the shadow, John guessed Amayon would have taken advantage of the moment to do more than sneer.

Among the stones all around the silvery glimmer of the demons flickered in the dry glaring sunlight. Dust-devils fleeted on the Blind Spot's edge like a deadly perimeter, rising and falling, little whirlpools of sharp pebbles stirring and settling. Waiting.

This, thought John, *is going to be bad.*

"Follow me," he said. "Keep them off me. The way into the Salt Garden opens only at noon, and only for a few minutes. If we miss it, we'll never hold out till evenin'."

"Tell me where it is."

"It's up your nose," retorted John. "Just follow me."

The dust-devils whirled up again, then settled—possibly at some spell of the gray thing's, though John as usual could feel nothing; in any case, the men of Bel were waiting, armed, tireless, many of them already dead. He thought there were fewer of them than even the fighting could account for, but it was still going to be a bad run to the gate.

"That bottle, now," he said softly, speaking over his shoulder. "If Folcalor should show up—"

"Folcalor will come," whispered the shadow, "when the way is prepared, when his power is at its height. I think not sooner. And I do not believe that his Greatness Lord Adromelech would tolerate it, should another trap the Arch-Traitor and deprive him of the pleasure."

John didn't even phrase his first thought—*Good*—in his mind. If worst came to worst, he'd been prepared to spend the rest of eternity trapped in the bottle with Folcalor, though with Adromelech loose and roving around it was half the battle lost right there: Now he only muttered truculently, "Well, I ain't keen on gettin' killed so his Greatness can have the privilege of trappin' Folcalor after I'm dead," a remark which the shadow ignored.

Jen, I hope you and Morkeleb got your spells in place while we were all hidin' out beyond the Gate of Winds.

Because if something had gone wrong, reflected John wearily, he was going to be in tremendous trouble when Adromelech pulled the stopper out of that bottle and disappeared along with his foe. *They're never gonna believe me if I say, "Goodness gracious, how'd that happen?"*

He wiped the dust from his spectacles, triangulated on the unmarked spot—he could see it in the distance, about half a mile to the south of the Blind Spot—and shifted the grip of his cramped and blistered hand on his sword.

The moment they stepped clear of the Blind Spot, Folcalor's demons were around them like sharks around a foundering raft. Whirlwinds and dust blasted them: pebbles, sand, what felt like razor-edged shards of glass. Spells of dizziness, nausea, pain. Counterspells darted, flames searing up through the sand only to be smothered with dust or swept away with wind. Blindness came and went, as if someone repeatedly caught the burning glare of the sun on silvered glass and directed it into his eyes. Out of the blindness and the dust swords slashed at him, never quite coming near enough to get in a counterstroke; he felt as he had when he was a child, when his father would thrust a sword into his hand and drive him hard against the courtyard wall. . . .

It had taught him. But he hadn't liked it.

Damned to you lot. If you didn't get me with semiautomatic sub-

machine guns in Corvin's laboratory, you're not going to do it with handfuls of pebbles in wind.

"Hold them off!" he yelled, barely able to see the pillar, the hill, the bulk of the palace foundation that told him where he was. He fell to his knees, dust and rock tearing him, demons shrieking. . . .

I'd better have this right.

The sun was overhead. On the ground he traced the sigil of the door, that Amayon had traced on every gate from the Wraithmire to Paradise and beyond. Shrieking whirlwinds tore the sign away, and he traced it again.

The demons swept past him, across the sigil.

And disappeared, leaving him alone to face blindness and dust and men slashing out of the whirling brown wall of blown sand with spears.

He killed one, two … then green fire roared up between him and them, and he dove over where the sigil had been and prayed to the Old God and the Old God's Granny that his calculations were right.

He was on his knees in the Salt Garden. Brushing the dust off his velvet doublet, Amayon sniffed, "Some warrior."

"All I need to do is get through it alive." John climbed stiffly to his feet. Beds of salt stretched in all directions around them, granite-bordered, like flower-beds in the Long Garden of the palace at Bel, decorated with winding paths of stepping-stones. The smell of salt burned in the air, and waves of heat breathed from the ground. It was always noon here.

Around them the silvery slumped demons were faded, ashen lizards slowly shriveling in the burning air. John couldn't see the gray thing, but guessed it was right there behind him as always.

"Let's go, you lot," he said with a briskness he was far from feeling. "I want to get done with this as badly as you do." Turning, he led the way into the Maze.

For days in Prokep he had studied it, trying this route or that one and making notes: Its pathways had changed their appearance from day to day, but the count of the turnings had remained ever the same. Through walls of gray rock or fog-netted hedge, he led the demons swiftly, listening behind him, around him, in the curious still-ness of whatever Hell or enclave or world constituted the world of the

Maze. He guessed that some of Folcalor's forces at least had followed them in, and prayed again that Morkeleb and the dragons had put his plan into motion—and that his plan would work. When he was younger he'd comforted himself going into battle by saying, *Well, they can't do more than kill you,* but lately he'd found out this wasn't true.

He wondered where Jenny was, and if she was all right.

And smiled, only thinking about her. That lovely, strange, and solitary lady, wherever she was, whatever she did. He'd kissed her in the alleyway behind the tavern, and felt her arms around him, and she was his lady again.

Blister the lot of you, he thought, glancing back over his shoulder—of course he couldn't see the gray thing, but the rest of the demons looked paler, smaller, and even Amayon seemed to have lost a little of his glossy look. *I'll survive this to have a life with her yet.*

As he threaded the paths of the Maze, and watched the demons around him fade and wither, he understood the wisdom of the mages who had died in the Henge, powering this whole system of traps with their deaths. Of course they'd needed a way to reach the Henge themselves, in case of unforeseen emergencies. The Maze fed on magic, as the demons did. The longer they stayed in it, the more it leached them, their own magic going to feed the strength of the Henge. He toyed with the notion of leading them here and there until they simply disappeared, but dropped it: With the talisman jewels as a source of power, he had no idea how long they'd last, and in any case his goal was to get the catch-bottle to Adromelech. Even without the gray thing's spells, Folcalor might very well be capable of breaking the Henge from the outside anyway.

The demons had defeated the magic of the wizards by sourcing their power in an alien star.

The answer was to combat them not with strength, but with a thing they did not understand.

The spring day faded, as they wound and rewound their way between the walls of the Maze.

The Moon of Winds stood cold as a bride's pearl in the dimming sky.

Above the hills—visible, as the broken pillars of the city were visible, as the barren, time-scored foundation of the old palace was visible—the Dragonstar flickered, a diamond speck in the deepening blue.

When they came out of the Maze, the Maze itself was no longer to be seen. Only a suggestion of smoke, glowing in the low places of the ground. The ruined city of Prokep stretched around them, as it had that first night, when Corvin had said, *I did not think that I had been gone so long.*

Around the Henge, the city itself lay motionless as stone. But moonlight glinted, here and there, on crystals: on the tops of the broken pillars, or on the foundation of the palace, or simply laid in the sand where the sand would cover them within days. More than once during the fighting retreat to the Salt Garden, John had glimpsed runes written on stones that had not been here when he'd searched the city three weeks ago.

Jen, he thought, his heart hammering, *this had better work.*

The night around the Henge flowed with demons, blue-shining and hideous, and stank of all the foulness of Hell. That cold, strong hand closed on John's nape again, and he stood still, looking into the ring, feeling the demons gather at his back.

Out of the puddle or ice-chip or whatever it was in the center, a firefly seemed to rise. It danced for a moment among the stones, and tiny as it was, its hot small light picked edges of white fire along the rough rune-scribed menhirs and on Amayon's smiling, boyish face.

Amayon took the talisman jewels from the gnomes—despite his greater powers he, too, had trouble carrying that many material objects—and moved around the ring, scattering them on the earth like a farmer seeding a field. Far away behind him John heard the gray thing singing, an eerie wail like a dying child, though the hand still gripped his neck. *Gaw, what if they decide to use my life as one of those they're getting power from?* He shifted his grip on his sword. *If it comes to it, Amayon's the one I'll kill.*

There seemed now to be half a dozen fireflies, drifting in the blue dusk within the Henge.

Where the jewels lay scattered, lines of light began to burn in the dust. Charred curves and sigils, fingerlets of fire burning up out of the ground. Threads of greenish lightning snaked over the stones; the air crackled with ozone. Somewhere within the Henge a deep voice called out, a bass echo of the gray thing's thin sobbing, an obscene chuckle mocking primal grief. The two voices merged, separated, and merged again, and white light flashed across the clear sky overhead, and underfoot the earth spoke, a sullen, terrible growling. For a nightmarish instant John had the sickened sense that the ground was about to give way.

The grip on his arms thrust him forward between the stones, and into the Henge.

As when he had stepped through Miss Mab's Sigil of the Door pasted onto the Burning Mirror's black surface, everything changed. Once inside the Henge, John saw how what he'd taken for a chip of ice or glass, or a small puddle in its center, was in fact a pool three or four yards across. Its surface trembled with a constant, shivering agitation, and steam billowed from it, flowing out over the ground and veiling the feet of the stones. *How many stones could I count from here?* John wondered frivolously, and dismissed the thought at once as something likely to get him killed. Through the steam he saw designs traced on the earth, sigils and power-curves and runes, fantastically intricate. If they made them like Jenny did, with whispered spells and power laid on every mark, they must have been at it for weeks.

Or years.

Or centuries.

In a chair beside the pool Adromelech sat. Gross, gelid, he glowed faintly, like rotting fish. He turned yellow eyes on John and the eyes made John feel cold and sick. They were eyes that cared nothing, that wanted everything, eyes that devoured everything they touched. Demon eyes. Eyes you couldn't look at because if you did, you'd understand things that would cause you to kill yourself later. . . . John moved his gaze quickly aside. And seeing this, Adromelech smiled, long silver tongue slipping out between dripping teeth.

So you have a sword that will kill, little friend? Amusement deepened in the flat, vile gaze. The smell of the demon was appalling, sewage and carrion and gangrene and carnage, and the demon-stink of burned blood. John knew without being told that what he smelled was the thing's soul. *But you know it won't be necessary, don't you? You leave us be, my far-wandering friend, and we'll leave you be. You've done us good service. We are fair.*

John clamped his mind shut against the words, *And I'm Queen of the May,* and said, "I don't give a shovel of mud if you're fair or not. Just get me home and leave us be. That's all I ask."

And tried very much to sound like the kind of man who'd believe what a demon told him.

Of course. Adromelech's voice in his mind was almost a purr. In the globe of the demon's huge belly John could see the half-digested shards of other wights: a staring eye here, a disembodied mouth screaming and another chewing on some organ that was all that it could reach.

Adromelech stretched out his hand, curiously white and childlike—a little girl's hand. John didn't exactly see the gray thing, but there was something there by the Arch-Wight's throne, something he couldn't look at properly, and a moment later Adromelech held the silver catch-bottle. He chuckled again, gloating, and John thought he'd suffocate, wondering if Adromelech guessed the nature of the trap. But the Arch-Wight stroked and kissed the silver bottle, wrapping his long tongue around it while Amayon prostrated himself at Adromelech's feet, kissing and licking and sucking, half-hidden by the drifting smoke.

Outside the Henge, silent lightning flashed in the empty sky. Though John could have sworn it had been the shadow thing chanting, now that the creature was inside the ring with him he could still hear its voice outside, calling down power, calling on the lightning, on the Dragonstar. Calling on the full moon and the deaths of those whose souls were locked in the final instant of agony within the talisman jewels. *Hothwais of death,* he thought, and saw how the jewels glowed on the ground outside, fire within them brightening and dimming in time to the cold far-off chanting voice. *No wonder they started with the magic of the gnomes.* Still delightedly caressing the catch-bottle, Adromelech began to chant again as well, a clammy bass that spoke like the rumblings in the earth.

Things were coming out of the pool. Curling silver things in glass shells that broke like eggs as the demons within them grew and uncoiled. Things that mutated in shape and in size, tentacled and rubbery, others like glistening lizards. Some floated in the air, blown up like bladders: grinning mouths yammering unheard random words, demon eyes. John glanced behind him and backed as close to the stones as he could, fighting the urge to bolt. In the moment that the Henge was broken, he thought, they would have power, over his body and possibly his mind as well. And he'd better not draw attention to himself one moment before they were completely occupied with other things.

Adromelech laughed in triumph. There were things outside the Henge now as well, glistening half-visible in the twilight, only half material. Grinning things, with eyes that shone like red mirrors. Human things holding jewels in their hands, and each jewel screamed and cried for pity with desperate tiny voices. Overhead, the Moon of Winds climbed to mid-heaven, and the Dragonstar's twin tails whipped and flickered in the dimming sky. The whole world smelled of scalded blood.

The sigils underfoot began to burn.

John stepped off the marks—it was difficult to find a clear space—and watched the tongues of fire dart from the talisman gems and run up and down those intricate lines. White light stabbed up from the pool, and Adromelech laughed again and raised his hands in triumph.

The heat inside the Henge coalesced, the air at flaming-point, like being bound to the stake again. Lines of ghostly fire crawled up the stones, sigils burning into the rock, as if brands were pressed on them from the inside, fire eating outward from the core. Half-suffocated, John could see Folcalor's demons outside, though, pressing against the invisible bounds. Shrieking cacophony, and spells of malice ready to pop like a rupturing blister, to pour poison inward and outward. Jewels glittered in the demon hands: stolen souls. Stolen deaths.

Another deep voice chanted, taking up the time of Adromelech's and the gray wight's. A flash of fire, and John saw between two of the stones a mirror with an iron frame, the black enamel of its surface cracked across and across and silver light pouring out of it and surrounding its conqueror in a halo of iridescent dark. Goffyer the gnome mage, arms outflung and Folcalor's demon grin transforming his wrinkled face. Power flashed around him like whirling knives.

On the edge of the world, the Dragonstar glimmered, a far-off mirror reflecting alien magic and alien hate.

Adromelech threw up his arms and cried out, calling the Dragon-star by its true name: the name it knew itself by, among all the true names of the stars.

With a searing crash the tallest of the standing stones exploded, red-hot fragments of rock spraying like bullets through the Henge. John ducked, sword still in hand, as burning shards tore his face and clothing. Closer to him another stone burst, and another. A column of light, solid as alien rock, burst from the pool and fire rushed into the Henge from outside, demons howling, flame searing up from the ground.

It was time to run for it, and John ran. He knew he'd have only minutes, maybe only seconds, before the demons had their first flush of greedy joy at tearing one another and turned to attack a human. He ducked between two stones as they went cherry-red with heat; they exploded behind him, the shock flinging him forward on his face. He scrambled to his hands and knees, caught up his sword, made for the point in the ring where it was possible to get closest at sunset.

And Jenny was there. She had run up in the very wake of the demons and was now on her knees, huge swoops of her arm sketching a gate-sigil in red chalk on the ground. A silver shape struck at her from the air, and John slashed at it, the scream as it shredded away into fire making the demons still swirling around the outside of the Henge turn, aghast, then flee. But few noticed, for between the red-glowing stones John could see Folcalor like a lean silver-green tiger, shedding Goffyer's body as Adromelech's spells exploded it, plunging through the chaos of struggling shadows, plunging straight toward Adromelech.

Jenny scrambled to her feet, looked around—stood still and looked around, and John knew she was looking for him. With what was about to happen, he thought, with what was already going on inside the Henge, she was *standing still* and looking for him.

She yelled, "John!" and they grabbed hands like two children, plunged away from the stone circle as fast as they could run. Nauseating pain gripped and snapped at him, ripples and eddies of it, and of searing heat, the un-Limited side slips of the demon spells. Magic spread out through Prokep, toxic magic, madness and hate that could cover the world if unchecked. Handfast, John and Jenny plunged away from the Henge, toward the broken shaft of a pillar on whose top gleamed an ice-white crystal, that caught the light of the Dragonstar.

Beyond that pillar they turned and looked back, in time to see Folcalor fall upon Adromelech in a windmill of adamant claws. The Arch-wight flung up his girlish little arms, cried something that John knew to be Folcalor's true name, the name Caradoc had whispered to the silver bottle. . . .

And both were gone.

Jenny cried, "Now!" her voice like silver lightning, slicing the night.

At the top of the pillar, the crystal flashed. On a promontory of a broken wall, a second crystal caught the glancing reflection, and on a knee of half-buried stone, a third. In and around the Ring the demons were crying out, shrieking, some still tearing at one another and others casting about, seeking their lords. Around the outer perimeter of the burning stones, crystal to crystal, the icy light flashed, silver light licking across the intervening space, until the Henge was formed again, irregularly shaped and about a hundred yards beyond the original ring: crystals set in rune-written rock, an impassable, burning net.

The whining vibration of ether-plasma stabbed through John's skull.

"Dear gods, you didn't tell me about that!" gasped Jenny, pressing a hand to her head.

"Sorry, love." John wiped the blood from his cheek with the back of his wrist, letting go of neither his sword nor her hand. He was trembling, sweat running down his face and so dizzy, he struggled only to stay on his feet, but could not take his eyes off the chaos within the Henge.

Out of the red-chalked Gate that Jenny had drawn in the ground, shining things were coming. Drawn by the smell of demons, they rose from the rock, and from the Hell beyond that rock: flashing wheels of wings and eyes, which rolled about among the shattered menhirs, devouring whatever they found. John saw the gray shadow-creature flee wailing, to be caught by a creature like a huge glowing slug, of the kind that had once nearly killed Amayon when the demon was guiding him through that particular Hell. Saw it drawn slowly into the slug's round, dark mouth. Heard it scream, with the panic agony of the dying, and it died slowly and hard. Smaller things, like burning hoops scattering lightning, darted in packs, encircling groups of demons and shredding them with claws of flame. Demons fled toward the smoking pool of the Hell-gate, but the Shining Things cut them off from it, pitiless and cold. Others tried to escape the Henge and into the outer world, but fell back crying from the burn of the ether, whose Otherworld nature they did not know or understand, and the Shining Things devoured them.

Jenny's hand closed tight over John's.

"Jenny!" Amayon fell to his knees only feet away from them, ichor streaming from his ripped back. Amayon as John had first seen him, the beautiful youth with the curly black hair, berry-blue eyes stretched with genuine terror, unknowable pain. "Jenny, let me out! I promise you, I swear to you, I'll be your servant, your slave! My love, my love, don't let them—"

Jenny turned her eyes aside, then a moment later looked back, in time to watch the great gleaming slug of silver take Amayon by the foot, and with inexorable leisure—one slow, terrible gulp at a time—draw him in.

The demon felt himself dying. John could see that in his eyes, the expression he'd seen in the eyes of men he'd killed in battle, all those years of defending the people of the Winterlands. He put his arm around Jenny, wishing she didn't have to see. Knowing there had been a time when she had loved the demon, not because she'd wished to, but because that is the nature of the bond between demons and men.

Jenny said nothing, but he felt her shudder as she pressed against his side.

By the time Amayon was dead, the other demons were gone as well.

The Shining Things rolled back and forth across the parched ground, like Snuff and Bannock hunting for the final crumbs of dinner. They paused, flickering, over the burned-out husks of the soul-jewels that had been crushed and exploded in the course of the fight, and passed on. They clustered briefly around the mirror, which lay knocked on its side between the stones of the old Henge and the chilly crystal lattices of the new, but did not seem to be able to pass through its gate. Nor did they enter the Pool. Gleaming with a skeletal light, they flickered out of sight, but the ozone whisper of their presence remained in the air.

Having been summoned to the Henge of Prokep, there they would remain.

The heat that had flowed out of the Henge dispersed rapidly. John didn't think he'd ever felt so cold in his life.

Jenny pressed her face to his shoulder, and brought up the end of her plaid, to cast around his shoulders to warm them both.

Then her breath caught and she stiffened, and John turned his head, his aching hand tightening again on the hilt of his sword.

He knew already what he'd see.

The Demon Queen stood in the moonlight, just where the shadow of a pillar laid a band of black on the lifeless sand.

John thought she'd been standing there for some time. She looked to him as she'd always looked: a tall, slim woman with an expression older than her face. Things moved in the dark chaotic coils of her hair. They stood up and hissed at him, exactly, he realized now, as had the worms in the black rotting hair of the graveyard wight that had slain King Uriens of Bel.

The gold eyes met his, and smiled.

She crossed the sand toward him, lazily, as if she had all the night before her. Though the air was still, all the smoky veils that wreathed her lifted and blew as if in some private atmosphere, as if she carried her own Hell about with her and was never completely free of it. She must have seen John use the demon sword, and knew its power, but she came straight up to him and stood before him, her smile lingering on her lips.

Then her eyes went to the Burning Mirror, where it lay within the new Henge of ether-light. It was a distance of nearly a hundred feet, from the edge of the Henge to the smoking surface of the enameled glass, and though the Shining Things were not to be seen, their crazy humming blended with the whine of the ether. They were near.

John smiled into her golden eyes and said softly, "Good luck, love."

And for a flickering instant her smile turned human, like a rueful girl's. "And you." She put her hands on either side of his face, and kissed his lips. Then she walked quite calmly across the boundary of the ether-Henge. She seemed to melt into shadow as the Shining Things flashed into being, rolling and swooping toward the place. John saw where her feet burned the sand in one place, two ... a flicker of silver mist played over the cracked enamel of the mirror. By the time the wheels of fire reached the spot, it was gone.

Long silence lay over the ruin of Prokep, broken only by the faint hum of the ether relays. Even the wind was still. The cold moon passed its zenith, and the Dragonstar slipped below the undulant dark horizon. For the last time, John knew from his calculations, in a thousand years.

A thousand years from now would the demons evolve some other scheme? It was a good bet they'd do it without either Folcalor or Adromelech, neither of whom—being demons—would release the other, or release the comfort of triumph at being the other's jailer.

As for the Demon Queen ...

Softly, almost below the level of the senses, music whispered in the night. Beautiful music, alien airs glowing like colors: blue and golden, pink and green ... black in black in black ...

On their broken pillars, their stumps of stone, on the rim of the palace foundation and the ruin of the gate where the Garden of Souls had stood, the ten ether-crystals began to glow more brightly still. The white-green ether-light was swallowed up momentarily in colors, flashing like a rainbow of mirrors. At the top of the pillar beside them, John saw the ghost-shape of wings, the uncoiling glitter of razor spines, catching the spectral moonlight: opal eyes, and the firefly halo of antennae lights. The dragon emerged from the crystal like a butterfly, no bigger than a man's crossed thumbs—John couldn't imagine how he saw it as clearly as he did.

But it grew like a silken cloud, rising above the pillar, weightless as shadow against the stars and beautiful beyond earthly conception of glory.

From each ether-crystal a dragon emerged, sparkling as if each scale were a mirror to catch the light of the stars that had been their first home. The night sang the music of their names.

Centhwevir blue-and-golden—John remembered, identified, the tune Jenny had long ago learned by rote upon her harp, in the days before she'd even known who Centhwevir was. *Nymr blue violet-crowned*–Ian's dragon partner. Hagginarshildim pink-and-green, and young Byrs of a thousand hues.

The dragons who had been possessed by demons, in the high brightness of summer, when the Dragonstar's first head had glimmered in the sky.

Morkeleb like a starry shadow, barely seen but in many ways more beautiful than all the rest.

And Corvin black-and-silver, reaching down with his long hind-legs to settle on the earth, tucking his tabby-silk wings against his sparkling sides. From pillar to rock the ether-crystals continued to burn, green-white again, the stream of their alien light unflagging, once called through from its distant world.

It is accomplished, said the dragon who had once been a scientist, and craned his bird-like head on the end of his long neck, surveying the ring of the Ether Henge. *The ether-flow from crystal to crystal is stable now, and it should power the spells of Ward indefinitely. Demon magic can't touch it, since it isn't of this world, and I think it will be long before any of them dares emerge into the Ring to be devoured by the Shining Things. I did not think they would be able to stand against the combination of magic and science.*

It was not your magic, nor your science, Black-and-Silver One, that wrought the doom of the Hellspawn. Morkeleb tilted his head to one side, a characteristic gesture, and the starlight twinkled on the points of his invisible horns. *What the Hellspawn could not fight against was the trust that our nestmates had in Mistress Jenny. The certainty that if they entered into the ether-crystals at her behest, to draw the ether from the Otherworld, that it was not a trap or a ruse to make them always slaves.*

Corvin's spines bristled and he said, *Trust?* as if the word were in an alien tongue. *In saving each of them from Folcalor, she held each by his name. They had to do as she commanded.*

But she did not command, pointed out Morkeleb. *She spoke no word of power, when she summoned each by his name.*

What are you saying? Corvin's nostrils rimmed with flame. *That now we must ... TRUST ... mortal men? Things that are born and perish like the grass, and like the grass change with every wind that turns?*

I say nothing, replied the Dragonshadow. *Only that trust is not a thing of dragons, and that tonight, it was the saving of us all.*

Wizard-woman, Dreamweaver, I shall be returning to the West, to the Skerries of Light. I have learned some things of humankind, and of the Hellspawn, and it is time for me to meditate upon that which I have learned. My nestmates and I shall bear you back to Bel, if you will, to wait upon the new King in his coronation. Or if you will, we shall carry you north to your Hold, if you have had your fill of Kings and demons, of war and grief and Hell.

John started to speak, then glanced at Jenny. "What'll it be, love?" he asked. "Tea and cream cakes in Bel with old Ector, or Aunt Jane's bannocks and another six weeks of snow?"

"Gar will need someone," said Jenny, "to help him order the Realm, in the wake of the damage the demons caused."

"That's enough to make me run screamin' in the other direction," John sighed, and dabbed a sword-cut tentatively on his shoulder with one hand. "I suppose you're right, love, if you can contact Ian by crystal, an' hear all's well there." He sheathed the demon blade he still held, and extended his bare arm to the light of the Moon of Winds. Beneath the grime, the silver marks the Demon Queen had traced on his flesh had disappeared. Somehow, he did not feel surprised.

He sighed, and turned back to Jenny. "Speakin' of cream cakes," he added hopefully, "I don't suppose, you've any food left, before we start back?"

Chapter 20

The dragons flew together as far as the end of Nast Wall, with the exception of Corvin, who remained in Prokep, guarding the great treasure-hoard within the palace's crypt. "So much for the greatest scientist an' loremaster of the star-drakes," John remarked, a little sadly, as he and Jenny climbed the wide stair to the top of the stone foundation and looked out for the last time over the ruins. "What good's his lore, an' all that he's learned an' known, goin' to do anyone now? He'll sink into his dreams with the gold, an' stay there forever, contemplatin' his magic dreams."

Never mind, said Morkeleb heartlessly, for he did not like the black-and-silver dragon. He waited for them at the top, sparkling like a mirror in the dry desert light and casting no shadow on the stones: barely more than a smoke-wraith himself. *We could not have appointed a better guardian for the ether-ring than the great and mighty scientist who devised it. Should any come who might interfere with it, he will soon deal with them.* And saying this, he spread his shadowy wings. The other dragons drew near the earth, weightless as flowers: Morkeleb gathered Jenny into his claws, and Centhwevir, an old and surprisingly sweet-natured drake, bore John up. Sometimes during the long flight to the West, Jenny would look across the distance that separated them and see her husband peering eagerly down through the winter clouds, taking notes on what he could see of the country-side beneath.

The star-drakes sang as they flew, making music with their minds. They made a song about defeating the demons, passed from mind to mind with laughing melody like a universe of silver bells, and another about being within the crystals and drawing the ether from the other universe into their own, to power the crystals forever. Sometimes they flew close to one another, enameled colors brilliant against the gray mists of the clouds; sometimes they spread out, until they seemed no larger that gay-hued birds among those towering columns of white and silver. But always the music surrounded them, golden and wild and sweet.

They sang older songs, too, the lore of ancient dragons, of things passed from mind to mind over the centuries, and Jenny heard again of the Dragonshadows who had been with them in the past, invisible and wise. She thought—but she was not sure—that the dragons regarded these creatures as curiosities, almost alien to themselves; creatures almost of jest, to be taken lightly. Yet, in flying, they gave Morkeleb wide berth.

Only when that golden flight came to an end, late in the afternoon on a deserted meadow high above the Clae woods within sight of the city walls of Bel, did Morkeleb speak of the Dragonshadows to her. The other dragons bade Jenny good-bye, their minds shaping *Dragonfriend, dragonfriend.* They rose into the air, circling, brilliant as flowers in the slanting gold light, and Morkeleb, who had faded in and out of visibility through the day, remained like a silken shadow on the earth. The snow had melted from this place not a day before, and still lay in patches in the shadows of the rocks. In places the thinnest fuzz of green showed among the flattened swathes of last year's brown grass.

"We'd best be careful how we approach the city," remarked John, seating himself rather shakily on a rock and pulling his plaids tighter about him. "They'll have us up as beggars." And he grinned, bruised and filthy and tattered.

"I'll speak to Miss Mab with the scrying-stone," said Jenny. "She will know if all is well, and if the last of the demons have in fact left the Deep. If that's the case, she'll send someone to meet us."

"It twilkin' better be the case," grumbled John. He took off his spectacles, looked around for a clean spot on his shirt to clean them with, and resignedly put them back on. "I can tell you now I'm gie wearied of adventures an' I will *not* appreciate another loose end to tie up."

All appears well within the city. Morkeleb settled on his haunches and tucked his wings close to his sides; Jenny could see through him, as if he were wrought of smoky glass. *Farmers go about their business in the orchards outside the city gate, and within the walls men raise banners, and put up platforms draped in bright colors. Tables are being set out in the city squares, and tuns of wine brought in wagons to all the fountains. Your little Princeling's red house-banners still fly from the palace jacks.*

"Good," sighed John. "The way things have gone I was afraid somethin' else awful had happened, though God knows what it *could* be after all this. You'll come to the crownin' with us?" he added, shading his eyes against the evening sun and squinting up at the dragon. Far off, a cow-bell clinked, tiny in the great silence of the meadow; a dog barked beyond the wood. "I'm to swear allegiance as Thane of the Winterlands, so Badegamus has got to let me bring a guest or two. It'd be the first time a dragon attended the crownin' of a King—first time anybody knows of, anyway. If nothing else, they'll serve up a champion lunch."

Even the prospect of a champion lunch, sniffed Morkeleb, *would not reconcile me to the spectacle of poorly writ allegorical plays performed on streetcorners, of hastily rehearsed hymns sung by amateur temple choirs in praise of a young man whose sole virtue seems to be that he is the son of Uriens. Why Kings wish to celebrate their entry into a lifetime of care by smearing oil on their heads, standing all day in a hot robe, and making their subjects all drunk, I have never been able to fathom.*

"Well, some would have it you don't remember a lesson properly unless you been flogged—me old tutor was like that—but they settled on bein' bored an' hungry for coronations 'cause the King's like to carry grudges." John yawned hugely—looking at him, Jenny thought he didn't look like he'd slept in days, never mind the shattering chaos they had just come through. Arriving in Prokep with Morkeleb after a journey of a day and a night, she had found John's tracks, and the bodies of two dead gnomes, but no sign of John or of the demons themselves. She looked forward to hearing what he'd done with them for three days. But it didn't look like it had been an easy time.

John went on: "Happen the oil on the head, an' the prayin'—an' maybe the amateur temple choir, I don't know—will bring back to the King's mind that he promised to answer for the lives of his people, when the time comes to really do it. God knows when you're actually goin' into battle you need somethin' to remind you. But our Gar's had a bit of practice at it now, before takin' it up as a full-time occupation, so I think he'll do. The lunch is the most important part," he added.

"There's no King properly crowned without there's a lunch to make it official."

I shall steel my mind with long meditation, replied Morkeleb, *to overcome the sorrow of missing the lunch.* And turning his diamond eyes on Jenny—the dragon eyes that mortals are cautioned never to meet—he asked, *And are you, too, Wizard-woman, gie wearied of adventures?*

For now, she said. *Though I suspect we will have some, riding back to the Winterlands when this crowning is over.*

I was not proposing, said the dragon, *to fly away with you on a re-newed quest, with your coronation sweetmeats still in your hands. But when summer has passed, or perhaps two summers, and peace lies on the land, will you grant a boon to me, you and your far-venturing Dreamweaver?*

For it is true, as you have said, Wizard-woman. I am not a dragon anymore. I have passed beyond a gate of being into an unknown self, and whether I am a Dragonshadow, or some other thing entirely, I now know not. While I watched for the Demon Queen in the Skerries of Light, I returned to the Birdless Isle where the Dragonshadows dwelled—where for years I had waited for them in meditation, seeking the answers to questions concerning my heart. By all the signs there they have been gone for many lives of men, far longer than ever they have gone be-fore. Many nights there I listened across the face of the earth for their thoughts, and found none.

And so I ask you this: Your Dreamweaver has ridden on errantry for pay, for the gnomes in the past and now also for the Demon Queen. What pay will you take, Dreamweaver, to go upon errantry with me, and seek the Dragonshadows through the gates of other Hells?

"Save a dragon, slave a dragon," John quoted the old spell. "It goes for the children of men as well, y'know."

Does it? Had Morkeleb had eyebrows, he would have lifted one. *I must have been looking in the wrong direction, for I had not observed this phenomenon.*

Jenny laughed, and said, "I think you were looking in the wrong direction, my friend—or looking at the wrong men. We bear much study, you know, men and women both. Even the worst of us. Even those of us who do no more than bear our children, and feed our cats, and live quietly among our friends. There is other music than that which dragons make."

So I am coming to learn.

The dragon spread his wings, and Jenny said, "Yes, my friend. Come to the North in a season or two, when there is peace on the land, and we will go with you through the gates of other Hells." And, as John had said to the Demon Queen, she smiled at him and said, "Good luck."

There was a time, she knew, when he would have sniffed at the concept of luck, for luck was not a thing of dragons. But he only looked down into her eyes and said, *And you.*

He rose in the air, letting the wind take him, and was gone from sight.

"You're not going to like this, love," John said two mornings later, as he turned from the door with the servant's tray of braided breads and honey in his hands. This time the butter was stamped in a fanciful design and embellished with violets, and there was a small copper pot of water, which John set in the fire, and a red bowl of coffee beans. These he dumped into a copper roasting pan, and settled down cross-legged on the hearth in his nightshirt to cook: It was only the most careless host who would have his servants make coffee for guests.

Jenny, sitting up in bed with the blankets around her, put her hands on her hips in an attitude of mock exasperation and said, "What did you accidentally leave behind in Prokep?"

John laughed. "Me innocence."

"You haven't been innocent since the day you learned to read." But she smiled as she said it and, gathering her voluminous nightshirt around her, went to sit beside him on the hearth.

Last night in nightmares she had seen Amayon die again. Waking, she had cried the tears she had not wept at the time, tears she still did not understand. John had held her, rocked her like a child until she'd slept again.

She supposed she would dream it again, and again, until the poison was all worked out of her. She could not tell how long that would be. She still could only work small magic, kindling fires, or a little healing—John's broken ribs seemed better—for the spells by which she had guided the dragons into the ether-crystals at Prokep had left her exhausted and drained. But that, too, did not trouble her as once it had. The strength was in her, pure and growing like a flower, her own magic, rooted in everything she was and had survived.

Her soul felt at peace. In the plantings of the palace's Long Garden outside the window, the first flowers of spring were beginning to show. "What won't I like?"

"I think I've figured out what that thing was, that killed Uriens," John said. "And why."

Along the garden terraces beyond the window, palace servants in red carried precious carpets, cushions, sprays of hothouse flowers to the banqueting hall. Feasting would begin that afternoon, and carry on all night to celebrate Gareth's coronation as King of Bel. Lying in bed at the first peep of the chill spring sunshine, Jenny had heard the footsteps of the chamberlains going down to the Temple of Sarmendes in the great Square of the Sun, where people had been waiting since dawn to see the Prince ride in procession, and behind him all the lords of the Realm. Past the wavery glass of the windows Jenny could recognize, by the colors of his fur jacket, the young Prince Tinán of Imperteng, who had arrived the day before to swear allegiance to his new King. He was talking to the tall, black-robed form of the Master of Halnath, the Lord of the Eastern Marches.

John would swear allegiance for the Winterlands, as he had sworn to Uriens after he'd driven Morkeleb from the Realm.

The Realm would begin to heal.

She looked sidelong at John, and raised her eyebrows, and he concentrated for a few moments on stirring the coffee beans—not that he was likely to maintain that concentration, she knew. He was no better a coffeemaker than he was a camp cook.

After a night's sleep in the Deep of Ylferdun—whence members of Miss Mab's household had come to meet them in the meadow—several baths and another night's sleep in Bel, John had lost some of his look of a mad hermit, though he was still red with sunburn and very thin. The hearth glow outlined his long, bent nose, and flashed rosy amber from the lenses of his spectacles as he turned his head. His expression was both bemused and a little sad. He said, "I think it was the Demon Queen."

Jenny stared at him. "Why would the Demon Queen . . . ?"

"As payment," said John. "To get me back on the good side of Ector, an' all them who'd said I was workin' for her. To let it be seen *by
all* that I slayed the monster that killed the King, rather than *me*
havin' to kill the King meself, which of course I would have had to do.
Because she was the only one in a position to give me back me good
reputation. An' because I think she planned the whole scheme of
Folcalor's defeat, from start to finish."

"*Aohila?*"

"I think so." John shook the pan and dumped the unevenly
roasted beans into a mortar to grind: "This was gie easier with an
ether-powered grindin' machine, let me tell you, love."

He gestured with the pestle. "I think from the moment Folcalor
seized Caradoc's body years ago, an' started puttin' together Adromelech's plan to break free when the Dragonstar came round right,
Aohila intended to use whoever came through the mirror. She knew
somebody would. Once Folcalor had the dragons an' the mages behind him, demon magic was the only way to fight Adromelech.
Whether Folcalor rebelled against his Hell-Lord or not, one or t'other
of 'em was bound to come after the Burning Mirror."

He went back to grinding the coffee, twisting and crunching the
beans in the marble dish. "Aohila tried her damnedest to make me
her slave, you remember. An' when I tricked her, an' paid off the teind
she didn't think I could pay, she worked out a way of makin' me think
I was comin' up with this plan of usin' ether-magic on me own. It was
she who put me together with Corvin, remember, so I could learn
about ether. An' I suspect, she who sent the rains to lay the gold dust,
when Folcalor's demons made a try to seize him in Prokep. It wasn't
so much she feared him puttin' her name in a catch-bottle because
her name already *was* in a catch-bottle. She knew he was a scientist
who understood ether—a force the demons neither understood nor
could control."

"That must have been what she was doing when I trapped her,"
said Jenny. "Sending the rains, I mean. The times fit."

She was silent, thinking about the ruin of Ernine. About the
burned-out soul-jewels, scattered upon the hills.

The demon commander deserved to be where he was, she

thought. Trapped in that silver tiny world, with no company but the vicious Adromelech, for eternity.

Do you like games?

And his shadowy lieutenant had been destroyed, as Caradoc's curse had required.

"You know," said Jenny thoughtfully, "I always felt I found that bottle a little ... *easily*. But she'd have to have known that she risked me using it on her."

"I think she counted on it." John dumped the ground coffee into the pot, and added too much water too fast. It was always safer to let him make tea, Jenny reflected with an inner sigh. And even then ... "She'd have known you *had* to use it on her, for it to be reprogrammed—spelled with another name"—he corrected the verb he'd picked up in his Otherworld travels—"to trap Folcalor. But she obviously thought you were intelligent enough to see that, alone, she was less of a danger to the world than Folcalor. An' that you were adult enough not to let your jealousy of her blind you to that fact."

Jenny was silent again, remembering the eerie silence of the catch-bottle. Remembering her jealous dreams.

They seemed to be part of someone else's life. But they, too, were a part of her, a part of what made up her magic. She would have to remember that, when next she drew strength from her own soul.

"I think ...," she said slowly, "I think I've just been complimented."

"You have, love." He leaned across the hearth to kiss her, the steam from the coffee misting his spectacles.

She'd spoken to Ian again that morning, through the white crystal that had been her master Caerdinn's: a delight beyond anything she could think of, to speak, as a mage, to her mageborn son. "Lucky you," the boy had said, "being in Bel where it's spring. We've got another storm going, and the snow in the courtyard is a yard deep." He'd reported that Muffle had dismantled the robot, and though he, Ian, had been able to detect no lingering magic anywhere about the pieces, or in the fragments of the burned-out moonstone, they would be hauled with the first thaw to the quicksands in Toadsuck Bog and sunk.

Meanwhile Adric was being kept away from them. As of yesterday, the boy was trying to convince Muffle to build another robot from scratch.

"But why?" Jenny asked later, when she was dressing to join the procession assembling in the palace hall. "What did Aohila gain? All that was ... for what?"

"For exactly what we're gettin' out of this, love." John paused in tying his shirt-points and looked down at her, the linen of his collar-ruffle startlingly white against his sunburned throat. "For a chance to go home an' know it'll be safe. For Happily Ever After. The Burnin' Mirror's safe in the Ether Henge: There isn't a chance another demon'll try to get into her Realm. She's the Lady of Hell, maybe the only complete consciousness in the place. She has there all she needs. She came out once, to conquer Ernine through Isychros a thousand years ago an' mix herself in the affairs of humankind, an' got defeat for her pains. Maybe she learned a lesson."

"I didn't think demons could."

John held out his arm to her, and she took it with a smile. In the plain black robe of a scholar, and a scholar's close-fitting velvet cap hiding his shorn hair, only the demon-killer sword he wore at his waist marked him as the warrior Thane of the Winterlands. He looked far more like precisely what he'd always wanted to be: a naturalist who'd rather talk to dragons than slay them, a reluctant warrior who'd sooner play the hurdy-gurdy than go to war, and design flying machines and parachutes and better ways of making coffee.

"I didn't either, love," he said. "I think, like Morkeleb, we may have been lookin' in the wrong direction, or at the wrong demons."

As they stepped outside into the garden, the spring breeze billowed their robes, for Jenny, too, wore the gown of a scholar, marking her true self for all the world to know. Thane and witch, tinker and hunter, they paused on the terrace steps to kiss in the changeable sunlight, partners who had never been quite what others expected them to be.

"Can we really go to seek the Dragonshadows?" she asked, as the trumpets sounded by the palace gates, calling all latecomers to the procession. Down at the end of the garden Badegamus appeared, gorgeous in green-and-purple satin so crusted with jewels that he seemed, in his fluttering mantlings, to be a dragon himself, hastening toward them with all the ribbons fluttering on his staff as he gestured for them to hurry.

"I wouldn't miss it for the world," John said with a grin. "Though God knows what we'll find—not what either of us expects, I daresay. Maybe not even anything Morkeleb expects. And what they'll think of him I can't imagine—always supposin' we find them. He's not a dragon anymore, as he said, no matter how much he tries to pretend he isn't interested in humankind or mortal lives. Whatever else he is . . ."

He shook his head, and finished, ". . . is what he is."

"I only hope he may find happiness in so being," Jenny said softly. "As I have."

Badegamus reached them, puffing so hard he could only gesture them toward the procession. Tinán, Prince of Imperteng, fairly glittered in his barbaric embroideries; the beautifully arrayed lords of the Islands bowed, looking like a flower garden when the wind passes. The Master of Halnath, like John and Jenny, wore scholar's robes, his long reddish hair trailing out from beneath his cap; Lord Ector stood beside him, erect and soldierly under thirty pounds of elaborately dagged satin mantlings and fussing over the proper order of procession.

Resplendent in a gown of ancient cut, Gareth led the way through the streets of the ancient city on foot, marking out, square by square, the place whose people he would be answerable for, even at the cost of his life. At each of the gods' twelve temples he was annointed, and swore before each deity—the Green God of Law, and the Gray God of Learning, the Blue Goddess whose name the city had originally borne and the Many-Colored Lady of the Wastelands, and all the rest—to stand in for the lives of the people, in all things touched by that lord. And before each god the rulers of the great fiefs and marches swore their loyalty: the Master of Halnath, and the Thane of the Winterlands, the Prince of Imperteng, and the lords of the various isles. And the people who followed the procession replied, in a many-voiced cry like the sweeping music of ten thousand blades of grass, "And so we swear."

Then there would be music and a little pageant by the local guilds and temple choirs singing slightly out of tune, and John and Ector discussing the history of the coronation rite under their breaths just as if Ector hadn't shoved a torch into a pile of kindling around John's feet a month ago: "... but accordin' to Tenantius, if the King is selected before the beginnin' of the world by the Spirit of Universal Justice ..."

"Yes, yes, but in Garuspex's *Rites* it says that no King is truly King until he is invested, and therefore ..."

Jenny shook her head, and looked at the young man standing before her on the steps of the Temple of Sarmendes, the last born and greatest of the Twelve. Gareth looked pale and haggard still in the red robes of the House of Uwanë, and in spite of the dignity of the day his spectacles flashed in the sunlight. He took the rite too seriously to risk offending any god by a single myopic misstep, no matter what he looked like in front of the people. The hooded priests of Grond and Ankethyes grouped around him, waving censers and mumbling rote invocations in a language that nobody remembered anymore, but when she scanned the crowd on the steps, Jenny saw little Millença with the nurse Danae and Danae's daughter, Branwen, all watching Gareth with mingled joy and love.

And around them, other people. Gareth's people, Jenny thought, the way the villagers of Alyn and Great Toby and Far West Riding were John's people. She could almost match them, face for face—old ladies who were certainly the spiritual sisters of Granny Brown, the rough-faced, smiling Cowans and Bills and Muffles of the world; girls in bright dresses and tight bodices like Mol Bucket, and innkeepers like Gowla and Grobe from the Silver Cricket, and the woman who'd been hawking hot pies in the alley behind Bliaud's house. She glimpsed Bliaud's son Abellus, in elaborate mantlings and a truly amazing hat, and Brâk with his scrollwork tattoos.

Weary faces full of hope, or red with free wine. The faces of those who'd come through plague and war and Rocklys's rebellion, through doubt and confusion and lies. The faces of those who'd lost wives and husbands and children to the plague—some who'd seen them return, only to be cheated and mocked by the demons who'd poisoned even their memories.

They deserved their celebration, thought Jenny. And their time of peace.

It would be good, she thought, to start for the North again.

She looked forward to teaching Ian, sensing that he was already a better mage than she and would be better still—that knowledge filled her with joy. To meditate in quiet in the house on Frost Fell, watching the luminous blue borealis ripple through the summer evenings when the birds sang through the hour or two of darkness, and the world smelled as close to God as it was ever likely to get.

To be with her children, and with John, and with herself.

With Morkeleb, too, she hoped—if not to go away adventuring, then to lie, as he had once said, in the thin turf of the downs, and to talk as friends of the endless lore of the star-drakes.

Time is long, she thought as her eyes turned to John once more— "—yes, but if the sceptre only dates back to the reign of Heskooth IV—" he was arguing, oblivious to the priests of Cragget investing Gareth with the keys and hammer of the Orange God in the name of the twenty-seven Guilds of the city. *Time is long, and the God of Time, the thirteenth God who dreamed the other Twelve, holds all things in his pockets. And no one knows what he will decide to bring forth.*

We all are what we are, and to fear that is to fear the stars in the sky.

The gnomes of the Deep came forward: Sevacandrozardus the King, who was called Balgub among men, in robes that seemed to be plated with gold and gems; the gnomish Wise Ones and the Patriarchs of the noble clans of the gnomes, Miss Mab's clan of Howeth-Arawan among them; Miss Mab herself, bowing with great dignity to the young man who had visited her in the slums when the dragon drove her and her people forth from the Deep.

Yet another hymn was sung by yet another ill-rehearsed choir. A face in the crowd caught Jenny's eye: a thin, small man with gray hair and eyes like the diamond labyrinths of the star-fields, and hands gloved in black, to hide his dragon claws. Morkeleb stood in the crowd, elbow-to-elbow with fishmongers and pork-butchers and the girls in their bright dresses and tight bodices, watching the King and watching the King's people with the fascination of one who has never seen such things before.

A dragon? she thought. *Never.*

A Dragonshadow?

Or one who was only the sum of what he had once been, and was now only what he was? *As are we all,* she thought.

The musicians broke into a fanfare, marred by a single out-of-tune hautbois; the children of the Weavers' Guild Choir lifted their voices in yet another hymn of banal praise. For one moment, across the crowd, Jenny met those diamond eyes.

Then Morkeleb lifted a hand to her, and smiled, and disappeared into the crowd.